The Crows

C. M. Rosens is an author of dark, genre-bending speculative fiction, particularly Gothic horror with tentacles and eldritch family drama, with body horror as a recurring theme. She is mainly to be found travelling between the hills of Wales and the plains of England, but loves visiting friends and family all over the world when she can. She has a PhD in a niche area of Medieval British Studies, and these days mostly applies her research skills in fiction rather than academia, which she enjoyed but doesn't miss. Her work is heavily influenced by the histories, mythologies and folklore of places she grew up in and lived as an adult.

T0182781

THE CROWS

C. M. ROSENS

San Diego, California

Canelo US
An imprint of Printers Row Publishing Group
9717 Pacific Heights Blvd, San Diego, CA 92121
www.canelobooksus.com

Printers Row Publishing Group is a division of Readerlink Distribution
Services, LLC. Canelo US is a registered trademark of Readerlink
Distribution Services, LLC.

First published in the United Kingdom in 2019 by C. M. Rosens. This
edition originally published in the United Kingdom in 2024 by Canelo.

Published in partnership with Canelo.

Correspondence regarding the content of this book should be sent to Canelo
US, Editorial Department, at the above address. Author inquiries should be
sent to Canelo, Unit 9, 5th Floor, Cargo Works, 1–2 Hatfields, London SE1
9PG, United Kingdom, www.canelo.co.

Publisher: Peter Norton • Associate Publisher: Ana Parker
Art Director: Charles McStravick
Editorial Director: April Graham
Editor: Angela Garcia
Production Team: Beno Chan, Julie Greene, Rusty von Dyl

Library of Congress Control Number: 2024933958

ISBN: 978-1-6672-0728-5

Printed in Faridabad-Haryana, India

28 27 26 25 24   1 2 3 4 5

Part 1

11–20 April

The Creepy Old House

In which Carrie Rickard has 33 days left to live

11 April

'You won't *fit in* there, Caroline.' Her mother issued her warning in the ringing, decisive tones of a fait accompli, the culmination of her ten-minute diatribe against Carrie's decision. Any anxieties she'd felt at passing her quarter-centenary faded away as her mother stripped her development back by ten years.

Carrie stood in one of the smaller back bedrooms of her new, finally-finished property, holding the phone away from her ear. Her lower lip had split from raking her teeth over it; blood tanged on her tongue.

'I'm *staying*,' Carrie repeated.

Few people tried to stand up to Margaret Rickard, and fewer still succeeded. The teddy on top of Carrie's wardrobe looked on, glass eyes dusty and judgemental.

A beat. 'You're not… punishing yourself, are you, sweetheart?'

Cold prickles washed down her spine. 'For what?'

Her mother backtracked. 'No, nothing. It's just… you put a lot on yourself. That's what I meant.'

Just hang up…

Carrie bit back the expletive-filled outburst that would give her mother the moral high-ground. From the moment she'd seen the ruin on a dull Spring day like this, almost a year ago, she hadn't been able to get it out of her head. The dying, lambent sunlight played across its broken windows, winking at her like a distress

3

call, a secret signal. She couldn't explain it, but for the first time in two years she had felt *seen*.

She hadn't wanted to go to that stupid house-warming anyway. Piddingdean was a tiny village in the back of beyond, she didn't even know Phil's cousins, and Phil had been in one of his moods. Then, like a magic star, that glimmer of light pierced her world through the passenger window of a blazer-blue saloon and changed everything. A week later she'd taken the train on her own from Victoria to Pagham-on-Sea Parkway and walked for miles until she found it again.

It had been waiting for her.

Carrie knew in that moment, standing on the nettle-strewn avenue looking up at the collapsed porch and broken windows, that she wanted that house more than anything. It had stood for hundreds of years against all weathers and all comers, stripped of its iron and lead, broken but defiant. It was the spark that finally set her resolve on fire.

If you can do that, she'd thought, *then I can leave Phil.*

The rest was history.

Even fully restored, Fairwood House was a lonely outpost, interrupting the sweep of agrarian melancholy around it. Huddling around its back lawns and curving up to the edges of Barrow Field were the trees of the public woodland called The Chase, once part of the Fairwood estate but now managed by the local council. The Sussex Weald lay above, the chalk-cliff coast below, the town of Pagham-on-Sea in between; a post-industrial twilight zone of soulless Brutalism and seaside Victoriana.

Fairwood was neither of those things, but rather an internal mess of architecture from previous centuries, dressed up in external Georgian symmetry. The main mass of the house was imperiously square, two shorter wings protruding on each side, symmetrical windows staring out in all directions. It had become known locally as The Crows, although no one could remember when. A murder of the big black birds nested in the trees behind the lawn, settling on the grass every day before taking to flight on

4

some cue Carrie couldn't read, like soldiers in her own private army. They were no help today, providing no defence against her mother's relentless logic.

Carrie stroked the window frame, running her fingers down the wood, looking out at the muddy disaster of the back lawns and the wishing well at the far corner.

'I love this house. I want a fresh start, I want—'

'Well, why can't you sell it on and buy somewhere more *sensible*? I thought that was the plan. Your grandad would have loved to see it, he left you that money to do something wonderful with, and you *have*. You used to love going to all those National Trust homes with him, didn't you?' Her mother's voice misted as it always did when she reminisced about Grampa Jim, and a lump rose in Carrie's throat. In a strange way, this had all started almost fifty years ago with another home, a modest council flat in Central London that her grandparents had managed to buy. Without that flat, the housing bubble (who could have predicted that in 1973?) and the staggering amount some banker had paid for it last year, she wouldn't be in this position, and her mum wouldn't be bloody lightyears away, running a bar in the Costa del Sol. If anyone should understand about following your dreams, it should be her.

'It's not just that. I *love* this house, Mum.'

'It's enormous, love, how can you afford to even *heat* it? What on earth is the point of all those rooms when it's just you? What about council tax – that must be extortionate! It would make a lovely bed and breakfast, or a spa or something. I'm sure you'll find someone to sell it to who'll make the most of it and love it as much as you.'

Carrie didn't have an answer. Her mother was absolutely right. It wasn't practical to live alone in a seven-bedroom house nearly an hour's walk from the nearest town when she couldn't even afford a car. She had no near neighbours, her job applications had all been unsuccessful, both her inheritance from her grandfather and her redundancy payment were all but gone, and she had nothing to keep her in Pagham-on-Sea whatsoever.

Her mother, an expert at exploiting a hesitant pause, shoved her foot in the crack and forced open Carrie's defences with questions she already knew the answer to. 'Have you met someone there? Made any friends?'

Carrie contemplated lying, but it never did any good. 'Not yet.'

'Are you applying for jobs in London? Why live there when you can live closer in?'

'I can commute in easily, there're trains…'

'I'm just worried you're running away from reality a little, that's all, sweetheart. I can see why you'd want to. What Phil did was *awful*.'

You don't even know, Carrie thought, rage building. *You don't know* half *of what he did.*

But that was not something she had the energy to get into over the phone. 'Leave it, Mum, I don't want to talk about it.' She rolled her necklace pendant between her fingers, her parents' graduation gift, its smooth, oblong edges reminding her that her mother was trying, that she cared.

'No, all right, I'm not going to say anymore. But I can see how you poured all your emotion and your energy into rebuilding that creepy old house, and I'm worried that it's – well, it's like… I, oh, I don't know what I mean.' Her mother's voice faltered. 'I just think – I mean, I don't know darling, it's getting a bit obsessive. And you *won't* fit in there, it's all just farmland and that *awful* rundown little seaside place. What are you going to do, work in a tea shop with your education? Who are you going to *meet* on your level?'

Carrie made a disgusted noise. That was rich, coming from someone who'd grown up on a council estate in Hackney.

'I went on a single's night,' she retorted, crossing to the window. 'I met a graphic designer called Ian.' Her pale reflection ghosted against the gloomy afternoon sky. As one-night stands went, Ian had been a solid four out of ten, but at least he'd made her laugh. Not a promising start, but a start. She fiddled with her ponytail, teasing out the silver streaks in amongst the blonde, wondering if she should try dying it again. Phil had flown into a rage the last time, accused her of cheating on him, said it was like lipstick on a pig, kicked a hole in the bathroom door. After their final split it had taken a month or so to walk past hair dye boxes in a shop without her chest constricting in cold panic, let alone buy another one.

Her mother sighed, as if she could see the grey hairs through the network. 'Oh, sweetheart, well, good for you. It's great you're getting back out there. I don't want to sound... I just want what's best for you, that's all.'

Is that a cliché every parent ends up saying to their child? Carrie wondered. *Does it come pre-downloaded at parenthood, playing on repeat?*

She stared out across her back lawn, a sloping, muddy expanse of dead grass hemmed in by a thin length of wire where the walls had fallen in. That was the next job, when she had the money: fixing up the lawns, the old 1920s greenhouse, the Victorian herb garden, the pretty little rockery. The builders had already broken open the boarded-up old well in the far corner, but the thickly wooded copse beyond the fence overshadowed it and gave Carrie the creeps.

'Caroline? Hello? Are you still there?'

'Still here,' Carrie said, wishing she wasn't.

She thought she could see something in the trees, a flash of grey between the trunks. Someone walking a dog, perhaps, but the figure – if that's what it was – was standing still. Fat droplets scarred the windowpane, a prelude to another April shower.

It's not him, she soothed herself, trying to believe. *It's not. He'd never wear grey.*

'Well, look, why don't you try it for a couple of months,' her mother said, sounding doubtful. 'I'm sure after a bit you'll see I'm right. You'll find a job soon, and then you can get it just right to sell it on. You'll make a nice profit on it, enough for a deposit on somewhere else.'

'Okay, Mum, look, the builders are just leaving so I'd better go and see them out.' It was only a partial lie. They were finishing up, but wouldn't be gone for another half-hour, at least. Carrie turned from the window, hearing the clunk of tools being packed away. 'Love you. Talk later.'

'Love you—'

Carrie hung up.

'Don't you worry,' she said to the bedroom, stroking the pale blue wallpaper, enjoying the curves of the embossed peacocks on the feature wall. 'I'm not going anywhere.'

–

He watched the house from his usual vantage point under the trees, acid-scarred hands thrust into his pockets. The builders had done a decent job. She must be almost complete by now, a brickwork phoenix rising from her nest of decay. He could feel her getting stronger, waking up, seeing the world again through clear panes of unbroken glass. Soon it would be just her and him, like it ought to be, the new owner surplus to requirements.

A few months ago, he'd lit the bonfire up on the Weald under the Blue Moon, cut open some girl and spilled her steaming guts on the frost-hard ground to read his own future in the firelight.

Thirty-three days left.

He'd been waiting for this for years, nearly all his life, what was thirty-three more days? From tomorrow, only thirty-two. Ditch-eels of excitement writhed in his chest. He considered breaking the owner's neck when it came to it, nice and quick, no need for a fuss. The 'how' had been vague, but the omens indicated he would bear a share of the guilt regardless, so it might as well be on purpose.

His fingers twitched.

The newcomer was a city-breed but not quite what he'd expected; there was an underlying brittleness about her, a frailty that Fairwood usually exploited when she found it. He knew the house's little tricks. She always called out strongest to broken things.

(*Not me, though: I'm the One and Only. Naun broken about me.*)

8

He shifted on the well-worn spot beneath his favourite tree, determined to believe his own assertion. She called to *him* because he was special. That was all.

Anyway. *Wyrd biþ ful aræd*, as the Saxons said, things always go as they must, and he was going to get everything he ever wanted. After sixty years, the protection that guarded against his blood-kin would be broken and he would be the sole master of the arcane artefact Fairwood protected. He giggled to himself in his soft, childlike way. Everything would play out in the next few weeks, and all he had to do was let it happen.

He could wait.

While he waited, having a neighbour was a novelty that hadn't yet grown old, no matter how long he watched. She had been sleeping underneath in the cellars or the old crypt, emerging bleary-eyed and hard-hatted in the mornings to wander around the rubble and builders' vans. His mother had always wanted a girl, heron-slender, vixen-light, and Ricky sometimes imagined his non-existent sister like this woman, only with the wide, straight Porter nose and darker hair. He was gratified to find the neighbour was nothing like his imagined sibling in many other ways. Attachment made everything more difficult.

(*Resentment*, he chided himself, *don't lie.*)

He shook off the darker thoughts and moved closer to the wire fence, watching.

Very soon, the builders would leave for the last time and the new neighbour would be all alone.

It started to rain over The Chase, cold drops splashing onto his hood, the shower building up to a deluge.

–

As the mercurial might of April assaulted the house, Carrie made everyone a round of teas and coffees, amused that the older men finishing up in the kitchen were dragging it out – normally, they couldn't wait to leave. Fred and Roy were the competent counterparts of Laurel and Hardy, and their apprentice Marty was a fresh-faced lad not long out of school. Fred called him 'McFly,' but Marty, to both Fred and Carrie's horror, didn't get the reference.

'How long has this clock been like that?' Marty demanded, finally noticing Carrie's joke from a week ago. The rescued grandfather clock didn't work, so she'd stuck the hands at two minutes to twelve in honour of his favourite Iron Maiden song after hearing it so often it had turned into an earworm. Marty refused to work in the house in silence. Too many noises sounded like whispers.

'Took him long enough,' Roy remarked, grinning at his apprentice and accepting his tea with calloused hands. 'Who had the last day on the job?'

'Fred did,' Carrie said, the keeper of the sweepstake. 'You owe him a pint.'

Marty took this in good humour. 'Who did that?'

Carrie slid by with two more mugs, her smirk giving her away.

The apprentice shook his head. 'Give over, Carrie. Roy's been leading you astray.'

'He wouldn't dare, I'd tell his wife,' Carrie retorted, as Roy feigned a cuff across Marty's head. She left them to it and went to find the master carpenter finishing up his last job.

Joe Lin was hanging a reclaimed chapel door to seal off the attic stairs. He gave her a thumbs-up as she approached with two mugs and accepted his with a grateful smile.

'Nearly done! Be out of your hair for good after this. What'll you do then? Sell it on?'

Carrie bit back the urge to ask if he'd been speaking to her mother. She shook her head. 'I thought I'd stay.'

'You sure? This house, it...' Joe shook his head with an awkward smile. 'It... changes people. I mean, that's what they say.'

'Change is good,' Carrie remarked, thinking that anything would be better than her current situation.

'No more sleeping in the crypt for you, anyway!' Joe laughed, sipping his Earl Grey. 'Keep the hard hat. Souvenir.'

Carrie allowed herself a smile. 'Thanks.' She paused, sorry to see them go. It had taken her weeks to get into the swing of the on-site banter, and after getting to know them all a bit better, only Joe lived locally. The rest of them were subcontracted from Bexhill and she was unlikely to bump into them again. 'I don't suppose you'll be sorry to see the back of us.' The 'us' slipped out before Carrie could stop herself. Joe looked at her strangely for a moment, but then his eyes slid back to the door and he gave the frame a pat as if to say he knew what she meant.

'Had a devil of a job getting locals to work on it,' he admitted, scratching his head. 'This stretch of road has... a bit of a reputation.' He gave a short, awkward laugh. 'The Bermuda Triangle of Sussex, they call it.'

'Yeah, the plumber said something like that. Why?'

'Oh, it's... It's just what they say.' He didn't elaborate further on who 'they' were, so Carrie assumed general folk-knowledge. 'Drivers go missing, they don't find the car, nothing. They say a lot of shit like that around here. They say The Crows is cursed, have you heard that?' He rolled his eyes, but there was a hint of uncertainty in them. 'Bet you've heard all the stories by now, hey?'

Carrie didn't answer. Since moving to Pagham-on-Sea, she had heard it everywhere. Locals clammed up around her with an almost guilty silence, and while most young professionals lived in the commuter's estate the other side of town, even they knew the place as 'that creepy old ruin'. Carrie hated that the most; the mix of the dismissive and the ghoulish, and the way they looked at her afterwards, like an unwrapped mummy displayed for their amusement.

Don't listen to them...

The thought – or was it a whisper? – slid in and out of her head as she sipped her coffee.

'I already lost my job, my savings and my boyfriend,' she muttered. 'I'll take my chances, thanks.'

Joe cocked an eyebrow at her. 'Your ex sounded like a right twat,' he said. 'Not much of a loss there.'

'Yeah, that one's more of a blessing.' She cracked a reluctant smile. 'You got any single mates?'

Joe grinned. 'You're not that desperate, trust me.'

Carrie spluttered into her coffee.

'Listen to that.' The rain picked up, lashing against the windows in the empty rooms, bouncing off the roof and echoing down through the attics. He swung the heavy door open and shut experimentally, muffling the tamping cloudburst. 'Perfect.'

Carrie wished she could summon more enthusiasm; it *was* perfect. The stained glass winked at her in the electric light.

'Yeah, thanks.'

'I'll invoice you. Exactly what we said – came in bang on budget for that last little bit, told you we would. Makes up for going over on the structural changes.'

Carrie hid the sickness in her belly with a fake smile. The final payment would bring her bank balance to almost zero. 'Yeah, fine.'

'How's the job-hunting?'

'Oh, you know, I've got a few interviews lined up, it's all pretty positive.'

She was on her forty-eighth job application and third unsuccessful interview since being made redundant. Most employers seemed to get no further than her address.

Joe took a satisfied step backwards. 'That's us done.' He packed up his toolbox and started off down the landing, the mug abandoned, half-full. 'Been a pleasure.'

She followed slowly. 'Hey, Joe – any more jobs going in town?'

Joe paused on the stairs. 'Maybe. My cousin wants a delivery driver – the Jade Emperor on Norman Way, best Chinese in town. You don't drive, though, do you? Kench Foods were hiring too, but you'd need to take the bus out there.'

Carrie shook her head. She had already applied for two positions at Kench Foods and not even gotten an interview for the night shift on the factory floor.

'SupaPrice are always hiring. The supermarket on the high street, you know? Shit pay, but they're always looking for people.' He frowned, one hand on the bannisters. 'You okay, Carrie?'

She tightened her grip on the coffee mug. 'Yeah, of course. I'm fine. Just, you know, asking.' She attempted humour. 'I guess it's too late – the curse struck already.'

People are pain...

As the thought slid into her head, Joe jerked his hand back.

'Ow!' He stared at the bannisters. 'Did you feel that?'

'Static?' Carrie asked.

'From wood?' Joe gave it a worried glance. 'No. Like – I don't know. Never mind.' He ran his fingertips along the polished surface of the rail. 'Carrie... tell me if I'm overstepping here, but are you *sure* you're okay?'

She pursed her lips, not knowing where to start. She didn't want to sandbag her carpenter with the chaos of her life. The lie slipped out, easy as an automated reply.

'Yeah. Fine.' He wasn't buying it so she distracted him with a question, a trick her mother had taught her. 'What's your favourite creepy story about this place?' she asked. 'You've never said.'

Joe laughed, embarrassed. 'Didn't want to scare off a good customer.' He was only half-joking. 'Dwelling on the past can get unhealthy 'round here. Anyway, Mags – the missus – works at the morgue, I get enough spooky stories at home.'

'No harm in saying now, though,' Carrie probed. 'Go on.'

He coughed. 'All right. There's one.' He looked doubtful but continued. 'There was this missing girl, I think in the Forties or Fifties – her mum was the cook here at the time. They didn't live in the house then; no one did, except for the mad old baronet and his nurse, and they lived in about three rooms, all the rest was shut up and rotting. Anyway, this little girl went missing. Last seen playing in The Chase, the woods back there.' He pointed over his shoulder in the vague direction of the public woodland that had once belonged to the Fairwood estate. 'There were search parties, all that, you know, but nothing. Local poachers got blamed, one family especially...' He tailed off, sucking his teeth. 'They found her when her mum tried to cook for the search party. Turned out, the kid had been stuffed up the chimney in the kitchen. Ex— what's the word, where you're drained of blood?'

'Exsanguinated?'

'That's the one. Weird marks on her, people said, cut into her arms. Gruesome shit.'

Carrie gasped. 'Seriously?'

'Yeah.'

'How long was she... up there for?'

Joe shrugged. 'Dunno, probably no more than a few days? Some people say months, but I doubt that.'

'Oh my God.' Carrie shook her head. 'Wow.'

'Yeah. Never caught who did it. I mean, the town's got a lot of theories, rumours, you know. Some reckon it was old Sir Jack himself. That's what they say, anyway.'

Carrie raised her eyebrows. 'God. That got left out of the brochure.'

Joe laughed. 'Yeah, I bet. Lots of deaths in this house over the years. That's the most sensational one, I'd say. I think that's when people started saying the family was cursed, or the house was cursed, or their luck was cursed, you know, stuff like that. The Sauvants were a weird lot. Growing up we used to—' He stopped and corrected himself. 'Kids used to dare each other to break in here, nick something, break a window, you know. Rite of passage stuff. If you took something out, the curse couldn't get you, something like that. We'd make up all kinds of stupid stories.'

Carrie folded her arms. 'You ever break a window?'

Joe snorted. 'Once, yeah. I was twelve, I wanted to fit in. Think I've done my penance now, though, don't you?'

'I don't know,' Carrie said, teasing. 'I think that's up to the house, not me.'

She thought back to things she had done to fit in around that age – scraping her hair back and gelling it in styles that didn't suit her, discovering weed and vodka in the park and learning lessons the hard way, chickening out of shoplifting cider from Mr Rao's at the last minute and being punched in the stomach by Megan Haines... She could easily imagine Joe, growing up in a not-so-diverse town, smashing the window of a derelict house because the other boys were doing it.

In the hall, Fred, Marty and Roy finished rolling up the dust sheets, bickering about the local football team.

Joe gave her a wry grin. 'Looks like we're off.'

'Thanks again.' Carrie put her mug on the stairs and wrapped her cardigan closer around her.

Marty opened the front door to a curtain of hammering rain.

'Blinking heck boys! Reckon we should've brought an ark, not the van.'

'See you, Carrie,' Roy called up the porch stairs, a cigarette behind his ear.

They let themselves out.

The front door slammed with a suck of air through the hall, as if The Crows had breathed a sigh of relief.

We're alone.

She looked down into the reception hall, listening to the rattle of the rain. The boards gave a contented creak as she shifted her weight. The Crows was all she had, but then, she was all it had, too. They each bore their life-scars behind a restored veneer, keeping their losses to themselves. It had stood, in various stages of its development, through the Reformation, the English Civil War and (comparatively more recently) the Blitz, extended here, remodelled there, now a bigger entrance hall, now a new conservatory, but always, Carrie imagined, fundamentally the same. The Tudor gallery on the first level had been converted into a wide landing serving the Georgian extension on the back comprised of additional guest rooms and the current kitchen, and it was one of these smaller bedrooms that Carrie had kitted out with the furniture of her London flat.

I am yours.

The Crows had told her, louder and stronger with every improvement, every contractor, every cheque. It told her again now, in the stillness, as she took in the quiet majesty of the refurbished house.

I am yours...

...and you

...are

...MINE.

A dull pain strobed suddenly behind her eyes. Carrie hissed in a pained breath, pressing her fingers to her forehead. The house gave a gentle creak as the pain eased.

She shook herself out of her reverie.

'Early night,' she announced to herself over the rain assaulting the masonry around her. 'That's what I need.'

She locked up the house, collected the mugs and dumped them in the kitchen sink, curled up in bed and streamed a film on her laptop. Things would get better, she promised herself. *Just you wait, Carrie Rickard.*

Just you wait.

A Town with Dark Secrets

In which Carrie gets a job

14 April

Carrie's lucky break was a zero-hour contract at SupaPrice, the supermarket on the high street. On the morning of her first shift, the dreaded message: *You are in your unarranged overdraft – charges are due to be applied to this account*, greeted her in text message form. Not the best start to her day.

She stumbled downstairs to the kitchen but even in her groggy, pre-caffeinated state she couldn't resist running her hand over the new bannisters, breathing in the smell of the fresh dawn on the cold tiles. This morning Fairwood seemed less friendly than usual, as if it knew she was going out and resented her impending absence.

Carrie glanced at the grandfather clock, its mournful mother-of-pearl face beautiful but lifeless. She contemplated selling it. It belonged to the house, but she needed the money.

Around the corner from the kitchen steps was the narrow servant's corridor, now partitioned into the utility and boiler room, the narrow spiralling servants' stairs leading up to the first floor, and trapdoor access to the coal cellar. Carrie's attention was drawn to the utility room door with a sense of foreboding thickening in her gut.

It was ajar.

She was sure it hadn't been the night before.

Instead of closing it, something drew her through it towards the disused back stairs and the trapdoor guarding the coal cellar steps. It was still closed, but Carrie had a strange urge to haul it open. She stood on the edge, dazed, staring at it.

The old trapdoor had been rotted right through, a gaping hole where, Roy had told her, some adventurous local kid had gone straight through while exploring the ruin and broken both their legs. She hoped he'd been exaggerating.

The coal cellar had been thoroughly cleaned by a team of burly suited-up men in masks with power hoses, blaring classic rock and dispelling the shadows. She'd had a go. It had been fun. Now it sat under the new trapdoor, pristine, and – she faltered over the thought – *awake.*

Angry.

Rage shot through her out of nowhere, incendiary and dry.

Those bastards will get what's coming to them…

Her own anger, at Phil, at her so-called backstabbing 'friends', at the gaslighting and the lies and the smug, cocky smirk on his face, boiled fresh and raw. But it was a picture of the town – the cold-shoulders, the refusal of locals to talk to her, the local builders not answering her calls, *that* was worse. It mingled with a host of imagined faces she didn't recognise, grinding into a throbbing headache.

Carrie backed away from the coal cellar and back into the soothing warmth of the kitchen, slamming the utility door.

Her headache subsided as quickly as it came. She played with her pendant, taking a few grounding breaths. The urge to call her dad left her torn; it was too early for him and he'd panic, think there was something wrong.

I'm nervous about this job, going into town, being stared at.

That was all it was.

'At least it's a job,' Carrie said aloud to the kitchen, her own voice reassuring as it broke the silence. She dumped instant granules into a chipped mug and the rich, bitter aroma hit her frontal lobe like a bolt from heaven.

The kitchen didn't judge.

She turned to face the hearth, nibbling a fingernail. Soon, she would have to leave the house and become a curiosity, open to the scrutiny of a thousand eyes.

'I hope the curse isn't a real thing. I already feel cursed enough.'

The original chimney breast had been preserved, a different stone to the rest of the walls, startling in the change of colour and texture from the brick and tile around it. Its yawn was stopped by the black range sitting in its gaping mouth.

Thinking about Joe Lin's story, Carrie wandered up to it and pressed her palm against the stone.

The hearthstone was original to the old gamekeeper's cottage, knocked down in the era of a particularly energetic lord of Fairwood, and the stone recycled for the kitchen extension. Roy had, grudgingly, told her that old Mr Pendle, the gamekeeper of the time, had 'taken on something terrible' over it, even though a new cottage was built for his family in The Chase. Bad luck of the catastrophic, apocalyptic, hellfire-and-damnation variety would beset the inhabitants of Fairwood House if they crossed the Pendles after all their years of service, old Mr Pendle had sworn, and his wife had made something to seal it with, some charm for good luck written backwards to reverse the intent.

Scratched into the limestone slab, barely visible now under all the dust and the shadow of the range, were symbols and initials, especially the letter 'P', over and over. Roy had refused to touch it.

Carrie leaned over the range and peered up at the flue. She had it for show, not for use, and now she knew the story of the cook's daughter, she was glad of her decision. A crow on the top of the chimney called down, startling her with the uncanny acoustic effect.

She jerked away. '*Shit!*'

Another of the large black birds swooped onto the path between the overgrown flowerbeds and hopped forwards towards the kitchen wall. As she came to the window to watch, mainly to prove to herself it was only a bird and nothing eldritch or frightening, it came closer, beady eyed. A little green caterpillar crawled across the broken stones, unconscious of any risk. Carrie watched with morbid fascination as it inched towards its own doom.

The kettle boiled and clicked itself off, distracting her. Carrie got on with breakfast, giving herself a pep talk in the process.

'I'm *going* to make friends here,' she told the kitchen, popping bread into the toaster. 'There must be *someone* who isn't scared of this place. Or me, for buying it.'

Her 'new' good luck charm, a corner from one of the broken tiles on the living room fireplace bearing a tiny four-leaf clover design, sat in a pot of odds and ends on the kitchen table. She fished it out and popped it into her pocket, then buttered her toast.

When she turned back to the window, both the crow and the caterpillar had gone.

–

Pagham-on-Sea's SupaPrice was the local branch of the budget supermarket chain located on the high street, spread over the ground floor of a few shops knocked through into one. It specialised in budget household items, basic groceries, a reasonable range of frozen food, and a cheap toy aisle.

'I don't know why anyone would come and live here,' Carrie was informed by the willowy sixteen-year-old hanging up her jacket in the upstairs break room. 'It's a shithole.'

Carrie smiled. 'Rachel, is it?'

The girl looked down at her name badge. 'Yeah.'

'I'm Caroline.' Carrie gave her an appraising glance. 'You can call me Carrie, though.'

Rachel nodded. 'You must live in the new estate, right?'

'Why d'you say that?'

'Everyone new lives out there.'

Carrie let Rachel think what she wanted, tucking her necklace into her blouse.

'We aren't supposed to wear necklaces,' Rachel said, eyeing Carrie's and tucking in her own half of a Best Friends Forever heart. 'But I won't tell if you won't.'

Carrie grinned. 'Deal. I feel naked without mine.'

Rachel's smile was warmer. 'Me too! Pauline's the worst about stuff like that, but Mercy's cool. She won't mind.'

'What don't you like about this town? It's not so bad, the bits I've seen.'

The high street wasn't awful. Aside from the pawn shops and shabby second-hand places on the dodgier end, it had a healthy mix of popular chains and independently-owned places. From what Carrie had seen there were plenty of shops and cafes, some tourist-kitschy but others, like the Sandbox, friendly and innovative. Carrie was sure Rachel bore a vague resemblance to one of its owners, with her long, sad face and light freckles peppered across her nose.

Rachel shot her a worn look but didn't answer. 'I want to do a gap year, travel an' that. Can't wait.'

'Still, you must know some interesting stuff about this place,' Carrie probed. 'Like... I don't know, there must be some urban legends and ghost stories, right?'

'About what?' Rachel straightened her tunic, avoiding Carrie's eye.

'Oh, I don't know.' Carrie cast about for some suggestions to mask her main interest. 'The local church, the smugglers... the big old house on Redditch Lane...'

Her informant shrugged, tossing her phone into her locker after sending one last message. 'Not really.' She shot Carrie another hard-to-read glance, as if she were trying to assess her. Finally, she asked, 'Have you ever heard people say, "Don't put in the ground what you don't want to grow"?'

Carrie thought back to the few local tradesmen chatting to her with their stoic reluctance, but couldn't recall anything like that odd little phrase. Rachel was staring at her like it was some kind of test.

'Can't say I have, honestly.'

Rachel blinked at her, relaxing, conker-brown eyes still dulled by the early hour. 'Doesn't matter. It's just an old saying. Good luck today, anyway. See you later.' She slid by Carrie and jogged down the stairs to the shop floor.

Carrie stared after her.

What was that all about?

Fortunately for her over-worked curiosity, there was no time to dwell any further on this point. The manager reappeared, polishing his bald spot with his shirt cuff in a harassed manner, to start her induction. If there really was a town-wide conspiracy not to hire The Crows' owner, Carrie thought, Mr Graham ('Call me Alf') had clearly lost that memo in the chaos of his in-tray.

The work itself was as mind-numbing as Carrie remembered from working part-time through her A Levels and degree. With a little practice and some adjustments to a new till system, it started coming back to her. Best of all, no one recognised her – no one whispered to each other in the queue, *That's the woman who bought The Crows*. It was like a superpower, a place to hide in plain sight and be paid for it. The only people who made eye contact were those who made a point of smiling at checkout girls, and those who wanted to be rude to them.

Her supervisor, Mercy Hillsworth, was a few years her junior and barely came up to her chest. Greeting Carrie with enthusiasm, Mercy elected to show her around again in a quick ten-minute break after the hour of till training.

'I never bothered with Uni,' Mercy said after asking Carrie about herself, brushing off Carrie's BA in English Literature with unintentionally crushing disinterest. 'I trained as a hairdresser, but there's not many jobs in town. Wanted to stay near our parents, since my brother moved to Australia.' She shot Carrie a brilliant smile. 'What did you do after that?'

'I... worked in insurance.'

'Oh wow.' Mercy looked up at her, a stray purple curl falling out of her hairclip. 'That sounds boring.'

Carrie's bubbling resentment towards this blunt, pixie-like person simmered down in a cold jolt. Under the platinum-blonde bob that looked like a unicorn had thrown up over it, there was fresh, crusting blood in Mercy's hairline and – now that Carrie was paying attention – the shape of a livid bruise spreading under the creamy layers of foundation and concealer.

Phil had never actually hit her – leaving external marks was not his brand of cruelty – but Carrie's first, instinctive assumption came as an imagined flash of violence. She focused on the floor and fingered the clover tile in her pocket, building up the courage to ask.

'Are you okay?' she managed finally, crowbarring the question into one of Mercy's short pauses, before she lost her nerve. 'You've got… um, there's something in your hair.'

Mercy tutted, raising a hand to the spot, fiddling with her hairclip.

'Oh! Oh, yeah, no I'm great, just, um, fell over on my way to work, that's all.' She gave a breathless laugh. 'Right, time to jump back on the till, Rachel needs a break, poor kid, she's been on since open.'

'But—'

'Off you go!'

That conversation was over.

Mercy gave her a strained smile and left her to it.

She opened the third checkout as security ejected a gang of punk teens, dog collars around their necks and metal chains swinging around ripped jeans. One of them waved a sandwich and peeled back his lips in a leer at Rachel on the next checkout.

'Fancy a bite, babe?'

The others howled.

'Give over,' the beefier of the two security men snapped, giving the boy a push. He dipped his red mohawk, snarling.

The guards threw them out onto the street, standing either side of the automatic doors to make sure they left, a rebellious huddle of angst and attitude.

'You all right?' Carrie called across her conveyor belt, swiping a jar of strawberry jam.

Rachel nodded, closing her till. 'They go to my school, think they're hard. They won't do anything.'

'Ignore them,' Carrie advised lamely, with no intention of becoming the shift's agony aunt. She swiped the other items through: a pack of cable ties, a special-offer box of ribbed condoms and a fret saw. Her elderly customer gave her a sweet smile, paid in cash, packed her own bag, and left.

Unfortunately, that was the most interesting thing to happen all day. By the end of her shift, she was stiff and starving.

Carrie dragged herself off to the break room as soon as she was relieved by a bored college-aged boy and grabbed her belongings. She stuffed down another breakfast bar, wondering what to do for forty minutes while she waited for the next bus.

As if in anticipation of her loose end, an unknown number flashed up on her phone.

Her stomach clenched.

It was a mobile number. As close as they had been before The Break-up, Jess hadn't called Carrie once since Carrie's move to Pagham-on-Sea. Maybe she'd got a new phone.

What if Jess had been shagging Phil, too?

It was an ugly thought, but Becky had been, hadn't she? Becky had spent the last two years siding with him, her 'married-woman-voice-of-reason' tactics making Carrie think she was being paranoid, unreasonable. If Becky hadn't forgotten her underwear – underwear that Carrie had helped her choose for Valentine's Day – she'd still be none the wiser and half-convinced it was all in her head.

Anxiety and hunger turned her inner voice into an inner snarl. *Answer the phone, stupid bitch.*

She caved.

'Hello?'

'Don't hang up.' The low, smooth plea was horribly familiar. Carrie froze, glued to the seat.

Shitshitshit…

'Carrie, come on, let's just talk? You still owe me for the deposit on the flat…'

She balled her free hand into a quivering fist, voice shaking. 'I had to replace the bathroom door, and I don't— I don't have any cash right now. No, no way. Leave me alone, Phil. You have to stop calling me.' Her voice broke. 'You promised.'

'I'm coming down to Piddingdean to see Tom and Jackie soon. It's not far, I'll pop by, you can give it to me then. We can have a coffee, or something. I don't like thinking of you down there, all on your own.'

Carrie's bladder turned to jelly. 'Please,' she said, voice hoarse, 'Please don't do that.'

'I need that cash,' Phil wheedled, trademark arrogance edging his whine. 'I've been so low these last few months, you really hurt me, Carrie—'

She jabbed *End Call* with a shaking finger. Tears welling up with the memory of bruising arguments, the realisation she'd been right all along when she'd found Becky's underwear under their sofa and realised the painful, burning humiliation of the sexual health clinic hadn't been because she'd got unlucky in the local leisure centre.

He made me think it was an infection I picked up in the swimming pool… I can't, I can't do it, seeing his car everywhere, the phone calls again, shit, he knows where I am, he knows where the house is…

'Carrie?'

Carrie started violently. Mercy was peering around the door, rainbow curls falling across one eye.

How much had she heard?

She swallowed. 'Yeah?'

'Want to go to the Ram?' Mercy asked, judging it safe to intrude. She unhooked her coat from a wall peg. 'I'll show you a bit of the town if you want.'

'I wasn't planning on eating out,' Carrie admitted, pretending to look for something in her bag. Her stomach growled, the ache insistent.

'Dinner's on me,' Mercy added. 'Like a welcome to SupaPrice present.'

Mercy looked different: in the space of a few hours, the bruising had disappeared, making Carrie doubt her own memory. She must have been mistaken, but it left her unsettled.

Carrie paused. 'Are you trying to stop me quitting?' she teased, trying to keep the suspicion out of her voice.

'Yeah, a little bit.' Mercy gave her an impish grin. 'It's not a fun job, and we're short-staffed.' She hesitated, glancing at Carrie's phone on the seat beside her. 'Do you… want to talk about it, or…?'

'Not much. Why are you really inviting me out?'

'You don't have to come.' Mercy stopped, a contained bundle of frenetic energy. 'All right, fine. You got me. I know who you are. You bought The Crows.'

Nearly. Carrie sagged, disappointed. She had nearly gone a full day in town without that *stupid* statement dogging her like an unspent criminal conviction.

Mercy had the grace to look embarrassed. 'I just had to know… I mean, I can't imagine anyone buying it, but everyone's been talking about the work going on up there and going to watch through the gate, and you're, you're working *here*, I can't believe it, you're like a celebrity.'

'A shit celebrity.' Carrie frowned, playing with the pendant of her necklace, her link to a more familiar home.

Her younger supervisor brushed this off. 'That's just because everyone's broken into it and stolen stuff over the years, that's all. And everyone's dying to know if the curse is real, if it's really haunted, what you've been doing in there, and if you're going to sell it…' Mercy trailed off.

Carrie blinked. She had finally met her match in the question department: a fellow curiosophile.

'Okay, look, fine. I'll come to the pub, and you can grill me.' Carrie folded her arms, stomach still fluttering. 'I've got some questions of my own, anyway.'

'Fire away!' Mercy flushed with excitement. 'Sure. I mean, I don't know if I can answer anything. This is so exciting, I can't imagine anyone *living* there, it was always this spooky old ruin, you know? Come on.'

Carrie forced a smile. 'After you.'

–

As they crossed the street, a young man approached them with an open hand, real fear etched in his eyes. 'Spare some change, ladies, please? Please?'

In all the months she'd been there, Carrie realised with a start, he was the first person she'd seen begging for money.

Coastal towns around the country had their fair share of deprivation and economic problems, but Carrie had thought Pagham-on-Sea was a quaint commuter town, a dreary middle-class hideaway off-season and in the summer, all fish 'n' chips and Union Jacks. In London, she had run the gauntlet of human misery in the few hundred yards between her office and the tube station, but here no one slept in doorways. She had thought that was a good thing, at first. Now she was thinking about what Rachel had said, wondering about the rumours about the Sauvants, the dead girl in the chimney. She remembered Joe Lin's cryptic comment about Redditch Lane – the Bermuda Triangle of Sussex, where people went missing.

The town seemed more furtive than before, the huddles of its buildings conspiring against her and all those who fell through the social cracks.

Carrie had next to nothing, but his haunted eyes made her look. 'I've only got twenty pence, mate.'

He nearly snatched it from her hand. 'I only need another fiver, and they'll let me stay the night,' he said, darting his panicked gaze from her to Mercy.

'Where're you staying?' Carrie asked, trying to judge his age. He couldn't be more than mid-twenties. A teardrop tattoo in faded blue prison-made ink was beneath his left eye.

He jerked his head in a vague direction. 'The hostel, by The Mermaid.' His Liverpudlian accent was out of place. He dropped his voice, quivering, knotting his fingers together. 'I can't spend another night out here. I seen – I seen stuff. Seriously fuckin' – 'scuse my language ladies, I don't mean to swear, but seriously messed up stuff. I'm not a junkie, honest. I literally want a room, that's it, anything you can spare, please. Please.'

Mercy thrust two notes into his hands, stiffening. 'There's extra. For the train. You should try and get to Eastbourne or Southampton.'

'Are you sure?' He looked at the notes. 'Aw, love. Thanks a lot.'

'Yeah. I'm sure.' Mercy was fidgeting, darting a worried look at Carrie.

He hugged himself, battered jacket filthy and wet. 'Just... you're the first person to speak to me, thank you, thank you for this, can I be a bit cheeky? Can I ask you a question? Nothing bad, just a question about the hostel said I could ask about a job here.'

He fiddled with an inside pocket, pulling out a tatty piece of folded paper. 'I dunno, I wanted to ask someone. I don't like the name of it. Hangman's Walk.' He gave a rough, nervous chuckle. 'Sounds, sounds a bit, whatsit, *ominous*, girls, know what I mean?'

Mercy backed off. 'Mate, you don't want to go there. And I didn't tell you not to. Get a train.' She tugged Carrie's arm. 'Good luck.'

The man clammed up then, taking the hint. He balled up the piece of paper in his fist, hurrying away in the opposite direction without a backward glance.

Carrie burned with curiosity and an odd sense of dread, but Mercy clearly didn't want to talk about it.

They marched off to the pub in tense, awkward silence.

–

The Red Ram turned out to be a chain pub off the high street, with a family-friendly atmosphere and big mullioned windows that let in the evening light, warming the rich mocha and red wine tones inside.

Carrie was left with her maelstrom of anxious thoughts as Mercy ordered their food at the bar. To calm herself down in the lonely flat she'd shared with Phil, she had walked herself through her childhood home, picturing it in meticulous detail. This time, she made herself imagine Fairwood, walking herself through the front door in her mind's eye and through the hallway, running her hand along the curve of the bannisters. She focused on the waxed surface of the wood under her fingertips, listening to the sound her footsteps made, inhaling the cold air and the smell of wood and tile. She walked herself through to the kitchen, the warmest room in the house. Dread knotted in her belly. She tried to shut the image down and return to the Ram, to reality, but she was stuck.

Her eyelids fluttered but wouldn't open.

The chimney loomed in her mind and something whispered, *They'll get what's coming...*

A faceless child tumbled out of it, hair matted with blood.

'Carrie?'

Her eyes snapped open.

Mercy was back. 'Are you okay?'

Carrie adjusted, shaken. 'Yeah. Fine.' She deflected before Mercy had a chance to sit down and ask her anything else. 'That was weird earlier, right? What's the deal with Hangman's Walk? Now I've come to think of it... that guy was the first person I've had ask me for money. I thought it was... nice, at first. But – it's creepy. Isn't it? What did he mean?'

Mercy took a long gulp of her cider and put the pint glass down a little too heavily. 'Um.' She scratched her head, fingers raking through her brightly coloured bob. 'The nightlife here. It's a bit... lively, I guess. We've had problems with anti-social behaviour, you know. Just. Normal. Normal stuff. And Hangman's Walk is the dodgy end of town. That's all. Just, um. Don't worry about it.' She took another sip of cider and changed tack. 'So! You're living at The Crows, right? And... you've not experienced anything...' She left her sentence suggestively unfinished.

'Anything...?'

'...Strange?'

Carrie shook her head.

Mercy sat back in her seat. 'Huh. Well, no, I mean. I'm being silly, it's all the urban legends we grew up on around here.'

'Like what?' Carrie leaned in. 'Go on. I'm really interested.'

'Well, you know, they say it's cursed. That's what we used to say, you know, in the stories we made up about it.' Mercy winced. 'I, um, broke in once and nicked a paperweight. Probably still got it if, you know, you want it back...?'

Carrie snorted. 'Is everyone in this town a vandal or a thief?' She meant it as a joke, but it came out harsher than she intended. Mercy locked her lips, eyes inflating with awkwardness.

On cue, their burgers arrived to rescue the conversation like tasty, steaming saviours.

Carrie tore into hers, the gnawing bubble of hunger under her ribs overriding everything.

'I can't thank you enough for this,' she managed around a mouthful of meat and tomato relish. 'Seriously.'

Mercy, her cheeks puffed with sweet potato fries, waved her hand. After swallowing, she muttered, 'Don't worry about it.'

'Do you know anything about the girl up the chimney?'

Mercy winced. 'Yeah – Cathy Ross the cook's daughter, there's tons of stories about it.' She frowned. 'I'm not putting you off the place, am I?'

'*Never.*' The vehemence in her tone surprised her. It almost came from somewhere else. 'Go on. Tell me. Is she anything to do with the curse, by any chance?'

Mercy swallowed, fidgeting. 'Um. Well. Yes and no. I mean, the Fairwood curse is a local legend anyway, ever since... I don't know, a few of them went mad and then the money ran out.

One of the lords, no, I think they were baronets? Is there much of a difference? Well, anyway, one of them did or said something to upset the Pendle sisters, or old Mrs Pendle, that's… that's one of the stories. There're the usual ghost stories about the place… Cathy was found up the chimney in the kitchen, it was horrible. The house was barely lived in then. Sir John, or Jack, I think – he wasn't well. He lived in one wing of the house and hardly ever left. It was pretty awful. They never found out who did it. There was all this vigilante action against the va—' Mercy bit back the end of the word and went pale. 'Va-n drivers. Van drivers, um. Sightings or something, something suspicious. And there's rumours about, um. One of the local families.'

Carrie leaned forwards. 'Who? The Pendles?'

Mercy frowned. 'There were three Pendle sisters who all married and there's only Mrs Wend left now out of the three of them. She's the matriarch, I guess. There's a few branches now but I wouldn't get mixed up with any them, if I were you. There's the Wends, the Wend-McVeys, the Porters, the Shaws and the Foremans. Not to, um, put you off or sound judgemental, it's just… not everyone's that, um, nice.' She concentrated on her food, dropping her gaze.

Carrie shook her head, remembering one of Ron the builder's stories. 'I've heard the name "McVey" before. Were they smugglers or something? That's another curse story, isn't it, the one about a smuggler who got trapped in the tunnel under the house?' She snapped her fingers. 'Oh! That's it, it comes up in the coal cellar. And there's meant to be a priest hole somewhere else in the house linking up to it, and the smuggler's tunnel was the old escape route for the Catholics.'

'I don't know,' Mercy said. 'We used to tell each other ghost stories about the house and a guy being buried alive under there but he was always a pirate in ours, I don't know about the actual *history*.' Mercy clicked her tongue, peering over Carrie's shoulder at the front of the pub as the doors swung open. 'You should try the Local History Society. Oh! Jazz! Sorry, Carrie, I hope you don't mind, my partner knocked off work so…'

Caught unawares by unexpected company, Carrie turned, plastering on a fixed smile. A lanky John Hannah-lookalike had entered the Ram, waving at Mercy with a cheerful grin.

'Hey, babe!'

His greeting carried over the babble of other customers, and Mercy beamed wider as he approached. His hard north-west London accent was music to Carrie's ears.

'Carrie, this is Jasper, Jazz, this is Carrie. She bought The Crows.'

He extended a hand, and Carrie shook it. He had the gaunt, grizzled appearance of the perpetually overworked, but even so she judged him to be older than Mercy by a good decade.

'Hey, how's it going?'

'All right, yeah.' Carrie smiled but shivered. His hands were icy.

Jazz laughed, nudging Mercy along the seat and stealing a chip from her plate. 'Sorry. Not a warm-blooded person. Work doesn't help.'

'He's a pathologist,' Mercy said, still smiling. 'I was just telling Carrie she should join the History Society.'

'Oh yeah? I joined that a few years back, it's an interesting area, this. But I can never go now. The pub changed the Quiz Night to Wednesdays.' He shrugged. 'Hang on.' He dug in his wallet and fished out a battered, dog-eared card. 'Yeah, thought I still had it. Drop them an email, I bet they'd be really interested in that house of yours.'

Carrie accepted it and grinned. 'Cheers.'

Mercy was smiling at him with warm affection. Their dynamic reminded Carrie of how she and Phil used to be at the start, when he still saw her as more than an ego-boost and someone to pay gambling funds into the joint savings account. The colours leached out of the Ram as the sunlight faded behind a bank of twilight cloud, her mood cooling just as fast.

Her mother's unhelpful comment rang in her ears.

Maybe if you'd paid your relationship as much attention as that old house, he wouldn't have slept his way around Wembley.

'You all right?' Mercy asked, noticing the change that had come over her.

Carrie shook herself. 'Yeah. Sorry. I'm tired, you know.' Enough was enough: the pub was filling up, her next bus was in fifteen minutes, and her head was buzzing. 'Listen, this has been really nice, thanks, I have to go but… thanks for all this. Really.'

Mercy looked a cross between relieved and stricken. 'Oh, Carrie, you don't have to go—'

'No, honestly, I need to… I've got a few things to do at home and I want an early night, that's all. I'm going to get the bus. You've been awesome.'

Jazz said his warm goodbyes and waved as she hurried out of the Ram and into the gathering twilight.

Carrie made it to her stop just as the bus pulled up, earlier than scheduled. She leapt on with a burst of relief, remembering the homeless man and the fear on his face.

Maybe it's not my house that's cursed, she thought, dazzled by the headlights as they rushed by. *Maybe it's this bloody town.*

The bus stayed nearly empty for the whole journey up to Piddingdean, the nearest village, and Carrie was the only person to alight at the secluded stop on Redditch Lane.

Someone stared at her through the misty window as the bus pulled off, unsettling her further, but she told her dancing butterflies to stop being paranoid. That didn't help. The passenger's blurry face smudged across her brain, accusing her of some mystery offence.

Everyone hates you, stupid cow.

The small tile chip was a comforting presence in her pocket.

You're fine. Nearly home…

Carrie wrapped her coat more tightly around herself, burying her chin in the collar. It was another fifteen-minute walk home. She set off, passing the ruined cottage on her right, half-buried in the woods, the streetlight gleam reflecting from one of the broken windows. She paused, shivering a little in the night air.

That must be Bramble Cottage, the 'new' gamekeeper's cottage, built after the original was torn down and Mr Pendle uttered his infamous (but most likely fictitious) curse.

It was bigger than she'd thought, now she was taking the time to look at it properly. The wall ringing the overgrown garden was the same stone as The Crows' garden walls, a local stone, Carrie guessed. Nature had attempted to reclaim the cottage itself, although there were ragged curtains in the upper windows, and dirty net curtains across the main window on the ground floor. Hands in her pockets, she rocked back and fore to keep warm. The chill was gathering around her, cold and sharp. Unlike Fairwood House, Bramble Cottage had a sinister aspect, as if it wanted to be left alone.

She thought she saw a movement in the garden, among the shells of old kitchen appliances and mounds of fly-tipped rubbish, and the shock it gave her made her start walking again.

Something grey flashed between the trees, in her peripheral vision.

Carrie sucked in her breath and unconsciously held it, lungs bursting in protest as she hurried on. Her first thought was that Phil had been watching her, was following her, and the fear stabbed down into her belly, turning it to water.

People go missing on this road.

Her hand closed instinctively over her house keys, pushing the long points between her fingers.

An owl's mournful hoot set her more at ease.

Oh God, it's an owl, she told herself, releasing the breath in a painful gush of relief. *Owls live in the country, I'm in the country now.*

But she wasn't happy until she pushed her way through her own gates and sprinted up the avenue to the embrace of Fairwood's porch, shaking, but safe.

Meet the Locals

In which Carrie joins the History Society
18 April

It had been a bloody awful day. His farsight was on the wane, as it usually was this time of year, and Gran had withheld access to the family shrine for the boost he needed.

(*No, Ricky, my lad, no going down the cellar for you, not until you promise.*)

(*Ain't promising you nothing, nothing, bloody old bitch, I'll do it another way.*)

The cottage door slammed, shutting out the world. He didn't bother to take his hood down indoors – it was as cold inside as it was outside, not that the temperature bothered him. His fever-flushes came and went in waves.

He was in the grip of one now, skin twisting under his clothes, iron-hard bulges pushing against his stretchmarks like writhing hernias. When he Changed for good, he would be a thing of beautiful monstrosity. He would bathe naked in the wintry sunlight on the Weald, drink in the whiplash-sweet salt of the sea and live a blissfully solitary existence.

His thoughts went to the house and its prize, *his* prize, but the comforting thoughts of future freedom were shattered by his present predicament.

'Richard! What did your gran say?' His mother's sibilant whisper slithered down the stairs, reminding him he was never alone, spoiling everything.

'Nothing,' he called back, heading for the trapdoor to the cellar. 'She's got her society meeting tonight.'

His mother took this in bad part. 'What the pest is the matter with you? Uncle David wants to see the omens for his business venture, have you forgot? He'll pay us well, didn't she help you?'

'I said leave it!'

He unlatched the trapdoor to the old coal cellar, taking care not to make too much noise. His mother wouldn't be coming downstairs. She was too weak. He had seen to that.

Rank wafts rose up as Ricky slipped inside, descending into the damp, fetid gloom. He inhaled greedily, knowing he was too old for this now, but nostalgic visits to his childhood friend relaxed him.

(*Burn it*, his father said, *what if it's found, who knows what it eats?*)

A glint of grey light wormed down through the floorboards and played over his needle collection: stainless steel, half-curved, double-curved, straight Glovers and families of circular cutting edge. He took his time to select the best for the task, threading it with care and snapping the length off with his teeth.

'How's the patient?' He turned to the figure strapped to the wooden wheel, its hooded head lolling forwards. 'Easy, Gerald. We'll patch you up. Don't you worry.'

There was no sound. Gerald flopped, limp, against the restraints binding him upright. Ricky experienced the usual twinge. He promised himself he *would* get rid of Gerald it couldn't last much longer. Eighteen was antique in stuffed toy years.

The rip in Gerald's side was quite bad this time, curled brown leaves sticking to the stitches. Ricky fingered these thoughtfully. Gerald never left the cellar. Where did the leaves come from?

He stuck his finger deep into the wound, poking a wriggling mess of maggots and putrefaction. He withdrew it and inhaled the stink that stuck jam-slick to his skin.

'Gran wants me to be her little spy,' Ricky complained, picking out the leaves and starting to sew, stinking gut-ooze coating his fingertip up to the first knuckle. 'I know her too well, she'd yank the strings of others' wyrds about like Punch 'n' bloody Judy, even mine, Gerald, even bleedin' mine. It's *my* skill, it's for *me* to know.

I'm the farsighted, *I'm* the soothsayer, *I'm* this fam'ly's One and Only, they'd all be mole-blind like the regulars of the world, were it not for me.'

The needle glimmered, stabbing in and out, drawing angry thread behind it like a dark comet-tail. The donkey hide was practically leather and worn smooth and bald in places, but Gerald had had this skin for a long time now, and he liked it.

Ricky sniffed, vision blurring. 'Fine, then, I'll let it fade an' stay blind myself, let it come back on its own, natural-like, it'll hurt them more'n it hurts me.'

(*Liar*, Gerald's caped skull accused, *without your farsight what are you? Naun but a maggot in my belly, Richard Edwin Porter.*)

'Don't be like that. I'll get you more innards, promise.' He gave the hide a little pat.

The deer skull nodded with the tremor, bobbing in mute agreement.

He dashed the back of his hand over his tear-stained cheeks.

'I'm a tool to them,' he sniffed. 'Ain't I? Just a tool.'

Gerald commiserated.

'What? *You're* not a tool,' Ricky objected, gravel-gruff.

Steel gleamed. The needle pressed a thin indent into his acid-white fingers.

'Nah, that ain't true. I'll sew you up and I'll unstrap you, see? Will you move for me, if I do?'

Gerald only shivered with the movement of the needle, antlers dipping.

Gerald never moved when Ricky was watching.

Never had.

'Nah, I know you're a toy,' he muttered. 'If you're a toy I should get rid of you, shouldn't I? Childish, stupid.'

He stabbed into the hide again, finishing off the repair with a vicious sniff.

'Well, fuck me, hey? Fuck me.'

It had been a while since he had allowed himself a good, self-pitying wallow. He put the needle away, pouting, round-shouldered.

'I don't know why I keep you around.'

He tilted the wheel on its axis, lying the six-foot figure flat on its back, antlered skull staring up at the floorboards above with cornflower-blue eyeballs. They needed replacing, too.

Ricky loosened the straps.

Long, mismatched canine limbs sagged, protruding awkwardly from the donkey hide.

'Look at you. Bag of bits 'n' bones.' He sniffed again, swallowing a lump of mucus. 'Heh, look at *me*. Fucking crying. Hell's bells and buckets of blood.'

Folding his arms, he regarded his amateur taxidermy creation. Gerald had seen much better days, once a magisterial sentinel in Ricky's father's old cape, towering over the much-younger Richard with a benevolent air, his only friend. Now he was a relic, a weakness, a bloated body full of straw and maggots.

'She'll let me in, soon, her next door,' Ricky said, thinking of the straw-coloured blonde with her long stride and sad eyes. 'Then I'll show them what I can do. I don't need Gran. I'm not the family toolbox. I'm my own, me.'

Gerald didn't blink. He stared at the dust and grime above, lifeless, chinks in the boards lancing him with stab-wounds of light.

–

Pagham-on-Sea's History Society met in the old scouting hall a good walk out of town, sitting on the end of a road that terminated at a fenced car park and scattered picnic tables overlooking the sea. It was a large, single-storey hall of dark green concrete blocks with a rusty tin roof, bearing the old remnants of the Boy Scout logo above the door.

Pushing open the heavy fire door, Carrie entered a musty land of electric heaters and utilitarian furniture, the space lined on each side with stacked tables and hard black plastic chairs that left scuff marks along the linoleum floor. The small gathering of people in the central ring of chairs turned as she approached, and Carrie found herself taking a step back.

Which one was Mr Bishop? Perhaps the older gentleman with the loud checked jacket and awful toupee. He stood up, approaching with an extended hand.

'Caroline Rickard, I presume! Thank you for your email, my dear. Welcome.'

Carrie's heart leapt into her throat and hammered for release. She shook his hand as firmly as she dared, while what felt like thousands of eyes fixed her with curious stares.

'Welcome to our happy little band.' Their self-elected spokesman released her from his enthusiastic grip, florid and jovial. 'I am the vice-chair, Mr Bishop's second-in-command, so to speak, widely knowledgeable on several topics, but Classical History is my specialist subject, as it were. Colonel Mark Curtis, at your service.' He stood to attention, a gentleman from another age.

Carrie forced her lips into a twitchy smile. 'Nice to meet you, Colonel.'

The Colonel's lively chocolate eyes twinkled over the bridge of his Roman nose. 'Not often we get new blood in our humble circle,' he said, offering her an empty chair. 'Do take a seat.'

Carrie, rubbing nervous hands along the seams of her jeans, made her way into the circle and sat down.

The woman across from Carrie, a severe-looking retiree with the uneven, weathered tan of a persistent gardener, gave her a faint smile. Her red blouse and high-waisted black-and-white striped skirt gave her a striking aspect.

'Lovely to meet you at last, Caroline,' the woman said, pleasantly enough. 'We've all heard so much about the renovations. It's all very exciting.'

'Yes, indeed, but now is the time for introductions, Beverley,' the Colonel admonished. 'Let's do this in some semblance of order? Ms Rickard, this is Mrs Sheila Azeman, our secretary.'

Carrie nodded in greeting at the next around the circle. There were already too many names to remember – new people on her shift, Mercy's partner from the other night, and now what felt like a whole roomful. She tried to focus.

A stout lady in a smart, cool-grey trouser suit that contrasted against her warm brown skin, perhaps in her late sixties or early seventies at Carrie's best guess, inclined her head.

'You'll need to fill this out.' She passed a form across to Carrie.

'Oh.' Carrie hadn't intended to join. 'I— I was only visiting, I don't think I can afford a membership fee at the moment...'

'There's no fee.' Sheila Azeman smiled, showing two elongated canines.

Carrie took the form.

'Pen, please?' It came out as a squeak.

Mrs Azeman produced one, seemingly from thin air.

Carrie signed herself up, handing back the pen and paper when she was done, and the introductions continued. Who had been around sixty years ago? She eliminated the younger members like Dev Syal, history teacher and another fellow Londoner, and a few others.

'...And that's all of our little group this evening,' the Colonel said. 'We're missing, let me see, two or three... and dear Mrs Varney, oh! Here she is.'

An elderly lady entered the hut with a friendly wave, moving with sinuous grace. She had the physique of a retired ballet dancer or gymnast, her hair swept into a sleek bun at the back of her head. She looked old enough to remember the murder first-hand, even if she had been a girl when it happened. Her nose wrinkled and she shot Mrs Azeman a sharp look.

Mrs Azeman eyeballed her, unflinching.

Mrs Varney growled – actually growled – in the back of her throat.

'Now, now, ladies,' Colonel Curtis said. 'I thought we'd agreed to put the tea rota business behind us. Janet, this is a new member, Caroline...'

Carrie gave a shaky smile, which was met with a piercing appraisal.

'New blood?' Janet Varney asked, gliding with long strides across the room. 'Colonel, you spoil us.'

'She's here of her own volition,' the Colonel explained with a bristling moustache. 'Bought The Crows, you see.'

'Selling it on, surely.' Mrs Varney eyed her with predatory suspicion.

Carrie shook her head, heart hammering. 'No. I live there now.'

Janet Varney stalked through the circle to sit by the lady introduced as Beverley. 'Fancy that.'

Carrie fiddled with her chain. 'I've got a lot of questions, actually—'

'So here we all are this week,' the Colonel cut across her, 'Except, of course, our fearless leader. Who is, as usual, ruddy late.'

'Coming from Barker Crescent, I'll be bound,' Beverley said with a suggestive cackle, patting the back of her untidy pile of sheep-cream curls. 'Chatting to the *lovely* Mrs Wade about the old theatre.' She pronounced 'lovely' the way Carrie's grandmother had always pronounced 'Jezebel'.

Carrie glanced around the circle again. It was an interesting group, she thought. This was as good a time as any to make a start in a new place. No one caught her eye except Beverley, who gave her a thin smile.

The door opened again.

'Sorry I'm late, everyone,' Guy Bishop said, striding into the midst of the Society.

Carrie flinched, digging her nails into the sides of her chair.

It was like a hipster version of Phil had entered the room.

Guy Bishop was in his mid-thirties, a close-cut beard framing his symmetrical features and bringing out the warm tones in his hazel eyes.

No, Carrie told herself. *No. He's not like Phil, calm down. Phil wouldn't grow a beard.*

He was looking right at her.

41

Carrie's cheeks blazed.

'Hi,' he said.

Carrie straightened up and gave him her best casual smile. 'Hi.'

'Guy, this is Caroline,' the Colonel said, gesturing towards her. 'She's come for a little look. Haven't you, m'dear? Bought The Crows.'

'Ah!' Guy even looked attractive when surprised. He stared at her. 'You're – not quite what I imagined, when I heard someone had bought it, and was actually living there, I have to admit...' He exchanged looks with Mrs Azeman, who shuffled the forms in her lap and looked away. Guy recovered. 'We'll definitely have a chat about it later, if you'd like.'

Carrie beamed. 'Sure! That's fine by me.'

Guy beamed back. Even his teeth were perfect. Nothing not to like. It had been ages since she had allowed herself to find someone attractive (Ian had been okay, not her usual type but a good reintroduction to the dating world) or been relaxed enough to let her guard down.

She filed the red flags away for later.

Once the meeting was underway, she got to ask her questions about The Crows, but to her surprise, no one seemed prepared to give her many answers. Guy suggested she buy his father's book on the subject, Janet Varney was keen to change the subject back to the campaign to save an art deco theatre, and Colonel Curtis, for all his welcoming bluster, shut her down when he got the chance.

'I just wondered about the, um, the girl they found,' she said finally, after being brushed over again by the Colonel. Beverley's focus became razor sharp. Carrie squirmed. 'Um. In my house, you know. In the Fifties...?'

'We don't talk about that, dear,' Beverley murmured, loud enough to carry across the circle. She spoke with a slight affectation, as if deliberately masking the more natural local accent underneath.

'*Miss* Rickard, some of us do not consider the Fifties *history* as such, given we lived through them,' Colonel Curtis said, raising his voice and taking odd punctuating breaths as his face darkened into an unhealthy beetroot stain. The switch from 'Ms' to 'Miss' didn't escape Carrie's notice. Her cheeks burned. The Colonel ploughed on, face darkening with effort. 'Apart from that, I for one, am of the opinion that *ghoulish* considerations of other people's misfortunes are, are best, best left to the gutter press.' His chest heaved.

Carrie quivered, falling back into the well-worn groove of appeasement. Phil had trained her well.

'I'm sorry, of course, you're right, I – it's just awful, I didn't want to upset anyone, I'm so sorry I asked...'

'It's all right, Uncle Mark,' Guy muttered, but couldn't quite meet Carrie's eye.

Carrie spent the rest of the meeting in silence, cheeks burning with humiliation.

By nine o'clock, the meeting was over, and Carrie had learned a lot about Pagham-on-Sea's theatre scene in the 1920s but very little of actual interest to her.

Guy and the Colonel stayed behind to stack the chairs. As the others filed out, Carrie busied herself with helping clear the hall to show willing and make up for her earlier faux pas.

Beverley approached her, not to help, but to point out she was stacking the chairs too high. Carrie flushed, but Beverley wasn't done. She hovered, observing.

'You're settling in all right, are you dear?' the older woman asked in tones of maternal concern. 'It must be lonely for you, all alone in that big place.'

'I'm not lonely,' Carrie insisted, lying. 'It's great here.'

Beverley studied her with a faint, disbelieving smile. 'Would you like to come for tea with me one day this week?'

Carrie wasn't sure she did, but it was the first invitation of the kind she'd had, so she smiled anyway. 'I'd love to, thanks. Um, it's Beverley, isn't it? Is there anything I can do? Do you want me to bring anything...?'

Beverley beamed, the apples of her cheeks growing pink with pleasure. 'Oh, bless you, no, I have my grandson for that. Ricky is ever such a good boy. Always brings me my shopping on a Friday.' Her watery eyes narrowed. 'He's our Letitia's boy. Neighbours of yours, Letitia and George are.'

'Neighbours?' Carrie didn't have any neighbours. She wondered how far away the nearest farmhouse was.

'At Bramble Cottage, dear.'

Something clicked. '*Really?*' She couldn't believe anyone lived there. The cottage was a wreck.

'Haven't you met our Ricky? Always in the woods, he is. Been telling me all about it up there, all the work.'

The grey in the trees, Carrie thought. *Not Phil – a creepy neighbour. Great.*

'Lovely boy. Always calls by once a week at least, drops my shopping off and has a bit of tea. Can't do enough for me. I wish the others were the same, but there we go, that's families for you, isn't it.' She sniffed, accent broadening as her tone darkened. 'You'd think our Ruby would call her old mother once in a while but oh, no, not her. Gone to be with rather bettermost sort of folks, hasn't she, marrying that Youngblood fellow and taking herself off to Lancaster. I could never a-bear that chap. Got a jacuzzi in the garden now, she has. In *Lancaster*. Imagine that! I says to her, Ruby, I says, it's a poor look-out for you if you want to swap the love and support of your own flesh-and-blood for a few bubbles up your—'

'Sorry to interrupt, Bez, but we have to head off,' Guy cut in.

Carrie winced apologetically, empathising with the errant Mrs Ruby Youngblood. 'Sorry, so do I. I'd love to come for tea, though.'

'Oh, well, when you're not busy.' Beverley squeezed Carrie's upper arm with a disconcertingly strong grip. 'Not a lot of meat on you, is there, dear? You're like our Katy, she's a scrawny little thing. Well, we'll fix that. Come over tomorrow at seven, I'm at the end of Sea View Road. Wundorwick, that's me.'

Carrie smiled. She finished work at six. 'I'll see you tomorrow.'

Guy gave her a shy glance. 'Can I give you a lift?' he asked.

'No thanks, I'm honestly fine,' Carrie heard herself say.

'Are you sure?' Guy's perfectly smooth brow creased in the middle. 'I'm dropping Sheila home too, it's no bother.'

Carrie hesitated, as if accepting would consign Guy to oblivion. 'If you're sure?' She tested his resolve. 'I mean, I do live in the Bermuda Triangle of Sussex.'

Guy laughed. 'Don't listen to all that. It's fine.'

If Carrie's inner voice had boots, it would have kicked her in the brain.

Shut up and get in the car!

'After you,' Guy said. He waved goodnight to the Colonel, who cheerily waved back. 'Night, Uncle Mark!'

Carrie, melting, scuttled through the door, the top-of-the-range sports car outside gleaming under the streetlight. Another red flag flipped up in her head. Booksellers didn't make *that* much money, surely? But perhaps business was booming, or Guy had an inheritance, or family money, or something like that. It wasn't any of her business. Then again, perhaps he was a lucky gambler (unlike Phil). Or a drug baron. She knew absolutely nothing about him. She tried not to show her discomfort as her imagination ran amok.

He was probably an axe murderer.

'I'll get in the back,' Mrs Azeman said, clutching her bag of folders and pens. 'What did Mrs Wend want?'

Carrie helped Mrs Azeman unload her things onto the back seat. The name rang a faint bell. 'Beverley? Oh, just being friendly, I think. Everyone's been really nice.'

'No, they haven't.' Mrs Azeman looked her dead in the eye with disconcerting shrewdness. 'I know the people in this town. You're lonely.'

Carrie froze, hand tightening on the edge of the car door. 'I'm fine.'

'No, you're not. I can tell.' Mrs Azeman gave her a small twitch of a smile. 'I suppose you've heard your house is cursed.'

'It isn't,' Carrie retorted, cheeks burning.

Sheila Azeman chuckled. 'Oh, I know. But people do believe a lot of rubbish. You'll make friends. Just be careful who with.' With that, she climbed into the back seat, letting Carrie close the door for her.

'Nice car,' she said, sliding into the front passenger seat, letting the luxury envelop her.

Guy patted the steering wheel. 'She's my baby. I saw her, and... yeah. Well, I'm sure you can relate, right?'

Sheila Azeman leaned between them, offering a packet of mints. 'I did warn him about buying *on credit*,' she said to Carrie. 'But he wouldn't listen to me.'

Guy shot her a sheepish grin and pulled off. They glided into town, headlights lighting up the road ahead. Carrie cracked the window and took a deep breath of salty air.

'Thanks for letting me join,' she said. 'It was really interesting. Is that all the members you have?'

Sheila sighed. 'We used to have a lot more, but these past few years have been very disappointing. A lot of the older members have passed on, you know. Younger ones come and go. My granddaughter used to come with me, but then she took up the guitar, started playing in a band at school.'

'You settling in all right?' Guy asked Carrie finally, forcing a cheerful tone. 'It's a nice place, once you get to know it.'

Carrie smiled. 'Yeah. Beverley invited me over, too, so that's nice.'

Guy turned in to a street that bowed like a crescent, bordered on either side by similar crescent-shaped streets. 'Great. Good to hear. Mrs Wend is a generous lady. Here we are, Sheila.'

This time, it came back to her in a rush: Mercy warning her against the Wend family over dinner at the Ram. Her eyes widened in the rear-view mirror, catching Sheila's amber gleam in the dark.

They pulled into the driveway of a block of flats, built in a style typical of modern private sheltered accommodation, a friendly light on in the foyer.

As Guy got out to open the door for her, Sheila leaned in close to Carrie's ear, her breath hot on the back of Carrie's neck. She tapped Carrie twice on the shoulder.

'If you go to Beverley's,' Mrs Azeman whispered, '*Don't drink the tea.*'

Jumping with surprise, Carrie twisted around to stare at her.

Guy opened the door.

'Have a good evening,' Mrs Azeman said at her normal volume, getting out and slamming the door.

Carrie's skin crawled where Sheila had tapped her. It felt like a signal of some kind, something she couldn't interpret. Another warning.

Guy didn't seem to have heard what she'd said. He saw Sheila into the foyer and returned to the car with long swift strides. As he got back in, Carrie licked her lips, shooting him a quick glance.

'Thanks for the lift.'

He coughed, suddenly coy. 'I, er… I don't suppose I'd be able to… see what you've done with the place, would I? Not now,' he added hastily, 'but, some time when it's convenient? I used to go there when I was a kid.'

'Don't tell me you nicked stuff too,' Carrie said, laughing.

Guy turned red. 'Oh, God. Who've you been talking to?'

'*Did* you?'

He made a strangled, guilty sound. His hands briefly lifted off the steering wheel.

'Sorry…' He gave an embarrassed chuckle. 'Never thought I'd meet someone who'd buy it,' he admitted. 'I never thought anyone *would* buy it, to tell you the truth.'

'I can't imagine why anyone wouldn't want to!' Carrie settled, watching the town speeding past them. 'I think it's the most amazing place.'

Guy's smile widened. 'I can't wait to see it.' He turned off at the roundabout. The Fairwood estate wasn't too far away from the town, but it was far enough off the beaten track for Carrie to be a little self-conscious about getting Guy to drive so far out of his way.

'Guy,' Carrie said, 'What do you know about the murder?'

'Murder... as in, a murder of crows?'

Carrie raised an eyebrow. 'No.' *People couldn't leave that pun alone, could they?* 'I meant, as in, the Ross murder.'

Guy shook his head. 'Ah. Well. It's all in my dad's book. It's a bit out-of-date now – he published it in 1987.'

'I don't know if I can afford a copy right now,' Carrie confessed.

He drove through the open wrought-iron gates and crunched up the gravel avenue. As the car pulled up outside, The Crows looked down upon them benevolently through newly glazed panes. While she fumbled in her bag for her keys, Guy got out and leaned on the car, staring up at the miracle the contractors had performed.

'Holy cow.'

Fairwood had been restored to its former glory, at least from the outside. The house surveyed its domain across the gardens, whole and complete. Three stories high in the central part with three gables overlooking the drive, the house wore a proud, concentrated expression.

Guy shook his head. 'I'll... I can drop the book up to you after work, is that all right? I'd – I'd love to have a proper look.'

No.

The disapproving thought jarred with her mood, as if it wasn't really her own.

She eyed him warily. 'Um... I work shifts though so I can't guarantee when I'll be in...'

'No bother, I'll pop it in your box.' He pointed at the vintage cast-iron postbox Carrie had splashed out for, hanging on the wall beside the door.

Carrie waved, letting herself in as he reversed out. Despite her reservations, she couldn't help but grin.

Don't overthink it. Let it be.

The house absorbed her thrill of delight, wood settling in contented creaks around her as she caressed the bannisters and made her way gleefully upstairs. Warmth flowed in her wake, coursing through the varnished woodgrain from her fingertips. It was cold for an April night, but Carrie didn't mind.

Life was finally looking up.

The Grande Dame

In which Beverley returns the Green Man and Carrie gets suspicious
19 April

Carrie decided against mentioning Beverley Wend's invitation to Mercy. Mercy seemed kind, frank and earnest, everything Becky and Jess had been. Carrie had already made that mistake once.

Besides, although Mercy's advice had been sincerely meant, every town had its scapegoats, every community had That Family. As an outsider, or as much as, she hated that designation and Carrie could approach people with an open mind. At least, that's what she spent the day telling herself, avoiding the obvious knot in this line of thinking: maybe Mercy was exactly what she seemed, and Carrie should stop projecting.

After work, armed with her Maps app that seemed to know how to get to Sea View Road without sending her over a cliff, she made it to Beverley Wend's cottage on time and without mishap. She took this as a good omen.

Set back from the road in the last crook of trees crowding around the lanes, Wundorwick was not the fairy-tale dwelling Carrie had imagined. It was a smart, two-storey detached house of dressed stone, matching curtains at all the lower windows and blinds upstairs. Carrie smirked at her own misgivings. The garden gate looked new, but the scream of its protesting hinges made her wince as she pushed it open.

Beverley Wend opened the front door before she was halfway up the path, looking like a model from a style-for-the-over-sixties catalogue. A ginger tomcat stalked out from under her long, high-waisted skirt, bottlebrush tail held high. He looked at Carrie with imperious disdain and streaked up the apple tree to leap onto the roof.

'That's Toffee, the little devil,' Mrs Wend said, as Carrie approached.

Carrie wasn't a cat person, but she tried. 'That's a cute name. He's lovely.'

Mrs Wend snorted. 'Don't let him fool you. It's short for Mephistopheles.' She beckoned her in. 'Come in, dear. I've put the kettle on.'

Sheila Azeman's warning punched its way into Carrie's mind. *Don't drink the tea.*

'Thank you,' Carrie said, wondering if she should take it seriously. 'Wundorwick? That's an interesting name.'

Mrs Wend followed her gaze to the sign on the wall. 'Old English, with a little poetic licence. Roughly, it means "wonder house". Everyone needs a little bit of wonder in their lives, don't they?' She gave Carrie a smile. 'Come in, I've got a casserole in the oven.'

'Could I get a glass of water, please?'

Mrs Wend patted her arm, squeezing a little unnecessarily, and led her inside. 'Of course. This way.'

Mrs Wend's living room was a gallery of amateur portraits and photographs. There were oils and watercolours of adults and children of various ages, all bearing some family resemblance: the nose, the cheekbones or the shape of the eyes. The framed photographs showed how closely the sitters had been captured.

One old photograph caught Carrie's attention. It was of a young, pale girl in a dark dress, straw boater set winsomely on her tight ringlets, standing by a rose bush. She was staring up at the camera with a hooded expression, a twisted smile of secret knowledge on her face. There was something malevolent about it that sent a chill up Carrie's spine.

'That's me, before I became Mrs Wend,' Mrs Wend said, peering over Carrie's shoulder and making her jump. 'Beverley Pendle I was then. I couldn't be more than, oh, eighteen there.

These are my sisters.' She pointed out a portrait of two girls, clearly an amateur's early attempt but showing promise in the passages of paint. The perspective was a little off, but they told a story of a quiet girl with sad eyes and a proud, younger girl with a strong jaw. It was the swirling background that made Carrie uneasy, as if the painter had been trying to capture something they couldn't quite see, something reaching for the girls with writhing, pale green coils.

'Did you paint these?' Carrie asked, looking around again. 'They're really good.'

'Oh, thank you, yes, I just do it for fun, you know.' Her hostess moved closer to the big portrait of the two girls. 'This is Olive,' Mrs Wend said. 'Olive-in-the-middle. And Eileen, the youngest. Got away with everything, did our Eileen.' She sniffed. 'Make yourself at home, I'll get you a glass of water.'

Carrie looked around, left temporarily alone.

Beverley Pendle.

Like the gamekeeper. The family connected to the girl's murder. Her kitchen chimney was literally built out of the old stones of the Pendle cottage.

What a strange coincidence.

Carrie looked around. The furniture seemed to be relics of multiple eras, none of which matched. A chaise longue by the window was heaped high with sewing boxes, rolls of material, and a reclining dressmaker's dummy. Two armchairs, one faded ox-blood red, the other smoker's beige, were positioned by the fireplace. An antique coffee table had been partially cleared of ladies' magazines, crossword puzzle books and old copies of the *Pagham-on-Sea Gazette*.

A prickling on the back of her neck made her look at the mantelpiece. A terracotta tile was propped against the wall with a Green Man face painted on it, the open eyes peering at her through the glazed leaves. It felt familiar. She crossed to the fireplace to get a closer look. It was warm in her hand, shiny and smooth, and as she turned it over she saw the marks on its edges where someone had chiselled it out of its place. It reminded her of the tiles around the fireplace in the living room of The Crows. Some had been missing, so she'd had to replace them. This one looked the right size, the right fit. She pressed her thumb against the glaze, stroking the leafy motif.

'Here you are, dear.' Mrs Wend re-entered, interrupting Carrie's curious contemplation of the tile.

Carrie put it back and took the glass with a grateful smile.

Her stomach growled.

Beverley smiled. 'Would you like some casserole?'

No one warned me against the casserole.

'Um, yes, please, that would be lovely.'

Mrs Wend nodded. She looked Carrie over with a shrewd, calculating expression. 'You know,' she said, staring straight through her, 'Most people looked at that old place, ruined and alone, so isolated, damaged, and they thought, *dreadful things have happened there* – and they'd be right – best to leave it be, let it decay… but not you, no. Not Caroline Rickard.'

Carrie's skin prickled. She sipped the water to mask her nerves.

Mrs Wend gave a short chuckle. 'Oh, don't mind me. I like to get to know people. It's what they do that interests me, you know. You can learn a lot about a person by watching what they do.'

What is it that you *do, Beverley?*

Ask her.

The question left Carrie's lips without going via her brain, and she only realised she'd said it out loud by the changing expression on her hostess's face.

Mrs Wend blinked. 'Pardon?'

'I mean, I'm sorry, I don't know why I…' The Green Man drew Carrie's attention again, prickles spreading over her face. It was looking right at her, mouth agape in the glazed wreath of leaves. She thought fast, recovering. 'I mean – what did your family do? Used to do. I heard the Pendles were gamekeepers for the Fairwood estate?'

Mrs Wend frowned, her accent slipping into a broader, older form. 'Oh. De Pendles were – yes, dat's true.' She caught herself, and the slight affectation returned. 'Then Sir James knocked down their home for his extension.'

Carrie pursed her lips.

'Oh, don't look like that, it weren't you.' Mrs Wend cast an eye around the living room, sweeping it suspiciously as if scanning for spies. 'Would you like to know more?'

'Absolutely. If you don't mind.' Carrie's glee must have shown, because Mrs Wend took a step back, appraising her.

'You really love it, don't you?' she murmured. 'Your face. It lights up when you talk about it. Like it's your best friend in the whole world.' She gestured at the tile on the mantelpiece. 'You can take that. One of the local boys gave that to me, years ago. I can barely dust it – allergic to the glaze or something, I think. It's yours.'

'Thanks.' Carrie picked it up again, warm and smooth. The Green Man smiled back at her, happy with this state of affairs.

'Caroline, dear,' Mrs Wend began, folding her arms, 'now, forgive me if I'm speaking out of turn, but I can see you're not happy. You seem under a lot of stress. And you're a curious person by nature, I think. Please ask me anything you like, and if you need something – well, I'd be happy to help if you wouldn't mind helping me out now and again.' She waved at the coffee table. 'It's a bit crowded in here. Let's eat in the kitchen.'

Carrie nodded, her stomach grumbling against her suspicions. 'Thank you.' She slipped the tile into her pocket, following her host.

Mrs Wend guided her down the hallway into a kitchen filled with mismatched pans and hanging herbs, a large kitchen table in the middle that reminded her of The Crows. A few places were set, and a casserole was bubbling fragrantly on the oven top, fresh out of the oven. Carrie's stomach flip-flopped at the smell. She sat, scraping up a chair.

She saw a handmade wind chime above the back door, a protection pentangle of twigs, small shells dangling from silken threads.

'Are you pagan, Mrs Wend? Beverley? Sorry, do I mean Wiccan?' She flushed, but her hostess didn't mind.

'Oh, goodness, no.' Beverley Wend laughed. 'No, I'm a bit beyond all that now. Not that I say anything against it, of course. Little Tina Harris, a friend of Wesley's, he's my Charlotte's oldest boy, she works at the morgue, you know, and not so little anymore, she's your age I'd say, or our Wesley's age, somewhere around there... they grow up don't they! Yes, I think Eglantine is something like that, though I've not really asked. Eat up, dear, you're skin and bone. There's plenty.'

Thinking back to Mercy's 'welcome to SupaPrice' pub dinner made Carrie realise she hadn't had a decent hot meal since the Red Ram. The casserole burnt her tongue and throat on the way down, but it was worth it. The meat melted in her mouth.

'This is amazing, thank you,' she managed, swallowing.

Beverley brushed the compliment aside. 'I noticed at the meeting yesterday you had questions about your house,' she continued, finally taking a bite of casserole and talking with her mouth full. 'You seemed put out that no one wanted you to ask them.'

Carrie fidgeted. 'I didn't want to seem rude, but...'

...*but you lot bloody were.*

Beverley smiled at her sullen scowl. 'Your house is full of secrets. Old ones. I can't tell you very much except that it used to be a monastery, founded in the eleventh century, I think. Quite poor, it was, never received many donations. By the Reformation, Henry VIII and his wives, you know, they only supported four monks. Thirteenth-century stone the crypt is supposed to be, and the king's men tore the rest down. The Sauvants were about five miles away then, they were given that land and built their "new" manor on top of it.' She paused, eyes raised to the ceiling, thinking. 'What else? Well, there's a smugglers' tunnel, but I suppose you know that already, going into the cellars on the other side of the crypt, and it's supposed to connect to the old priest hole somewhere near the grand staircase, well that's Elizabethan. And then the "E" shaped building went out of fashion, and they turned it into a square, and that was when Sir James decided to do a lot of remodelling and pulled down the old Pendle cottage and built the new one. I suppose you want to know more about the Pendles, and their cottage, is that it?'

There was a strange tension in the older woman now. Mrs Wend's eyes were cold, with a dark red gleam that was surely just Carrie's imagination. The brown of Beverley's eyes had a reflective sheen that must come from somewhere, Carrie reasoned, but there was nothing that would make chestnut shine like ruby.

Beverley's smile was colder. 'Suppose you tell me what you already know. Then I won't be boring you.'

Carrie blinked, putting her fork down. 'Well. I know it's an origin story for the curse. Mr Pendle is supposed to have cursed the Sauvants when his cottage was pulled down, that's all I've really heard. I noticed the hearthstone in the kitchen has the letter "P" carved into it – I assume it was theirs?'

At the mention of the hearthstone, the tension increased. Mrs Wend went deathly still, rigid in her seat.

Carrie swallowed. 'Were they gamekeepers for a long time?'

Her hostess gave her a pinched nod, relaxing slowly into nonchalance. 'Oh, four or five generations, yes. Bramble Cottage was built for us, and was signed over to us eventually, when the Sauvants lost all their woodland and farmland. Crippled by death-duties, they was.' She seemed to be waiting for something else, reading Carrie's face in case she missed something written there. 'My father, he was a Pendle.' She smiled, but the corners of her eyes didn't crinkle. 'My sisters and I loved those woods. We played there all the time, me, Olive, and Eileen. It was where we grew. Where we fell in love.' That smile should have had fondness in it at least, but instead it sent a chill through Carrie that cut her to the core. The red sheen seemed to glow darker. 'I married

Mr Wend, of course. Couldn't have babies out of wedlock, not back then.' She sniffed, pausing, suddenly sly. 'Our Letitia and George have it now, Bramble Cottage, I mean. Their son, Ricky – he's a good boy, really, and such a good-looking boy I think, if he looked after himself a bit better. But he has his little schemes. Not the best influence on people. I wouldn't call him a catch, I'm afraid. I do *try* with him, but...' She shrugged sadly.

Carrie sensed she was being warned off and wrenched the conversation in another direction.

'Mrs Wend... what about the girl? The girl in the chimney?'

'That poor lamb? Oh, yes. Terrible. Terrible thing.' Mrs Wend shook her head. 'I don't know much about that. Nobody does.'

Carrie resisted the urge to play with her necklace and dropped her hands to her lap. She licked her lips, watching those unsettling eyes. 'Why was she up the chimney? It's bizarre. If you were trying to hide a body, surely it would take more effort to—' she stopped. 'Unless... that was the *point*. The chimney was *important*.'

'I can't imagine how,' Mrs Wend demurred.

'I heard she'd been drained of blood,' Carrie said, wondering what she had gotten herself into.

'Yes, well, people say all sorts of things.'

Carrie's eyes watered as she realised she had asked the wrong question at the start. It slipped out before she could stop herself.

'What *did* you do, Mrs Wend?'

Beverley Wend's lips twisted in a flicker of her youthful malevolence. 'I just helped people, dear. That's all I've ever tried to do.'

'I'm sorry.' Carrie couldn't shake the uneasy feeling. 'It's just, um. Bit of a coincidence. I'm just wondering – I've got this weird feeling.' She stopped. 'I'm going to shut up now.'

'Before you accuse anyone of murder?' Mrs Wend chuckled. 'Probably wise, dear.'

'It's not haunted, is it?' Carrie asked abruptly.

Mrs Wend gave a thin little shrug. 'Old houses have person- alities of their own,' she said. 'So full of memories and energies that there's no room left for spirits, sometimes.' She gave Carrie a sweet, pearly smile, her gaze flicking over the green and white shop uniform. 'You'll see that for yourself, I've no doubt, if you can even afford to keep the place, of course. What will you do if you can't find a better job?'

Carrie blinked at the change of pace. 'I – what do you mean?'

'Well.' Beverley's shadow loomed over the table as if it had a life of its own. 'Minimum wage isn't enough to run that place, is it? It's barely enough to live on, never mind the heating bills in the winter, the electricity... How are you going to manage?'

Carrie thought about the applications she'd sent off to no avail. She might as well have thrown her CV into an abyss.

'I'll manage. It's only temporary.'

'There's other places, dear. Now you've renovated, you could always move on. Get the heritage lot to take it over. Or the History Society here, we have good connections. If you ever did need to move away for work, or for your health, or your family... we'd be happy to help you out.'

The Green Man tile, secreted in her pocket, pressed itself firmly against her thigh.

It came to her less as an assertion and more as a burst of emotion, something hot and angry balling itself up in her stomach. '*No.*'

Mrs Wend blinked. 'No?'

'*No Pendle is setting foot in my house.*'

Carrie barely recognised her own voice, it was so guttural, so cold. The words scraped against her tonsils, sharp-edged and hard as brick. She clapped a hand to her mouth, but it was too late. Too stunned to even say sorry, she stared at the older woman in mute horror, fingers clamped to her lips.

Mrs Wend didn't react as if she had said anything out of the ordinary – rather, she sat back in her chair with something akin to satisfaction, as if she had found something out.

Ruby glinted in her eyes.

'Only a suggestion, dear,' she murmured, studying Carrie as if she were reading the inside of her skull.

The garden gate screeched and two teenage girls burst in through the front door.

'Gran! Are you in?' The first girl was tall and slim, with straight brown hair and the same sulky cast to the face that Carrie had noticed in the family portraits.

'Kitchen!'

The other girl, jogging in behind her, waved at Carrie with some surprise. It was Rachel, from the supermarket. 'Oh! Hello! I didn't know you knew Katy's gran.'

Carrie exhaled in a rush and stood up, nearly knocking her chair over. 'Oh, hi! I'm just going, actually.'

'This is Katy,' Rachel said, threading her arm through the first girl's. 'Katy, this is Caroline, she's the lady who bought The Crows.'

Katy gave her a nod. 'Hi.' Her attention was short-lived. 'Gran! Is there anything to eat? I'm starving.'

'Isn't your mother feeding you?'

Katy shrugged.

Carrie took the opportunity to make her escape. 'I'll be going, Mrs Wend – Beverley…' She had almost forgotten about the Green Man until it knocked against her hip as she took a step forward. She made it into the hall, peering back to the kitchen.

'But you've not long arrived!' Mrs Wend nudged past the two girls, making Carrie back off to the door.

'Thanks so much for dinner, but I need to get back…' Carrie covered her pocket with her hand. 'Can we do this again?' She had no intention of ever going back to Wundorwick, but instinct told her to keep things calm and casual.

Mollified, Mrs Wend frowned. 'Well, of course, but—'

Carrie edged to the door. 'Lovely to meet you, Katy. Nice to see you again, Rachel! Beverley – I'll see you next Wednesday, at the society, I guess. We'll sort out tea again. Okay? Thanks. Sorry. Bye!'

Katy gave her a polite smile. 'Nice to meet you.'

'You too.' Carrie managed to leave the cottage, heaving a sigh of relief as the front door closed on her.

It was getting dark.

Carrie couldn't shake the feeling of being watched the whole way back, although there was no one around and Redditch Lane was deserted. She kept looking over her shoulder for traffic or cyclists, or any other living soul, but only the bus passed her, half empty. Red brake-lights flashed as it slowed but didn't stop.

Carrie tried not to think of them as glowing eyes.

A prickle on the nape of her neck made her turn and stare over the fence into a field. It was deserted, the cropped grass stirred by the breeze. People disappeared on this road, the locals said. Cars and all. Gone.

Carrie shivered, clutching her keys in one hand. She pushed the sharp edges between her fingers and made a tight, hard fist. The breeze died, the grass was still. She carried on walking, following the distant glow of the bus's lights as it trundled through The Chase up ahead.

The great wrought-iron gates of Fairwood greeted her as she cleared the field and came to the high stone wall ringing her property, twisted metal birds in the arched tops aping the real crows coming home to roost. Carrie pushed the gate and set off up the gravel driveway, the sense of an invisible watcher disappearing with the beating of strong black wings.

The house had an expectant air about it.

As soon as the front door swung shut behind her, she knew she was safe. The ominous feeling left her. The hall enveloped her in the smell of dry wood and dusty tiles like an invisible embrace, drawing her into the living room.

The Green Man was warm to the touch when she pulled it from her pocket and placed it on her own mantelpiece. The ceiling beams settled above her in a long, contented creak, the chandelier swaying in a draught Carrie couldn't feel.

'I was right,' Carrie mused, looking at the painted tile, its eyes softer, mouth agape in a slight smile. 'You do belong here.'

You *belong here.*

The thought slid into her mind like an echo, fatigue washing through every joint and muscle. She dismissed it as a product of her own exhaustion.

'I'm so tired,' she whispered to it, overwhelmed by a yawn.

Sleep.

The tile smiled at her.

Foot-sore, she clicked off the light and trudged up the stairs, trailing weary fingers up the smooth bannister rail. There was too much to think about.

What was going on with the Pendles? What was wrong with the town?

Carrie fell into bed without eating anything else, her alarm set for the morning, and was asleep before ten o'clock.

–

In her dream, she was standing in the attics all alone. The part she was standing in was kitted out like a Victorian study, complete with a fireplace – the living room fireplace – that shouldn't be up there. Book spines of hunter green and dusky blue filled the shelves, and on the desk was a music box and a posed, taxidermy cat wearing a child's waistcoat and little leather boots. It was Toffee. Someone had sewn antlers on his head, too big for the little skull. His forepaws had been replaced with the tiny hands of a human child.

He was posed above the box as if pouncing on it or trying to keep the lid closed. Carrie moved the box away from those creepy little cat-fingers, and taxidermy-Toffee meowed angrily and toppled over.

She leaned into the cold fireplace with her hands on the mantel, waiting.

He was behind her.

It was impossible to fix him in her mind, but there was a new presence in the room that had not been there before. She never heard him enter, but he always came.

She was wearing some kind of old-fashioned beige garment with buttons down the front: the buttons sprang open but she couldn't see his hands. His heat warmed her, reassuringly real as sun-warmed bricks and copper piping, but she only felt his touch when she closed her eyes. His hand was smooth as the bannisters down the stairs, like polished wood gliding over her skin. The invisible cheek against hers was rough like unfinished stone, gritty as granite. He smelled like a library in summer with undertones of a loamy, overgrown garden, filled with night blossoms and flowering weeds.

She knew that smell.

Mine, *he whispered in her ear in a deeper register of her own voice, guttural, sharp, the way it had sounded in Mrs Wend's cottage.*

Carrie closed her eyes, pressing into him, feeling him there as fragile as a pane of glass. She wanted him badly, an ache of longing glowing through her thighs, but as she pushed herself back against him, he crumbled into plaster dust and chimney soot, leaving her alone in a cloud of chalky air.

Something in the Attic

In which Carrie finds a music box and Guy brings a book
20 April – Morning – Afternoon

As Carrie peeled her eyes open the next morning, the dream evaded recollection. She was left with a compulsive urge to go into the maze of the attics, but what she needed to find there escaped her. Heavy-limbed and on automatic pilot, she padded along the landing.

When she got to the narrow doorway leading to the stairs, she stood in front of the stained glass with some confusion, expecting to see a different door. Her head swam.

I'm dehydrated, she thought. *I slept for ages.*

Still, not quite knowing why, she pushed the door open and ascended the stairs to the airy eaves.

There was no fireplace up here, no Victorian study, no books with blue or green dustjackets. Those details returned to cycle through her mind, out of context. Carrie shivered, disorientated.

Something metallic clunked quietly a few yards away.

A water pipe? Carrie rubbed her face, trying to shake off the feeling that someone was behind her. She turned around, but there was no one there. *Am I dreaming, or what?*

The attics felt as inviting and comfortable to her as they always did.

She had to get ready for work.

Turning to go, the same sad little sound came again, off to her right, somewhere near the wall. Frowning, Carrie dragged herself over to investigate. If it was anything complicated or expensive, it would have to wait. Indefinitely.

The cardboard boxes were full of off-cuts of material, things that had been rescued from cabinets and cupboards during the building repairs, and some newer tins of paint. Carrie pulled out as much as she could to make sure there was nothing that required her immediate attention. The boxes had blocked a hole in the wall, but that was all.

Look…

It was an urge more than a command, and it pulled Carrie to her knees as if tugged by an invisible cord. Her hand reached into the hole before her conscious mind caught up with all the usual reasonable objections: her fingers hit something hard inside the wall before she could pull her hand away.

Carrie had visions of a skeleton, yanking her hand back as the mystery object dislodged. A box slipped between the insulation and thudded with a quiet *plink* onto the floor, where Carrie could see it more plainly. It reminded her of something. Gingerly, not keen on spiders or any other creepy-crawlies that could be lurking on the object, she drew it towards her. It was a dusty, battered music box, its key snapped in the lock and crusted with the grime of ages.

Carrie had the strangest feeling that she had seen it before.

The déjà vu was a bit much on top of the tendrils of emotion her dream had left behind. Carrie turned the box over in her hands, noting the dirt coming off on her fingers in the process, and decided to take it downstairs and worry about it later. For some reason, Phil was on her mind. The dream she couldn't quite remember made her feel like she had been cheating on him, too.

That's ridiculous, she chided herself. *You can't cheat on someone with a house.*

It was half-past six: there was time for a quick run to the beach, if she hurried. She jogged down to her bedroom to deposit the music box, ignoring the chirpy morning text from her bank – *Charges are due to be applied to this account, please top up your balance by 00:00 to avoid additional charges* – and got ready to face the day.

By ten past eight, Carrie's life had taken another downward twist, but now the calming crash of the rising tide breaking over the beach made Carrie forget she'd spent the past hour in tears. SupaPrice had called to say they were sorry, the rota had changed at short-notice and they wouldn't need her for the next two days after all, could she stick to weekends this month. Maybe the manager had finally got the Don't-Hire-The-Crows-Woman memo.

Carrie's calculations, based on her initial number of shifts, were sliced in half. She now couldn't afford the electricity and gas bill. She couldn't face calling either of her parents – it wasn't fair, they weren't exactly well off, her dad would only worry himself sleepless and hypochondriac and her mother would be more triumphant than sympathetic. Something might come up in the meantime.

She burrowed into her trusty grey Bruce Springsteen hoody, head down against the brisk wind, the long walk working its calming magic.

Mercy came jogging over the smooth pebbles, slim figure bulked up with wellington boots and a parka jacket, hair covered by a snug, pink crocheted hat. She was followed by an eager Golden Retriever. 'Hey! Carrie!'

Carrie waved, squinting as the wind lashed her hair across her eyes. 'Hi! Who's your friend?'

Mercy grinned, stretching. 'This is Branston.'

Branston nosed Carrie's pockets, tail thumping against Mercy's straight-cut jeans.

'Branston!' Mercy grabbed him by the collar and hoisted him back, but he battled her to thrust his muzzle in Carrie's midriff.

Carrie grinned, hunkering down to his level to make a fuss of him. 'I don't mind,' she said, scratching his head and fondling him behind the ears. 'He's a lovely dog!'

'He's a daft old thing.' Mercy thrust her hands into her coat to produce a sad looking tennis ball. 'Branston! What've I got? What's mummy got? Look Branston! Ball! Who wants the ball? Who wants the ball?'

The dog bounded back and forth in front of her, salivating with joy. His gleeful bark carried along the strand as Mercy threw the tennis ball as hard as she could. He shot off like a golden bullet.

'Look, um. I don't know if they've already called you, but… I'm glad I bumped into you. How random is this!' She gave an embarrassed laugh, caught off guard. 'First, I didn't do the rota this month. That was Pauline.' Mercy winced. 'I'm really sorry, Carrie, but…'

'You've cut my hours,' Carrie finished for her. 'Yeah. Thanks.'

'Look, people call in sick or don't show up a lot,' Mercy said, frowning. 'When they do, I'll text you first. I don't understand why they've done it, to be honest. We really need an extra person in the week.'

Carrie nodded, biting the inside of her cheek, willing herself not to cry. She looked out at the sea, the grey breakers lapping at the shingle.

'Have you walked all this way?' Mercy asked, looking up at the cliffs behind them.

Carrie nodded.

Mercy gestured to the grey, unpredictable waters. 'We always come out for a walk along here. Branston loves it. How's it going? Did you go to the History Society meeting?'

Carrie watched the dog running off after some interesting scent, the coveted ball firmly gripped between his teeth. 'Yeah, they were very unhelpful. No one wants to tell me anything.' She paused. 'I forgot to say… Mrs Wend invited me to Wundorwick for tea and, um. I went along yesterday. And it was… weird.' She chanced a glance at Mercy's face. Her elfin features were frozen in a pale, wide-eyed stare. 'I didn't want to be rude and turn her down,' Carrie added, trying to smooth over the fact that she had ignored Mercy's well-intentioned advice.

'No, no of course not.' Mercy frowned. 'No, that was the, the right thing to do, I guess. Did you… eat or drink anything?'

'What's that about?' Carrie asked, folding her arms. 'That's… Mrs Azeman the secretary, she said exactly the same thing. "Don't drink the tea." Why?'

Mercy pressed her lips together.

'Mercy, come on. What is it?'

'People… go strange.' She winced. 'Gosh, that sounds mad when you say it out loud. People get *attached* to her.' She watched her dog bounding happily in the shallows, chasing waves. 'She's got this little group of people who follow her around and treat her like a queen. They start off normal, and she invites them over, and then they start… acting out of character. I can't explain it. They'll do anything for her, it's weird, it's little things, I've seen people give up their places in line at the shops, if she needs something they're all falling over each other to help her out, it's… it's creepy. I can't explain it. I'm talking about people who used to *hate* her. They go for tea and a chat or they… eat some of that gingerbread she makes for bake sales and things, and then… total change. *Total three-sixty.*'

Carrie assumed she meant one-eighty but didn't correct her. She raised her eyebrows. 'Well, *I'm* not rushing to go back there or help her out. Just let me know if I start acting out of character.'

Mercy brushed strands of hair from her eyes as the breeze picked up, buffeting them. 'Yeah, 'course. Have to get to know you a bit better first, though.' She grinned. 'Hey, if you want, you can come over ours on Monday? I've got the day off next week.'

'Or you can come over mine?' Carrie balked at the idea of spending an evening away from The Crows. The evening was her favourite time, where she could curl up and savour the peace of the place. 'We could watch a film or something.'

Mercy nodded. 'Sounds good. I'd love to see the house. I could bring Tina, too? She's just split up with her partner, so she's really down at the moment. We could have a girl's night.'

Carrie wondered if this was the same Tina that Mrs Wend had mentioned. 'You know what, that sounds lovely.' It didn't. It sounded like something she *ought* to do, and the eel-slither of panic at the idea of guests slipped into her chest. Carrie took a deep lungful of sea air and wet dog, steeling herself.

'Fab.' Mercy whistled and Branston tore back over the sand with happy, easy bounds. 'We're off! Come on, my little pickle! Let's go home! Do you want a lift back, Carrie? I've got the car.'

Branston woofed at her, tail thumping.

'Nah. I'd like to keep walking for a bit. Thanks, though.'

'You sure? Okay. See you soon!'

'See you,' Carrie said, as Mercy clipped Branston's lead back onto his collar.

Mercy trotted off, Branston loping beside her.

Carrie set off in the opposite direction feeling sick, chancing a glance up at the cliffs above. The bank of smothering clouds hung over the sea, flat and grey like a tin lid on top of the world. She thought she heard someone calling, but there was only a lone figure walking the path in silence.

As she looked up, the figure stopped, hands in their pockets and hidden by their quilted coat, watching her. Prickles washed along Carrie's back, lapping at her fight-or-flight response.

It wasn't the right build for Phil.

She thought she could hear a whistle on the edge of her hearing, sounding shrill and faint from some distant, invisible source. The figure jerked into a crouch, reaching for her across the gulf with crooked gloved fingers like talons.

It was the pose of a pounce.

–

Carrie called her dad as soon as she got home, hoping he wouldn't hear the anxiety in her voice, and chatted about his medication and her stepmother's latest redecorating spree for half an hour.

'Are you *really* all right down there, love?' Her dad sounded concerned. 'Your mum's been on the blower to me five times trying to get hold of you. She says you haven't called her for over a week.'

'Yeah, I meant to, I've just been busy,' Carrie admitted, hugging a sofa cushion into her chest. The sofa was too small for the living room, like all of her other furniture. It looked lost in the middle of the vast space, unopened packing boxes dotted about it like rocks around a tiny island. 'I *did* email her, actually, but she probably hasn't read the message.' Her mum was less techno-savvy than she liked to think she was. 'I really miss you guys.'

'We miss you too, sweetheart. We've all been so worried about you! Do you need me to come back and look at the plumbing again? Ann wants to know if you're eating properly. Why didn't you call? We could've covered your rent for a few months...'

'I don't want to worry you... and I don't want to keep asking for money, either. I just...' Carrie shifted position, flopping full-length on the cushions.

'Come off it love, it's not charity is it? And don't be spending more than you need to, calling up a plumber when I'm still fit to work...' Her dad started to cough.

'Dad! You still smoking?'

'C-ut down...' The reply was choked, but the coughs tailed off. Carrie heard her mother in the back of her mind: *George Rickard, you stubborn old goat...*

She shook her head, but before she could nag him about looking after himself, someone knocked on the front door. The hollow booms made Carrie start.

'Dad, stay on the line a sec? Someone's at the door.'

'I don't like thinking of you in that big house all by yourself, Caro. That waster hasn't been bothering you again, has he?'

'He – he's rung once.' Carrie rolled off the sofa and pushed herself to her feet, thinking about the stranger on the cliff. 'I... I told him to get lost.'

'Good for you. Listen, love, you call us, any time, and we'll be straight in the car. How far out are you from town?'

Carrie listened to her own footsteps echoing through the house as she crossed the hall. The grand staircase behind her responded with a creak, wood swelling in the afternoon sunlight.

'Takes about thirty minutes or so to walk...' It was a deliberate underestimate, but he was already worried.

'Let us give you some cash for a taxi, Caro. Or bus fare, or whatever. You can pay us back when you're on your feet again.'

Carrie swallowed. 'Hang on a sec, Dad.'

She opened the door and Guy Bishop smiled at her, book in hand. 'Hi.'

'It's okay, Dad,' Carrie said quickly into the phone, 'Look, can I call you back in a minute? Someone's popped round, from the History Society, that's all.'

'Oh – well, all right. Love you too sweetheart, speak to you later.'

'Bye!' She hung up. 'Hi!'

'So, um, I thought I'd pop over a bit earlier on the off-chance you'd be in,' Guy said, looking coy. 'Sorry, didn't mean to interrupt.'

Carrie shook her head. 'That's okay. Thanks for this! Do you want a cup of tea or coffee or something?'

Guy beamed at her, his eyes bright and warm. 'Great! If that's not any trouble.'

'No trouble!' Carrie stepped away from the door, and Guy stepped over the threshold, book in hand.

'I was going to leave it in a bag on the porch for you,' Guy said, handing the volume over. 'If you weren't in, which you were, so that's good'…'

There was a honey-coloured blend of blonde and auburn in the brown curls of his short beard, hair gelled darker into a deliberate messy ruffle, which Carrie hadn't noticed the other night. He had what her father called a 'book-lovers' tan', that is, the creamy shade of someone who spent most of their time indoors under a reading lamp. Phil had been the robust, quick-bronzing type who spent even mild spring days baring his chest to the world, but Guy looked as if his tailored shirt was a secondary skin. She was willing to bet if he rolled up his sleeves there would be an even paler line around his wrists.

He strolled around the entrance hall in a glazed state of wonder. 'Oh wow. It's phenomenal. It's like I imagined it when I was a kid.' He shook his head, craning his neck back to take in the restored beams of the ceiling. 'I can't believe this.'

Carrie beamed with pride. 'It's taken a while, but these last two weeks everything's pulled together. I think the builders felt sorry for me.' She hesitated. 'Do you want to… have a tour…?'

Guy's rich hazel eyes were lit with enthusiasm, but the atmosphere in the house was becoming strangely oppressive. Carrie felt something heavy descend on them like a shroud.

He frowned, shaking his head as if something was in his ear. 'I would love to, but – I have to go to the Home, see my dad. Another time?'

'Oh, yeah, sure! Just a coffee, then?'

But Guy was shifting his weight, glancing around with less enthusiasm than before. 'You know what – I've got something I need to do, just remembered. Can we do this again?'

Carrie blinked, folding her arms to hide her disappointment. 'Sure! Yeah, of course. Thanks again for the book.'

'No problem!' He stepped out again onto the porch.

They stared at each other a fraction too long, then both looked away with shy smiles.

Guy blushed. 'I could… show you around the town a bit? I know a great place by the pier. Have you seen the Historic Docks yet? If you'd like to get lunch, or a coffee, or something?' He looked hopeful.

The house creaked behind her.

'Maybe, yeah.' There it was again – that long pause, the locked gaze held for too long… Carrie's heart fluttered. 'Maybe I could text you when I'm free?'

He got the hint and jumped on it. 'Great. What's your number?' He pulled out his phone, prepared to type it in. Carrie reeled it off. He called it, then hung up. 'That's mine. So, I'll see you soon, then. Enjoy the book.'

Carrie nodded and he jogged down the steps. This was going far better than she had expected. She had almost forgotten the incident on the beach that morning, the sunny afternoon putting her at ease. It seemed like months, not hours, had passed since her mini-meltdown that morning.

As he turned to wave at her, he looked up at the porch, and his face paled. 'My *God*. I'm so sorry about people in this bloody town.'

Carrie frowned, puzzled. 'What?'

'The graffiti.' He scowled, gesturing at the portico surmounting the Doric pillars. 'Sorry, I only just noticed.'

She came to stand next to him and followed his pointing finger. Her hand flew to her mouth. 'What the— *who* would *do* that?'

A stepladder lay on the gravel around the side of the house, under the window on the left. That room had been the dining room, big enough for a banquet, long enough to dance reels. Carrie kept it empty, not knowing what to do with it.

Sell it to a spa chain, her mother said. *Sell it on, to someone who can appreciate it.*

Her eyes travelled from the ladder back to the porch, and the big red letters sprayed on the stone like a slap in the face.

GET OUT

Be Careful What You Wish For

In which Ricky Porter introduces himself and Carrie finds the priest hole

20 April – Afternoon – Evening

Carrie decided to check the garden once Guy had reluctantly left, taking a hammer from her toolbox with her. There was nothing her inexperienced city eyes could see, no footprints or cigarette ends that might denote miscreants on her property, but all the same she wasn't entirely satisfied.

Walking around the garden gave her a strange, isolated feeling that she never got from the inside.

She skirted the wall of local stone that was twice as tall as she was, touching the smooth metal hammer head for comfort. Birds whistled, out of sight. Mud crept up her shoes and splashed onto her ankles, cold and wet.

Fairwood watched her, protective.

Carrie felt safer knowing the house was keeping a lookout. That made no sense, so she put it aside and shrugged off the unease.

Further along, the wall crumbled and ended. A thin wire stretched from one heap of stones to the corner of the broken back wall, marking the boundary but easy enough to duck under and no real deterrent.

She squelched back onto the thin gravel path and headed towards the wishing well in the far corner, overshadowed by the crowding trees. The weather was changing again, another light drizzle dampening the ground.

73

Carrie perched on the edge of the well, wondering how you got spray paint off old stone. In her peripheral vision, The Chase was silent, green and brown with a glimmer of grey.

The grey moved.

She jumped up, a shiver racing down her back, the stone scraping the backs of her legs through her jeans.

Someone was standing on the other side of the wire, face lost in the shadow of their hood, watching her in the gloom. Fear prickled over the nape of her neck.

The figure waved.

'Wotcher, neighbour.' It was a man's voice, gruff, but young.

Carrie stood perfectly still, trying to make him out.

His hood was in her eyeline, she guessed. He couldn't be taller than her. He wasn't much wider than her, either. Not the markers of what she considered a threat (Phil's height, Phil's build, embedded in her brain), but she knew better than to underestimate people. In her experience, lads dressed like that moved in packs, but he seemed to be alone.

'This is private land.' She backed off a few steps, running nervous fingers over her gold chain.

'This isn't,' the man said with a cocky sneer.

She tensed to run, but he didn't move.

'It's all right love,' he called across to her, face still impossible to see. 'I ain't after you.'

It was hard to tell if he was mimicking her accent on purpose, or if he had a more Londonized version of the local one.

'What *are* you after?'

'Just out for a wander.' He nodded at the well. 'Dropped some money, there.'

Carrie slapped her hand to her pocket, the hammer a reassuring weight. She hadn't had any money in her jeans, she was sure. Almost sure.

She turned.

A five-pound note fluttered on the stone, but before she could make a grab for it, it sailed into the well and disappeared.

'*Fuck!*' An actual fiver. Carrie felt sick.

'Hope you didn't need that,' he said.

Carrie rounded on him, remembering the flash of grey she had glimpsed in the trees. 'Are you stalking me?'

'Hardly, love. I live here.'

Carrie kept her distance and took a wild guess, putting two and two together.

'Are you – ha, um, sorry, are *you* Ricky Porter?'

The mystery man took his hands out of his pockets, treating Carrie to the glint of gold signet rings on all his fingers and the curl of a tattoo spiralling under his sleeve as he stretched.

'Yeah. That's me. If you couldn't afford to lose that cash, I'd make a wish, if I were you. So it ain't wasted.'

She snorted. 'A wish?'

'Yeah. Go on.'

'You're serious, aren't you?'

Ricky shrugged. 'I'm a serious man, me.' He took a step back, appraising the house behind her. 'They did a good job on 'er, didn't they? Nice to see the old girl looking smart.' There was a catch in his voice, and he cleared his throat as if caught out, the cockiness turning shy. 'We're neighbours, you know that? I live right there.' He pointed behind him. 'Bramble Cottage,' he added. 'That's us.'

Carrie's eyebrows shot up. 'Should have introduced yourself before,' she said, keeping one hand on the hammer. 'I had tea with your grandmother yesterday.'

'That's brave.' Ricky Porter rocked back on his heels. She caught a brief glimpse of a stubbled, angular chin, and then his head dipped down again into shadow.

'Did you see who scrawled over my bloody porch?'

He shook his head. 'No. But they ain't gone. I'd get back inside, if I were you. Good time for the flittermice, this.'

'The what?'

'The bats. Bloody big 'uns.' He pointed up to the trees, but Carrie couldn't see anything. 'They got rabies.'

Carrie looked around but there was nothing to see. The garden was quiet in the drizzle, but it was always quiet.

'Well, thanks for the neighbourly concern.'

He nodded, missing the sarcasm. 'We got to watch out for each other out here. Who'd you run to in the night? No one else for miles.'

That was true. She rubbed the top of the hammer.

'Cheery. Thanks for that.'

He half-turned and jerked his head. 'Follow the track through the trees. I keep a light on. You'll find us, if you need us.'

Carrie realised she hadn't introduced herself properly.

'I'm Caroline, by the way.'

'Yeah, I know.' He turned to go. 'Be seeing you, Mistress Rickard.'

Her surname sent a chill through her, but she reasoned his grandmother must have told him. He wandered off down a well-trodden track into the trees. She was left staring after him, wire biting into her hands as she leaned against the fence. Shaking her head, she turned back to the well to see if she could rescue the precious five-pound note.

The well was dark and deep, the note floating in the gunge near the bottom. She licked the light, mizzling droplets from her lips and placed a tentative hand on the damp stone. The note folded up as she watched, as if someone had reached through the ooze and pinched it in the middle, drawing it below the surface.

There was a slow ripple as the money disappeared.

'*Shit.*' It really wasn't her day. 'Fine.' She slapped her palm against a damp slab. She hadn't made a wish since she was little. Wishes didn't work. Throwing pennies into wells and blowing out birthday candles in one big breath had not kept her parents together, nor stopped the rows, nor prevented her mum moving in with Reg from Peckham. Not even prayer had done that, because sometimes you just didn't get what you wanted.

'I wish… I don't know. I wish my dreams come true, how about that.'

Nothing replied.

Carrie stared into the silent well, wondering where she could find a long-handled net.

From the trees behind her, something fluttered from one branch to another.

Carrie jumped at the sound of its wings, trying to catch a proper glimpse of it. Her creepy neighbour was probably pulling her leg, and it was just a crow. She hadn't seen a bat in the wild before; foxes, yes, but only the urban kind. Meeting a rabid bat would be just her luck today.

The weather was worsening, bigger drops splashing cold and wet down the back of her neck and dribbling through her hair. She dashed back across the lawn and let herself into the kitchen, the warmest and most comforting room in the house.

It took her a few minutes to calm down, and then, convincing herself she was safe inside with all the doors locked, she returned to the living room with the book.

It was a first edition, written by Harry Bishop, Guy's father. According to the introduction, the house had stood empty since 1979. Goodness knows how many kids had broken in over the years, stealing a little bit of the house each time. Who knew where all the pieces had ended up? She was willing to bet her neighbour, Ricky, had nicked something – latent prejudice and past experience convinced her he'd be one of the first to strip it for whatever he could sell. He wasn't in his grandmother's good books, that was for sure.

With the *History of Fairwood House* in her hands, she felt the pieces returning. In the black and white print and glossy photographs, the renovated estate became more alive, as if she was restoring the soul of the house. She had a strange urge to read out loud.

One paragraph in particular caught her attention.

> Sir Peter Sauvant (d. 1892) was the leader of an occult group who called themselves the Eleusinians, after the ancient rites performed each year in Ancient

Greece by the devotees of Demeter and Persephone, based at Eleusis. Such an agrarian cult suited the surroundings of the East Sussex coast, but the name was a pretty deceit and had less to do with the harvest as it did with tampering with things men ought to leave alone. As far as this author can tell, it is from the activities of the Eleusinians and their own enacted Mysteries that the curious local phrase, 'don't plant what you don't want to grow' originates. Although this appears to be nothing more than agrarian wisdom, folk legend has it that during the time of Sir Peter and the Eleusinians, the soil around the town, situated in the South Downs below the clay of the Weald, became increasingly – some might say aggressively – fertile.

She flipped to the colour plate of Sir John Douglas Sauvant, a direct descendant of Sir Peter and the last baronet, square jawed and stern.

'You attract all the good-looking blokes, don't you?' she remarked dryly to the house.

Carrie read aloud to herself and the listening room until her throat dried out and her voice cracked, and it was time to put the kettle on. She had never felt more at home, nor had the empty old place seemed more alive. It was as if The Crows had woken up, a yawning Sleeping Beauty from its bed of weeds, and she was its Prince Charming. Except some coward with a mysterious grudge didn't want her administering that kiss of life.

As she stood and stretched, something small bounced off the window behind her.

Carrie spun around, but the night had drawn in and the glass only showed her own reflection. A big moth, maybe, attracted to the light. Swallowing, she went to draw the curtains.

There was a movement out on the lawn.

Carrie froze, trying to see what it had been, but there wasn't anything to see. As she squinted, a tiny pebble flew from nowhere and hit the pane again.

Carrie leapt backwards and collided painfully with a packing box.

Someone was messing about, and it wasn't bloody funny. Not Phil – this wasn't his style. The figure on the clifftop resurfaced in her mind, and a chill shot down her back. Someone was trying to freak her out. The culprit with the spray paint, most likely. Or her creepy neighbour. She grabbed her phone, wondering how fast the police might get there on a Friday night.

She couldn't remember the hump of grass about ten feet away from the window, on the edge of the gravel drive. Carrie gripped the curtains, about to draw them properly, when she realised there had never been a hump of grass there. Not that big. She froze, staring.

Two amber points stared back in the dark.

Carrie swallowed.

That's a bloody *big dog.*

It reared up on its hind legs in one fluid movement, long-limbed and enormous.

Rabid fangs leered out of the darkened garden.

Carrie stumbled backwards, kicking boxes out of her way, and huge paws slammed against the window at head height, making the whole frame shake.

She tripped over her own feet with a yelp and nearly fell, heart pounding in her ears.

Call 999, part of her brain told her, but the rest of it had shut down. She tried to focus on the screen and getting to the door at the same time, but the door was her first priority.

As she made it out of the room, something smashed through the window in an explosion of glass. Carrie slammed the door shut and jabbed at the screen in a blind panic, ringing a completely random number.

A deep snarl from the living room paralysed her with fear. All she could think about, bizarrely, was that she had left Guy's book on the sofa.

'*Hello?*'

'Mer-Mercy?' She recognised the voice, and her heart dropped like a stone. Not Emergency Services then. How the hell had she called her supervisor? What the hell was wrong with her damn phone?

Something thudded towards the door with a smash and a crunch, and then there was silence. Carrie backed off along the hall, breathless and cupping her shaking hand over her mouth as she whispered into the phone.

'Mercy? *Shit,* shit, shit…!'

'Carrie?'

'Oh God…'

It scratched at the closed door, dragging claws down the wood. Carrie's throat constricted as she backed away as silently as she could, fumbling down the panelled hall.

'Carrie, are you okay?'

She forced herself to answer, voice coming out in a scratchy whisper. 'It's in the house, shit it's in the house, it's, it's a dog, or a… I don't know but it's *bloody huge* and it, it's broken the window, oh my God, it's in the house…'

The living room doorknob rattled and Carrie stood frozen, every muscle rigid.

There was silence.

All Carrie heard was the ticking of the rescued grandfather clock, counting down.

It doesn't work, Carrie remembered. *How can it be ticking?*

She lowered the phone, eyes watering, and forced herself to look over her shoulder. The gold pendulum was swinging side-to-side.

Tick.

Tick.

Tick.

The time was still wrong: two minutes to midnight.

A shiver crawled down her back.

A heavy weight hurled itself against the living room door, the shivering wood bowing and splintering outwards with the impact. Carrie threw herself backwards against the panelling with an instinct that wasn't hers.

Something clicked behind her in the wall.

The panel slid sideways under her weight. Carrie pitched back through an empty space, and the panel closed up as she stumbled into a narrow cavity in the wall, coffin-deep, plunging her into darkness. She gagged on dust, half-choking.

Outside, wood splintered.

There was a low growl from the hall, muffled through the thick panels.

She squeezed her phone so tightly she was sure she'd crack the screen. The signal had gone: the call was dead.

There was another *thud*, and the sound of scraping, something long and sharp being dragged across the panels in the hall.

Something sniffed along the floor, snuffling outside her hiding place, inches from her feet.

You're in the priest hole.

Carrie knew that thought wasn't her own. It sounded like her voice, but it wasn't. The susurrus suggestion was made all around her, from the wood itself.

She couldn't think.

Something scraped vertically up the wood, lining up with her rigid body, from her feet to her throat. It knew where she was.

Step right.

Carrie could feel the solid wood to her right, and there was nowhere to go. She slid her foot sideways and stumbled as the floor dropped away.

What the hell?

The smuggler's tunnel, Carrie.

The panel pounded, inches from her face.

A tiny burst of light came through as a claw punctured the oak.

'*Shit!*'

She dropped down the hole, feet finding rusty iron loops set at intervals like a ladder, or perhaps they found her feet, it was hard to tell. Wriggling her way down the narrow shaft into the greedy darkness, Carrie's eyes burned with dust and darkness as a trapdoor slammed shut above her head. Her hand struck something metal and cold on the way down, knocking it off its hook and sending it smashing to the ground a few feet below.

When she hit the floor of the tunnel, she remembered too late the tales of old Seamus McVey, buried alive.

Move!

That came from above her, this time.

Carrie groped for whatever she had dropped and scooped up something cold, cuboid and squat, which imagination told her could be almost anything, but common sense suggested was a lantern. Any oil or candle it had once contained was gone.

She tried her phone, but there was no flashlight app, and the screen light was faint and weak against the pressing blackness. It was still better than nothing.

Above her, there was a muffled crunching sound and a yelp. The beast banged against constricting walls. A howl shivered into the tunnel, cut off by an angry wooden creak.

Carrie stumbled further back into the dark, tripping over loose stones. She found the tunnel wall, dry and dusty and shored up with old brick.

'This is mad,' she whispered to herself, groping her way along as fast as she could. 'This is mad, this isn't… this isn't happening.'

Something dropped into the tunnel behind her with a sickening thud, claws clanging on the metal rungs on the way down. Carrie switched her phone off and buried it in her pocket. She didn't want it to see her.

She closed her eyes to readjust to total darkness – not that it made much difference – and listened, everything on high alert.

Dead, surely. It's dead, right?

Something scraped against the floor at the end of the tunnel. It was still moving.

Carrie forced herself to think.

Screwing her courage tighter by a few turns, she grasped the lantern ring like a kettlebell, swinging it experimentally. McVey had met his death in this tunnel, and that meant the cave-in was somewhere along its length. If there was a cave-in, she was trapped down here, and the only way back up was past the thing that had fallen down after her.

Quivering, she softened her knees, bracing for impact from the Thing she couldn't see.

A light flared behind her, a dim orange glow dazzling as it cut through the total blackness. It picked out a dark, hairy, human-limbed mass at the end of the tunnel, finding its feet.

'Wotcher, neighbour. In trouble already?'

Carrie spun around to find her hooded neighbour with an old wind-up torch. Suspiciously, he didn't sound in the least surprised.

'Drop that, it won't do any good.' He grabbed her roughly by the arm. 'Come on,' he said, dragging her after him. 'Quick, afore she Turns back properly.'

'Turns back…?'

'*Shift.*' Ricky dug soil-packed nails into her arm, tight as a poacher's trap, dragging her behind him.

Carrie couldn't breathe.

Sprinting around a rockfall down a narrow, cleared stretch forming the remaining fork in the passage, they came to another shaft near a pile of rubble.

'Up,' Ricky ordered, pushing her in front of him.

Adrenaline gave Carrie speed.

She broke into the sharp night air, hauling herself up and into the woods. Ricky threw the torch up and was right behind her, as something scrabbled at the rungs of the old shaft behind them.

They were never going to outrun it.

Carrie's legs worked like pistons, forcing her on, but she wasn't fast enough. Behind her, she could hear something big bounding over the grass and crashing into the undergrowth. It was powerful, and it was gaining.

She could see Bramble Cottage in the trees up ahead, one flickering candle flame in the upper window like a guiding beacon. She crossed a line of white beach pebbles scattered over the ground and nearly reached the low stone wall when Ricky caught her around the waist and threw her to the ground. Carrie gasped, her phone flying out of her pocket, and with it, the small piece of tile from The Crows.

Foul-smelling fabric pressed against her mouth as he held her down.

'*Shut up*,' he hissed into her ear, breath reeking of bad fish. Carrie gagged. '*Not a sound.*'

The thing on their trail howled again, right behind them, and Ricky's hood came down. Carrie wasn't sure what she saw – he clamped a hand over her eyes, but between the cracks in his fingers she saw black coils rising above them like eels, writhing in the night air.

Silver glinted in the darkness.

The howl turned into a piercing shriek.

Carrie pushed Ricky off and rolled to the drystone wall and out of the way as Janet Varney tumbled in a heap on the ground, blood pouring from her open throat.

The eyes turned from amber to brown. The jaw began to pull back into the skull. The teeth – no, fangs – remained the same. Mrs Varney's slack mouth was filled with razor-sharp incisors. Her tongue lolled out of the side of her mouth, and Carrie thought of Branston. It was such a stupid thought, and the contrast of normalcy versus… *this*… made her double up with a sudden wave of nausea. She staggered blindly to her feet, retching, but her stomach was empty.

'Oh my God…'

'Carrie!'

She recognised the new voice, even though she had never heard it before. It resonated deep within her, the sonorous ring of a pipe being struck and the dryness of a creaking floorboard.

Carrie couldn't move. Her words dried up before they reached her tongue.

Inexplicably she could hear Grampa Jim, goggling at him in her head.

Bloody hell, Caro, he's built like a brick shithouse.

The stranger standing before them was enormous. He towered over her, wide shoulders, broad chest, a sword sticking out of his sleeve, glinting silver-sharp as it changed in the pale moonlight. The tip of the blade, dripping blood that was almost black in the dark, flattened into a palm, long fingers unfurled. It was her imagination. It was just a hand, an arm. There was nothing silver about it. But the blood... the blood dripped onto the grass, and there was a dead woman on the ground.

Her brain tried to process what it had seen but failed.

She looked back up at his face. Something wasn't right.

He's covered in tattoos?

But that wasn't it.

No, she corrected herself dreamily, a fuzzy vice around her forehead. *He's engraved.*

Deep livid sores ate into the skin, etched across his cheeks in raw, indented teardrops, cutting down into his neck with pale forks of scar tissue. It was as if something had gouged chunks of his flesh away, dug out the fibres for sport.

'Who *are* you?' she heard herself whisper.

The apparition stared at her. 'Fairwood, of course.'

She stared at him, taking in the deep gouges. The ones on his forearms had perfect corners, chiselled in wide lines like the steps of a staircase. They should have gone all the way down to the bone, but Carrie had the oddest feeling he didn't have any. Beneath the white shirt, the triangle of torso on display was stippled and rough like the surface of brick tiles and natural slate, colours mottling and hard to see in the dark. She looked back up at his scarred face, where his eyes – bright, alive, and clear as water – stared patiently into her soul like windowpanes. In the corner of one iris, a jagged cobweb of blood vessels had burst like smashed glass.

'You're... *Fairwood*?'

The man looked back through the trees in the direction of the house, a faraway glaze in his brilliant grey eyes. 'Yes.'

She knew the face. It was the same as the last colour plate in *The History of Fairwood House*: Sir John, or Jack, Douglas Sauvant, who had spent his final days addled with whiskey and tertiary syphilis.

That's where being handsome gets you.

Her mind whirled, body shivering out of her control. A small First Aid recollection piped up in the back of her mind: *You're going into shock.*

She tried to warm up her arms, rubbing them ineffectually, forcing herself to breathe in and out in a set rhythm, but kept losing count.

'All right there, neighbour?'

Ricky Porter, who had stayed a safe distance away, approached the garden wall at a casual swagger. His hoody and grubby tracksuit bottoms had taken the brunt of the arterial spray, but that didn't seem to bother him. He regarded her with a cocky leer, features masked in shifting shadows. In the centre of his pupils, two cherry-red dots burned. She could have sworn she was making it up, but then, she could be dreaming it all. He cracked his knuckles, the popping sound they made making her queasiness worse. 'Cor, that worked out even better than I expected, not going to lie.'

'What – what just happened?' Carrie pointed back at the dead woman on the ground. 'I know her. I've met her. She – she was at the History Society.' She glared at him. 'Why were you in the tunnel? You *are* spying on me. I saw you in the trees, watching the house…'

'Wasn't breaking the law,' Ricky said immediately, signet rings gleaming as he rubbed his shaved head. 'And I knew where you'd be, if you got into trouble. Just went straight there. Think that earns me brownie points, don't it?'

'*How* did you know?' Carrie didn't wait for a reply and turned to the giant, silent as an empty room. 'And – *you* – you…' She trailed off.

Fairwood watched her with its usual patience.

Her neighbour licked his lips and sidled up to her, keeping an eye on the hulking statue. He moved like a boxer, chest up and limber, but as she glanced down at him, she realised he was shorter than she was. She shook her head in flat denial.

'This is mad. I'm seeing things. Oh my God, this is, this is lucid dreaming or, or – this isn't real, I'm not well. I've, I've eaten something, drunk something…'

'It's real all right.' Ricky peered at Mrs Varney's body. 'Good job your dreams weren't all marshmallows and unicorns, or you'd be in deep shit right about now.'

She stared at him, growing cold. 'My dreams?'

'I got good hearing,' Ricky said. 'Though as wishes go, that was pretty bloody vague. Glad I set those stones up, now.'

'Mr Porter,' Carrie said, breathing hard through her nose, her voice tight and quiet, 'if you don't tell me what is going on, *right the fuck now*, I am going to—' She gulped a breath.

'Ha!' He burst out laughing, loud and hard. 'You'll do what?' He took a step back. 'Come on in, since you've crossed the boundary line.'

Carrie turned to look at the white pebbles on the grass behind her. Some of them seemed to have marks scratched on their surface, but that could be a trick of the light, seeing patterns that weren't there. She didn't trust her own eyes. 'What're those?'

'Wishing stones. Tell you inside, come on.' Ricky pushed the broken gate and beckoned them in, but she didn't move.

'Are you all right?' the avatar of her house asked.

'*No.*' She turned back to the corpse. 'What the *fuck* is that?'

'That's a werewolf,' Ricky put in, as if that were obvious. 'They don't always need a full moon, if they're in the mood for fun and games.'

Carrie's trembling knees gave out.

She sank to the ground with a small moan, only now aware of the nettle rash burning her arms.

'Oh my *God.*'

If it wasn't for the pain, which was *very* real, she would have been completely convinced this was all some kind of horrific nightmare. As it was, she was only half-convinced. It was all so bizarre that she laughed. She couldn't help it – it was involuntary, rising out of her churning stomach like bile.

'Bloody hell.' Ricky pulled his hood up as if he meant business and heaved Carrie to her feet. 'Come on, love, let's get you a cup of tea.' He nodded at Carrie's phone, lying on the grass a few yards away. 'She'll be wanting that.'

Don't drink the tea.

Sheila's warning returned like a sucker punch.

'No tea. I'm fine.' She let him lead her through the gate, tripping over the cable of a broken fridge.

Ricky kicked a tin can out of the way. 'Give over, I'm not going to poison you. Forgive the mess, we're all of a dishabille, as they used to say. Mum and Dad don't do visitors.'

'I don't want to be any trouble,' Carrie said automatically, bravado wearing off as her laughter subsided, but Ricky scoffed.

'Too late for that.'

The interior of Bramble Cottage was as bleak as its exterior. Carrie wasn't sure what she had been expecting, but the stink of damp and mould, mingled with the cloying stench of rotting meat, hit her full in the face as soon as she stepped through the door. She clamped a hand to her nose.

'I'm going to be sick.'

'No, you ain't. Breathe through your nose, nice and deep, it gets better.'

Ricky pushed her fully inside and sat her in a sagging armchair near the broken window – his mother's sewing chair, he said – and went around lighting the lamps. The apparition of Sir John Douglas Sauvant, a bad statue of angles and lines in an approximation of a human shape, ducked through the door, and Ricky stayed at least three feet away from it as if it gave off a repelling aura.

Dull, flickering light twisted the remaining darkness into uncanny shapes around them. The furniture was sparse but the place was tidy, without a single thing to suggest anyone lived there. Carrie thought she saw something uncurl beneath the hood at the back of Ricky's head, but it could have been a trick of the pale flames.

'Right.' She dug her nails into the greasy arms of the chair, staring from him to the bulky protector of her dreams. A house within a house. Her head swam. 'What's going on?' Carrie paused. 'Do you know what, I'm going to record myself saying that and play it on repeat until I get some answers.' She shook her head. 'Your parents had better be alive, Ricky, I swear to God this had better not be like *Psycho* or some shit.'

'Keep it down, they're upstairs,' Ricky said, drawing up a wicker chair. 'It's fairly obvious what's going on, I'd have thought. The old girl tried to kill you, except you made a wish first. Ain't that lucky.' He shot the scarred stranger a meaningful glance. 'Wonder who put that in your head?'

Carrie tried to piece the night together, furrowing her brow. She looked at the bulky humanoid figure. 'All right, let's say you are my— no, that's stupid. I can't believe I'm saying this. Let's say you *are* Fairwood. Why didn't you stop her breaking in?'

Fairwood shrugged. 'I hid you. I... shouldn't be like this. I don't know why I'm like this.' He looked at the scarred arms and hands. 'I am condensed. My rooms, my... I'm collapsed in on myself. How did this happen?'

'All right, I admit it, I confess,' Ricky said, raising his hands. 'I may have... given your wish a little more juice. Got her *over the line*, so to speak. But in fairness to the well, you did only throw in a fiver.' He looked the figure up and down and whistled. 'Cor, she's come out looking like the last bloke, hasn't she? Too big to be his double though.' He chuckled to himself, or possibly at himself, it was hard to tell.

'She?'

'The house, I mean. Everything's a "she" down here. Excepting a tomcat, an' she's a he.' He grinned.

Carrie ignored him, focusing on the phrase nagging at her memory.

Over the line?

She remembered the white pebbles in the grass, an unlikely thing to find in the woods. 'If I hadn't crossed the pebbles...' Carrie said slowly, 'What did you call them? Wishing stones? Would it have...?' she struggled with a word.

'Manifested?' Fairwood suggested, trying to be helpful.

Ricky gave a short bark of laughter. 'For a five-pound note? Nah, not a chance. What the hell have you been dreaming about? Gets inside your head, don't she, old Fairwood House.'

'Great. I can't even afford my own wishes.'

Fairwood gave her a strange look out of the shadows, blending in with the peeling, mouldy wallpaper. 'You should dredge the well,' it – he? she? they? – said, in that deeper, scratchier version of her own voice.

'Why?' Carrie shivered, wrapping her arms around herself. 'What else is down there?'

'By the family's count, about ten thousand pounds worth of old wishes,' Fairwood said, 'In old money. I can't swear to the price of the antiques.'

Carrie stared at him. 'Whoa, wait, what? Isn't that – isn't that what they call a treasure trove? What kind of antiques?'

'Oh, *now* you believe you're talking to your own house?' Ricky looked from one to the other. 'That didn't take long.'

'I'm broke,' Carrie snapped. 'I can't afford to live here. I can't— *shut up*, Mr Porter.'

Her neighbour blinked. 'I saved your life, you know.'

'My *house* saved my life,' Carrie pointed out. 'This isn't even happening, anyway, it's a nightmare, some kind of fucked-up dream.' The smell of the cottage hit the back of her throat. 'Eugh, God. Some kind of lucid, rancid, rotten dream.' The candlelight flickered in the space between them, Ricky staring at her in complete surprise as if he hadn't expected her to speak to him like that. Carrie broke eye contact first, turning her attention back to the building in human form. 'So? Can I really afford to keep it? *You?*'

'I can dredge up the memories and do an inventory.' Fairwood's bright grey gaze held hers.

It was too good to be true.

I bet people have already nicked it.

Fairwood's eyes twinkled in the lantern light. 'Not a chance. It's too deep down. You need to dig it out.' It paused, examining its arms, how they bent in the middle. 'Or I could, I suppose.'

'*Stay out of my head!*' Carrie slapped her hands over her ears, rocking forwards. 'Don't do that. This – this is too weird. Don't.'

Fairwood retreated back against the wall of the cottage, abashed. 'Sorry.'

'Aw, look at him,' Ricky exclaimed. 'Like kicking a big concrete puppy.'

'*There's no concrete in Fairwood House,*' Carrie and Fairwood snapped in one voice.

Ricky balked. 'Bloody hell, all right. Calm down. Well, congratulations Mistress Rickard, your dreams have come true and now you can skip off into the sunset and take it home to meet the parents. Not that I can talk, you understand. Our lot like to keep it in the family so much I'm lucky I only got away with an extra mouth.'

'What?'

'What?' Ricky returned with swift, sugary innocence, leaning back in his seat. '*I said*, congrats on the new guardian angel and the big pile of cash. And the dead old woman. We're going to have to do something about her, by the way.'

Carrie stared at the shadowy space in the hood, trying to make out his expression, but failed. She settled for answers to her other questions.

'Is she really a— wait. Werewolves, they're real?'

Ricky sniffed and hawked, spitting phlegm on the floorboards. 'Real enough. Anyway, not to worry. Knew she wouldn't get you. Saw it in the entrails.'

Carrie blinked. 'Saw it – in the entrails?'

Ricky cupped a hand behind his ear. 'Is there an echo in here? Yeah. Entrails. Omens were all good. I'm a soothsayer.'

'A *soothsayer*.'

'There it is again.' Ricky shook his head, dislodging the hood a little. Something flicked around his cheek, thin and pinkish-brown. Carrie couldn't tell if it was a tongue or a tentacle, or just her imagination. He reached over to the stained table for a small bag and shook it at her. 'Bones, too. I do a good line in bone readings. Want me to say your sooth?'

'You think you're funny, don't you?'

'Who, me? Nah. Told you, I'm a serious man.'

'What'll it cost me?' Carrie was catching on to the way Ricky operated.

He shook his head. 'Nah, first one's free. Like smack.' He snorted. 'Go on. Have a quick read.'

Before Carrie could say anything, her phone lit up. Mercy was calling. She answered with relief.

'Mercy! I'm okay.'

Mercy sounded close to tears. 'Oh, thank God! Where are you? The gate's locked...'

'Bramble Cottage?' Carrie shot a glance at her hooded host. 'Um. With Ricky Porter.'

'*Shit!*' Mercy was horrified. 'Don't eat or drink *anything*.'

Ricky bounded to his feet and swiped the phone from Carrie's hand. 'You got a motor?'

Mercy went quiet.

'Oi! I said, you got a car? Only there's a corpse here that needs disposing of. Not your mate's. Mind the jaws, though. They'll still give you a nasty bite post mortem. Cheers, sweetheart.' He hung up on her and tossed the phone back, glowering.

Carrie set her jaw.

'Naun wrong wi' the victuals in this house,' Ricky muttered. 'I ain't gonna poison you. Why would I? You know what a soothsayer *does*, don't you? Tells the fucking truth.'

'Why would Mrs Varney try to kill me?' Carrie retorted. 'I never met her until the other night. What have I done to her?'

Ricky mooched back to his chair in a sulk. 'Lots of secrets in that house, ask it. Go on. Plenty of people want you out of there, I'd say.'

Carrie put her head in her hands. 'I'm going mad. Aren't I? This isn't real. This can't be happening.' She rubbed her face, gritty dirt on her hands sandpapering her cheeks. It certainly felt real. 'Wishes come true. Werewolves are real. You're some kind of magician.'

'*Soothsayer.*'

'Right.' Carrie pinched the bridge of her nose. 'So, what was the bat you mentioned earlier? A vampire?'

'Nah. Just a bat.'

She huddled over her knees, head in her hands.

He leaned forwards, watching her. 'C'mon Caroline. Get it together, love. We've got a body out there. Let's not get on the coppers' radar just yet, shall we? I can't say I want them round again.'

'Why?' Carrie asked, hugging herself. She attempted humour but was only half-joking. 'Who's under the floor?'

Ricky fidgeted, managing to look both hurt and shifty. 'Why? What've you heard?'

Headlights streamed into view, flooding the front of the cottage with their brilliant glare as a car screeched to a halt.

'Ho, heads up boys, cavalry's here,' Ricky remarked with dripping sarcasm, bouncing off the chair to fling the door open. He tweaked the hood further over his head. 'This way, roll up, roll up, all the fun of the ghost train.' He waved his arms, indicating the body lying outside the garden wall.

Jazz and Mercy burst out of their car, scrambling through the trees to the cottage.

'Carrie!' Mercy screeched, skidding to a halt. 'Mr Porter, where is she?'

'I'm here, I'm fine.' Carrie came outside to join them and motioned for Fairwood to stay behind her, hidden behind the door. 'I think... I killed a werewolf.'

Ricky Porter gave a strange, childlike giggle.

Mercy narrowed her eyes. 'Carrie?'

'*She* didn't kill anything,' Ricky said, gulping down his mirth, 'Her house did.'

Jazz, who had evidently seen a lot of strange things in his time, stood slack-jawed with his eyes flicking from Ricky to Carrie. He reverted to pragmatism. 'Is she dead, or not?'

'Oh, she's dead,' Ricky assured him, snorting. 'Antique-silver-blade-for-hand dead.'

'Right then.' Jazz swallowed and turned back to the car. 'I don't know what that means, so I'll get the dust sheets and a shovel.'

Mercy ran forward to give Carrie a hug but trod on a tin can and fell headlong into her. 'I'm so glad you're okay,' Mercy gasped, wide-eyed, squeezing her around the waist. 'I thought you were going to die.'

'Thanks?' Carrie couldn't handle being touched. She pushed Mercy away, skin crawling. The nettle rash still burned.

Mercy raked the messy waves of her rainbow bob. 'Your *house* killed her?'

'Not exactly...' Carrie beckoned Fairwood forward, wincing. 'Um. I made a wish...'

'A wish...? What, like, that it would protec—oh my *good God above*, what is *that?!*'

Mercy backed off as Fairwood ducked out of the cottage, and Ricky's hard, hysterical giggle made Carrie flinch.

The upstairs window lifted up a crack.

A sibilant voice drifted out, accompanied by the faint smell of mothballs and sickly-sweet decay.

'Richard? *Richard!* What's going on down there? Your father has the hot-chills. He needs his rest.'

'It's all right, Mum,' Ricky called up, getting control of himself. 'Go back to bed. Everything's fine.'

The window juddered back down.

'Keep it down, ladies,' Ricky instructed, jerking the edges of his hood. 'The old man's trying to sleep.'

'Is your dad ill?' Carrie glanced up at the window. 'Is there anything we can do?'

Mercy stared at her.

Ricky looked at Mercy. 'She's serious, ain't she?'

Mercy nodded, struck dumb.

Ricky scratched his chin. 'That's sweet. No, don't you worry about it, neighbour. Let's get back to introducing your friend to your house, it's a better laugh.'

Surrounded by so many humans, or what Carrie assumed were humans, the house seemed to make up its mind about its appearance. The scars stayed the same, but the surface of what passed for skin, stippled like brickwork, smoothed into pinewood tones.

Jazz had returned from rummaging in the car boot and was inspecting the body. He had found a metal medical bracelet on her wrist.

'Janet Varney, Second Pack. Shit, she's DNR. We've got to cut her head off.'

'Cut her *head off*?' Carrie didn't think the night could get any worse, or any weirder. 'Doesn't DNR mean "Do Not Resuscitate"? Why have we—'

'If we don't, she'll Rise. Trust me, the only thing worse than a werewolf trying to kill you while they're alive is one trying to kill you after they're dead. Werewolf zombies are the absolute worst. Don't put in the ground what you don't want to grow.' The shovel bit down and finished the job. Mrs Varney's jaws snapped shut.

'You've done that before,' Ricky commented, and Jazz gave him a wry smile.

'Comes with the territory, I found.'

Carrie had had enough. 'Okay. I want to go home now.'

Fairwood stepped forwards, crushing the can underfoot.

Mercy shuffled uncomfortably, thrusting her hands into her dressing gown pockets. 'All right. Look. Let's… let's go. I'll… put the kettle on, and – we'll talk. Okay? And we can clear up all the mess. Let's… let's leave them to sort this out, shall we?'

'Not me.' Ricky shook his hooded head, looking uncomfortable around so many people. 'Nah. Done my bit for tonight.' He nodded at the house's manifestation. 'Don't you forget that, neither.' He strolled back into the cottage, leaving them in the deathly quiet of the woods. The door closed behind him.

'I need a torch here, guys,' Jazz called. 'Babe? I gave you the torch?'

Mercy dug it out of her dressing gown pocket and handed it over.

'And a hand would be nice.'

Carrie quickly learned there was nothing like disposing of a body to bind relative strangers. Jazz explained that 'mindless resurrections', which seemed a weird qualifier, now only happened at certain times of the year thanks to the rituals performed in the town, but they had to wait for the full moon before all Risings could be limited to the mortuary itself. Until then, the Crematorium on the outskirts of the town was operating at all hours.

Jazz called ahead and drove off with the body in the boot, while Mercy led Carrie back to The Crows, its personification in tow.

'I'll help,' Mercy said, and Carrie didn't protest.

It was going to be a long night.

Real After All

'What a night.'

Carrie mutely concurred.

Once they had located duct tape and flattened a few boxes to fill the window gap, Mercy had eventually got Carrie nestled on her sofa, staring into her mug. The manifestation had blended back into the fabric of the house, which was disconcerting. Mercy had been rearranging the rest of the furniture and unpacking forgotten boxes, anything to avoid sitting in silence. She had dug out a rug from the old flat, spreading it out in front of the hearth. Her newest discovery, a beanbag Carrie had forgotten all about, was plumped beside the fireplace.

'So, let me see if I've got this,' Carrie said, putting her hot mug down on the floor. Mercy dove for the newly unearthed stack of coasters as the floorboard complained. 'Pagham-on-Sea is…' she paused, 'not your average town. In fairness, I think I got that. I just didn't know *how* odd it was.'

Mercy retreated to her seat, smoothing the pink streaks in her hair. 'Yeah.'

'I'm guessing there's lots of things I probably shouldn't do.'

Mercy pursed her lips. 'Mm. A few.'

'What about wishing wells?'

'Don't use them?'

'Too late for that.' Carrie sat back. 'This is completely insane.'

'Ricky Porter told you to, didn't he?'

Carrie nodded, her side of the story already told.

Mercy shook her head, not meeting her gaze. 'Can I tell you a story about Ricky Porter?'

'Sure.' She wanted to know who she was living next door to.

Mercy twiddled a strand of pastel-purple hair. 'My friend Tina used to play with his cousin Wes when they were, like, six. Wes was pretty fond of Tina. They were down on the beach one day and Ricky wanted to play with them, you know, but even then he was weird. Like, weirder than... I don't know. Anyway... Tina had a puppy. You know what Ricky did?'

Carrie pulled a cushion onto her lap and hugged it.

'It's going to be grim, isn't it?'

'Ripped it open with a pocketknife to read its entrails before anyone could stop him. You know why?'

Carrie shook her head, numb.

Mercy studied her pink pumps, mud splattered and scuffed. 'He... wanted to know if they'd be friends. Apparently, liver said no.'

'No shit.' Carrie thought of Ricky's shifty eyes, his full lips parted and sad. He hadn't been faking that, but Mercy – Mercy had been hiding a lot of things from the moment they met. Carrie tried to concentrate. 'I'm guessing he doesn't have *many* friends.'

Mercy wrinkled her nose. 'Not really.'

Carrie blew out a slow breath. 'So, there are soothsayers, werewolves, wishing wells that *work*, houses that...' she stopped. Mercy was looking anywhere but at her face. She narrowed her eyes. 'What are *you*?'

Mercy's shoulders squared, but her voice rose an octave. 'First of all, that's not something you come out and ask. Even I don't come out and ask stuff like that. You work it out from context, like, the street they live on, or their name, or physical characteristics, hobbies, interests, social circles, that kind of thing.' She glanced through the open door into the passage and lowered her voice. 'I didn't even tell Jazz outright for about three months, and *he* saw me get off an autopsy table.'

Carrie froze.

'It's not like that.' Mercy nibbled her thumb nail.

'But… you're not… you're not human either?'

Mercy sighed. She opened her dressing gown and lifted the bottom of her pyjama top to reveal a rosy birthmark above her hip. It looked like a number in a rough, port-wine coloured splodge, like a child's clumsy crayon writing.

'We – we're called a lot of things,' Mercy said quietly. 'We're all born with one of these.'

'A number?'

Mercy dropped her top. 'It's… it's how many years we have before we die.' She swallowed. 'And… until those years are up, we – can't.'

'Can't… *die*?' Carrie couldn't quite take this in. 'You just… what, you're indestructible? Like the Terminator?'

Mercy snorted. 'No, I wish. I got hit by a car the other week.'

The bruises. Carrie remembered her on the first day they met, how her face had healed under the makeup, how she'd stopped limping. Carrie had almost convinced herself she'd made it up.

'The day I started work?'

Mercy blinked. 'Yeah, could've been. I was running late. Anniversary of Granny Hillsworth's death, my dad's mum. I drive him to the cemetery every year. I dropped him home, couldn't find anywhere to park, legged it across the road without looking…' she trailed off and frowned. 'Driver didn't even stop, imagine if he *had* killed me permanently? Bastard.'

Carrie leaned forwards, staring at her. 'So, you – just wake up, do you?'

'Yeah. Eventually. It's hard to heal from really bad stuff, so I have to be careful. Broken bones are fine, internal bleeding, that's okay… werewolf bites…' Mercy winced. '*Not* okay. We can't Turn. But we also can't die. But we also can't heal, because of the enzymes in the saliva. So.' She winced. 'And don't get me started on zombies.'

Through the broken window and strips of gaffer tape, they heard a car crunching up the gravel.

Mercy sighed with relief. 'Good, Jazz is back.'

Carrie's brow creased. 'What... what's your number?'

Mercy inhaled slowly, stretching back in the chair. 'Ninety-two.' She saw the relief relaxing Carrie's face, and it made her smile. 'Yeah, I know. I've got a good one. Gran's was thirty-two. Dad came home and found her dead in the chair one day. It was such a shock because she was the kind of old-fashioned Resurrectionist who didn't ever share her number with anyone. "Only God knows the numbers of our days," she'd say. She didn't leave a letter or a note or anything, which was a bit cold. Dad was only a little kid – he found her.' She nodded down into her lap. 'It's not like you'd think, being different.'

I don't want to be different, Carrie thought. *I don't think I ever wanted that.*

Jazz knocked on the front door before entering, his footsteps echoing through the hallway. 'Only me,' he called, unnecessarily.

'Living room!' Mercy jumped up.

He stuck his tousled head around the door. 'Hey, babe. All sorted. Sorry it took so long, had to give the Alphas a bell and let them know. The Wades were *really* pissed off.' His frown lines deepened. 'All right here?'

'I think so.' Mercy crossed the room to wrap him in a tight hug, burying her face in his skinny chest. 'I told her everything.'

Jazz nodded at Carrie over Mercy's head. 'Sorry about all this. My first day here wasn't much better, although I am on the cutting edge, so to speak.' He cleared his throat.

The Crows creaked around them, boards bowing impercept-ibly above and below. Mercy squeaked, huddling on the beanbag, but Carrie didn't react. She barely heard the creak over the voices. They were starting up again, familiar as her own thoughts, but this time she knew they weren't.

'Can you guys stay tonight?' she asked. 'I don't... I don't want to be alone... and I know it's weird, but I don't want to leave the house, either. I feel like we've both been through enough for one night.' She shivered.

Mercy nodded. 'This beanbag is pretty comfy.'

'There's… there's, um, there's an… airbed,' Carrie said, trying to concentrate. Fairwood was whispering, whispering inside her head. She couldn't hear the words, *if* there were words. There were layers to the whispers, layers on layers, room upon room, in concert with each other, all whispering, whispering…

Mercy hurried after her. 'Everything will seem so much better in the morning!'

That was usually true, but Carrie suspected it would take more than a good night's sleep to make this all right. She had a dreadful idea, currently buried under layers of denial but slowly burrowing up to the surface, that nothing was going to be all right again.

She caught a glimpse of herself in the bathroom mirror before she stumbled into her room and hit the mattress. The woman in the mirror with toothpaste around her mouth was bedsheet white except for the blotches of nettle rash and tired purple saddlebags under her eyes. A few silvery threads glistened in the messy ponytail. The white peppermint foam made her look rabid, a zombie-shell of her old self, clawing its way into a life it didn't understand.

Mercy tucked Carrie in with maternal concern, and Carrie had to remind herself that they had only known each other a week. She was too tired to think it was creepy.

'That's a cute music box,' Mercy whispered, leaning over Carrie's bedside table and turning something over in her hands. 'It's really pretty.'

'What music box?' Carrie mumbled into her pillow. 'The one I found… in the attics… it's—' she yawned. '—down, downstairs…'

Mercy put the box back on the dressing table.

It gave a soft twang.

'You know what,' Mercy whispered, 'I'm putting that in a cupboard for now.'

'Knock yourself out.' Carrie was too exhausted to care. 'Night.'

She turned over, cuddling her spare pillow, and sunk into deep, soothing sleep.

He whirled around the coal cellar in a silent, triumphant waltz, Gerald flapping over his shoulder in a fireman's lift, appendages flopping, antlers shivering. An eyeball popped out, dangling from the skull by the optic nerve and a shred of duct tape.

They spun around to no particular beat, Ricky's insides squirming with anticipation.

She was nice.

The thought came out of nowhere. It stopped him dead.

Gerald slid off his shoulder and crumpled in a limp heap on the floor.

'Must be one o' your thoughts,' he decided finally, running a hand over his shaven head, unsure. 'She was all right. As they go.' He didn't hold with being 'regular'. Regularity was petty and mean, small and powerless. He couldn't imagine going through life ignorant of the intricacies of the wyrd, blind to the woven threads of fate glistening within constellations of arcane knowledge.

He giggled to himself.

'She won't be reg'lar much longer, Gerald,' he whispered, bending low to the balding fox-ear glued to the deer skull.

Gerald listened to all his secrets but never told Ricky any of its own.

'I'll get you fresh kidneys, how about that? I'll plump you back up again. Looking thin and poor, you are.'

The skull lay at an awkward angle, uppermost cornflower-blue eye gloopy with decay. Ricky had managed to make eyeballs last a good few months, but these were at their limit.

'Stay there,' he told the pile of parts, still giggling to himself. 'I'll be off to my bed.'

Gerald didn't move, a hulking, shapeless heap.

Ricky closed up the trapdoor after himself and trudged upstairs to his own room, filling his lungs with fungal moistness. The wrought iron bedframe of his childhood bed was a fraction too short even for him, and, after stripping off at the door, rubbing his flat, muscular belly as something rippled inside, he assumed his usual foetal position on the stained mattress. Lying in the dark with his head pillowed in the crook of his own arm, a thin brown blanket only half his length pulled over his naked skin, he listened.

His own breathing filled the room.

There was a suck of skin as his other lips parted, mucus-slick, the scratching quest of his air-roots as they coiled up from inside him, squeezing their way along his spine and twanging his oesophagus on their way out. The mattress behind his head felt spongey, tasted sour under the tongue-like lengths as they spread out behind him, seeking protein.

(*Feed, it won't be long now, the Changes will be done soon.*)

That thought was certainly his own.

Moths were chalky, woodlice bitter.

His other tongue tickled. Maddening. He raked it with his teeth, tasting five or six parts of the room at once.

From downstairs, there came a muffled scrabbling.

Ricky froze, tendrils in mid-coil and spreading out over the bulging damp of the wall. He scrunched the edge of the ragged blanket into his hand.

The scrabbling came again, a muffled squeak, a small crunch of bone on bone.

Ricky's chest hollowed.

Gerald never moved for him.

Perhaps it wasn't Gerald, he consoled himself, aware it had been a long time since he last *minded* Gerald's determined inanimation. Just an owl.

Ricky remained in his foetal curl, mechanically comfort-eating his way through the fat, dark moths in his dank bedroom until his aching belly stabbed at him to stop, their dusty wing-scales waltzing through his intestines, sour-sharp as broken glass.

Part 2

24 April – 06 May

Inbred and Evil

In which Ricky Porter comes for tea
24 April

That weekend, Carrie called in sick. She needed to think.

Around her, Fairwood breathed. Wood creaked, bowing in and out. Open windows sucked in the outside air, blew out deep sighs. Doors clicked and swung without her touch.

The dead clock in the hall ticked steadily, an impossible heartbeat.

The house was in her head, rifling through her subconscious with fibrous fingers, picking over the images it needed and absorbing her into the mortar, scrapbooking her between the pages of its history.

The voices were worse. She'd almost prefer the manifestation, at least that was only one thing to focus on, but at the same time she couldn't cope with something bulging out at her through the walls. It seemed as though Fairwood could either be condensed down into an avatar or be alive in its own construction, but not both at the same time: when the avatar was around, the rooms stopped whispering.

For the most part, Fairwood communicated in ideas and vibes, not words. Mainly what it communicated was a simmering, migraine-inducing indignance.

Hatred for the town, for the despoilers and the vandals, for the attack on its current possessor, roiled up from the coal cellar in choking billows of flammable rage. Next to this, the medieval crypt, the only remnant of the original monastery on which Fairwood was built, chanted softly of peace and forgiveness.

The upper floors had vengeance glinting in their windowpanes, shard-sharp. The living room, which had seen the worst of Janet Varney's attack, nevertheless held out as the moralising centre, providing strains of structured rationality.

Mercy had called, but Carrie couldn't face her.

Guy had texted her, apparently oblivious of the night's events, to ask about a house tour, and Carrie had laughed hysterically and thrown her phone across the room.

For three nights she lay awake inside a sleeping house, listening to its ticking heartbeat keeping time to her pulse and striking the hours.

On Tuesday morning, Carrie looked out of the window and saw Ricky Porter, hood up and hands in his pockets, behind the wire fence. As she watched, he gave it an experimental twang, lowering his ear to the vibrating length.

'What the hell is he doing?' Carrie wondered aloud.

She could feel the house watching him too, concentrating its focus through the window she was standing at, as if trying to borrow her eyes. Ricky straightened up, apparently satisfied with his test, and climbed carefully under the wire to stand on the lawn. He thrust his hands into his pockets, stamping the moist grass.

'Does he... want to come in?' Carrie scratched her head. 'Should we offer him tea, or something?' She had always talked to herself in the house: that, at least, wasn't new. It was natural as breathing.

The house didn't reply.

Ricky had turned his back on the wishing well and was taking slow steps across the lawn, as if navigating a mine field. He seemed to be calculating a route towards the back door, avoiding dips in the grass and things she couldn't see. He reached the rockery and uncultivated garden, where he stopped, and looked up.

He waved.

Carrie pulled back and headed downstairs.

He was waiting at the back door when she opened it, shifting from one foot to the other. Ricky was a far less intimidating figure in daylight and familiar surroundings, a grubby, slouching young man around her own age in stained clothes and muddy shoes. He didn't take down his hood, but she could see him far more clearly now. His eyes weren't red today, his lips parted in a faint, crooked smile.

'Hey,' she greeted, raking her fingers through her hair.

'You're alive in there, then?' He peered around her at the range and the hearth. 'Haven't seen you go for your walks. I was beginning to wonder if you'd been took bad.'

The flash of grey between the trees flickered through her memory. 'So you *have* been watching me.'

Ricky cleared his throat, accent broadening as he feigned nonchalance with painful transparency. 'Doant flatter yourself, I just 'appen to go out same time as you, s'all.'

Against her better judgment, she stepped back from the door to allow him entry, but he hesitated on the threshold.

'You can come in,' she prompted, watching his expression.

He tilted his unshaven chin and scratched at his stubbled neck. 'Ain't up to you. Never has been.'

'How d'you mean?'

Ricky reached out with both hands, winced as though he encountered invisible resistance, then stepped back. 'All right. You still don't trust me. I'll be completely honest, will that help?' He wasn't talking to her. He glanced around the walls, scanning the windows and casements. 'I been naun but good to you, haven't I? Pendle blood or no, you can't say as I didn't help you out time to time, chased kids off for you, never broke a window, never overstepped my bounds except that once and I paid for it without complaint, di'n't I, got my fingers burned and serve me right, but I only ever asked nice.' He put his head on one side. 'You called *me*, not the other way 'round. You can choose, now, Mistress Pritchard never thought of that, did she? Well. Here I am.'

Carrie heard the house muttering in concert with itself, all the layers of history and personalities of its rooms chiming in all at once. She stepped away from the door and covered her ears, wincing, but the voices were inside her head.

'Please stop.'

'I ain't said nothing.'

'Not you…' Carrie pressed her palms tight around her head, but it didn't help. The house felt her pain, and quiet descended. It picked a spokes-room.

He never despoiled. Never fractured. Never hurt.

…Only for today. Then, we'll see.

Carrie swayed, feeling sick. 'Okay,' she breathed. 'Okay, go for it.'

Ricky nodded. 'I had a word with Gran. She don't know anything about Janet Varney's little stunt the other night, and I believe her, for what it's worth. Jan was acting on her own.'

Carrie folded her arms. 'Okay.'

Ricky let out a sudden boyish giggle, running a hand over his shaven head under the hood. 'This is the closest I've ever been allowed,' he admitted, face lighting up like a child. '*Ever*. I couldn't even get across the lawns before today.' He grinned at her, full lips parted in a bright, happy smile. 'Are you gonna let me in? You said 'okay', but—' He sucked air through his teeth. 'You're still standing in the way, like it's not. That ain't very hospitable.'

'That's it?' Carrie didn't move. 'Your gran isn't responsible, you think she's telling the truth, and that's it?'

He thrust his hands back in his pockets, rocking back on his heels. 'What else d'you want to know?'

'Why won't the house let you in?'

He coughed. 'Long story. Be comfier inside. Neighbourly to let me in first, offer me a pot of tea, say "thank you, Mr Porter, for your life-saving assistance", I don't know, just throwing ideas around.'

'Thank you,' Carrie said, and meant it.

Ricky studied her, seeking sarcasm, and blinked when he couldn't find any.

Carrie stepped back from the door. 'Come on in. Just for today, though, Fairwood says. I want you to explain why, the house isn't – isn't very clear, today.'

'Understood.' His eyes were moist, wonder-wide, about to cry. He held it together.

Carrie backed off as he put a careful hand on each side of the doorframe and climbed in as if encountering slight resistance, lifting one leg high above the step and pushing through into the kitchen, leaning in, half-in-half-out. He pulled the other leg through as he pushed himself all the way in, like a diver in a submerged vessel.

Bizarre performance complete, Ricky Porter stood triumphantly in her kitchen, looking around at the door with a flicker of gleeful surprise. He bounced on his heels a couple of times, then, to her amazement, took off his muddy shoes and deposited them on the mat. His feet were calloused and bare, streaked with dirt.

'Well, ain't this a turn-up for the books.' He sniffed, crooked smile splitting wider into a sharp-toothed grin. 'First of us to set foot in the place since 1958. Making history, I am.' He laughed again in that sudden, unguarded way, releasing a childish bubble of joy. 'The old girl didn't make much of a mess in here, at least. Could murder a cup of tea, by the way.'

'I cleaned up,' Carrie muttered, not registering his request as his comment triggered the memory of Mrs Varney, lying open-throated on the ground. 'I didn't just… I couldn't just leave it.'

Jazz had returned briefly and taken the splintered remains of the living room door off its hinges, the boards now blocking up the broken window. She still needed to ring Joe Lin and ask him if he could sort it out. Carrie shivered, twisting her necklace chain around her finger. 'I've never seen a dead person before.'

'What, *never*? I take it black, by the way.'

His determination to get a cup of tea out of her made her laugh. It bubbled out of her nerves, louder than she intended. She'd laughed like that in the hospital, the night her grandad died.

She hadn't meant to then, either, but it had burst out, dark and mirthless, and too loud for the late hour. 'Grampa, yeah, but he was – I never saw anyone die like *that*.'

Ricky relented, dropping the acidity. 'All right, sit down, bloody hell. I'll do it myself. You look all in.'

'I'm fine. I'm going into work later.' Carrie rubbed her forehead. 'Someone called in sick so Mercy texted me.'

'Yeah. Do you good.' Ricky strolled around the range, taking in the layout, and found the teabags. 'See, I'm helping,' he announced to the wall.

'I've probably got some beer Dad left here, somewhere,' Carrie said, sliding into a chair. 'If you want.'

'I don't drink.'

This surprised her. 'No?'

'Not a drop.' Ricky made the tea in pious silence, stroking the worktop with light, quick movements, as if afraid he'd be burned if he touched it too long. His fingers wandered to the tiles on the wall, tracing the contours of the ceramics and grouting until the kettle boiled. She watched, her limbs too heavy to be useful.

'Is that… because you're a soothsayer?'

'That's right.' He turned to her with strong, black tea and dumped the mug in front of her. It slopped over the sides and onto the table, nearly scalding her wrist. 'Hi-ho, hi-ho, an ascetic life for me. No sex, no drugs, no rock 'n' roll. No processed sugars either, in case you was thinking of inviting me to a party, as would be neighbourly of you.' His accent wandered around the British Isles with mocking ease, settling back into a version of Mrs Wend's, a more neutral version of the local dialect. 'Shouldn't be having tea at all, not technically, but I'm doing you a social courtesy.' He slumped down into a chair. 'Right, I'll be honest with you. You ask, I'll tell.'

'All right. Why aren't you allowed in the house?'

'A certain meddling old hedge-witch, name of Miss Eglantine Valmai Pritchard, if you please, thought Gran or her sisters had killed the kid,' Ricky said promptly, jerking a thumb at the chimney. 'She stopped the Pendles setting foot here again. You have to tie a curse like that to something, some sort of condition. She thought she'd let the house decide to let us in, thought she was being clever. Of course, Fairwood wasn't properly alive then, not like now, so she couldn't *decide* shit. Oh, she called out, lured people in, but not, you know, coherently. Bit of a bitch for us, since that hearthstone from the old Pendle cottage is imbued with energies we need.' He grinned. 'Bet no one told you *that* at the auction, did they? *Caveat emptor* applies, and all that.'

Phil would have used the Latin to show off, but Ricky slipped it in without anticipating applause. Some people had a way with words; Carrie was coming to appreciate that what Ricky had was more of a spaghetti junction. Carrie couldn't help but grin. She glanced at the hearthstone, covered by the range.

'That has magical properties?'

'Didn't say that. Said "energies", didn't I? If I meant magic, I'd have said magic.' Ricky sipped his tea. 'It's the difference between poison and venom, know what I mean? Two different types of toxin.'

'But they can both kill you,' Carrie remarked.

Ricky rolled his eyes. 'In certain doses. All right, I'm just being *accurate*. Said I'd be honest. Doing my best.'

Carrie frowned. She stared down at her tea – black, the way he took it, since he hadn't asked her what she liked.

Cocky sod, she thought, and the well-bred snicker of the smoking room filtered into her consciousness. She decided to play him at his own game.

'Can you put some milk in this?'

He blinked. 'What?'

'Milk. I take tea with milk, thanks for asking.'

'I'm off'ring you *answers*, here. *Magic*. A whole new bloody world. I'm not your tea boy.'

Carrie kept up her poker face. 'Thought you said "energies", not magic. The milk's in the fridge.'

'Fuck me.' He went to the fridge with bad grace and poked around inside, taking longer than necessary. 'Oi. This mince is out of date.'

Carrie narrowed her eyes, prompted by the kitchen's instincts towards hungry occupants. Her own appetite was severely lacking. 'D'you want it?'

'Maybe.' He turned the packet over. 'It's not bad quality, this.'

'Knock yourself out.'

Ricky was salivating. She could see the trail of dribble dripping down his chin. 'Deal. Not like my farsight isn't wrecked as it is. Won't do any more harm.' He pulled it out with the milk, sliding the bottle across the table to her and ripping off the plastic film with sharp, dirty nails.

Carrie concentrated on her tea as he shovelled a handful into his mouth.

'Okay, your farsight, can you… tell me more about that? You saw my future, that's why you were in the tunnel…? You thought, what, if you helped me, the house would let you in?'

Ricky wagged a finger at her, chomping on the meat. ''xactly.'

She waited for him to swallow.

'And…?'

'And, it's fading. The farsight. Does that sometimes, natural cycles, but it's inconvenient when it goes. Asceticism helps, keeps my head clear, but—' he shovelled another handful in, chewed and swallowed, '—if I can use the Pendle Stone, I can get it back up to scratch wi'out having to resort to the more, let's say, *drastic* methods to boost my abilities, since they're labour-intensive and a right pain in the arse.'

'Drastic how?' Carrie remembered the stink in Ricky's cottage, the sweet reek of decay.

'Carrie,' Ricky put the mince down, picking bits out of his teeth. 'I can't tell you that. Let's not run before we can walk.'

'Tell me or get out.' Carrie folded her arms, taking him in.

Ricky paused. 'She puts up a good front, don't she?' he asked the house. He reached for the mince, but Carrie lunged across the table and snatched it out of range. 'Oi!' He saw she was serious. 'Fine, all right. If you must know, I do rituals to channel forces from, well, let's call it Outside, as in, not of this reality. Sometimes I kill people and eat bits of 'em.'

Carrie willed her face into a tight mask, her bladder melting into ice water. '*Seriously?*'

'Yeah.' He wasn't joking.

'*Why?*' Carrie knew she should be horrified, but she was too numb for that.

Ricky grinned, sharp and bloody. 'I ain't praying to *benevolent* deities, here. None of that "blessed be" bullshit.'

Carrie shook her head, half-convinced this was something her sleep-deprived brain had conjured. 'No, see, you're doing it wrong. You don't admit you kill people if you want to make me like you.'

Ricky frowned. 'Honesty's the best policy, that's what they say, right? Read that somewhere.' He reached for the mince and she didn't stop him. 'The thing is,' he said, tapping the table, 'the thing is, if I lied to you, said it was all herblore and starlight and all that airy-fairy crap, you'd find out eventually. I *could* spend my time tiptoeing around cleaning up the corpses and pretending to be vegan, but to tell the truth, love, I really can't be arsed. It's a lot easier for me if we all know what we're signing up for at the start.'

'And what I'm signing up for,' Carrie said slowly, 'is some really dark shit, am I right?'

'Basic'lly. The kind of dark that leads to subtle madness, that sort of thing.' Ricky licked the bottom of the pack, watery blood dripping down his chin as he tipped it up. Carrie looked away until he was done.

'*Why* would I ever agree to that?' she asked. 'Why on *earth* would I ever let a self-confessed cannibal in here to do God knows what in my kitchen for – why, exactly?'

Ricky blinked. He put the packet down. 'What d'you mean, why would you? It's the right thing to do. Fair's fair. Pendle Stone belongs to us. I saved your life, boosted your wish. Doant you go forgetting that. All I want is access to what's ours and been denied us. That strikes me as fair, and what I want to *do* with it ain't your business.'

'Why shouldn't I call the police?'

'Police won't do shit. I've lived here my whole life. They're an inconvenience, not a threat.'

'Ricky, that's not…'

'Tell you what,' Ricky said, leaning forwards, biceps bulging under his thin grey sleeves. 'I'll do you a favour. Every time I use the Stone, I'll owe you something. You can't say fairer than that, can you?'

Carrie set her jaw. 'Suppose I said yes,' she muttered, reluctant to even entertain the idea. 'But only to use it once, and definitely not for anything involving body parts. What about if you tell me why Janet attacked me, and if I'm in any more danger?'

Ricky sniffed. 'I can't, can I?' He tapped his temple. 'I don't know.'

'The girl up the chimney, then,' Carrie snapped, losing patience. 'What about her? What kind of rite was she part of? Was that to see the future, too?'

Ricky shook his head. 'Nah, a kid's not much good for that. Best guess is, some sort of bastardised youth rite that went a bit wrong. Kid got found too soon, something like that. You need to hang 'em up for a while to get all the juice out of 'em, it's time-consuming. And maybe old Jan, she knew something, and she was hoping you wanted to sell it on. Then you show up to the History Society and tell them you want to live here, and, knowing you, start asking questions, Jan gets the wind up and decides to scare you off. Except, you know, that goes a bit wrong too.'

'What d'you mean, "knowing me"?' Carrie demanded. 'You don't know me.'

Ricky chortled. 'You're joking. You've been asking nothing but questions since the moment I introduced myself.'

That was a fair point. She rolled her eyes at the self-confessed cannibal sitting across the table, nursing his own mug of tea. 'Phil always said I asked too many questions. I can't help it.'

'Who's this?'

'My ex.' She dropped her focus to the table. 'He'd have a right go at me if he could hear me. Say it served me right.'

'Yeah, well. Fuck him, hey,' Ricky advised sagely. 'If you hadn't pissed Mrs Varney off, I couldn't have ingratiated myself into the house, so—' he beamed '—worked a treat, as far as I'm concerned.'

Carrie sat back. 'Are you flirting with me, Mr Porter?'

The effect this had was stunning.

Ricky's face stiffened into a horrified mask, eyes widening as his cheeks went pale, then red.

'You what?'

'Relax!' Carrie giggled, as his stare gave way to mild panic. 'Ricky, I'm teasing, I'm sorry, your *face*…' She coughed, trying to stop laughing.

'Don't… that's not nice,' Ricky mumbled, flushing. 'Don't laugh at me like that, it's… you can't laugh like that, I just *told* you I kill and eat people.'

'Sorry.'

Ricky cleared his throat. 'Look, I've got things to do, so unless you're happy to give me a shot at the Pendle Stone now…'

'No.'

'Suit yourself.' He stretched out and gave her a mocking salute. 'You'll agree anyway.'

'Sure, of course I will. Written somewhere, is it?'

He ignored her and went to put his shoes back on.

'How about I come to you next time and meet your mum and dad?' Carrie suggested with heavy sarcasm as he left by the back door. 'Since your invite's rescinded.'

'Be seeing you, neighbour,' Ricky shot over his shoulder.

He skulked off across the lawns with a few furtive glances back at the kitchen door, and each time he saw Carrie still watching he gave her a wave until at last she waved back.

She watched him disappear into the trees, her thoughts jumbled.

'He really thinks I'll let him in again,' she murmured. The empty mince packet was the only proof he had been there at all. 'He eats people. Ha, he eats people, of course he does. My neighbour's a chavvy Hannibal Lecter.' She frowned. 'Don't tell him I said that.'

He doesn't lie.

Carrie steeled herself.

'Right,' she said. 'Come on out.'

The house was still.

'I'm serious. Let me see you. Come on.'

The wall bulged, the form of a head pushing through the wall, a body pulling away from the cupboards, until it stood there in the form of the last Sauvant of Fairwood.

'This is new for me, too,' 'Jack' said in her voice as if reading her mind, with the petulance of the master bedroom and the patience of a stone. 'I'm… not used to having my personality consolidated like this. It's like being condensed into a… a mobile outbuilding. And I did save your life.'

'I'm not *un*grateful,' Carrie said, stung by his expression. 'I'm not. It's just…' She trailed off as he turned to face her, arms folded across his chest and eyebrows raised. 'This has all been a bit much. Thank you, for − saving me.'

'Thank *you*,' Fairwood intoned, 'for saving me.' The look he gave her reminded her of the sorrowful way the windows of The Crows had stared down at her before its restoration, broken panes and empty frames expressing grief it had no words for, a house full of stories but no one to tell. It tugged at her heart. She got up and took an involuntary step towards him, coming closer than she intended.

His arms were smooth like polished wood, shirt painted on but doing a good imitation of real cotton. Carrie couldn't help it; she had to touch him. As she moved her hand up the sleeve, the fabric parted from the arm, until it was an actual shirt. She stepped nearer, tracing light fingertips over the chest where the gouges bit deeply into the plaster-flesh. She had too many questions.

'Can we trust Ricky? What do you think? You must know everyone in this town.'

'People are pain,' Fairwood murmured, reasserting its experience. 'But Ricky Porter isn't a thief. Not a vandal. Not a disfigurer. He never touched me. Never broke a window.'

'Yeah, but... what do you *know* about him?'

Fairwood pressed a palm to her forehead.

Carrie gasped, flooded with a series of images, static lines zipping through her vision like flies, swarming with energy.

A group of children jostled each other far below her, wide-eyed and perspiring. A young boy threw a stone, hitting her square in the eye. Her vision splintered. Her remaining eyes overlooked the lawn where another boy was watching, staying away. His rage boiled with her aura of pain, she felt it as he circled the perimeter and got the stone-thrower alone, heard the scream and snap of bone.

The sun and moon cycled across the sky in a dance, shadows sailing over her rough, crumbling skin. Her vision was blurred, distorted with dust and grime and a thousand cracks. She could see in all directions from the broken shards of her eyes lying on the ground, the reflections bouncing and light dazzling her, a thousand eyes in all directions.

He was always just on the edge of her vision, always almost out of sight. Sometimes he disembowelled squirrels for something to do. A few years later he left lager cans behind, washing down pills that made him unpredictable and telling her it was his fifteenth birthday. She couldn't reply, but the gaping wound in her kitchen mourned the absence of cake. He was not allowed to come closer. He slumped by the fence and watched the crumbling walls, longing in his glazed, wild eyes.

Carrie gasped, her eyes constricting back into two points at the front of her head. 'Ohh—' She swallowed. 'That's... wow, that was weird. Poor Ricky.'

The sun came out from behind a cloud, showing up the streaks and marks on the window glass. She closed her eyes, and for a moment she felt the same excitement as in her dream, the same thrill of knowing her desire was made flesh and in the room with her. Her lungs filled with the same smell: a warm library and a summer garden. His hand on her arm was smooth and cold, quickly warming from her own heat. A light shiver shot down to her groin, pulling her forward until they were pressed together. It was like leaning into a solid wall. Anger surged up at the thought of stones flying at the windows.

'Poor *you*.'

'Your heart is fast,' Jack commented, concerned. 'The doctors say that isn't good.'

Carrie felt suddenly sick. Fairwood's memory flashed into her head, an elderly doctor with a brown leather bag and a stethoscope listening to the heartbeat of a sickly child in this very room, as servants and cooks bustled about.

She pulled away.

'What about Cathy Ross? Can you show me what happened?'

He shook his head. 'Cathy Ross was not killed here.'

'Who stuffed her up the chimney, then?' Carrie reached out and took his wrist, hoping for another insight into the house's past. 'You know that, you must do.'

'I don't.'

All she sensed was a frustrating web of static. The rushing in her ears made her wince and let go. 'What's that?'

'I don't know.' He caught her worried frown. 'A psychic block. Someone cleaned up after themselves pretty thoroughly.' He dropped his head, window-grey eyes sorrowful. 'I'm sorry, I can't help. I've wanted to speak to you for such a long time.'

Carrie stared, mesmerised. 'I know.'

There was a moment of comfortable silence.

Fairwood was the first to break it. 'You have to go to work.'

'I wish I didn't have to,' Carrie murmured. 'I don't... I don't know what to do.'

Fairwood let her go and moved off down the hallway, a spring in his step that made her feel lighter.

'You should ask Cathy,' he called over his shoulder, before he walked into the staircase and disappeared back into his larger self. 'Let her out and ask her.'

'What? How?'

But Fairwood was whole again, and the rooms replied in their harmony.

In the box…

They couldn't get rid of her, she's still here…

Carrie stood still at the bottom of the stairs.

The music box?

That made sense, too, in a light-headed way.

'With any luck,' she remarked, heading up to her bedroom to get changed, 'I'll get some breathing space before anyone else tries to kill me.'

She needed to know what was going on: finding out Janet Varney's secret was now top of her list.

Bad Omens

In which Guy Bishop brings Carrie flowers

26 April

On Thursday, Guy Bishop called round with a bunch of flowers from the History Society. Janet Varney's death was now common knowledge, but the circumstances had apparently been spread around a select group.

'So sorry about what happened, Carrie,' Guy said from the porch, bouquet like a barrier. 'Beverley thought we should send you… well, a token really, no hard feelings about what happened, I hope? It must have been *so awful.*'

Carrie loosened the tie of her dressing gown so he could see she was fully dressed and not lounging around at two in the afternoon, even though someone else had pipped her to the post for a cover shift she'd wanted and she had nothing else to do.

'Um. Thanks.'

His earnestness grated on her, as if sincerity was something he'd picked up with his weekly shop and brought along with the flowers. The way he emphasised the *awfulness* of the incident – Carrie struggled with this word, it sounded like a police report that happened to someone else – made her cringe.

She accepted the bouquet with bomb-disposal delicacy. Three striking lilies made up the centre, a dusky purple with delicate scooped petals, each with a trio of pollen-dusted stamens that Carrie made a mental note to avoid. The rest were pretty things she couldn't name, except for the dark pink ones she knew were roses.

'D'you… want to come in?'

'Sure.' He accepted so readily that she was certain he didn't know about Fairwood.

Carrie stepped back, letting him over the tiled threshold. Smart brown shoes scuffed over the marble-whites and duck-egg blues.

You don't trust him, do you? She asked the house. A wall of animosity exuded from the walls, passing through her in a wave of rage. She caught her breath, fists balling at her sides.

Liar, vandal, thief!

Says he cares, he doesn't care.

Send him out, get him out.

…People are pain.

Carrie swayed, concentrating on her own body, her own poise, and it ebbed away. She indicated the living room, off the reception hall to the right, but Guy was enraptured by the great staircase up to the gallery and first floor, the great curved uprights of the bannisters, the shut-up rooms to the left. He hadn't noticed her discomfort, at least, so that was good.

'Guy?'

He shook himself but continued to stare. 'This is incredible. I mean it. I couldn't have imagined…' He shook his head. 'How did you… how did you escape?'

'Escape?' Carrie stiffened. 'Well. I – went down the priest hole.'

'The smuggler's tunnel, that's real?' Guy's eyes lit up. 'It's, wow, we heard so many stories about this place. I never dared come in.'

LIAR.

A door slammed upstairs, emphasising Fairwood's fury.

Carrie glared at Guy, indignant. 'Yes, you did. You said as much in the car!'

Guy flushed. 'Oh, well… I mean…' He stopped. 'Can I look around?'

NO.

The refusal gusted through the house in a huff of cold, eddying air. It pushed Guy backwards, but Carrie caught his elbow and laughed it off, sounding fake and shrill in her own ears. 'I'll put the kettle on.'

She didn't trust the living room to be hospitable, but she thought she could trust the kitchen. She directed Guy along the hall, but even the kitchen felt a little colder than it usually did. 'Just – have a seat! Warmest room in the house.'

His cardigan gave off a darkly spicy scent as she bundled him through to the kitchen table, some expensive antiperspirant mingled with peppermint breath mints and undertones of bourbon.

Who drank bourbon at lunchtime?

Filing this as another potential red flag, or at least a puzzle piece whose shape she didn't trust, she cast about for positives. Few men could pull off a cardigan, Carrie thought, but Guy Bishop was one of those men. He suited his surroundings better than Ricky Porter, slouching in the same chair with raw beef blood dripping down his chin.

'This is lovely.' Guy's voice sounded strangely strangled as he shifted in his chair. He glanced over his shoulder at the chimney, gave her a wincing smile, and shuffled around to face her.

'Creepy, isn't it?' Carrie remarked, watching him. 'Don't suppose you'd know anyone who could do a séance, do you?'

He shook his head. 'Can't say I do, no.'

'I just… I want to know what's going on,' Carrie said, watching him. 'I don't want to hurt anyone, or cause trouble or anything like that, I literally just need to know who the fuck is trying to hurt me.'

'And do what?' Guy looked at her, drumming his fingers on his arm. 'Ask them nicely to stop?'

Carrie shrugged, taken aback by his tone. 'I don't know. Maybe.'

'And if they were involved in the kid's death all those years ago, you would hand-on-heart not report them?' Guy gave her a disbelieving look.

This was a sticky point. She fidgeted. 'Well. I mean, I don't know, I *should*, I guess, but... I don't... I mean, yeah, I guess I'd have to.'

'Do you believe in destiny?' Guy asked, staring at the table.

'Destiny?'

He picked at a stray thread in his sleeve. 'The Anglo-Saxons called it your wyrd, you know. Your wyrd is unchangeable, but not unknowable, and that's a curse as much as a blessing, you see.'

Carrie wondered where this was going. 'Have you been talking to Ricky Porter?'

'Good grief, no.' Guy shook his head, wrinkling his brow in profound distaste. 'I take it you've met him?'

This rubbed Carrie up the wrong way – *now I know what people mean by that cliché*, she thought, her back stiffening. She'd take Ricky Porter over Guy Bishop right now. Ricky was creepy, unhygienic, and had more than a touch of the dark and arcane about him, but at least he was honest. Guy was hiding something, and Carrie was sick of people lying to her face. 'Yeah. I gather he's an acquired taste, though I could say that of most people.'

'Do you think you can change your fate?' he asked her, not listening.

'I don't know, I've never really thought about it,' Carrie confessed, deciding to play along and see where this went, if anywhere. 'I always thought you could make your own.'

'I thought that.' Guy glanced over his shoulder. 'But – supposing wyrd is like elastic, no matter how you try and change it, it just... pings back into shape.'

'Eloquent.'

Guy missed the sarcasm. 'Like this house. It went to wrack and ruin, but it always knew what it wanted to be, and... here it is. Like nothing happened.'

'I'll put the kettle on.' Carrie slid out of her seat.

Guy was silent for a moment, huddled in his chair as if afraid of what might come down the chimney and get him. Carrie made the tea, listening to Fairwood's mutinous whispers of vandalism and treachery.

Guy looked up as the kettle boiled. 'Thank you.' It was hard to tell how sincere his earnest politeness was: it sounded mechanical.

Carrie took her time. 'So, you think it's all meant to be? Me coming to this house, Janet… is that meant to make me feel better?'

'Not really. Well, perhaps. You mustn't upset yourself about it. I gather you understand that Janet… well, she was…'

'A werewolf?' Carrie drummed her fingers on the worktop. 'Yeah, got that.'

A door slammed somewhere above their heads. Fairwood's upper rooms were particularly vicious where it came to past sins. Carrie cocked her eyebrow at the ceiling as the floorboards bowed, mimicking heavy footsteps.

'We're alone,' she assured Guy, pursing her lips around the rim of her own mug. 'Don't worry about that, it's a… draught.'

His face paled, to her amusement, but he cleared his throat. 'I don't suppose you've come across any old letters or diaries, things like that?'

'There's loads in the attic. I haven't thrown out anything that wasn't totally unsalvageable.'

Guy nodded. 'D'you fancy… I don't know, going for coffee sometime? Or dinner, maybe, if you eat… dinner.' He caught himself and groaned. 'I mean, obviously you eat dinner…'

Carrie nearly snorted her tea. Recovering, she asked, 'What has dinner got to do with old letters?'

Guy flushed. 'Well, you know, we could look over some stuff? Dad's book – he found a lot of things out about the house, but it was too dangerous to have a really good poke around and find all the paperwork, you know. I wondered if you wanted to go through it properly? I mean, it's local interest, maybe dad's book is due a revised edition, might be a fun project, that's all. And, I, um—' he took a deep breath '—I feel bad about what happened, I can't believe Jan would… I mean, I *can*. I think she was trying to scare you, that's all, but I'm… on behalf of everyone in the society… I'm so sorry.'

Carrie sat a little straighter in her seat. 'That… yeah. Thanks for, for, um, coming over. And that does sound fun, what exactly are you thinking might be here?'

Guy gave an awkward grin. 'Well, maybe something from the 1880s, Sir Peter Sauvant's stuff, especially. It's fascinating, the secret society of farmers, just a rumour, but…' He shrugged.

Carrie recalled the passage in Harry Bishop's book. 'The… what was it called? El-ewe-something?'

'The Eleusinians. All about fertility rites, the goddesses, you know. Classical education that went a bit awry, I think. Sir Peter… well, he wasn't the leader, I think there was a "priestess", you know.' Guy's face lit up as he warmed to his theme, chasing away his unease. 'I mean, no idea who it was, no idea who any of them were. But the dead started walking not long after the society or cult or whatever you like to call it, after that disbanded. And there's… well, newspaper articles, I mean, Dad didn't put them all in the book because they weren't relevant to the history of the *house*, but—'

'That's what Jazz meant,' Carrie leapt in. 'She was DNR, Janet, he cut her head off and took her to the crem—' She stopped, too late. 'Oh, God, Guy, I'm sorry, that was really blunt. I forgot you knew her, that was tactless.'

Guy was tight-lipped. He shook his head, avoiding eye contact. 'No, no, it – it's okay. But, um, yeah. You don't want people dying around here in the spring or summer, it gets, well, I mean, you've seen the films, right?'

Carrie shuddered. 'Shit. Are you serious?'

'Deadly.' Guy twitched in his chair. 'Don't plant what you don't want to grow, that's what they say.'

Carrie had heard this before. She recalled a throwaway line in Harry Bishop's book, the tragedy of losing the old parish church to a mysterious fire in the 1960s, and with it a lot of Sauvant family monuments when the roof and bell tower caved in. 'Is that why the church burned down? Something to do with who they buried there?'

'The graves all had iron grids across them, not just to deter body snatchers, but more so the dead couldn't get out,' Guy said. 'You can go and have a look, the ruin's still there. It burned down in the Sixties. They, well, there's lots of stories about why, but all the witnesses either went mad, catatonic, or became alcoholics, so I mean… who knows.' He scraped his chair back. 'I have to get going, but you know, if you find anything, let me know.'

Carrie nodded. 'I will.'

'And how about dinner?' He shot her a pearly-toothed smile, the kind that would have set her heart skipping if it didn't carry associations of profound mistrust.

In that moment Carrie knew she couldn't do it.

'That… would be nice,' she started to say, the 'but' on the tip of her tongue, but he gave her a brilliant grin and headed for the hallway.

'Great! I'll text you.'

Carrie stared at the back of his head, kicking herself. Her throat constricted around her protestations, fear welding her to the floor.

What was difficult about a date?

She saw him out, forcing her limbs into action, her head spinning.

The flowers were still sat on the small telephone table by the front door, and she wasn't sure what to do with them.

As he turned to wave, he pointed at the porch. 'Glad you managed to get the graffiti off all right. See you.'

Carrie watched his car crunching down her drive and came out, puzzled, looking up at the stone. He was right: the red letters were gone, and the stone was wet.

Carrie waited until she was sure Guy had left, then went up to the offending room above the kitchen, a bathroom with an antique bath she never used. The door opened to a cloud of steam. Carrie groaned.

'Fairwood…'

There was someone in the bath.

A slim hand, a familiar hand, was draped over the edge. Scars ran along the fingers to the wrist. Claw marks, fresh and deep, gouged up the arm to the elbow. The hand splashed down into the water, fingers beckoning.

Carrie steeled herself, coming all the way into the room. Despite the steam, her throat was dry.

The figure in the water was totally submerged, ravaged with lesions and gouges, eyes open and surrounded by a floating cloud of greying blonde hair. Red swirls of paint dirtied the water.

Carrie was staring down at a version of herself.

She dropped to her knees with a sharp gasp, shoulder against the tub. She shivered, steeling herself, and eased herself upright, eyes closed.

When I open them, it won't be me.

She opened them.

Her own body was still submerged, still ravaged with scars.

Of course it isn't you, she heard Fairwood say.

'No, it's—' she stopped. 'It's you.'

Her doppelganger rose from the water leaving traces of red paint behind, swirling like ribbons. The skin was all wrong, white-washed and stippled like painted brick, lips a dusky pink of curtain fabric, eyelashes stiff with gloss paint. The eyes were still window-grey, clear, questioning. Carrie let her eyes travel down.

'Oh!' She swallowed. 'Is that a – a gargoyle, you've put there?'

'Drainage,' the house's most recent avatar corrected, in her voice. 'You don't like it?'

'It's, it's, it's… nice,' Carrie said, not sure what else to say. The open-jawed lion gaped at her from between the gouges running down both slim thighs, custom-made sandstone. 'It's just… my, um, my "drainage" is, is on the inside.'

Fairwood-Carrie blinked, patient. 'This is not you.'

'No.' Carrie swallowed. 'No, this is not me.'

'Sir Jack served a purpose. He is not my owner now.' Fairwood ran its hand – Carrie's hand – over its new form. Carrie found herself mirroring the gesture, fascinated, a strange excitement filling her.

The steam inflamed her cheeks. 'Don't you... don't you own yourself, now?'

Fairwood blinked again, the windows shading in the bathroom as if briefly tinted. The condensation on the inside was wiped clean. 'The contract has your name on it.'

'No, well, yes, but you're – you're alive, aren't you?' Carrie faltered. 'Living things generally... belong to themselves.'

Fairwood gave her a look of incomprehension, a perfect mirror of her own version of that expression. 'No, I don't think so.'

'They do,' Carrie insisted.

'No.' Fairwood shook its – Carrie's – head. The hair was still floating, Carrie realised, floating in water that wasn't there. It shone in the light like a halo, insulation foam-yellow, fibre-fine. 'Because everything belonged to the lord, and what didn't belong to the lord belonged to god and the king. And they had to sign for the new small lives and keep their contracts safe.'

'No, those are birth certificates, not contracts,' Carrie protested, realising she was fighting a losing battle. 'That's not how humans work.' But wasn't it? She stopped, thinking. In a literal sense, the Sauvants had profited, directly and indirectly, from people believing they owned other people. Anyway, hadn't that been Phil's problem? Wanting control, possession, treating other people like toys? No. Fairwood was right. It was *exactly* how humans worked.

Carrie gave up. 'No, you know what? People *are* pain.'

Fairwood paused. It didn't refute this or reassure her that she was not. 'When are you going to repair me?'

'I'll call today.'

'Good. Mr Lin understands me.'

'Okay, I'll call Mr Lin.'

Fairwood folded its arms under small, polished, wooden breasts. 'I want more oak.'

'More oak. I'll tell him.' Carrie hesitated. 'That's expensive, though.'

'There's a few spent wishes I think will cover it. From the well.'

Carrie nodded, as her house stepped closer until they were nose to nose.

'This is weird.' Carrie traced her fingertips over Fairwood's grooved plaster flesh. 'So weird.'

Fairwood copied her, light touch gliding smoothly over her skin and her clothes, tracing her shape with possessive curiosity.

Mine, they thought in unison, reflected in each other's eyes.

–

By four o'clock that afternoon, Guy Bishop was at the residential home in which Harry Bishop, historian, author and avid bibliophile, now resided. His mind was still full of The Crows, the feeling he'd had inside the house, the boards covering Janet Varney's break-in, the graffiti on Caroline Rickard's porch.

Sitting in his car in the car park, he toyed with his phone. He thought about Janet, about the bourbon bottle in the glove box, how one wouldn't hurt. He hesitated, unwilling to break his promise to his father, face the crushing disappointment.

The Home was a blackspot for signal, so when his phone rang, he fumbled it in surprise and dropped it onto the passenger seat. It answered on its own.

'*Stop it*,' the voice told him, coming loudly and clearly through the speakers. '*You're thinking too much.*'

'Don't *do* that!' Guy slapped a hand against his chest, heart racing. 'Bloody hell—!'

'*What is taking so long? You gave her the flowers, didn't you?*'

'I did! Yes.' Guy squirmed, jabbing the End Call button. It did nothing, the screen frozen. 'I don't know what happened to Janet, I don't know what she knows, I don't think she *knows* anything, but she, she, said something about a séance, and I, I tried to dissuade her...'

'*Did you.*' The voice sniffed, disapproving. '*I hope you're not going to play the hero, Guy. That would be very foolish. Let it all run its course, is my advice.*'

Guy jabbed the End Call harder, to no avail. 'I can't talk right now,' he said desperately. 'I have to go and see dad...'

'*Harry will tell you the same thing.*'

The phone went dead.

Guy forced himself to get out of the car, leaving his phone on the passenger seat.

He was torn between buzzing in at the reception and turning around and going back.

A nurse made up his mind for him, approaching silently from the flowerbed. 'Mr Bishop?'

'Oh! Yes. Sorry, I was miles away.'

'Didn't mean to make you jump.' She smiled at him, and he smiled back. 'Your father's waiting for you in his room. His friends have just left. He's been looking forward to your visit all day.'

Guy grinned, a little sheepish, and looked down. 'Great. Yeah, great, I'll just sign in.'

Once his name was in the logbook, the nurse took him down the familiar stretches of fresh blue carpet and peach blush walls, towards the lifts. There were residents heading towards the dining room, some requiring more assistance than others, and apart from the odd whiff of something not too pleasant, the Home was a welcoming place.

'Would you like a drink?' The nurse asked, leaving him by his father's open door.

Guy felt his father's eyes on him. 'Oh, yes. Tea, please. Milk, two sugars. That would be lovely. Thanks.'

She disappeared, and he looked in to see his dad in his usual chair by the window, staring down at a solitaire chess game. He had once had a fine thick head of glossy dark hair, but that was thinned and soft and white now. His eyes were rheumy and tired from years of straining in the dim light to read small print. Plagued by arthritis, his swollen fingers no longer cooperated when it came to turning pages.

'Hi, Dad.'

His father looked up at Guy's approach, and a thin smile spread over his face. 'Pull up a chair.'

Guy dragged one up to the table, also looking down at the board. 'Who's winning?'

The old man snorted and ignored the quip. 'What's the latest?'

'Nothing much. Shop's doing fine. Uncle Mark is doing an excellent job with the society programme this year, of course. We've got a new member at the LHS, though. That's news.'

'A new member?' Harry Bishop squinted at his son. 'Not that dreadful woman from the planning department.'

'Mrs Rumbold? Oh, no.' Guy shuddered at the idea. 'No, no. Her name's Caroline. She's nice.'

His dad jerked his head, the corner of his lips twitching down. 'Caroline, is it? Not a regular, is she?'

Guy pulled the cushion out from behind his back and put it on the floor. 'Yes. No. Well, I don't rightly know yet.' He looked out at the landscaped gardens beyond the window, framed with chintz curtains and stained wood. 'She's... she's the lady who bought The Crows.'

This time, the silence fell on both sides. They stayed quiet until one of the staff came in with the tea, and Harry cast a baleful glare at his cup.

'Bloody kids,' he grumbled. 'No idea how to make a decent cuppa.'

Guy bit back a laugh. 'Dad! She might hear you.'

'No.' Harry dismissed the idea with a pained wave. 'Not a chance. Got their earbuds in all the time, listening to whatever passes for music nowadays.'

Guy rolled his eyes. 'You're such an old fart, Dad.'

'Don't you call your father an old fart, you ungrateful little sod,' Harry reprimanded his son. 'You watch, I'll still have you with my slipper.' He grinned, showing all his dentures. Then a thought returned and settled in his mind. His face clouded over. 'What did you say this woman's name was...?'

'Caroline, Dad. Caroline Rickard.'

'Caroline Rickard.' Harry rolled the name on his tongue, trying it out. He didn't seem too impressed with it. 'She on her own in there? Well, of course she is. She would have to be, wouldn't she? Can't see it taking to more than one person at a time. Jealous type of place, it felt like to me.'

'She's done it up beautifully. I mean, it's pretty perfect.'

'So, you've been in, then.' Harry's good eye became flinty. The other watered down his cheek, and he managed to tug out a tissue from the nearby box. 'What's it like?'

'Stunning.' Guy shook his head. 'She's really got a feel for the place.'

'That's not what I mean,' Harry said. He shifted his weight in the chair, pulling himself further forwards and closer to his son. 'I mean, the house, what does it *feel* like? Does it feel…' He lowered his voice to a scratchy rasp. '*Angry?*'

Guy swallowed. 'Yes.' He fidgeted, and his father noticed. 'It felt like it didn't want me there.'

'What did she say?'

'Said she wasn't leaving.' Guy avoided his father's scrutinising stare and studied the ornamental birdbath outside on the patio. Three sparrows were splashing about, fluffing their feathers in dips of spray. A few crows alighted on the lawn, hopping forwards.

Harry seemed lost in thought. Then he raised his head. 'You'd better take care of her, son.'

Guy gave a short, strained laugh, betraying his nerves. 'All right, Dad. No need to worry.'

'Who's worried? Why would I be worried?' Harry raised his hands and shook his head. 'What does a dying man have to worry about? Read to me.'

Guy pulled out his slim pocket volume of Coleridge.

*'In the open air
Our Myrtles blossom'd…;'*

'Not the Conversation Poems.' It was close to medication time, and Guy could see his father becoming tetchy. '"Kubla Khan", read that.'

All Harry Bishop wanted to do was to pick up a book and read it for himself again. He wouldn't touch audio books and was brutally scathing of any suggestion of a Kindle: the one Guy had bought for him remained in a drawer somewhere, and as far as Guy knew, had never even been switched on. He knew better than to bring it up. He went into his father's shelf and took down *The Complete Works of Samuel Taylor Coleridge*.

A sharp *smack* at the window made him jump and turn, the book slipping from his grasp and thudding to the carpet.

The crows were perched on the weathered stone rail in a line, laughing with wicked beaks agape. A frightened sparrow had smacked right into the glass leaving a crazed circular crack, a smudge of blood, and a single brown feather.

Guy lunged at the window, thumping on the frame with his fist, the cracks spreading.

The murder took off in a stiff fluttering of glossy black feathers, leaving the small brown body broken on the flagstones, one wing twitching slowly into the talons of death.

'Bastard things!' Guy thumped the sill at the last to take off, and it cackled one last time at him before joining its brethren. 'I'd shoot the bloody lot of them.'

'That's a bad omen,' Harry said, unexpectedly. He was leaning over the chessboard with a deep frown of concern.

Guy paused. 'For whom, dad?'

'The Crows' woman, I hope. The little girl who bought it.'

'She must be about my age.' Guy shook his head. He attempted humour. 'Are you saying I'm a little boy?'

His father didn't answer that, so Guy tried reassurance. 'Nothing's going to happen, Dad, I promise. It's just a house, and all the memories were put to bed a long time ago.'

Harry's knee quivered and he turned away, back towards the garden, his view now spoiled by the cobweb of cracks, the smudged spot of fresh blood. 'Read.'

Guy read. And read. And read.

They stopped for some sandwiches and a piece of Mrs Emory's birthday cake, the sun went down, and Guy read some more until it was half eight, his voice had all but gone, and he had to go home. He patted his father on the shoulder as he left, and Harry Bishop covered his son's hand with his own arthritic claw.

'See you next week?'

As if he had to ask. 'Sure. Bye, Dad. See you soon.'

'Don't shut the door behind you.' Harry pressed his buzzer for assistance, and Guy left quietly, as he did every week.

Brain Fever

In which Carrie is unwell and Ricky starts a fire
28 April

As the moon waxed, Fairwood fell into a quiet stupor. The voices quieted in Carrie's head, rooms whispering less and less. On Friday, she woke up with what she thought was the beginnings of a head cold, but by Saturday it was more like the flu. The flowers in the hall filled the house with a sickly fragrance, and Carrie couldn't summon the energy to get rid of them. She still went into work, groggy and full of Lemsip, a gnawing in her bones.

Saturday was a busy shift.

She struggled to swipe products, her shoulder burning with effort, wondering who the hell needed six litres of bleach, a roll of duct tape, a box of matches and seven refills of lighter fluid. Her arm dropped with relief as the harassed young mother packed her own bags and handed them to identical, curly-haired twins, barely tall enough to peep over the conveyor belt. Carrie wondered if there was a helpline or something you were supposed to call, but her sinuses were full and her eyelids heavy, and she couldn't bring herself to care.

'Have a lovely day,' she said, and the twins gave her identical blank stares over their shoulders as they left the shop.

Primary colours flared in her vision. Too many, too bright.

Mercy's vanilla perfume throbbed in her sinuses as she slipped behind her. 'You look rough. Do you want to go home?'

Carrie shook her head. 'See how I am.'

'Take these.' Mercy handed her some painkillers, and Carrie could have kissed her.

She took two with a quick gulp from her water bottle stowed under the checkout, but it took another two customers before her hands were steady and her headache had started to subside.

Only three hours to go. I need the money.

It was getting quieter. Not long now, a nice and easy end to the shift—

'Wotcher, neighbour!'

Carrie looked up. 'Oh, no.'

In the raw strip-lighting of the supermarket, Ricky Porter cut a far less intimidating figure. Slight enough to slide by taller, bigger men, it was harder to see why anyone would take him seriously, but a few seemed more afraid than indignant. Ricky Porter was clearly a well-known figure in town for all the wrong reasons.

''Scuse me, till's closing, there we go,' he muscled up to the end of the checkout, pocketing a bag of tobacco and a lighter he'd lifted from their rightful owner.

'Till isn't closing,' Carrie muttered, scanning items through. 'Give those back.'

Ricky sniffed, jumping onto the plastic bag pile and sitting on them. He eyeballed the bigger man he'd taken the tobacco from. 'Smoking'll kill you, Frank. Doing you a favour. You can come and take 'em back, if you want. Had a lot of fun last time, didn't we?'

The big man visibly paled under his beard. He mumbled something and ducked out of the line to the back of the next queue, although it was longer.

Carrie glanced at the SupaPrice security guards who were keeping an eye on their unwelcome patron but making no move to do anything about him. Her current customer, a tall, middle-aged woman in heels, had backed up against the next checkout, gripping her purse tight to her chest. If Ricky hadn't been sat on the end of the checkout, he wouldn't be able to look her in the eye.

'Why are you still working?' Ricky asked Carrie conversationally, as if the queue he'd jumped didn't exist. 'You look like shit.'

He looked around for corroboration and his eyes lit on a terrified Rachel in lane four. 'Don't she?'

Rachel nodded, sinking down in her seat.

He dipped his hood in satisfaction. 'See?'

'I'm *fine*. That's seventeen pounds and sixty-three pence, please.'

The lady handed her a note with trembling fingers. Security approached a few paces, but Ricky shot them a look and they thought better of it. The only sound was the background music playing at half-volume through the shop.

'Here's your change,' Carrie said, her own voice ringing in her ears over the chirpy strains of the chart music. She counted it out and handed it over. 'Have a nice day.' She turned to the next people in the line. 'Hello—'

They had scooped their items up off the belt and were scurrying to the end of the next line.

'I'm not here to make trouble,' Ricky announced to the world at large. 'Can't a man go to the supermarket anymore?'

'Mr Porter, you know you technically shouldn't be here,' Pauline ventured from a safe distance, appearing from the freezer aisle. She raked manicured nails through her long grey hair. 'You were banned last month, remember? I'm sorry the other gentleman was rude to you, but you can't do things like that, not in the shop...'

Ricky glared at her. 'Yeah, well, it's a new month now, ain't it?'

Carrie folded her arms as her customers disappeared. 'What the hell is wrong with you?'

'I just want these.' Ricky waved a pack of sugar-free mints at her.

'D'you want to get the back of the queue?'

'What queue?' Ricky gestured to her abandoned checkout. 'Ring 'em up, there's a love.'

Carrie snatched them with bad grace and swiped them through. 'How are you paying today?'

'Paying?' Ricky snorted. 'You're funny.'

'You're an arsehole,' Carrie returned, prickles of embarrassment surging over her face. Her words rang into tense silence. 'Sixty pence, please.'

Nobody moved. The ones who had no idea what was going on were smart enough to know it was nothing good, and the ones who did were not about to intervene.

The other two cashiers were frozen at their tills. Carrie glanced over her shoulder and saw Rachel's mask of horror.

She's Katy Porter's friend, Carrie's inner voice reminded her. *She must know the family pretty well, and look at her face...*

Ricky cleared his throat, grinning broadly, savouring all the attention. With exaggerated care, he produced the exact change and handed it over.

Half of it was in coppers.

Carrie groaned inwardly and let him tip the jingling fountain of coins into her cupped hands, glaring at him.

'You're doing this on purpose,' she muttered.

'Just shopping,' he replied loudly over his shoulder, more for the benefit of the security guards. 'How are you getting back?'

'Bus.' Carrie pinched the bridge of her nose, a flower of colour flashing in her peripheral vision. The headache blossomed back.

'She ain't well,' Ricky announced. 'She'll get paid anyway, right?'

You tosser, Carrie thought.

'Yeah, yeah, yeah, of course,' Pauline stuttered, 'She's worked the whole shift, Mr Porter. Course she has.'

Carrie heard murmurs of agreement.

'Carrie, you okay?' Mercy sidled up as close as she dared.

Ricky fixated on Mercy and grinned like a fox who had learned to open a cage of battery hens. ''Allo again, love,' he leered in a passable Cockney accent. 'What's *your* number?'

Mercy blanched.

Ricky sniggered, digging Carrie in the ribs. 'Even if you put 'em through a wood chipper, they stay conscious for fucking *years.*'

'She's my *friend*,' Carrie muttered, trying not to broadcast it to the whole supermarket. 'Back off.'

'All right, bloody hell. Calm down. Have a mint.' Ricky offered her the foil tube.

Carrie pushed it away. 'I'm going to go home,' she told Mercy, realising Ricky wasn't going to leave of his own accord. 'Please don't sack me.'

'Yeah, don't sack her,' Ricky said louder. 'She's getting paid for the whole day, right?'

Mercy nodded. 'Go on home. I can give you a lift...'

He shook his head. 'Nah, I'll take her. We're good neighbours together, ain't we, Mistress Rickard? She'll be all right wi' me.' He stepped back, not touching her, and Carrie stumbled for the door. 'As you were, folks, don't let us keep you.'

The beep of items began before the murmur of conversation, but by the time Carrie was out into the street it had become a buzz of gossip.

Her cover at work was blown. Everybody in town would hear about this in sixty seconds flat.

That checkout girl, she's the one who bought The Crows...

She knows Ricky Porter...

Carrie fumed. She really *couldn't* fit in here.

On the other hand, he'd wangled her a half-shift at full pay.

Swings and roundabouts, her inner voice shrugged.

Ricky kept his distance, letting her lead the way to the bus stop.

Carrie looked back a few times to see if he was still following, but he was always there, a few paces behind, a faceless figure in grey.

She flopped onto the bench, already feeling better for the fresh air.

He joined her, keeping a gap between them, and they sat in awkward silence for a few minutes. After a while, Ricky's filthy, acid-burnt fingers emerged from his pocket with his packet of mints and a waft of something unpleasant.

'Have a mint.'

'No, thanks.'

'La-di-dah. Paid for 'em, didn't I?'

'Oh, for fuck's sake.' She gave in and took one, fiddling with the foil around the tightly-packed tube, popping the mint in her mouth.

They sat for a few minutes in moody silence.

'You look rough,' he said eventually.

Carrie levered herself stiffly off the bench as the bus came into sight, tensed muscles protesting. 'I'm fine.'

'Nah, you're not. I can see that without casting bones.'

Her phone chose that moment to ring.

Carrie glanced at the screen. '*Shit.*' She hit reject, the unsaved number sending a shockwave through her sensitive stomach, head swimming.

Not Phil again, not now, please not now...

The dreaded happy ping of her voicemail alert made her turn her phone off and push it deep into her pocket.

Ricky tilted his head. 'Best mate?'

Carrie snorted. 'It's... nothing you'd be interested in.'

Ricky shrugged. 'Suit yourself.' He waited.

'It's... I don't even know where to start. My ex is an arsehole, and apparently he's coming down here because he wants money off me that I haven't got.' She stared at the bus further down the road, waiting at the traffic lights.

'*Do* you owe him the money?'

'What? No.' Carrie fiddled with her handbag strap. 'He wants, like, five hundred pounds. Might as well be the moon, even if I *did* owe it, he can't have it. He's probably in debt to the bookies again. They beat the shit out of him, once. They aren't proper bookies, you know, they're dodgy blokes down the pub he goes to, they'll let you bet on two flies crawling up a wall as long as you pay up.'

Ricky considered her for a moment. 'Bloody hellfire. And I thought our Layla was full of drama.'

'Is that your sister?' Carrie asked, doubtful. She couldn't picture Ricky with siblings.

'Nah, cousin. I'm a rare beast. The only only-child since 1879.' A hint of bitterness soured the pride.

The bus finally made it to their stop at a reluctant crawl. It stopped and its doors opened, and before Carrie could protest, Ricky had hooked his arm under hers and hoisted her in with him. The smell of stagnant water wafted from his tracksuit's unhappy fibres.

'Two for Redditch Lane.'

The driver, a young man not long out of school, took one look at his passenger and nodded. Ricky bundled a protesting Carrie towards the back with a smirk, pushing her purse back down into her handbag. For a man so close to her own height and build, she thought, what he lacked in physical size he made up for in bossy determination.

'Like the glory days,' he whispered in her ear, minty-freshness masking the underlying moist reek of warm dog food. Carrie held her breath until he bumped her into a window seat and plopped next to her, his tracksuit giving off another stale waft in the process, and stretched his legs out in the aisle.

Carrie rubbed her nose, breathing through her fingers, head foggy. 'I've never not paid for a bus ticket.'

'You haven't lived, love.' Ricky turned away from her, and there was a movement under the hood at the back of his head. Carrie stared, but it squirmed once more and then was still. 'What're you going to do about this dickhead, then?'

'I don't know.' Carrie rubbed her arms. 'I don't want to see him. I don't want him anywhere near me.'

Ricky dug in his pockets and produced the pilfered pack of tobacco containing some filters and crisp white paper. 'Can I make a suggestion?' he asked, starting to roll a cigarette on his thigh. Carrie nodded, suspicious but game.

'You tell him exactly what you said to me. Tell him he's an arsehole, and he can piss right off. If he starts something, you're not on your own, are you? Apart from Pixie Dust there at the supermarket, that house of yours will give him a right bannicking if he tries anything in there.' He lifted his head and lifted an eyebrow, treating her to a not-unattractive angle. 'Oh, and me, of course. If you ask nice.'

Carrie couldn't help but smile, watching him expertly compensating for the bumps in the road as the bus trundled them through the town in a stop-start-stop-start of traffic lights.

'Don't suppose you *could* give me a hand, could you?' She asked without thinking. It was the sly smile and ruby gleam as he slid her a slow glance that made her remember what he did.

I kill people and eat bits of 'em.

'Oh, God, no, not like that,' she blurted out, whipping her head around to stare out of the window. 'No, I didn't mean that.'

Ricky's shoulders shook. 'Yeah, you did, deep down.'

Carrie raked her nails up and down her arm until Ricky tapped her hand. She knotted her fingers in her lap.

He leaned into her ear, his breath hot and wet on her earlobe. 'You *really* want me to help, you ask me again. We'll come up with something. I mean, I've already declared my vested int'rest.'

Carrie shivered, but he didn't seem to notice.

He didn't budge as the bus started to fill up, his legs still stretched in the aisle. Passengers had to practically climb over him to get at the seats behind, but most of them bunched miserably in the front so they wouldn't have to. It made her think of the reaction in SupaPrice; her response to him was in such contrast that it was no wonder she was attracting baffled, hostile stares by extension. It must be like watching a suburban cat lady who had wandered into a jungle and rapped a man-eating tiger on the nose with a newspaper while all around them its victims screamed and groaned and tried to reload.

Carrie gave him a sideways glance. 'Do you care about anyone else, at all? I bet you don't even smoke, do you?'

He scoffed. 'Don't be daft. Course I don't smoke. It's not for me.'

A middle-aged woman overladen with shopping nearly tripped over his ankle, and Ricky gnashed his teeth at her as she clambered into a free seat, pale and profusely apologetic.

'You're a bit of an arsehole, aren't you?' Carrie remarked, watching him.

He tucked the rolled cigarette behind his ear and gave her a clumsy wink. 'Just your type, by the sounds of it.'

'Oh my God, you *are* flirting.'

This time, Ricky grinned. 'Don't flatter yourself.' It came out oddly rehearsed, as if he had read up on plausible responses since the last time and memorised one.

Carrie managed a grin back. 'Careful,' she said. 'People might think we're mates.'

Ricky stared at her, the ruby red fading from his eyes.

Finally, he muttered, 'No. Course not. This is about me getting in that house. That's all. Like I told you.' He pressed the bell, swinging himself upright and offering her a gallant hand like a Victorian gentleman.

Carrie noted the other passengers – a total of five, now, and she was almost sure some of the others had alighted a few stops early – were taking pains not to look in their direction. The only exception was the middle-aged woman with her shopping piled on the next seat, but her nervous darting looks juddered away out of the window when Carrie caught her eye. The bus slowed, reaching their stop, and Ricky was blocking her way with his outstretched hand.

Carrie took it reluctantly, their stop lurching towards them.

Ricky's fingers closed over hers, spring-loaded and tight. He pulled her up in a fluid movement and released her to swing his way down to the front. Carrie watched him squeezing out before the doors had opened all the way.

Carrie stumbled down the aisle in his wake, shooting the driver an apologetic look. 'Thanks.'

He didn't acknowledge her, eyes fixed forward on the road.

She hopped down and the bus jolted away.

'You still look like shit,' Ricky said, hands in his pockets.

Carrie swallowed. 'If I have a lie down, I'll feel better.'

'I'll walk you home, shall I? Show your lovely abode I'm a trustworthy sort of neighbour, right? Got you off work, and everything.'

Carrie was too bone-tired to argue. 'Yeah. Okay.'

He kept his distance, and Carrie willed herself to stay upright, feet floating somewhere below her on the dark tarmac road.

—

The neighbour was due to die in fifteen days and he *still* hadn't got what he wanted. Fairwood's aura repelled him again – he had tried his luck at the back fence, to no avail. His farsight was almost totally gone, and, for the first time in a long time, he was anxious. What if the wyrd were not as immutable as it ought to be? What if it was fixed for everyone else, but not for him?

He'd seen a single magpie on a branch that morning, black and white feathers ruffled in moody silence.

(*One for sorrow, that's how the rhyme goes.*)

The crows had mobbed it, chasing it off in a flurry of feathers, dropping a scrap of thin, paper-lined foil on the ground, the kind used in sweets packaging. Without his farsight, that omen was hard to interpret.

Should he have gone into town at all? He could feel the threads of his wyrd constricting around him, warp and weft trapping him like a fly. The town made him feel like that, too, claustrophobic amid the concrete. He hadn't been in for a long time. He didn't like the noise, the pavements, the traffic, the people. He hated the buildings and the loud accents that had no business there. (Not as bad as his mother, who considered Hampshire foreign and classed anything above Winchester as 'the North'.)

He glanced over his shoulder at her, hand in his pocket gripping the tube of mints, rubbing his thumb over the protruding foil at one end.

She looked rough. Every step was stilted, slow. There were tiny purple pinpricks all around her eyes, covering her eyelids in a rash of burst capillaries. Her lips were paler than they ought to be for a breathing woman. He'd seen healthier-looking corpses.

(*Oh, yeah, need another one of those, promised Gerald – what about that older woman on the bus?*)

He went towards the main gates of Fairwood, Carrie's shoulder grazing her front wall.

'Bloody hell, love,' Ricky said, put in mind of Rising season. 'Climbed out the wrong side of the grave this morning, did you?'

She didn't crack a smile this time.

Ricky wondered if she was feeling too ill for that, or if he had made the wrong joke.

A tingling in his extremities, the greasy static of live electricity in the air, set him on high alert. His belly gurgled, sloshed, as he peered down the drive. He pressed his hand to it, feeling the bulges within writhe and settle.

(*By the pricking of my thumbs, something wicked this way comes.*)

He licked his lips, tasted the air.

Fairwood wasn't herself, he felt it plainly. He gave the gate an experimental tap. It stung but didn't burn. 'You should let me in,' he advised the iron. 'You're both under the weather, ain't you? I can help, you know I can.'

Never trust a Porter.

Not one of his thoughts, he knew them too well.

'How very dare you? I been naun but honest.'

'Let him through,' his neighbour said (favours bestow on her), stumbling up to the gates and pushing them open.

Touching her didn't make his skin crawl as much as it had the first time, although it still wasn't comfortable. He hoped he hid it well. He hooked his arm under hers, so Fairwood had no choice but to admit them together. The gate creaked open a fraction, but still needed a push.

'She ain't well, either,' Ricky said, out loud this time, meaning the house. He wondered if his neighbour had noticed.

They got to the front door, where she dropped her keys.

The smell was stronger now. What *was* that? Liquorice. Treacle. Gangrene. Something floral.

He knew what was going to happen before she stepped inside, but it was gratifying to have an intuitive guess proven right, showing he didn't need farsight for everything. He could have guessed earlier, maybe, but there was always next time.

Caroline Rickard got through her front door and passed a pretty floral display of pinks and dark purples, gave a wheezing gasp, and collapsed on the tiles. It was fascinating to watch. She crumpled, every joint loosening at once, tumbling in a heap the way Gerald did, a bag of bits and bones.

Unlike Gerald, who never made a sound, she continued to wheeze, each breath building to the gurgling death-rattle he loved best of all, but he couldn't let her do that, not now, or the house would never let him in again. Besides, if she croaked here on the hall floor, he'd have to bury her in The Chase somewhere if he wanted to carry on being neighbours. That wouldn't be any good. The Chase was the first place they searched for missing persons and dead bodies, predictable as the warrant they served him with as regular as a season ticket.

(*Ought to invite us to the policeman's ball, Detective Inspector, the amount of time your lot spend around our place, Mum'd love to get dressed up for something.*)

No, no good having Caroline Rickard die yet, and anyway, it wasn't her time.

Ricky sighed.

He scooped up the floral arrangement in both arms, cradling it like an infant, and, with the finesse of shot-putting a baby, threw it out of the door. The lilies bruised their delicate petals, roses bending and snapping on impact. Ricky gave it a stern look, and it obediently burst into flames.

Smoke purled upwards, all the colours of a dark rainbow.

'Hair of the dog what bitten,' he muttered, playing with dialectic tense to amuse himself. He could still hear her wheezing behind him in the hall, fighting for air.

That was all right. There was time.

Ricky strolled over to the burning bouquet, sniffing deeply.

'Yeah, it was gangrene, that's it, little frisson of it there. Knew I recognised her.' He squatted down, jabbing at the shrivelling lilies with his bare finger. 'Sorry about Janet, Gran. This your little vengeance? Or is it something else? What'll she let out into the world that you want staying put?' He scooped up the ashes in his hands, hawked and spat, and turned back to the porch and his stricken neighbour.

'Nah, this is for your fine abode, not for you.' He jogged back up the steps as she tried to ask for help, rolling onto her front and reaching for the open door, choking on the words. 'You don't want to know where these hands have been.'

The house wasn't too keen either, he felt the resistance as he pressed his sticky palms to the door frame, stabbing splinter-cross into his skin.

'Oh, come on now, don't be putting on airs. Take your medicine.' He rubbed both palms down the frame and scraped the ashy mess off onto the door itself. 'There, see how you go with that. Now then.'

Fairwood let him in. All business now, he gripped his neighbour under her arms, dragging her down the hall into the long, empty dining room she never used. He dropped her unceremoniously, stepping over her gasping torso in a quest for chalk.

(*Like a fish, ain't she? Just like how they suffocate up on the bank, juicy things.*)

'Going to have to take your clothes off,' he warned her. 'This bit's tricky.'

He thought she was going to protest, but she did as she was told. Or attempted to. Her arms were uncooperative, struggling with her uniform as she burned up in a flush of fever, still gasping for proper breaths.

Ricky rolled his eyes. 'Don't panic, I'll do it, bloody hell. Wait there.'

Her wheezing was easing now, but he had no way of knowing how advanced the curse was.

(*Could always ask her, of course, this one's still alive.*)

'When did you get the flowers?' he asked, not used to Gran's victims answering back.

'Thur–Thur–Thurs–day.'

(*Two days ago, she'd be dead as dust if it wasn't for the house taking it in as well, Gran didn't factor that in did she, losing her touch the daft old bint.*)

Ricky started to hum, an atonal improvisation around a sparrow's song.

He stripped her with his usual efficiency, marvelling at how much easier it was when they cooperated. Her bare body made little impression on him. He noted the darker veins, joined by a network of blue arteries as the skin turned translucent, like tracing paper. He could see through several layers of the dermis, which wasn't a good sign.

'Here we go,' he muttered. 'No chalk, so, I'll have to improvise.'

He crushed the mints in his fist, feeling the foil and paper split. His muscles bulged iron-firm when he did that, eliciting a shy smirk of accomplishment. He liked this body, its proportions, its capabilities. He liked honing it, improving it, sculpting it. He would like what was underneath just as much.

Sprinkling the mint-dust in a rough circle around her, he said, 'I know you'd be asking questions right now if you could, so this is what I'm up to: it's a basic containment, you can knock one up with anything. Use a sharpie if you want, it's all the same, but I like the feel of powder, so that's my preference.' He sniffed, dusting off his hands, and pulled the hood down. 'To be honest, it don't actually achieve much, I just like a circle for working in. Tradition, superstition, call it what you will.' His back lips parted and champed, tendrils readying to taste the open air. They wormed upwards, tickling his vertebrae.

'This?' He asked in response to her imaginary question. 'Oh, don't mind this, it's just a quirk.'

Her eyes were closed, anyway.

The coils snaked out, circling his head in a squirming halo.

'You may feel a slight prick,' he murmured, and giggled, letting three of them slither down and trace their soft tips over her body until they found a strong vein. A small stab brought an ooze of deoxygenated blood, dribbling from the puncture dark and slow. The tendrils converged, slurping a taste, and withdrew.

Ricky smacked his other mouth, tasting it.

'Shit, yeah, you are a bit far gone.'

The tendrils began to secrete their mucus, snail-silver, the halo stretching into a canopy and dribbling down onto her skin. She was still breathing, but barely.

'We'll wrap you up,' he advised, 'And maybe we'll call a doctor in. A *real* one, not one of your regular GPs.'

There were dustsheets draped over ghosts of furniture, so he whipped one away from the old damp-riddled piano and bundled her up.

Carrie was floppier now, more of a dead weight.

The dustsheet was soaked through with sticky silver.

'Let's lie you down somewhere better,' Ricky muttered, scooping her up with a practiced lift. 'You'll be right as rain.'

(*Don't lie*, he reprimanded himself, *don't say things like that*.)

She whimpered, surprising him. She was heavier than Gerald, but not by much.

Ricky rubbed the part of her back he could reach. 'Easy, now,' he muttered again, soothing, almost expecting her to smell of donkey-hide. 'We'll patch you up. Don't you worry.'

Damsel in Distress

In which several days pass eventfully
29 April

The ceiling was white, tube-like, bowed in an unhappy frown. There was a sense of weightlessness, of herself, of what was beneath her, of the whiteness above, of the thoughts in her head. Floating. Lost in space.

No air in space, she recalled. *No wonder I couldn't breathe.*

She didn't know what time it was.

Pilots must do more than one journey in a day, back and fore, back and fore, three hours this way and three hours that, the time zones shifting and unstable, forwards, backwards, until time was fluid and meaningless and there was no need for it anymore, and clocks melted like water down the dashboard and dripped onto your face...

'I dare say you've seen many a person die in this room,' Dr Monday said conversationally over Carrie's head, wiping the beads of sweat from her brow. He had his own unique scent, filling Carrie's head with peace; sepia film reels and withered violets, her father's old jumper and peppermints masking forbidden Camel cigarettes, warm mahogany and washed linoleum, unused cardboard and Bakelite appliances. The smell of memories, not all of them her own. She sifted through the odours, sorting them one by one into drawers, wondering where to file them all.

Alphabetically or thematically? Or both?

The ceiling straightened, little by little, bending back into shape.

Ladies and gentlemen, we may now experience some light turbulence, please fasten your seatbelts...

The swimming vision brought with it a nudge from her bladder.

...during this time the use of the toilet is not permitted...

'Deaths? Oh, yes.' Her own voice, but deeper. Fairwood's voice.

She was home.

Carrie's eyes fluttered, but her neck was sore and her muscles felt like she'd been repeatedly run over.

'Not this one, though.'

The doctor leaned over her, so close she could see the edges of the skin-mask he wore, but not what was underneath. She let this information wash over her, happy to accept whatever came her way. Dr Monday had been her doctor for years: Dr Monday had known her all her life. Dr Monday was perfectly normal.

I don't think that's right, a tiny voice itched in the back of her mind. *I don't think that's true at all...* An image popped into her head with a wave of familiarity.

Dr Monday, stepping through Regency London with his cane and the dignity of a forgotten god, walking Victorian streets chameleonic in borrowed skins, on house-calls tapping along to Charleston rhythms in his black and white spats.

Dr Monday had been her doctor for years.

Dr Monday had known her all her life.

Dr Monday was perfectly normal.

'You did exactly the right thing, Mr Porter, of course.'

'Obviously,' Ricky scoffed, from somewhere in her room.

Carrie focused, and her fingers twitched. She tried to move her arm, but it wouldn't budge. Something was pinning it to her side.

'Don't try to move,' Dr Monday said in her ear. 'I've had to bind you, for your own protection.'

Her body felt strange, her skin tight and dry. There was an odd sensation of pressure all over her, which she couldn't understand.

'It's called the Sarcophagus Wrap, but don't let that worry you.'

Carrie blinked, the world swimming into focus. 'Wh-mmf?' Clean fibres with an oily texture smothered her mouth.

'Oh, I wouldn't try and talk, you're not meant to *eat* the preparation. This is a relatively old technique, courtesy of my colleague, Dr El Sayed. His workshops are always greatly illuminating.' Dr Monday nodded to Fairwood, whom Carrie still couldn't quite see. The bedroom ceiling shimmered above her as her eyes played tricks with her mind – unless that was ectoplasm she could see.

She hoped not.

'Keep the protection charms going overnight. I'll ask Miss Harris to drop by – she's good with protection.'

Fairwood melted into the walls, the house breathing softly around them.

'What d'you need that meddling medium for?' It was Ricky Porter's voice, coarse, indignant. 'I found her, she'd be dead if it weren't for me. *Again.*'

Dr Monday disappeared from the field of Carrie's vision, his cane tapping on the boards. 'Yes, thank you, Mr Porter, but the house has made its feelings clear. It distrusts your uncanny ability to show up when needed, like an orchestrator.'

'That's *bullshit*. I'm a soothsayer, I see the bloody *future*. I tell people the *truth.*'

He sounds really angry, Carrie thought, numb. *Poor Ricky. No one gives him the benefit of the doubt, do they?*

They all know what he is, The Crows re-joined.

Carrie didn't doubt that, but it was too big, too macabre, to grasp.

No, I want him to stay. It wasn't his fault… I'm pretty sure…

No more Pendles!

He helped, I feel better with him around, he knows his shit…

But—

Please! She needed Ricky there. He was selfish and dangerous and entirely invested in keeping her alive. *Besides, he's an outsider, too, like us.*

The house grudgingly relented.

Dr Monday's rich lilt broke into her discussion as if reading their thoughts. 'Yes, Mr Porter, thank you for your assistance, and while I am fully aware of your position, it's not me you need to convince. Miss Rickard, please do drop by the surgery on Mill Street when you're up and about. I'd like to see you for a follow-up. Rest today, and the bandages will be changed tomorrow.'

Carrie tried to protest, or wriggle, or – something, but the bandages held her tightly in place.

'Sleep,' said Dr Monday, and Carrie couldn't fight the sonorous command.

The darkness closed in again, obliterating her worries and aches and the worrisome void of white in a rising tide of blissful black.

29 April – 02 May

He had never spent three nights away from the cottage before.

(*Where? Nowhere to go.*)

Fairwood wouldn't let him in half the rooms, thwarting exploration. The Pendle Stone was his consolation, the kitchen always welcoming, and, when he wasn't cleaning the neighbour up (the bandages needed changing, same with the waste bags, and, somehow, he had to feed her those clear plastic bags of nutrients on the tall beeping stand) he sat on the kitchen floor stroking the hearthstone and muttering Gaffer's favourite incantations over and over and over, precious rhymes he'd never thought he could use alone.

The energies were bringing on his Changes, faster now, and about damn time. Imagine pushing thirty and not fully Changed yet – they thought he'd done it, that was it, to Change again so late was unheard of.

(*No, my dears, no, there's more to Cousin Ricky than you think, he ain't done yet, we're far from finished…*)

Stroking the Pendle Stone was his solace, and slowly, slowly, achingly slowly, his farsight crept back. His third eye was only a metaphor (unlike his second mouth), but he felt it opening again and blinking into the warp and weft of the wyrd.

He didn't mind the other stuff. She even had a bookcase with her own books – some he'd never read – and that was, in itself, a minor revelation. Like his own library, without the need to slip in after hours to be alone.

Dr Monday had done all the technical things, the medical things he didn't understand, clever old shadowman with his face collection. Miss Charlotte, devil-woman in white, clinically polite, came to check on him, shrieked about hygiene, and made him wash his hands.

Ricky saved the waste bags. He didn't see why not, and sometimes, if you waited, fermented it all down, what was left could be pretty potent in ways other than smell.

(*No, I'm not like Gran, I don't go in for all that controlling stuff, take it back.*)

(*Wish we'd had a girl, George, a lovely little girl with lips honest as rubies.*)

Ricky wrestled with his shadow of a conscience.

He kept the waste bags anyway.

At night, stripping off in his usual fashion and leaving his folded clothes on the floor, he slept on the mattress beside the bandaged coma patient since it didn't occur to him to sleep anywhere else.

If he closed his eyes, he could imagine it was Gerald there, still and quiet. He hadn't had Gerald in his bed since he was twelve, and his dad told him he was too old for all that. That was the night Ricky had poisoned his parents for the first time. Gerald had not been burned, but he hadn't dared keep him in his bedroom after that, all the same.

It was odd, sleeping next to something after so long. Even odder to be next to something warm, something breathing.

Ricky forced himself to touch her, only gently, to prove to himself he wasn't afraid. She made a small sound, and it jolted through him with a static charge, hair-raising, nape-prickling. Exhilarating.

After that, he slept with one arm carefully positioned around her middle, feeling the deep diaphragm pulses of her breath. He counted them, steady, like a metronome. She talked in her sleep sometimes, he caught odd words, and each time that happened he would jerk awake in a kind of panic. Bodies didn't talk. Then he'd see her in the dark, smell the bandages and the preparation, relax his muscles one group at a time, let his tendrils fall back over the pillow and crawl up the wallpaper.

He toyed with the idea of keeping her like this forever, slipping a tendril into her ear and through to her brain, piercing something vital and locking her in her dreamworld for good, but it seemed disloyal to Gerald (the first Gerald, at least, if she was to be Gerald the Second), and Miss Charlotte was not easy to fool. On the other hand, keeping her like this, a Second Gerald, meant no complications, no conversations, a warm body instead of a cold one. No dogs, no warrant, no DI Paula Parsons. But even if he could convince Miss Charlotte and Dr Monday that this bandaged, comatose condition was naturally prolonged, Fairwood wouldn't tolerate that. He could feel the house scratching inside his brain like an earwig, digging out the thoughts he tried to hide from it.

After four interesting days and three blissful, sleepless nights, Gerald the Second relinquished its name and was declared ready to be de-tubed and unwrapped. Away went the IV stand and its bags of liquid nutrition. Out came the other tubes and there would be no need for any bags anymore.

Ricky realised she might not want him to sleep beside her once she was better, once she was Caroline Rickard again. The moment approached, dull like a drill, and the closer it got the deeper it hollowed out a cavity in his chest.

He buried it deep and, unable to block out the summoning tug he'd started to feel, went to tea with his grandmother.

Granny Wend's door was always open to family in the same way that Fairwood was always closed to them. Ricky came in without knocking, sullen at being summoned, rubbing his breastbone where the pinch of Granny Wend's insistence had him in its grip.

She had a visitor.

'Richard, you're late.'

'Don't have a watch, Gran.'

'Very funny.'

He took in the scene: the homely atmosphere, poky compared to The Crows, the mean little range and well-used paraphernalia, and Guy Bishop at the table with a bottle of whiskey.

(*There he is, Gran's little delivery boy. Should thank you, Mr Bishop, thank you very much.*)

'Back on the bottle, Mr Bishop?' He patted his tight, flat belly. 'Pardon me if I don't join you.'

'Don't be rude, Richard. Sit down.' She had let her hair down, long and grey, flowing in waves down her straight back. 'Where've you been?'

(*Does she know? She can't know.*)

He edged in, letting the door bang behind him, and took a seat opposite the younger Mr Bishop, wary. Whiskey rankled in his nostrils.

'Around.'

'I couldn't see you anywhere.' She ladled soup into a bowl, her tone level. 'Davey was looking for you, couldn't find you in the cottage. George and Lettie didn't know where you were.'

(*Shit, Uncle David. Stay quiet you can't lie.*)

She set the soup in front of him, her lily of the valley scent overpowering the whiskey for a moment. 'The only place I can think of is the long barrow,' she continued, still in the same gentle tone. 'You wouldn't be messing with things in there, would you? You wouldn't be looking for Mr Wend's signs, not without explicit permission.'

'No, Gran.' Ricky stuck to the truth. 'Wanted peace and quiet is all. Lost track of time.'

(*Peace and quiet would be over when Mistress Rickard started talking again. Should've taken a chance, gone through her ear or tear duct.*)

'Hm.' She wasn't convinced and he knew she was more powerful than he was. Even now, even with the Pendle Stone energies opening him up to the Outside, she was older and stronger, had had those energies coursing through her frame for so long, and spawned the children from her own womb.

He waved his spoon at Guy, who was sitting immobile, staring into his glass. 'The fuck's he doing here?'

This earned him a cuff around the back of his head, right across his sensitive lips. It stung. 'Language, Richard.'

Guy stirred but said nothing.

Ricky recalled a distant memory of teenage rebellion before his first Change, topless on the beach and two six-packs of lager down, necking neat vodka in the sun. Fuck the farsight, fuck the family, fuck 'em all. Baseball cap instead of a hood. Nothing on the back of his head but hair, thick and brown. Had a nosebleed, why? Someone had punched him, some nine-to-five family man, didn't appreciate the puking, the littering or the language. Ricky dimly remembered kicking the shit out of him in front of his screaming kids. He grinned to himself, slurping at his spoon on purpose. This earned him another cuff around the head.

The soup was lukewarm. Bland. Watery. Nothing to distract him, nothing to drag him into the present.

'What d'you want me for, then?'

She loomed behind him, watching her visitor. 'Poor darling's a bit desperate. Terrible debt.'

Ricky sniffed, biting off a chunk of bread roll.

Stale.

'Wha's that t'do wi' me?'

Another cuff.

'Don't talk with your mouth full.'

(*Bloody old bitch.*)

'I took him down the cellar. It's always harder on them, the third time, I don't know why.'

'Wha's wrong with him?'

'Oh, the usual. He was catatonic, earlier.' She moved around the table and pulled up a chair. 'Poor dear.'

Ricky snorted.

'Do you have it back yet?'

That was it. That's what she wanted. What they always wanted. He snorted. 'If he's done the ritual, he don't need it.'

'He couldn't finish it,' his grandmother said, leaning over to pat Guy's sleeve. 'Too much for him, this time.'

'Luck ain't the easiest thing to harness. Like lassoing the business end of a hydra with only one rope.' He leered across the table, enjoying the pallor of the bookseller, entitled young tosser who wouldn't let him take his books. 'Once, that's easy. Twice… trickier. Three times…' He leaned back, sucking in air through his teeth. 'Luck don't like that.'

'Don't tease him, Richard.'

She kept using his full name. Uncle David was 'Davey' today, but he was 'Richard' and this drunk was 'dear'. Not even blood, not even bone, but he was 'dear' and Ricky was 'Richard'. Venom bubbled hotter than the soup.

'I ain't got the farsight back. Not prop'ly. An' if I did, I wouldn't help.' He pushed the bowl away and shot the remains of the bread roll into Guy's whiskey tumbler.

(*Not fair, you owe him, furthered your cause no end.*)

His grandmother tutted. For a moment, he saw the energies pulsing under her skin, tar-black. '*Richard*. I'm sorry, dear, let me get you another glass.'

Guy took a slow drink from the bottle.

Ricky leaned over, studying him. 'What does he want? Grand National's been an' gone. What's next? World Cup? Lottery numbers?'

'He'll lose the bookshop this time,' his gran said, with galling sympathy. 'Poor boy. So much pressure. And Harry hasn't long.'

(*Oh, sympathy, is it? Too much pressure? Fuck me, though, hey, your own grandson, bloody old bitch.*)

'This meant to be a reward for something?' Ricky asked, innocent. 'Did you a favour, did he?'

(*Delivery boys deserve tips.*)

'Dad'll be upset,' Guy slurred slowly into his lap, before she could answer.

'Can't let your father down,' Ricky mocked, but he relented. 'All right. Let me down there, Gran. No promises, just a quick one. An' I'll tell him something special.' He eyed the whiskey. 'I'm not promising nothing, though.'

She smiled, that twisted, malevolent smile. She loved chaos, stirring other people's lives into maelstroms until she was their only anchor. 'Don't worry about that. Just this once, you go down. But only quickly. No getting greedy.'

His jaw clenched and fluttered.

(*Not greedy, am I, bloody old bitch, want what's mine is all.*)

But a quick blast of her shrine's energies was all he needed. The Pendle Stone had already opened him up a little. He'd have to be careful, not indulge himself in how soft she was (*shut up, shut up*) not think about the Second Gerald he was losing the next day (*stop it*).

'You seem a little upset, dear.' Her endearment was a honeytrap. She didn't switch from 'Richard' to 'dear' without wanting something.

He scraped his chair back. 'I'm tired, Gran. Haven't been sleeping.' He moved towards the cellar steps, where the shrine awaited. All it would take was a bit of extra energy, in a place where the veil between worlds was thinnest. The Pendle Stone was imbued with much older energies the newer shrine couldn't channel yet, but it had been dormant for sixty years. Waking it up fully would take more time.

I know what you're doing, Richard.

That wasn't his thought.

He chanced a look at his grandmother again, stroking Guy like a cat. Toffee sat under the table, evil eyes staring at him from between the chair legs.

'Did you hear something, Gran?' he asked.

'No,' she said, and he didn't think she was lying.

Come down to the cellar, my lovely lad, tell your Gaffer all that's bad.

Ricky went down the steps, buoyed by a rare frisson of excitement. If that was the Voice, then it was speaking to *him*. The shrine welcomed him, shutting her out. His pulse quickened with his breaths.

(*Mine.*)

He hurried downwards and let the cellar's gloom consume him.

02 May

On Wednesday, Mercy turned up with Tina Harris, the mortuary assistant, as the bandages came off. Tina Harris was a plump, busty woman in a tight-fitting vintage dress, russet hair rolled up in a Forties style with makeup to match. She looked like a plus-size pin-up model. As she bent over Carrie to unwind the bandages, her cleavage nearly took Carrie's eye out.

Carrie shut her eyes, letting the woman do her work.

Tina was not used to dealing with living people: she stripped Carrie of her bandages with rough, cold hands, talking over her as if forgetting Carrie was conscious. Her glossy pink lips bowed in a tight frown.

'I'd rather not get involved in this,' she complained. 'Burt's moved out, Meredith bloody Blake is breathing down my neck about mysterious deaths connected to Barker Crescent, and honestly, Mez, I'd rather not be here. Curses give me the creeps.' She gave the last bandage a sharp tug, jerking Carrie unpleasantly in the process. Tina ignored Carrie's grunt of surprise, bundling the used strips into a ball. 'Right, there we go. I'm dying for a fag, can you hold the fort here while I go outside?'

Mercy took them gingerly, wrinkling her nose. 'Uh, sure, yeah.'

'Don't mind me,' Carrie muttered, sitting up.

Tina didn't. She bustled out of the room, already rummaging in her handbag for her cigarettes and a lighter, leaving Mercy behind to bag and bin the bandages.

Mercy had dressed for the occasion using an ice cream parlour palette, as if combatting a dark curse could be achieved through the power of pastels alone. Today, she was experimenting with hair extensions.

'Carrie? How are you feeling?'

'I'm fine.' Carrie startled Mercy by standing up, rubbing the remains of the canary-yellow residue into her middle. It was bacon-grease thick, squidging under her fingertips. She missed Fairwood's solid, concentrated presence, and, for some reason, Ricky Porter's gruff banter. She rubbed her waist, for a moment feeling a warm pressure there that she couldn't explain.

Carrie wondered who had been changing her underwear, but Tina had mentioned that Miss Charlotte (whoever that was) had been nursing her for the duration of her Wrap. She was in desperate need of a shower, but the instructions had been not to get wet until the preparation had all been absorbed into her skin. She wasn't sure what it was supposed to *do*, nor if Dr Monday was, strictly speaking, a proper doctor, but either way things had gone beyond the NHS. She stood in her bra and knickers without a shred of self-consciousness, which wasn't like her at all, watching Mercy blush. That was weird. Fairwood watched her all the time and it never blushed about anything.

People are weird.

'Oh, gosh, sorry.' Mercy hovered by the bed. 'Um. Do you need clothes? Can I help?'

'Tina can go if she's got better things to do,' Carrie remarked, grabbing a top from the clean pile on the chair. 'Dr Monday said something to Fairwood about protection.'

'Oh, yeah, Tina's got something for you.' Mercy held out a bracelet. 'You'd better wear it, just in case.'

The bracelet was simple enough and looked handwoven from strands of hair. Beads of semi-precious stones and healing crystals were set at intervals along it. Carrie took it and looped it over her wrist, letting Mercy tie it securely for her.

'What's it made of?'

'Um.' Mercy shrugged. 'I'm not sure.'

'Is that human hair?'

Mercy blushed red. 'Possibly.'

'Where'd she get it?'

'It was given to her. Look, we think we know who did this to you, Wes Porter pretty much said—'

'Porter?' Carrie pulled her wrist back. 'Ricky's cousin?'

'Yeah. He's on Tina's pub quiz team.' Mercy fidgeted with the lace on her skirt. 'Wes thinks… he thinks his gran is up to something.'

'No shit,' Carrie snorted softly. She probably knew a little more than Tina, but that didn't help. 'What the *hell* is going on? Why are members of the History Society trying to kill me?'

'Better ask Ricky that, hadn't you?' Mercy asked, disapproval clouding her face. 'He's taken a real shine to you, hasn't he?'

'Only because I've got something he wants.' Carrie didn't want to get into all that now and couldn't explain why she was helping him. Mercy, an insider all her life, couldn't possibly understand. Carrie finished dressing, taking a deep, satisfied breath. 'That's better. Thanks. Thanks for, for coming over.'

The clouds scudded away as Mercy smiled. 'Sure thing.'

'Now Tina's here,' Carrie said, new life flooding her veins, 'I'd like to ask her about the séance. Can you grab the music box? I haven't moved it.'

Mercy scratched her head. 'Oh, um, really?' Her voice had risen. 'Um. Okay.'

She scuttled off to locate the airing cupboard, while Carrie finished making herself decent and headed downstairs.

She's in the kitchen, with company I am not allowing in.

Carrie burst into the kitchen door to see Tina, a magnificent vision in green, chain-smoking out of the back door.

'I told you,' Tina announced to someone standing beyond it, 'she's not here. Push off.'

'Christ, she always did have a shit taste in friends. I'll be back round later,' a rich, familiar voice promised, full of sneer and swagger. 'I know you're there, Carrie!'

The sound of her name sent paroxysms of panic through her, her limbs reacting faster than her brain. She dropped behind the table.

'Piss on off then, darlin',' Tina said, ample frame filling the doorway, blocking his view. She blew a long jet of smoke in his direction. 'Good boy. That's it.'

The figure marched away around the corner towards the front of the house, where, Carrie just knew, a blue saloon would be waiting on her gravelled drive.

Carrie forced herself up as her knees protested their brutal treatment.

'Shit.'

Tina turned, surveying her with a cocked eyebrow but not, Carrie felt, without an edge of sympathy. Tina wielded sympathy like a scythe.

'I'm guessing that's someone best consigned to the bin of history?'

Carrie found herself recalling the chilling reputation of her stretch of road, and wished Phil would drive away into oblivion, disappear without a trace and be gone from her life forever.

No, mustn't make wishes. They might work.

Tina exhaled a smoky jet of commiseration, correctly interpreting her silence. 'We've all been there, love.'

Carrie looked away. It was all so *mundane* – how could something as simple as a knock on the door open the gateway to your own private hell?

Mercy jogged in and dumped the music box on the table, rubbing her hands together vigorously. 'Here it is! Oh! What have I missed?'

Tina let Carrie tell it, although she didn't want to.

'Oh. Um. Just an unwanted visitor.'

'Ricky Porter?' Mercy guessed.

'My ex.' The words burned like bile, throbbing in her throat. She wondered if anyone had noticed Ricky coming and going, if anyone knew he was the exception to the curse.

Tina rolled her eyes. 'Ricky can't set foot in The Crows,' she told Mercy, answering at least one of Carrie's private questions. 'Great-Aunt Eglantine saw to that, after the... you know.' She pointed at the chimney, and then upwards.

Mercy winced. 'Oh! Right.' She fidgeted with her lacy skirt, frowning. 'Speaking of which, Tee, um, Carrie was wondering about, about having a séance.'

Tina looked from Carrie to the music box, and back again. 'I'm not sure that will help,' she said slowly. 'Is this about the girl in the chimney?'

Carrie nodded.

'Look, um, if her spirit's trapped in there, that's bad news.' Tina moved around the table, the music box sitting innocently between them all. 'Great-Aunt Eglantine used to trap spirits that she couldn't help cross over, the ones that were... *resistant*, let's say, and tough to exorcise. That's a bad sign as far as we're concerned. Who knows what will happen if we let it out?'

'She was just a little girl,' Carrie mumbled. 'And whoever wanted that ritual done now wants to kill me, and I want to know why.' She raised her voice a little, afraid of being too loud. 'Can you put her back in the box afterwards?'

Tina winced. 'I don't know.'

'Can we try? I mean – maybe that's it, maybe once the ghost is out of the box, she'll tell us what happened, and we can...' Carrie trailed off. *Can what? Go to the police? With what proof? Set the ghost on her tormentors? With what consequences?*

Tina was watching her, her expression asking all the same questions.

Carrie shook her head. 'What should I do, then? Chuck it down the well? Not make a wish, obviously.'

'I don't know much about this house,' Tina admitted. 'We moved away from here when I was ten. I haven't been back in town for very long. But – you're in a lot of trouble with someone, that I know. And I'm not making a secret of it, it makes me uncomfortable, and I don't want to be here. I don't know you,

you don't know me. I'm doing Dr Monday a favour, because he asked.' She paused. 'Getting at someone that way is just cowardly.'

Carrie realised she meant the cursed flowers. 'It's the History Society,' she said. 'I don't know what they did, or who exactly was involved, but… it's the History Society. That's the link. A few of them are old enough to have been around at the time.' She steeled herself, locking stares with Tina. 'I just want names, or, or *a* name. Or a clue, a hint, or something. I want to know who *exactly* is *doing* this to me, and why. If I'm going to be targeted for something they think I know, then I want to bloody well know what they think I know.' She paused. 'If that makes sense.'

'Damn it,' Tina muttered. 'Fine, all right, we'll try. But if Great-Aunt Eglantine couldn't get anything out of her, I don't think we'll get much either. At least if we get a name out of her, you'll be more… prepared.' She played with her own bracelet. 'That ought to keep the Wends and the rest of their clan at bay, anyway.'

Carrie rubbed the beads on her wrist. 'Thanks.'

'I learned "best practice" from my mum, and she learned from her great-aunt,' Tina said. 'She was pretty formidable. Bit of an oracle, was Great-Aunt Eglantine.'

'Eglantine… Pritchard?'

'That's her. You've heard of her, then?'

Carrie nodded. Oracles and séances seemed the thickest end of the wedge now, compared with werewolves, sentient houses and doctors who wore masks of human skin.

'So, what do we do?' she asked. 'Shouldn't there be more of us?'

'Three is a good number.' Tina glanced through the open door at the hall, the tiles and panels reaching up the dizzying heights of the grand staircase, then looked around the kitchen itself, casting her curious gaze over the freshly painted ceiling. 'And this house… is a good location. It's alive, is that right?'

Carrie nodded.

'Houses are alive in lots of ways,' Tina said, as if she had rehearsed this before coming. 'You can feel their energies, their characters, sometimes even before you walk in the door. Animists believe even rocks and stones have a life force of their own. I suppose this one just… crossed a line somewhere and became alive in a different sense. A – dare I say it – more "mainstream" sense.' She looked at Carrie. 'I take it you wouldn't ordinarily be emotionally attached to a building.'

Carrie shook her head slightly, almost afraid that The Crows would be offended by her past insensitivity.

Tina nodded. 'Is there somewhere we can go? An empty room is best. Less to hurt ourselves on.'

'There's nothing in a few of the guest rooms. We could go in one of those.'

'Are we using Ouija boards or something?' Mercy had grown pale.

'Bitch, please.' Tina rolled her eyes. She motioned for Carrie to lead the way, stepping back to let her pass. 'After you.'

Mercy scooped up the music box and scuttled in their wake.

Carrie was glad of the activity after days of bandaged sleep. She didn't have the drugged wooziness of sleeping pills or illness, nor the gnawing ache in her stomach that she should have after her lack of food. She didn't even feel particularly thirsty. Her skin was smooth and supple despite her need of a shower, the preparation now fully soaked into her pores. If anything, she felt refreshed, light on her feet rather than light-headed.

'Do you know what Dr Monday did to me?' Carrie asked.

Tina followed her up, Mercy bringing up the rear with tentative, slow steps.

'No,' Tina admitted. 'I work with the dead. But I'm pretty certain it's a preventative.'

'How does it work?'

Tina waited until she was at the top of the stairs to answer, catching her breath. 'It renders you dead to the one who cursed you. It makes you a new person, for all intents and purposes.'

Carrie could believe that. She certainly felt like a new person. 'All right. And this bracelet…'

'That'll ward off the Evil Eye and anything stronger. Or stranger.' Tina ran her fingers over her own. 'I learned pretty fast that if you're going to have anything to do with the Porters, the Shaws, the Foremans, the Wends or the Wend-McVeys, you'd better have one of these.' She caught Carrie's expression. 'They're all related,' she supplied, and Carrie decided to pretend she was hearing this for the first time. 'Ricky Porter, Mez said you've met, well, he's their current – I don't know what, but they all seem to look up to him. Spiritual guide of the clan? Truth-teller?'

'Soothsayer,' Carrie supplied.

'That's what *he* calls it. He's only about our age, but don't let that fool you. There's a lot of rumblings in the clan at the moment. I don't get involved and I don't ask, but when you've got Wes Porter on your quiz team you learn stuff.' She shrugged. 'Where are we doing this?'

Carrie led the way to an empty guest room. 'Here?'

'Perfect.'

Tina invited Mercy and Carrie to sit in a rough triangle in the middle of the guest room and took a small polished stone from her pocket. The stone had a hole in the middle, almost a perfect circle. 'I'd usually draw on the floor in chalk,' Tina said. 'I don't know if the house would mind that…'

The friendly creak as the floorboards bowed slightly beneath them made Carrie smile in spite of the weirdness of it, but Mercy sprang to her feet and Tina closed her eyes, palms flat on the floor, looking sick.

'That's fine,' Carrie interpreted. Mercy passed her the box.

Tina nodded, still with her eyes shut, round chin tilted slightly upwards as if in silent prayer. She moistened her lips and slowly brought a piece of chalk from her voluminous skirt, as if asked to empty her pockets by a paranoid gunman.

'I'll be gentle,' she promised.

Carrie swallowed a grin. 'The floorboards don't mind.'

The encouraging creak made Tina fumble the chalk, but she managed not to drop it. She put the stone in the middle of them all, positioning it carefully and drawing a circle around it.

'God, this is weird. Normally I'd have a candle, the flame is… never mind. We'll do that later, if the ghost doesn't want to go back in the box.'

Mercy, uncharacteristically, was tight-lipped and saying nothing at all. With longer hair, she looked much younger, more vulnerable.

'You don't have to do this,' Carrie said to her, but she shrugged and settled, staring at the floorboards.

Tina drew the protective symbols on the floor and others Carrie didn't recognise.

'Right. Open it.'

Carrie pinched the stem of the broken key, the nub sticking out a little way. To her surprise, it turned easily, the lid springing open with a rusty click. A broken ballerina with half her skirt missing and the rest of it sadly torn, face obliterated with age and grime, twisted drunkenly on her platform. One little arm swung from a dislocated shoulder, and all the paint had been worn away. It was playing *Three Blind Mice*, flat and out of tune.

Yet another thing to feel sorry for.

Tina sat back down in her place and held out her hands for Mercy and Carrie to take one each. Her hand in Carrie's was clammy. Mercy's was similarly unpleasant to grip, but there was little choice. Carrie sat still, the energies of the house rippling up through her, palms hot, part of a sorority of strangers bound by sweat.

Tina took in three deep breaths with slow exhalations, each one longer than the last. An expectant, pregnant silence fell over them. Tina muttered something in what Carrie thought was German, but then she caught the words *gaast* and *cargást*, and realised it was Old English. It was one of those rare occasions when an English Literature degree came in handy.

Still muttering, Tina opened her eyes and stared directly between Carrie and Mercy, over their joined hands, to a place behind them about halfway up the wall. Her eyes followed something moving further up to the ceiling, until the mortuary assistant was staring directly above the little pebble lying on the floor.

'Speak to us,' Tina commanded in modern English and the chalk quivered by her side.

Mercy was looking decidedly grey.

Carrie could hear the buzzing of fat bluebottles in the room, distracting her. She turned her head slightly, not wanting to break the circle for fear of what may happen if she did, trying to find the source of the irritating buzzing sound. A thick mass of flies crawling up and down the wallpaper in a river of tickling legs and vibrating wings made her flinch. Tina clamped Carrie's hand in hers, while on her other side Mercy's hot, slippery fingers nearly slid from her grasp as Mercy let out an involuntary squirming whimper. Maggots dropped out of the wall, curling and writhing on the floorboards and disappearing in the cracks.

Carrie shuddered.

'Speak to us,' Tina repeated, her fingers white with the effort of holding on.

The chalk beside her quivered. Their eyes travelled down to it as a small fly landed there, wringing its front legs.

'What is it?' Tina asked. 'Is there something you need? Something we have to do?'

The chalk rolled away from her towards Carrie, leaving tiny flecks of white dust in its wake.

Carrie closed her eyes, excitement building in her body, the energies of the house flowing through her in waves. The wooden boards beneath her were pulsing with life, the grain carrying messages to her like nerves, not words but sensations, images, colours. They flooded her, growing in power and urgency. The chalk bumped against her foot.

She let go of Mercy's hand and picked it up. Images of the empty house, its rooms shut up, its furniture covered with dust sheets, its reclusive owner cloistered in three rooms and seeing no one but the cook, crowded her mind and obscured her vision. She was aware of the current room, the chalk signs on the floor and the flies on the wall, Tina and Mercy staring at her from their positions on the bare boards, but all this faded and closed into a pinprick of restricted, blurred myopia. It wasn't *her* hand that took the chalk – this hand was too small, with nibbled nails and freckled, sun-tanned skin that had spent a blissful summer out of doors. Yet it belonged to her, somehow. Her rosebud-pink smock dress was covered in blood. She couldn't speak: warm liquid filled her mouth, but she could taste nothing. It was only when she started to choke that the sensations left her, vacuumed right out of her body with an abrupt rush.

Carrie slumped forwards, only coming to her senses as her cheek hit the floor.

The circle broken, the flies dispersed, the room still.

A dull headache assailed her temple. She groaned, letting Mercy heave her up. 'What the hell? Why keep picking on *me*?'

'Look at that!' Mercy gave her shoulder an unsympathetic shake, the words on the floor more urgent than Carrie's latest trauma.

Carrie focused, the painful throbbing in her head now concentrated behind her left eye.

The words were not in her handwriting, although there was chalk-dust on her fingertips. They said:

Can't tell – find my tongue.

Haunted by the Past

In which Carrie gets a visitor

03 May

There was no such thing as central heating in The Crows, but that didn't matter even though it was on the chilly side for the start of May: the kitchen was the warmest room in the house. The evening was dying quickly, a sea mist rolling in from the coast and already creeping up the lanes, and the kitchen with its single naked bulb felt in need of cheering up. Something wasn't quite right. Carrie was used to the house having a warm, friendly atmosphere, but after the séance the house seemed tense and troubled.

'Fairwood?' she asked, keeping her voice level. 'You're right behind me, aren't you?'

Carrie-Fairwood unfolded herself from the too-small chair, causing it to tilt and almost topple. Today it was the same size as 'Jack' had been, and for such a big avatar, so square and solid, it moved quietly – moments of clumsiness reminded her that it was not used to having limbs. Even with that disquieting thought, Carrie couldn't help a quick smirk. It was a little endearing.

'I made the well part with three of these,' the avatar said, setting out three antique snuff boxes on the table. Its eyes flashed with binary code. 'Charles II. Restoration age pieces. Those were good times. One of these sold at auction for a thousand last month.'

Carrie stared. 'Seriously? That's – that's amazing. I'd ask how, but... d'you know what, never mind. What do I have to do?'

'Thanks for the broadband,' Fairwood said, answering that for her. 'You need to get them valued... I can arrange that.'

'I'd have to be in, though… or go somewhere…?'

'There's a place in town. Some of me ended up there intermittently, they are very careful. Very considerate. Blackberry Antiques.'

Carrie nodded, a flush of hope glowing through her. 'I wonder if I could get anything for the music box, while we're at it.'

Something cold snaked across Carrie's back, a light breath frosted with fury. She spun around, but there was nothing there. The kitchen was pregnant with an alien tension.

'Okay. What's wrong? Why do things feel… *different* here?' She watched the avatar get a clean mug out of the cupboard for her, deliberately dragging out the silence.

'Things are bound to be different when I've never… manifested before,' Fairwood said after thoughtful consideration.

'I can't get my head around that,' Carrie admitted. It was insane. Maybe she *had* lost her grip on reality somewhere along the line, with all the stress, and this was all a dreamworld she had constructed for herself, a parallel world of supernatural dangers to make the real-world problems fade away.

The doorbell rang.

Carrie frowned. 'Hold that thought, I'll deal with this in a minute.'

Ghosts she could handle, she told herself. It was living people who were the problem.

The house grew still. Fairwood sank through the floor as Carrie hurried down the passage to the reception hall, not bothering to pick up her keys. The door unlocked for her before she reached it.

'Hi—' Her greeting died a strangled death.

Phil posed on her porch in an attitude of false diffidence, statuesque as Michelangelo's David but better dressed, all sharp suit and chiselled cheekbones, chin and nose knapped to flinty perfection, chestnut curls gelled into an obedient halo.

Carrie couldn't move, muscles cemented in place.

Fairwood felt her panic. She sensed the house allowing its more aggressive features to take charge.

'Dropped in on the cousins in Piddingdean,' Phil said, giving her a cold grin. 'Thought I'd stop by on my way back, since I missed you yesterday and you're not answering my calls. It's a beautiful house.' He sneered. 'Good to see you spent our cash wisely.'

Carrie balled her fist at her side with a gut-punch of hatred. '*My* cash.'

Phil frowned. 'Oh, right? Must be some mistake there, Carrie, because I thought the joint savings account was ours, it's got both our names on it.'

The savings account? Shit.

'I was the only one putting anything into it,' Carrie pointed out, wrapping an arm over her stomach. 'And don't think you're getting the deposit back on the flat, because that's gone. I don't have it. And you trashed the place out of – out of sheer *spite*, Phil, and you kicked a hole in the bathroom door. There is no way you're getting a penny.' A surge of hot fury flooded her from the floor upwards, the anthracite-hard anger of the old coal cellar ripping through her blood. The house hissed around her in multitudinous layers of white noise.

Not mine! NOT mine…

NOT HIS.

Phil's eyes narrowed, trying to catch the whispers on the edge of hearing. 'What's that noise?'

Carrie trembled. 'Draughts.' Her voice was cold as the crypt. 'You're wasting your time. I don't owe you a damn thing. I can prove the money I took out of that account was mine, I took photos of the flat, and this house is *mine*. Entirely mine. It's nothing to do with you.' She gripped the edge of the door.

Phil's face darkened in a crimson flush.

Fairwood glowered down at the intruder on its porch, the upper windows gleaming with malevolence.

'Come on, Carrie,' he said, tone deceptively light. 'Just dropping by to see if we can sort stuff out, that's all. I need the cash and looks like you're doing all right now.'

Appearances can be deceiving, but you'd know all about that.

'What d'you need the cash for?' Carrie could guess, but she wanted him to admit it. 'Who do you owe this time?' She shook her head. 'Oh, let me guess, your cousin wouldn't lend you any money either. Tom doesn't even like you, does he?'

Phil took a menacing step forwards, prompting a suck of air out of the door, gusting cold around his ankles.

Keep out!

He stopped, broad brow furrowed with confusion, as if encountering resistance.

Carrie let go of the door – Fairwood didn't need her to hold it – and folded her arms in the safety of her hall. 'You can't intimidate me into giving you cash I don't have and you're not entitled to.'

He lunged forwards and the front door swung violently shut on his hand. There was a crunch of bone and a roar of pain, and the top of Phil's middle finger dropped onto the tiles.

Carrie stared, open-mouthed, as the wood drank up the blood and the small puddle on the tiles seeped into the grouting.

Phil was shouting and swearing, kicking at the door.

'Oh my God!' Carrie burst out laughing. She couldn't help it. '*Fucking bitch!*'

Phil – the real Phil, the man behind the classically handsome veneer – was screaming through the wood. It locked itself, the bolts sliding across.

Carrie forced herself to breathe. 'Fairwood? Let– let's get rid of him,' she managed, and felt the house manifest its enormous Sir Jack-shaped persona through the walls.

She tipped forwards as the manifestation formed through the pillars of the porch, opening her eyes as the cool air licked her face, looking down on a purple-veined Philip Hoskins gripping his bleeding hand.

Carrie cleared her throat, brick-dust dry.

Phil turned his head, the swearing drying up as his finger spurted. Carrie saw the square, stocky hulk of the scarred figure reflected in Phil's eyes. She thought she could see her own face in Fairwood's grey irises, a tiny smudge trapped behind the stare.

Fairwood gripped Phil by the collar and dragged him wordlessly down the steps.

Phil kicked and struggled, his heels leaving twisted troughs in the gravel, but Fairwood marched down the drive with relentless solidity, towing its bleeding burden towards the gates. The blue car was parked up outside, blocking the entrance. After they split up, Carrie had seen it everywhere, driving too slowly along her route to work, parked up by the train station when she went to stay with her dad, cruising around the local supermarket car parks. The sight of it was a cold pinch in her stomach.

Fairwood wrenched Phil through the gates in a brutal underarm swing, tossing him into the road like a rubbish sack. The gates clanged on his departure, and Fairwood melted through the stones, running like a grey river back to the porch where it dissipated into the pillars and steps, pouring back through the walls.

Carrie gasped, rocking back on her heels. She was in the hall, still staring at Phil's bloodless fingertip snapped off at the top knuckle joint.

She stared at it for a moment, gathering her scattered thoughts. Phil wasn't going to be back, not now, she was almost sure. He'd think the scarred giant was lurking somewhere, he wouldn't be able to believe a man stepped out of stone. Or maybe he'd sell his story to some wretched little rag and she'd have ghost hunters turning up and camping on her doorstep.

Or he'd call the police.

That chilled her. She stood rooted to the tiles, knotting her hands together as the knuckle oozed. Had he even left? She didn't dare look outside.

Yes, he's gone.

Fairwood reassured her, but Carrie wasn't convinced. He might come back.

'How do you get rid of a finger?' she asked the house, finally. 'What if he does call the police, does me for assault?'

They won't find any blood.

Carrie wasn't so sure. 'I'll get the bleach.'

She returned with kitchen towel and a box of cleaning supplies, wrapping up the finger and scrubbing at the door and the floor tiles until her thin latex gloves were wrinkled with sweat and slippery on her hands.

The finger sat on the hall table, packaged and oozing a little into the kitchen towel.

'I don't want to bury it or bin it,' Carrie thought out loud, imagining her garden churned to mud by tramping boots and police tape. She wasn't sure how much of this was rational and how much was her anxiety throwing her into paranoia. Who was going to believe that a scarred giant had melted out of the stone and thrown him out? No one, that's who. But his finger… he could say she did it on purpose, get her arrested, take her away from the house.

The obvious solution presented itself, slithering into her mind as she stared at the paper.

'I did *say* I'd go over,' she muttered.

Upstairs, a door slammed.

Carrie knew instinctively that it wasn't Fairwood.

She looked at the floor, the bleach and the finger, then back up to the staircase. 'Right. Can I be bothered to see what this is about?' Her voice quavered, spoiling the bravado. 'It's just a door, right? No, probably not just a door, probably a ghost I released from a music box.' She pursed her lips, closing her eyes. In the relative safety of her own head, she counted down from ten, the cleaning products a reassuring weight in her hand.

'Okay.' She took three steadying breaths, deep and slow, from her diaphragm, a tried and trusted technique. 'I'll come up there and get changed. And if anyone wants to… talk to me, about any of this—' She gestured at the hall. '— or what happened in the Fifties, that's fine. We can do that.' Putting the finger in the cleaning box for the time being, she rubbed her hands on her thighs and steeled herself. 'Okay. Coming up now.'

Carrie walked slowly around the empty rooms, treading the sanded floorboards with care. She preferred the rooms without furniture, even though they had been robbed of their functionality. They were blank canvases, the house stripped to its bare bones, waiting for something to fill the space and, in the meantime, the pure essence of what a house should be.

'He's gone,' she announced into an empty bedroom. 'If there's a ghost in here, I'm alone again now. It's just us.' She paused. 'I'm going out in a minute, so if you've got a message for me, now's the time.'

There was silence.

Carrie stroked the vintage wallpaper, head cocked for the slightest sound. The little blue flowers were warm and smooth under her hand. She thought she heard a creaking in the corridor, a gentle leading series of steps; but when she came out to look, there was no one there.

She crossed into her own room, the bare boards creaking under her weight, the house settling and full of now-familiar sounds as the wood settled. She changed into warmer clothes more suited to trudging through The Chase, something she wouldn't mind getting slime or animal guts all over. Bramble Cottage seemed like that kind of place, even if the inside was neat and tidy. She was in that much of a rush, she barely checked the mirror properly. Something flickered behind her reflection, a vague shape in white.

Slowly, the hairs on the back of her neck standing on end, she turned back to check.

Directly behind her, reflected in the glass, she saw the pale shape of a child's legs clearly visible between her own.

Carrie jumped and spun around with a sharp gasp.

There was no one there.

The prickles washed over her, crawling over her skin like flies. She swallowed. There was a *presence* in the room with her, a malevolent, frustrated, cold presence, nothing like the house. It was close – so close, she felt its frosty touch chilling the room. She spun around to face the mirror and came face to face with a pair of dead, whirlpool eyes.

With a hoarse scream, Carrie dropped her clothes and punched out. Her fist connected with nothing, but the featureless face, blank and paper-white, evaporated without a sound. Carrie took a shaking step backwards, straight into Fairwood's avatar. She lurched forwards again immediately with a frightened yelp.

It held up its hands to stop her from lashing out at it as well. 'I don't think she can hurt you.'

She pointed. 'I saw in the mirror… oh, God. Look at that!'

Across the glass, in her only tube of lipstick, sticky pink letters had appeared.

KILLHIM

Fairwood patted her carefully on the shoulder. 'It'll come off.'

'I'm not bothered about *that*.' Carrie swooped down to grab a top and force it on. 'Shit.' She shook her head, heart fluttering. 'Kill who?'

She ran her hands over her sides, rubbing her palms into the material, trying to cleanse them of the fact she had nearly punched a vengeful spirit in the face.

That cold, dead face.

She shuddered.

'We *might* have a problem,' Fairwood admitted. 'But if she wanted to occupy your form, you'd be vomiting on a three-sixty rotation by now. It's had all this time to get into your head.'

Carrie frowned at the *Exorcist* reference. 'Really? Head spinning round, projectile vomit… all that happens, does it?'

Fairwood avoided the question. 'It depends.'

'Depends on what?!'

'How badly it wants to break your neck.' He leaned over and checked the mirror again. 'It's still watching us.'

'Oh *God*!' Carrie dropped her voice, eyes wide and staring. Her hands balled into white-knuckled fists at her side. 'Where? Where is it?'

Fairwood jerked its head at the doorway. Carrie turned, but she still couldn't see anyone standing there.

'I need to get out of here,' she whispered, nearly crying. She didn't care if bursting into tears at the sight of a ghost was *pathetic*. Little faceless kids with vortexes in their eye sockets freaked her out, apparently.

Fairwood stared at her in horror. '*Out?* You mean – you want to leave?'

Carrie was already out of the door. 'I– I'm going to Bramble Cottage.'

She was halfway down the corridor when she looked up and saw, reflected behind them in the mirror at the end of the corridor, a small pale figure standing some way back. The eyes stared, and it lifted a pink stained finger.

Carrie yelped and tried to sprint down the stairs, but Fairwood stepped out of the staircase and locked her in place with arms like steel bolts.

'Carrie, slow down, you'll fall...'

She didn't fall. She wriggled out of Fairwood's grip and ran downstairs.

'I want to go for a walk.' She slammed into the unyielding front door. 'I'm not *leaving*, I'm coming back! I just... I need a breather.'

The door remained stubbornly shut.

Carrie raked a hand through her hair with a growl of frustration. 'Come *on,* Fairwood, please, give me a break. I'm not running away, I just... come on. Please open the door.' She rattled the handle. 'I just want to go for a walk.' She made a show of putting the finger joint in her handbag, dumped under the coatstand, and unhooked her light cardigan.

The door slid open a reluctant inch.

Carrie sighed. 'That's more like it. Don't let anyone in while I'm gone, okay?'

The door closed behind her, and she faced her empty drive with a prickle of fear.

–

He flicked the old police stinger out across the road at the right time, letting the speeding car roll right over the spikes. It was easier than going all the way to Piddingdean or taking someone off the street. The omens were all bad for those options, but the good old-fashioned way promised better results.

The omens were *so* good, in fact, it was like someone *wanted* him to do it. Ricky was content with that.

Wyrd bið ful aræd. No one could escape their wyrd.

The tyres blew out with a satisfying sound, the driver lost control, and the car skidded into a tree further down the road.

Reeling his contraption back in, Ricky sniffed the air and gave the driver enough time to come back around and escape the car.

Above him, a pair of magpies chattered, another good sign.

The driver's door opened and a curly-haired Adonis crawled out, the kind of man Ricky's cousin Jem Foreman had aspired to be until the Changes put paid to those ambitions with a bad case of gelatinous ooze.

(*Bloody hell, it was a bigger bloke than I was expecting.*)

He sniffed, spat on the ground, and headed over, all concern. 'You all right?'

The man was groggy, shocked, staring around in confusion. 'What the hell happened?'

'You wrecked your tyres, mate,' Ricky said, with an air of wisdom.

The big man swore. He was clutching his hand – must have hurt his wrist on impact, Ricky guessed. Blood was in the air, a rich, familiar smell.

'Need to call the garage?' Ricky came around the steaming engine. 'Want to borrow my phone?'

'Yeah.' The man limped away, following Ricky further into the trees off the road. He kept looking back at the wrecked car, too shocked to realise his unlikely good Samaritan was not the kind of person he should be following into the woods. 'Fuck!'

Ricky watched him, an amusing idea bubbling up. Normally he was all business (*I'm a serious man, me*), but something about the neighbour's humour was infectious. He pushed his hood down.

'Fuck indeed,' he said solemnly, hefting a stone from the ground and testing its weight in his hand.

'Fucking bitch,' the man muttered, holding his injured hand into his shirt. 'Fucking hell,' He turned on Ricky with an ungracious snarl. 'Give us your phone, then.'

Ricky smiled, sweet and dirty. He let his tendrils loose, whipping around his head in their dark, angry coils. His pulse quickened with rare enjoyment, watching the man's jaw slacken first in disbelief, then in horror, his eyes growing wide and glassy.

'You don't talk like that to the One and Only,' he growled, gruff and low. 'You get on your knees.'

The man dropped like a puppet, pallid and sweating.

'Ooh, look at that,' Ricky said, still testing the weight of the stone. 'Himself in the Outside would like someone like you. Family are so bloody *irreverent*, that's half the problem with kids today.'

He came closer, the tendrils thirsting for a taste of his spinal fluids. The thick muscular rings of the largest and longest opened and closed, revealing tiny mouths slavering their anaesthetic silver.

'Got something for you,' he whispered, as the man twitched in terror. 'Not a phone, though. Want to see?' Then, giggling with the irony of it, Ricky swung the stone and bashed him into unconsciousness.

The man dropped to the ground.

Ricky chortled, wiping his eyes. 'Oh, I crack myself up. Sorry mate, were you expecting something a bit special? Ha!' He let his tendrils suck the stone clean of blood, hair and any other DNA, gave it a wipe and dropped it back in place. 'Right son, let's get you home to mother.'

He would usually call Uncle David to get rid of the car, tow it and strip it and flog the parts to several dodgy garage owners he'd met in his own teen joyriding days, but time was of the essence. He chanted a few choice incantations instead, smearing a triangulation of silver mucus across three trees. Reality began to twist and rip in that spot, perception distorted and rippling. The

183

Others, translucent priests of his grandsire, voracious lovers of the metals found in this plane of existence, were on Their way. Their time here was limited, but it should be time enough to polish off a saloon.

The man was heavy, but Bramble Cottage wasn't far. He'd stow him in the cellar for later, get his mother off his back about having no real meat in the house, and show Gerald he hadn't forgotten him. He had entrails to read, first and foremost, and now he'd gotten into the house and been messing with the Pendle Stone, he was sure he'd be able to read them just fine.

Whistling a jaunty birdcall, Ricky rolled up his sleeves to his elbows, baring his arcane symbol tattoos, and started dragging.

–

Carrie didn't go for her walk immediately. She was too nervous about meeting Phil somewhere in the woods or along the lane. A thought, ugly but sincere, played on loop in her head.

I hope the Bermuda Triangle of Sussex is a real thing, I hope he drives into oblivion and never comes back.

She did a few laps of the back lawn, forcing herself to sit on the wishing well and practice some grounding techniques (What can you feel? What can you see? What can you smell? What things can you taste?) but with limited efficacy. She played on her phone, exposed, on edge.

Eventually, she decided on a course of action.

Ducking under the wire fence at the back of her property, heart hammering at the thought of Phil lurking somewhere in the woods, she tried to shake off the fear, but it jangled in the background like tinnitus.

Carrie wrapped her cardigan around herself and followed the winding track through the undergrowth of The Chase until the cottage came into view, the upper windows shuttered this time, and no line of pebbles, white or otherwise, to step over on the approach.

She could hear the muffled sound of violent swearing.

Concerned, Carrie picked her way through the debris in the garden, approaching the cracked lower window where Ricky's mother's 'sewing chair' was placed. The stained net curtain made it nearly impossible to see in, except through the rips and tears. She was about to rap gently on the glass when she caught a glimpse of a cleaver slicing through the air and slamming into the table top.

Carrie dropped to her knees under the window and peered through the largest rip in the curtain, as Ricky Porter, topless and bloodstained, cursed and swore at the remains of a badly butchered badger.

'*No! No!* Damn it to bloody Hell! *Fuck!*'

'You lost it,' a gruff male voice said from the dark corner near the window where Carrie was kneeling. She couldn't see who it was. 'Useless, addle-headed fool you are. What're you going to do about him in the cellar? Your mother wants her pie.'

Ricky's angular face was distorted in a sharp-toothed snarl, purple bags puffing under his eyes. He put on a posh voice, dripping with strained patience. 'I'm bloody trying, pater dearest, it's the liver, it's—'

'Doant you arg wi' me.' The voice in the shadows rumbled low and dangerous. 'You cut out talking like that, putting on airs. You look again. That liver's fresh.'

Ricky poked about inside the animal with increasing frustration. 'Naun here. Nothing. It's telling me *nothing*!' With a howl of visceral rage, he started to change. Something was sprouting out of the back of his head. Tentacles writhed like snakes, coiling around him like a dark halo. Carrie clapped a hand to her mouth to stop the scream bubbling up inside her, unable to tear herself away from the chink in the curtain.

Ricky smashed the badger with his fists in a blind rage, pounding into the carcass and sending chunks and clots of blood splattering across the room.

'You got too cocky, didn't you?' The older voice of Ricky's father was accusing, sneering. 'Think you're special, our One and

Only indeed, your mother and me 'ud swap that any day of the week for a nice lot of childer, looked up *and* down on we are, letting you run wild around the place.'

Ricky stopped pummelling the dead badger, panting with rage. His chest was smeared with dirt and blood.

'Shut up, old man,' he snarled, pointing a quivering finger into the corner Carrie couldn't see. 'You shut your abuseful mouth. Get thee upstairs, you mortal old fool, or I'll read *your* bleedin' liver!' He wrenched the cleaver free of the table and hurled it.

Carrie flinched, and Mr Porter bellowed in pain.

'George!' A sibilant woman's voice whiffled down from the upstairs. 'George, what's he doing to you?'

'I'm going out,' Ricky yelled, fists clenched. 'Stay out of it, Mum!'

Carrie pulled away and pressed herself against the crumbling wall of the cottage. She heard the door slam over the muffled curses of Ricky's father. Before she could scramble up, Ricky stalked by her, hurling the shell of a washing machine out of his way. Carrie couldn't stop the muffled squeak that came out as he passed.

There, in the back of Ricky Porter's shaved skull, was a large gaping mouth. Thick white lips like tapeworms opened and closed, silvery mucus strands laced between them. They chomped on the air as Ricky ranted at the woods, a string of colloquialisms and swearwords assaulting the silent trees.

At the sound she made, Ricky spun around, nostrils flaring, face dark with anger. When he saw Carrie, he stopped. His eyes widened in horror, mirroring hers. He reached automatically for his hood, only to realise he wasn't wearing it, or anything.

Carrie raised her hands. 'It's okay,' she whispered. 'Ricky, it's– it's me, it's okay.'

Ricky's brown eyes burned a dark ruby red. His hands cupped the back of his head, protecting it from her rather than the other way around.

'Seriously,' Carrie whispered, getting shakily to her feet, 'It's fine, I'm just gonna go, okay, I'm just going.'

'You can't be here,' Ricky growled at her, lowering his bloody hands. 'What're you doing here? I'm busy.'

'I – you invited me, remember?' Carrie pointed out. 'You said I could come over for tea...'

Ricky jerked his head at her, then lunged forwards to pull her away from the cottage when she didn't take the hint. He glowered, smearing her cardigan with badger blood. 'Now's not a good time.'

He tugged her over to the wall and let her go.

'Ow!' Carrie rubbed her arm, getting blood on her own fingers. 'Oh, great. Thanks.'

'You're remarkably bloody calm,' Ricky commented, crossing sinewy arms. His tattoos spiralled up to his shoulders, two sleeves of symbols exuding a sinister, otherworldly menace.

'I'm not, I'm just really good at hiding it,' Carrie said. 'Or maybe it's the stuff the doctor gave me. I feel... I don't know. Different.'

He eyed her sullenly, shoulders dropping. 'I'm going to wash this lot off,' he mumbled. 'Just – wait there.'

He ducked under the washing line before she could pull the finger out in its paper towel, heading around the corner, and proceeded to wash the butchery from his body with the water from a rainwater butt.

Carrie waited.

Ricky came back with a ragged towel in one hand and his grey hoody, tugged from the line, in the other. He looked much better, except for the bags under his feverish eyes and haggard complexion under his stubble.

He balled the towel up and threw it on a broken refrigerator lying in the grass, pulling the hoody on over his bare chest and tweaking the hood up.

'What d'you *want*?' he demanded. He dropped his weight onto the garden wall, adding moist dirt to the badger blood on his trousers. 'It's private property, this.'

Carrie clambered over the wall to the other side. Ricky turned to watch her.

'This isn't.' She echoed his own words, putting her hands behind her back.

He tried not to grin but couldn't quite fight it.

'I just popped over to say that there's a ghost in my house now, I let it out of a music box by accident and I'm pretty sure it's Cathy Ross.'

Ricky grunted, leaning forwards despite himself. 'Bet she's happy.'

Carrie paused. 'And. Um. Phil did show up. I told him to piss off, and, that… did not go so well.' She dug in her bag and fidgeted with the bloody paper towel. 'That's… also sort of why I came. I didn't know what to do with it, so, um, I brought you something.' She drew it out, hand trembling as she showed him.

Ricky grinned, eyes alight with sudden interest. 'What's that tasty little scrap of a thing, then? *Please* say it's his cock.'

'Calm down.' Carrie had to laugh. 'Just the top of his finger.'

Ricky wrinkled his nose. 'Shame.'

'D'you want it?' Carrie held it out. 'I don't mind what for, I just, I know it's silly, but I don't want it in the house and I'm scared that… he'll call the police or something.' She looked away. 'Anyway, I wasn't sure what to do with it and then I… I thought of you.'

Ricky considered it for a moment, then burst into a childish giggle, with all the bashful delight of a child surprised with a treat. He snatched it from her and unwrapped the knuckle, studied it for a moment, and popped it into his mouth.

The bone and fingernail splintered and cracked between his teeth.

'Mm. Ta.' He slurped it down and burped on purpose. 'It ain't even my birthday.' He cleared his throat, taking a few beats, and changed the subject. 'So, got a ghost now? What's the plan with that?'

'Don't know,' Carrie said, fascination wrestling her horror. She pressed her hand to her stomach to quell the nausea. 'I guess I should try and communicate with it?' She cocked an eyebrow, recalling something she'd overheard. 'So… who's in the cellar?'

Ricky turned himself all the way around to face her, feet dangling over the woodland side of the wall. 'You done a séance yet? Tina's good at those. And none o' your bleeding business, as it happens. Mum's dinner, that's all. I promised her some real meat for a, well, it's the old girl's birthday and she don't want a fuss, so.' He shrugged.

'Real meat, like, beef, right?'

He laughed. 'Come and see, if you want.'

Carrie stayed where she was. 'You're not trying to get me down your cellar under false pretences, are you, Mr Porter?'

'False pretences? I'm hurt.' He patted the wall beside him. 'Why would I do that?'

'I don't know.' Carrie approached gingerly and sat beside him, staring at the trees. 'I think you should keep your lower ground floor to yourself.'

There was a long pause.

Ricky's tendrils snaked out of the back of his head, licking at the air.

'Was that... was that an innuendo?' he asked eventually.

'It wasn't great.'

'Hell's bells, you're not scared of me at all, are you, neighbour? That's funny.' He scratched his forehead. 'Look, I got a badger to bury. You want to come, say a few words? That's pretty dead, too.'

'Over the badger?' Carrie wondered if this was a test. 'Sure.'

Ricky nodded, and waved her back into the garden. 'The old man'll have cleared off by now. Come on in.'

The cottage was worse than last time. Globs of blood flecked the floor and the walls. Parts of the dead creature had been smashed to raw mince, and its head dangled sadly off the edge of the table. The cottage stank of blood and badger faeces, and whatever had been in the badger's stomach.

'Can't you do this outside?' Carrie asked, holding her nose.

'Nah. Some do-gooder always calls the police.' Ricky dug a sack out from under a pile of mouldering newspapers and plastic bags. 'Hang on, let's get her in here.'

From under her feet, she thought she heard something muffled, growling and shuffling, an angry animal, or maybe a human being trying to be heard as they struggled with their bonds and gag. She shot a glance at Ricky, who didn't seem perturbed.

Should I ask?

She bent her head and tried to see between the boards where the cracks were bigger, but there was nothing down there but the dark. There was a bump and a low moan, which sounded more human than animal.

Carrie straightened up, hairs prickling up. 'What was that? Ricky, shit—'

'Go see if you want,' Ricky said, busy scooping badger guts into the sack with his bare hands. 'Go on. Steps are down there.' He nodded at the trapdoor in the floor some way away, around the side of the stairs. 'Naun to be afraid of, promise.'

He wouldn't say that if it was a person, would he?

Ricky's face was a picture of honesty, but fear snaked up her back.

'I'll wait outside,' Carrie said, stomach roiling. She rubbed her middle more firmly and fought the tightening at the top of her throat, stepping out to take a deep breath of fresh air.

He joined her shortly afterwards, and took her around the side of the cottage, through a squeaking back gate and into The Chase.

It was a bright, sunny day for once, and if they hadn't been carrying a leaking sack full of bits of badger it would have been a pleasant walk. The crows followed their progress, flapping from tree to tree, branch to branch, calling softly to one another above their heads.

Ricky found a spot and unshouldered his shovel. 'Here'll do.'

Carrie dumped the sack on the ground as he dug a shallow hole between the roots of an old, gnarled tree. She squinted up at it. 'What kind of tree is this?'

Ricky wiped his brow with the back of his hand. 'She's a beech. Don't you know how to tell?'

'Londoner.' Carrie dropped the bag into the hole as carefully as she could. 'So, um, rest in peace, badger. Thank you for...' She looked at Ricky for inspiration. '...your sacrifice?'

Ricky snorted. 'I was only kidding about saying something, it's a bloody badger.' He started back-filling without ceremony. When he finished, he stood back, looking at her. 'Go on, love, say it. Let's get it all out there.'

'You know that's horrible and disgusting.' Carrie wiped her hands on her jeans. 'I'm not judging, well no, I guess I am a bit, but... that is *revolting*.' She shuddered.

Ricky slammed the tip of the shovel into the ground, leaning on the handle.

'Come on love, that's a bit weak. Let's hear all of it.'

'That's — that's about all.' Carrie wrinkled her nose, brow furrowed.

'No, it's not. Come on. Let's have it.' He tugged his hood down and slapped the back of his skull. 'Come on! You've seen this. What am I?' His eyes throbbed a darker ruby red. 'Say it! What does this look like to you?'

Carrie rubbed her arm. She should have been afraid, but she wasn't. He wanted her to call him a monster. He was daring her to say it, his whole stance one of aggressive challenge. If this was the council estate where she'd grown up, someone would have taken their top off by now and there'd be real trouble. She shook her head, refusing.

'I have no idea,' she admitted. 'I've never met anyone like you before.' That wasn't strictly true: she'd met a lot of lads like Ricky Porter, but none with quite the same — for want of a better word — physique. She threw out a distraction, raising a hand cautiously towards him.

'It doesn't hurt, does it?'

Ricky stabbed the shovel into the ground with an angry grimace. '*Does it hurt?* No, it bloody doesn't. Why are you asking me that? "Does it hurt", are you serious?' He jerked away from her hand even though the gap between them was considerable.

She lowered it. He shuddered, dropping his voice and rubbing the top of his head.

'D'you – d'you want to touch it? No, of course not.' He faced her, blowing out a shaky breath, eyes clouded with something that looked a lot like hope. 'Do you?'

Carrie blinked. She didn't, but there was something in the way he'd asked. It was important to him. She moistened her lips. 'Yeah, okay.'

'You do?' This threw him. 'Bloody hell. All right.' Ricky beckoned her forwards, not quite looking at her.

Carrie steeled herself, reaching out to his face. He flinched away.

'I'm not going to hurt you.' Carrie kept her hand where it was, letting him haltingly lean towards it, until her fingers were brushing his temple. His short-cropped hair was soft, like a baby hedgehog's spines. It was his turn to close his eyes.

Carrie's sympathy over-spilled into a grudging smile. 'Is that nice?'

Ricky moved his head against her hand, furrowed forehead smoothing as he relaxed. 'I don't... I don't dislike it. We're not as you'd say, an affectionate family.'

'When was the last time you had a hug?'

Ricky curled his lip. 'Steady on.'

Carrie stroked the side of his head, moving her hand further around the back each time, until she could feel the rounded, smooth upper lip of the second mouth, puckered skin like a fat scar. 'You won't bite me, will you?' she asked.

He gave a boyish giggle, pulling away. Carrie hesitated, surprised, but continued when he pressed his head back against her hand.

'You said "you",' he explained, letting her explore the wide ridges on the back of his skull. 'Not "it". Most everyone says "it", like it ain't a part of me.'

'Oh my God, Ricky,' Carrie murmured, heart clenching. 'Oh. Wait, something's got my wrist, you've got hold of my wrist.'

She had held a king snake once at the reptile house in London zoo, letting the length of rippling muscle wrap around her arm and push its way up to the top of her sleeve. This felt almost the same, except the snake had been smooth and dry, while this was slick and slimy.

'Sorry, it's a defence mechanism, it's when I get emotional...' Ricky cleared his throat, closing his eyes and focusing. She watched his face grow still. The tentacle, or tongue, or whatever it was, released her and withdrew. Her skin tingled.

Carrie gave the lips another gentle stroke before withdrawing her hand. Sticky snail-thick mucus coated her arm, the tingling spreading up to her elbow. 'My arm feels weird.'

'Anaesthetic.' Ricky pulled up his hood. 'It's all right, just wash it off. Won't last long.'

'Hah.' Carrie let the mucus catch the sunlight, watching it shimmer. Numbness rippled over her forearm until the patch was dead to the touch, spongey but firm as she poked it. 'That's pretty cool.'

Ricky fetched the shovel, trudging back through the trees. Carrie jogged after him.

'Don't go getting ideas,' he warned her. 'Don't you be telling anyone about this, either, you know I'm not meant to get invested.'

Carrie smirked. 'Thought you said we're just neighbours.'

'Yeah. Well.'

They walked on in silence.

Within sight of the cottage, he stopped abruptly and jerked his thumb in the direction of The Crows. 'You can bugger off now.'

'Yeah, I will.' Carrie waved. 'Be seeing you, neighbour.'

Beast with a Human Face

In which Fairwood finds a clue and Ricky has a confession

04 May

As the moon sailed beyond the middle of the night, Ricky couldn't sleep. He had spent more time away from home in the previous few days than he had ever done in his life, and his own bed was a stranger to him. (Had they done something to it? His father was well enough to be downstairs yesterday, had he gone across the landing and done something, changed something?)

(*Sleep well, son*, George had gurgled that night, clots still dribbling from his chin.)

Ricky bounced onto all fours, spine curved, and tore the mattress apart. The springs pinged hard against his nails, mildewed guts spilling out of the tear. He ripped it open and flung it off the bed frame, but there was nothing to find.

Breathing hard, Ricky towered, a lean, tattooed titan, in the wreckage of his room. It was difficult to 'tower' at five foot five, but the ceiling was so low he managed it in fact as well as in his imagination. The damp was eating at the walls, fungi sprouting where the wallpaper had curled away. The mattress was beyond repair. His bed stood immobile, inflexible, too small.

Ricky snarled at it. He had better things to do with his life than stay at home, dosing and nursing his parents, outgrowing them and this cramped life. The ruin he'd had his eye on since he was a boy was open to him now. What could be more fitting? She wasn't a ruin anymore, either: fully restored, she was, and thirsty for vengeance.

(*Carrie Rickard understood, saw Fairwood for what she was — had seen him, all of him, now, too.*)

(*Shut up*, shut up, *shut up.*)

Still comfortably naked in his goose-fleshed skin, Ricky stalked downstairs to the cellar where he'd stashed the motorist from that afternoon. He'd do him in now, skin him and carve him, then curl up with Gerald like he used to as a little boy (like he'd done the last few nights with— *shut up shut up shut UP.*)

No wonder the badger hadn't shown him anything. He'd used up his energies giving Guy Bishop the winning horses at Ascot. Was this what he was reduced to?

(*No: heard the Voice, have been for a while. He's watching me, waiting. I'm part of the wyrd, part of the plan, I can wait.*)

He sighed, descending into the cellar in the dark, and struck a match to light the lantern. The light flared on a trussed-up man at least twice Ricky's size, struggling and mumbling through the gag. The light also flared on Gerald, tied securely to the wheel in the corner. One of Gerald's bonds had come loose, the fox limb torn partially out of the donkey-hide shoulder, as if Gerald had attempted to escape.

'Did you do this to him?' Ricky demanded, inspecting the tear.

(*Could be mice, hard to tell in this light.*)

The man shook his head vehemently, sweating bullets, muffled swearing pouring through the gag.

Ricky scowled. 'Never mind.'

He was off his game, and he knew it.

He unrolled his toolkit, selected a sharp, curved blade, and prepared to get to work.

Some of his cousins liked to strip off when they had a job like this to do, standing amid plastic sheeting partially or fully erect, getting off on the blood or the pain or the noises. He viewed the meat they served up at family dinners with mild suspicion and distaste: it always tasted better when you knew the butcher hadn't fucked it first or wanked himself off during the process.

Ricky was naked, the way he usually slept, but this was a job to him, and nothing stirred beyond the occasional growl in his stomach.

The man wrenched his hands free in a desperate swipe and charged, head down, catching Ricky around the waist. Ricky gripped the man in a dancer's hold and spun him around, jerking his shoulder out of its socket with a satisfying crunch of bone. He buried the knife in the man's shoulder, which proved to be a mistake.

The man bellowed with pain but kept going, flailing, punching out.

Ricky dodged the other fist with ease, barely moving, until the man threw himself into Gerald's corner, looking for a weapon. He clearly knew better than to unplug the wound by taking out the knife, or he was running on adrenaline and had forgotten it was still in there.

'Don't you bloody dare,' Ricky growled, seeing the wild-eyed glance at the antlers. 'You keep your hands off of him – don't you bleedin' dare.'

The man, his right arm swinging limp and useless, made a grab for Gerald's skull.

Ricky lunged forward as he managed to snap an antler off, and the man plunged it right into Ricky's eye through to his brain.

(*Fuck me…*)

Time stopped. So did pain.

For a moment, Ricky hovered on the edge of the Outside.

Slithering sounds came towards him in the green-black of the darkness. Grandad's worshippers slapped their way out of the void to his aid, drawn by the tattoos burning a message into their dimension.

It wasn't the first time they'd dived into his mind, but he hated feeling them in there, crawling, worming through his cerebral cortex and drawing him back into the light of his own reality.

When he came to, the man was trying to break his way out of the trapdoor.

Ricky sat up, head pounding.

Gerald's bloodied antler lay discarded on the floor.

'Where the pest d'you think you're going?'

The man blanched, clutching his dislocated arm and nearly falling in shock. He was a striking-looking bloke, even from that angle. Ricky had once flicked through a book on mythology with laughably inaccurate pictures, and the chiselled jaw of Apollo with his short curls was uncannily similar.

He ignored the man's frantic attempts to escape (padlock was new) and got up in one fluid movement to select another knife from his table. While he'd been out of it, the man had done the same: his least favourite blade was missing. Wes had given it to him on his seventeenth birthday, a blunt blade with a flashy handle.

'You shallow twat.' He shook his head, smirking. 'You had all these beauties and you picked the shit one.'

The tendrils slithered out like anacondas. They withstood the attempts to fight them off, the knife-bites stinging no worse than pins and needles. The man howled as he was dragged back down the steps, the silvery mucus blinding him and gluing his limbs rigidly in place.

Ricky tossed him back into his corner, taking his knife back in the process, and got on with it.

He took the organs he needed, ignoring the frantic struggles and gagged screams, carved some sinewy bits off for mother, and readied the guts like a string of slippery sausages. The stink of faeces and urine joined the sweeter reek of putrefaction wafting from Gerald.

Ricky mentally made his clean-up list as he worked, trying to remember where he'd put the man's wallet and ID. It would be easier to think without all the noise.

Fortunately, the man passed out not long into the job, around the time Ricky fished out his right kidney. It was only when his intestines were in a pile ready to be packed into Gerald and Gerald's straw-stuck, maggot-infested guts had been piled into the man's stomach cavity, that Ricky noticed his unlucky motorist was missing the top joint of his finger. He was pretty sure he hadn't lost it in the fight or by crashing the car.

'*Fuck's* sake!'

He had a nibble of another finger joint, just to be sure, clamping down on the pinkie and chewing it off. There was no doubt about it – he had tasted this before.

'Well how was I to bloody know?'

He'd just gutted Caroline Rickard's ex-boyfriend.

Ricky sighed. 'No hard feelings, mate. I still can't see too well. Starting to think I been short-changed by that bloody shrine, to tell the truth.' He studied the gory remains. 'Should be thanking you, really, breaking the right bits of her, bringing her to me. I'm no-ways ungrateful.' He gave Phil's lifeless legs a kick. 'All I need to do is keep tellin' her the truth.'

Gerald was watching him.

He looked up into the oozing eyeballs. 'Doant you be a-looking at me like that.'

Gerald said nothing, filling the cellar with his accusatory silence.

'Piss off,' Ricky muttered, suddenly out of sorts, and collected up the organs for his mother.

–

Cathy's ghost was getting impatient. Her sullen figure appeared in the bathroom mirror as Carrie passed by, watching silently. Her presence was in the kitchen, chilling the usually warm space with an unnatural speed, and draining Carrie's phone battery as it sat in the middle of the kitchen table.

Carrie went to find her charger, and when she came back her phone was lying on the floor with a cracked screen.

'Oh, *come on*.' Carrie was glad she had insurance. 'Come on, really?'

The utility door slammed.

Carrie stood her ground. 'Look, I'm trying to help you. I promise, I'm looking, but… I've got literally nothing to go on,

I'm trying to hold down a job, I've already been cursed once, can you give me a break?'

The door banged again, making her jump.

'Okay! Fine, I'll try harder.'

She turned around, and Cathy's vortex eyes burned into hers inches away.

Carrie leapt back, heart in her throat, swiping at the air. 'God, this is weird!'

Let me help.

She got herself a slice of lemon cake from the counter, her treat courtesy of Mercy, and devoured half of it in one go. 'Bloody hell.'

She went into the living room, where the Green Man stood propped on the mantelpiece.

What do you think? Did you know Janet?

I remember Janet Varney. Despoiler. Thief. Yes, I remember now.

What did she do to you?

Broke in. Took linen. Ornaments. Things she said no one was using. Left scars, like the rest of them. Thieves, vandals, fools.

Carrie shared the flash of anger.

What a bitch!

I can see into her kitchen from here.

Carrie frowned, taking her time with the crumbs. *From where?*

There was a pause.

She kept something of mine. It's in the kitchen.

The house is empty.

Are you sure? Carrie asked, without thinking.

She felt the withering pity of The Crows rush through her mind, as if the house had raised a gable in place of an eyebrow.

I know houses.

All right, keep your slates on.

Carrie grinned down at her plate, tickled by her own joke.

Okay: can you manifest there? Look around? We're looking for anything that might connect her to you. I mean, how old was she? She couldn't have been involved with the Ross murder, could she?

The Green Man smiled.

Carrie let her hand close over the tile. Her vision blurred. The world spun into a pinpoint, sucking her up and throwing her out into a vortex of shape and colour. She opened her eyes in a new world of a catalogue kitchen, matching beige everything, looking out of the eyes of a Toby jug.

'When Ricky said he was going to show me a whole new world, I'm not sure he imagined this,' she remarked.

'We can do better than Ricky Porter,' Fairwood said primly. Square, stocky and too big for the miniature elegance of Janet Varney's kitchen, Fairwood's avatar scraped its head against the aertex ceiling. Carrie saw the claw scars, fresh and deep, running down its neck. Since the living room window was still broken, a craze of silver webbed in the corner of its eye.

'That's the master bedroom talking,' Carrie retorted, recognising the tone, the sides of her ceramic cheeks growing redder under the glaze.

Fairwood sniffed. 'Well? What are we looking for?'

'I'm a jug. Where're my feet? Ugh, I'm hollow. This is… this is bloody weird.'

Fairwood picked her up. 'I'm not sensing anything else belonging to me.'

Carrie knew it wasn't going to be easy. 'Okay… let's go for her papers, her mementos, things she's hidden away. Maybe tried to destroy? I don't know…' She rolled her eyes around, trying to take in as much as possible, catching their reflection in the window. 'Oh my God, I'm a talking Toby jug. I don't like this.'

'Let go of the tile,' Fairwood advised. 'I'll see what I can find.'

Carrie didn't have any hands. She couldn't let go of the tile. She had left the tile in the living room. 'What do you mean, let—'

She woke up on the floor.

Trances were a bitch.

Her cheek felt numb. The pain came a few moments later, bursting around her head where she had hit it against the fireplace on the way down. The mirror reflected the violent beginnings of a colossal bruise.

'Not again, bloody *hell*!'

She tugged her bobble out of her ponytail and ruffled her hair around her face to see if that would cover it. It didn't. 'Oh *God*, why is this always happening to me? Can I please not be knocked out or attacked or cursed for *five fucking minutes*, this is getting *ridiculous*.' She wasn't sure what she'd even done – there was some blood on the grate, so she assumed she had bashed her face on that when she'd collapsed.

Her right eye was puffing as she watched, she could feel it swelling, tender, the slight graze on her cheek already scabbing over. 'I'm going out into the garden,' she announced. 'I need fresh air. Fucking hell.'

Fairwood did not answer.

'People *bleed* and *bruise*,' she shouted at the living room. 'We're not like wood or stone or plaster, we get hurt! So just – can you just remember that, please?'

She tidied up her cake crumbs and the broken plate, smashed in two on the grate, located the fork with some difficulty, and dumped everything in the bin (including the fork, which she would regret later).

The garden was cool, the wishing well as innocent as any garden ornament, the sun shining.

She sat on the grass, head spinning, hoping that once she got the hang of her new-found skills (abilities? curse?) she would be fine, it would all be fine, her life would go back to some semblance of normality, and there would be fewer injuries and far less pain.

'Wotcher, neighbour.'

Carrie flopped back onto the lawn, shading her eyes with a hand. 'Bloody hellfire.'

'Oi! That's my line.'

Ricky Porter crossed the lawns and stopped, casting his shadow over her. Carrie glanced up at him.

'Should I start charging you rent?' she asked.

He grinned. 'Think of it as – what's the word – acclimatisation, that's it.'

'Don't worry,' Carrie said dryly, 'you'll get used to me.'

Ricky giggled delightedly in his unguarded, childlike way, the wrong kind of laugh for a man like that, but she was getting used to the cognitive dissonance it engendered.

'The sun isn't even behind you,' she said, squinting. 'You're doing this on purpose. This whole, eldritch thing.'

Ricky dropped into a squat, and his shadow went away. 'Yeah, you got me. Showing off.'

'It's not − it's not things-that-go-bump-in-the-night that bother me,' Carrie muttered. 'It's people. Social crap. I used to be fine, and now... now I'm not doing so well again.' That was an understatement. The anxiety was there in the background of her life all the time, spoiling the quiet moments with its constant, static vibrato. Dr Monday's preparation had helped, but now she felt it coming back, seeping upwards from her subconscious in a slow, relentless, insidious flood.

Ricky grinned, lying down beside her and stretching out with one arm behind his head, the other shading his eyes. 'You seem all right with me. Does that mean I'm not "people", then?' He didn't seem offended.

She noted how close he was lying, not quite touching, but comfortably close. It tugged at Carrie's mind, as if they had done this before, but she knew they hadn't. Maybe she was thinking of the bus journey.

'Neighbours are different.' Carrie put her arm under her head and stared into the clouds. The sunlight bothered her − she winced, cupping her free hand over her damaged eye.

He glanced at her and did a double take, moving her protective hand away from her bruises. She turned her head as he sat up, head on one side.

'Cor, you've been in the wars. What's wrong with your face?'

'Nothing.'

He jabbed at her cheek, forcing her to jerk her head back and knock his hand away.

'Stop it!' She rolled her eyes or tried to – her right eye was too puffy to roll and the headache was getting worse. 'Fell over. Bashed my face on the fireplace.'

He sniffed, businesslike. 'You know, I could see my way clear to, you know, move in. Lodge. Could be useful, if you're not a hundred per cent.'

Carrie stared at him. 'Seriously, what? You want to *move in with me*?'

'Yeah, well, things aren't exactly working out at my parents' place right at the minute.' He avoided eye contact, running his fingers through the grass. 'Had a bit of a... set-to yesterday with the old man, and... well, you heard all that. Don't mind paying rent. In kind, obviously, I don't have any money.'

Carrie continued to stare, speechless, propping herself up on her elbows.

'All right, all right, I won't darken the upper floors, don't you panic. Happy in the cellars, me. And I'll clear up after myself, no blood, no nothing, naun for the Old Bill to find even if they turn up with a full SOCO team.' He paused. 'That's actually happened,' he added with a hint of pride, as if that were proof of his thoroughness. 'Twice.'

'What are you – what are you going to pay with, if not money?' Carrie had no intention of saying yes, but the idea was horribly fascinating. 'Because you know, it's money I'm short of. And you're already owing me favours from the Pendle Stone, so...' she trailed off, leaving it suggestively unfinished.

Ricky shrugged. 'How about the lottery numbers? Or I can tell you who's going to win the World Cup.'

'Are you joking? You can't do that, there's got to be... rules.'

'Why not? Future's immutable. You can think of that one of two ways – problematic, or lucrative.' He jumped up, stretching in the sunlight. 'If it can't be changed, you might as well bet on it.'

Carrie struggled up too, a whole inch taller than he was. 'I'll think about it.' She didn't fancy the idea of an eldritch horror in her cellar, and she didn't really believe he'd tell her something so mundane as the jackpot numbers. Of everything she'd seen and put up with over the past few weeks, that one was too unlikely.

'Nah, say yes,' Ricky insisted, backing off a few steps. ''Cause I've got a… bit of a confession to make and I'd rather you—' He sucked air through his teeth. 'You know, agree first.'

'Oh *God*.' Carrie groaned. 'What now?'

He hunched his shoulders, hood twitching as the tendrils pushed at the fabric.

'Funny story…'

'Oh *God*.'

Ricky squirmed. 'Mother was on about meat pies all bloody week, right, and I needed something for − for a rite, yeah, and there's this bloke with a puncture. Just stood there.'

'Just *happened* to have a puncture?'

Ricky squirmed. 'Well. You know how it is, who am I to change another man's wyrd? I'm just an agent of destiny, me. Anyway, I bash him on the head and take him to the cottage, right? Well then I had to read livers and that didn't work out, and you turned up, and—'

Carrie held up a hand. 'Whoa, whoa, whoa, you abducted a bloke, bashed him on the head, and he was in the cottage the whole time I was with you?' She groaned. 'Oh, God, this is the man in the cellar, I knew it, I should've…' She trailed off. *What? Rescued him? How?*

He frowned, concentrating on his train of thought. 'Yeah, that's what I said. Well, anyway, last night I can't sleep so I remember this guy, and I go down to the cellar, make a start, flay him a bit, carve up some cuts for mum, take out his spleen—'

'*You what?*'

'His *spleen*,' Ricky repeated, louder, 'get a kidney, you know, while I'm in there, and he's a feisty bastard, doesn't bloody shut up the whole time, so it's not until a bit later I noticed… he, er, he's missing the top of his finger.'

Carrie went cold. 'What… what colour was the car?' she croaked, praying the answer both would and would not be blue.

'Can't remember,' Ricky said.

Conga eels writhed and knotted in the pit of her stomach.

Ricky fished a driving licence out of his pocket, holding it out to her. 'I'm going to put her with the others, but first I thought… I wanted to check if I should put in a bit more work covering up this one, since I… don't want to get you in any bother.'

With the others?

She imagined handmade mobiles of ID cards, twirling in draughts on catgut strings, macabre tributes to their missing owners.

She didn't want to touch it.

The familiar face drove the wind out of her. She stumbled back a pace. The picture was an old one, she could see it from there, exactly as she remembered: he had joked he looked like a junkie in the harsh light and they had both laughed. She let the knowledge seep in, stared it in the plastic face.

Phil. He's killed Phil.

It was the relief, the treacherous wave of relief, that hit first. The dread, the self-hate, the horror, all that would follow, but not now, not yet, although it churned like flotsam and when the wave broke, she would have to deal with the wreckage. She stared from the card to Ricky and was overwhelmed with the mad desire to kiss his crooked smile, kiss him hard on the lips, break his teeth, rip his tongue out, smash his cocky face in.

She didn't know why she did it.

One minute she was staring at a driving licence, the next her arms were around Ricky Porter's neck and she was clinging to him like a life-preserver, locked in a throttle-hold.

Ricky went rigid.

His shoulders and back were iron-tense. He gripped her upper arms and prised her off him, holding her at arm's length as studs of pain blossomed in her flesh around his fingertips.

'Ow, Ricky, *ow,* you're hurting me…'

He looked genuinely shaken. She grabbed his arms at the elbow to push him off, wincing with the tightness of his grip, and he took the hint but didn't let go entirely. They stood apart, locked in their strange wrestle, until Ricky cleared his throat.

'So—' His voice was still gruff, but there was a fragility in it that she hadn't heard before. 'We're all right then?'

His breath hit her, spearmint-sweet.

He freshened his breath before he came over? He must be serious.

(*"I'm a serious man, me."*)

'Yeah.' Carrie was too numb to think clearly. 'Yeah, I think… I think we're all right.'

The tension bled out of his body, muscles un-bunching a group at a time, going from iron to putty. He quivered at her closeness, eyes wide, their central dots blazing.

They released each other, and he nodded.

'Ricky, his cousin lives around here, people will be asking for him, they'll come to the house…'

He scoffed. 'Nah. They won't find anything. Promise. Mention my name, tell 'em to ask me if I saw anything, and I guarantee you they won't be bothering you again.' He eyed her, a smile playing on his (visible) lips. 'That is… I *can* help, *if*…' He shrugged, willing her to complete the sentence.

Carrie's world closed in, one choice at a time.

Ricky's sly smile chilled her to the marrow. 'So, what do I call you? Landlady?'

Shit! Carrie rubbed the left side of her face, the bruise almost forgotten in the rollercoaster of the last few minutes. 'Yeah, you've got me there, haven't you?'

He grinned.

'Look, you know it's not up to me. If the house says yes, then I can't really say no.' The words pinched in her throat, she nearly gagged on them. 'Have you got… much stuff, or…?'

Ricky crowed his delight to the bright May sky, grabbed her by the shoulders and bounced up on the balls of his feet to plant a smacking kiss on her forehead. It was so out of character that Carrie forgot Phil was dead. He pulled away immediately, taking a few steps back and burying his hands in his pockets again, but it was too late.

The kiss burned into her skin like a brand.

Her hand flew to the spot automatically, but she caught his eye and scratched her head instead. She itched to rub it away, rub the skin off her forehead, rub a hole straight through the bone into her brain and rip out the knowledge he had saddled her with, but she couldn't do that.

'No kids up the chimney,' he said, solemn, 'I swear. I mean, I'll give it my best shot. Until my farsight's back up to speed I can't *swear* I won't have to, know what I mean?' He beamed at her. 'Just one more rite, that's it, to that I *can* swear, and my third eye will be wide open for the foreseeable.'

Carrie nodded. 'Okay. Okay, just, um. Please don't let them arrest me for something I didn't do?' *Oh my God did I really say that? Is that all I have to say? Do I call Phil's mum? How can I when she doesn't even know he's missing yet? Who do I tell? No one! I can't tell anyone! Oh God, oh God, what do I do?*

He gave her a smile that was almost fond. 'Don't you fret, neighbour. I'm here to help.' He frowned, rummaging in his other pocket. 'Speaking of which…' He pulled out a clear plastic packet, containing what looked like tobacco, a note inside. 'This is for you. One of the favours I owe you. Get anxious, do you? Not medicine, more a pick-me-up, but this will help.' His childlike giggle escaped again as she took it. 'See you later.'

He waved at the house with all the energy of an excited schoolboy on his first parentless trip and strode off across the lawns into the trees.

Carrie studied the packet. It looked more like a bag of iron filings than shredded tobacco now she had it up close, but as she pinched the plastic, she saw the dark greens and purple-blacks, a muted rainbow of dark shades. Inside was a handwritten note in large, carefully rounded writing, unevenly spaced.

It hadn't occurred to her until then, but from the way he spoke and the casual references he made, Ricky Porter must be well read even though she hadn't seen a single book or magazine in the cottage. What did he read? Where did the books come from?

Who had taught him to write this way, the handwritten version of cut-and-pasted letters in a kidnapper's note?

Taketwopincheswithtea.

Blacktea is b es t.

Twiceaday.

Free Refills. My Favour.

Carrie hesitated.

She headed back into the kitchen, the packet clutched in her hand.

"*Don't drink the tea.*" "*Never trust a Porter.*"

Why not? What was he going to do? And what did it matter now, anyway?

She took two pinches as directed and stirred them into a cup of tea. As she drank it slowly, calm and clarity re-entered her world. The overwhelming, storm-tossed breakers of her life settled into lapping waves, easily navigated. Things began to slot into place.

There's nothing I can do, so we'll worry about that later, one thing at a time.

Her stomach settled. Her mind eased.

That's it. One thing at a time.

Carrie took a deep breath. 'Find anything at Mrs Varney's?' she asked out loud.

Fairwood materialised through the oak panelling of the stairs, striding down the steps into the kitchen to join her. 'Not much. I looked in all the usual places, Owners hide things. This was in the wood-burner.' He laid down some scraps of burnt paper, and an old photograph, curled and scorched. 'The house was not so old – it put on a few airs, but it knew better than to cross me. It showed me this, up in the attic.' It was a box of mementos, which Fairwood also laid on the table for Carrie to peruse.

'What was she burning?' Carrie picked over the papers and photograph first. The paper looked like old newspaper, brittle and yellowed. It fragmented at her touch, so she tried not to poke it. 'Must be a one, and a nine, nineteen... And... um.' She struggled to concentrate, trying not to think about Phil. 'Fifty-eight? Yeah, so what happened in 1958?'

'Cathy Ross,' Fairwood said promptly.

'She kept the newspaper report? And now she burns it? Then attacks me. Us. That's not a coincidence.' Carrie tapped her nails against her mug. 'This photo... what's this? Is that the Colonel?' She peered at a group of serious looking adults gathered around a table, the Colonel front and centre with another lady kneeling on the floor beside his seat.

'What's he holding?' Carrie tilted the photograph to catch the light. 'Her wrist? That's weird.'

It looked as though the Colonel had the woman's arm across his knees, her sleeve rucked up to the elbow. His big hands had closed around her elbow joint and her wrist, exposing her forearm to the camera. There was a mark on her arm that she couldn't make out. A bruise? A stain on the photograph?

'It's like a big game trophy photo,' Carrie muttered, thinking of the pictures she had seen on social media and the scenes in period dramas at the time of the British Raj. 'God, that's awful. What's he *doing*?' She scanned the photograph again for anyone else she knew. 'Mrs Varney would have been a kid then, wouldn't she?' There were three people with vintage-style dresses in the photograph, but Carrie couldn't make out who they were.

She chewed her lip.

'Do you know her?' she asked.

Fairwood's head, her scarred, gouged twin, lowered close to hers, his soft scent light and soothing. She filled her lungs with it, light-headed.

'No, I've never seen her,' Fairwood said finally. 'She looks familiar, but she never passed my gate, never set foot inside.'

'Yeah, you know, she looks familiar to me too,' Carrie said, trying to place the round, white face staring into the camera. 'I can't... It's her expression that's throwing me off, I think.' A chill trembled through her as she realised what it was. 'It's terror. Isn't it? She's terrified.'

Fairwood studied it. 'It is a look I've seen humans make,' he conceded, 'when they know they are going to die.'

Carrie gripped the edge of the table, digging in her nails. Had Phil had that expression on his face when Ricky Porter came for him in the night? Locked in a cellar for hours, not knowing what was coming?

'I could have saved him,' she whispered, staring at the photograph without seeing the faces. 'I should've… I should've gone down there…'

'He knew you wouldn't.'

Carrie shook her head. 'No, I – how, how would he know that?' She caught up with her own train of thought. 'Oh. Right. Farsight.' She rubbed her forehead. 'He said it like he didn't care. He didn't. It didn't matter, whatever he said, he knew I wasn't going to…' She swallowed, a shiver setting her limbs quaking. 'What about the police? Can we trust him, can we… they'll know, they'll come round, won't they know? If I tell them to ask Ricky, they'll just know, won't they?' She couldn't think. 'They'll know it's me. I did it.'

'You did nothing,' Fairwood said, trying to comfort her.

'Exactly! I did *nothing*.' Carrie couldn't stop shaking. She started to laugh. 'I did… nothing! I might as well have, I'm an accessory, right, I knew! I knew there was someone down there, and I walked out and *left him to die*. His blood's in my hall…' She couldn't stop. The laughter bubbled out, dark and ugly. The tea wrapped itself around her brain, soothing scent driving out the guilt little by little.

Her doppelganger circled behind her chair, wrapping solid arms around her. Carrie was pinned to the chair, choking on her laughter as it devolved into manic sobs. Was it relief? Horror? Shock? Nothing? Maybe it was the tea, but everything was ebbing into numbness. Fairwood encircled her, comforting, enclosing her all around with warmth and solidity. 'They, they, they'll take me away, a-way from here,' she choked out, trying to breathe as a new spike of terror undid the tea's good work. 'They, they'll take – take me away, they'll take me—'

'You're safe,' Fairwood creaked gently. 'You're safe here. No one can take you from me. They won't find him. He knows what he's doing, does little Richard Porter.' That sounded like a quote. It chilled her.

'What do I do?' she whispered, closing her eyes, safe in her small dark space. '*Tell me what to do.*' Her face throbbed where she'd fallen, the ache pulsing through the bone.

'Find out who killed Cathy, who polluted my stones and left her there. Give me my revenge. And you'll be safe, and you can be with me, and they won't take you away.'

Carrie huddled into the safety Fairwood offered, letting it soothe her. 'Promise?'

'Promise?'

'Like a contract. Will you make a contract with me? Do you promise?'

Fairwood considered. 'Yes.'

'You're mine.'

'Yes. And you are mine.'

Carrie nodded, eyes screwed tight. 'Yes.'

She forced herself to relax, as Fairwood held her lightly. When she opened her eyes, the photograph on the table arrested her attention, drawing her into something else, something untainted by Phil or her old life.

'I wonder if there're more copies of this photograph? Maybe the Colonel has one?' Her voice was too bright. It didn't fool her.

'The Colonel has nothing of mine,' Fairwood said. 'I can't help you.'

The kernel of a plan began to form in Carrie's mind as she dragged herself into this pressing problem. 'Then we'll have to get you in there, won't we,' she muttered.

Victory is Mine

In which Part One of Ricky's prophecy is fulfilled
05–06 May

On Saturday, the soothsayer moved into the cellar. He came via the smugglers' tunnel and frightened the ghost into hiding. Carrie didn't mind that: she hoped he would keep to himself. He didn't bother to talk to her all day, but she could hear his gruff, low voice carrying on a one-sided conversation when she opened the utility room door. At least, it sounded like a one-sided conversation until she tried to catch the actual words, and then it was garbled nonsense. He was speaking Old English, to himself mainly, but although muffled, the repeated Modern English phrase 'eight days' made it up to her ears like a chant.

He didn't come up to eat or say hello, but she could hear him scraping things across the cellar floor until she went to bed.

Against her better judgement and the repeated warnings not to drink it, the only thing that worked for the guilt and the nausea was Ricky's mystery tea. Its calming numbness spread over her mind and left her fearless, her stomach settled, her mind blissfully blank. The white noise of anxiety and guilt reverberating in the background of her life died and went silent. Fortified by its calming balm, Carrie rang Ann just to hear her stepmother's voice, and they talked about her dad's health and curtain fabric and where Carrie was spending Christmas, while Cathy Ross dripped ectoplasm down the chimney breast behind her and the serial killer from the woods made himself at home under her feet.

Sunday was meant to be her shift to work, but Pauline called and said they didn't need her. Zero-hour contracts were a bitch.

Carrie was already halfway into town, so she carried on walking in and decided to visit the library instead.

The library was instantly welcoming, a building designed to help you forget about the outside world, an escapist luxury in beige and cinnamon. The glass foyer glinted out onto the central square, opposite the town's morgue, a palatial building that also housed the council offices on the upper stories. The library seemed a tad embarrassed by the ostentatiousness of its neighbour, its own Georgian features heavily remodelled in a modest, accessible fashion. There was a small counter selling coffee and snacks, a seating area replete with charging points, and three floors of books. The town records, Carrie was informed, were on the Lower Ground floor.

Chest fluttering, Carrie's alarm bells were jangling all at once with nothing to pull the cord. The librarian was an elderly retiree and perfectly lovely. There was not a shade of judgement in her voice, not a question mark around the makeup covering the latest bruises, not a whisper of gossip about her house or her neighbour or the man her neighbour had (most recently) killed.

Carrie asked about the History Society records and whether there were back copies of the *Pagham-on-Sea Gazette*, and headed to the Lower Ground, where there was nobody to be seen or heard and the air was soft with old leather, sleeping pages and clean carpet. The idea of talking to anyone or asking for help filled her with low-level dread, despite the tea.

Must go to the doctor's, can't go on like this, Ricky said the tea wasn't a replacement.

The newspapers were on microfilm, right at the back of the reading area. Fortunately, most were digitised, and the library computers had a subscription to their digital repository. She did a quick search for names, starting with Col. Mark Curtis.

It came up with three hits: the first was a report on the History Society being (temporarily) disbanded in 1943, after its sixtieth anniversary. Carrie blinked. Clicking through, she was directed to the highlighted section of the scanned paper, where a photograph of the remaining members stared sombrely out at her.

This must be some mistake: Col. Mark Curtis, Roman nose and all, was front and centre of the group with a man the caption named as Lionel Bishop. It was undoubtedly the same Mark Curtis that she had met at the History Society, but that couldn't be possible.

There behind him were another three familiar faces, faces she recognised from Beverley's living room. The Pendle sisters, Mrs Wend, Mrs Foreman, and Mrs Shaw. There were others, too, surnames she vaguely recognised.

Carrie changed her search.

She looked for any reference to Mrs Wend, and the *Gazette* obliged with a number of hits including another two pictures. One was a flower show, also in 1943, the headline proudly stating *The Show Must Go On!*

According to the article, Eileen Foreman had won first prize for her black roses for the fifth year in a row. Eglantine Valmai Pritchard, Tina Harris's formidable ancestress, had come second, and (oh dear) Beverley Wend had taken third.

How old was Mrs Wend really?

The picture showed three unsmiling women clearly uncomfortable with standing next to one another. Eileen Foreman was, again, recognisable from the portrait hanging in Wundorwick, a determined, proud jaw raised above her trophy, a woman in her thirties. Miss Pritchard was a large, stout woman of middle age, severely clad in tweed with her hair piled in a no-nonsense bun. Tina had certainly inherited her physique. Mrs Wend looked the most displeased with her prize, piercing gaze staring straight out of the photograph at Carrie as if to say, *What are you looking at, dear?*

Carrie hastily clicked back and checked the other photograph. This was from 1998 and had something about a charity bake sale record.

Carrie changed 'Wend' to 'Pendle' and tried again.

This time, only one picture.

Carrie clicked on it and nearly fell off her chair.

There, from 11 June 1888, in a piece on the inaugural Pagham-on-Sea flower show, was the same photograph Carrie had spotted in Beverley's living room. ("*I was eighteen there, Beverley Pendle I was then…*")

A young girl in a straw boater standing by a rose bush, a malevolent smile of secret knowledge on her face. Beverley Pendle, then a budding gardener, and winner of the Best Rose in Show.

Carrie closed her search and stood up so abruptly she nearly knocked over her chair. This explained something, but she had no idea what. She either needed a stiff drink or something sticky-sweet to shove in her face. The tea wasn't cutting it.

Grabbing her bag, she headed out into the open air, practically jogging across the street to the Sandbox Café where Rich and Jerry Ashdown's homemade muffins would smother some of the insanity with their salted caramel filling.

Ricky had said something about a youth rite, hadn't he? Well, the Colonel looked exactly the same in 1943 as he did now, but he wasn't *young*. Was he undead, or immortal, or what? And what the hell did this have to do with anything? A bunch of immortals or gods or whatever they were converging in a perfect storm, all to kill a little girl in 1958 and reap the eldritch rewards? What were the rewards? Longer life? Why kill Cathy Ross? Convenience? *Where was her tongue?*

She ordered a coffee and a muffin from the owner, Richard Ashdown, while his husband Jerry gave her a wave and started getting her order ready, hoping they wouldn't ask about the bruises under her makeup or try and chat. She didn't have the capacity today.

She retreated to a corner table with a limited view of the street and wished she'd bought about five more muffins.

Ricky hadn't seemed remotely bothered by the idea his gran or her sisters were responsible. Although, he had abducted and tortured a total stranger to death for his mother's pies and some bloody ritual, so why on earth would a dead child up a chimney bother him?

No – not just any stranger, although that was bad enough. Phil.

He'd abducted and tortured Phil. The man she'd lived with for four years.

It was the stab of relief that prompted the guilt.

Carrie rubbed the less tender side of her face, wishing she hadn't made that connection. The tea was wearing off. The enormity of what he had done was returning to haunt her.

She shoved the muffin in her mouth and the first bite hit her tongue with an explosion of rich, sweet heaven.

Energies.

What was it Ricky had said about energies? Channelling them, opening something... she nearly had it, it was close, a whispered suggestion out of earshot. No. She didn't have it yet.

Energies.

Something jolted through her, a static charge, sending the café spinning out of reach then snapping back into focus.

Whoa, love, what just happened?

Carrie blinked. Absently, she rubbed her midriff where some memory pressed against her skin.

I feel different, what happened?

Her phone rang – an unknown number.

She answered it without worrying about who was on the other end.

'Yeah?'

'Hi, is this Caroline?'

'Yeah, who's this?' She grabbed her coat, folding it over one arm.

'Um, this is awkward, it's, it's Tom? Tom Hoskins, Phil's cousin? I don't know if you remember, we met a couple of times...'

'Oh, sure, Tom, hi.' She waved at Richard, heading for the door. 'How are you?'

'Um, I'm fine, thank you, but, this is a bit awkward, it's just that Phil didn't show up at work today and, long story short, his mum's been calling me so I – I know he left ours and he, well, I overheard him on the phone leaving you a voicemail message…'

'I got that, yeah, but I don't know where he is,' Carrie said, voice steady as a rock, telling the absolute truth. 'You know what, he did come by, but we've got nothing to talk about and he didn't stay. My neighbour might have seen him go, want me to give you his address? They don't have a phone, I don't think.'

'Oh, right. Yeah, sure, I'll get a pen.'

Carrie wandered down the street, expecting the guilt to hit any moment, but it didn't. Something in the back of her mind, some tiny voice, whispered from the void, *This is wrong. Something's wrong with us.*

'Okay,' Tom said, after some muffled rummaging.

'It's Bramble Cottage, Redditch Lane, Pagham-on-Sea.'

There was dead silence.

Tom hung up.

Carrie smirked, the relief crashing back, but the flotsam of remorse and fear was nowhere to be felt or found.

Like magic, she thought, *Ricky was dead right. Dead, ha.*

What's wrong with me?

Nothing, it's – what's it called, acclimatisation.

She waited for the bus at the stop and was almost offended when she had to pay.

–

The ritual was done.

She was out, of course, but that was fine, he hoped she'd stay out long enough for him to clean the eyeballs off her kitchen counter. Gerald would have liked them, but they were necessary for this last bit. He had folded his clothes up on the table, knowing the full-body Change was close.

Fairwood had completely accepted him. The Pendle Stone was attached to the house, as much a part of it as all the other bits cobbled together, all of it adding layers of life and personality, all of it now one cohesive whole. His energies flowed through it, and he was now a part of her, a part of them both, though it was getting hard to see where Fairwood ended and Carrie Rickard began.

The house spoke to him now, whispering to him like it did to her.

Ricky sank to his knees in rapturous delight, head lifted to the ceiling, letting her speak in all her voices, her rooms, her whispers. He choked on joy. This was all he had wanted, all he had ever wanted, ever since she'd called to him through the trees and then wouldn't let him in.

(It wasn't personal, it was never personal.)

His guts gave a sudden, painful twist.

The skin over his stomach stretched transparent-thin, sweat beading through his pores, dry heat filling him up. Smoke purled through his mouth, ash coating his throat, the taste of his own flesh burning up inside him, paired with the rusty tang of his own hot blood. For a moment there was no more pain.

The front door opened and shut.

Her footsteps made him smile. She would be the first to see him Change. That felt fair, somehow.

'Oh my God, Ricky!'

Her hand reeked of processed sugars, but he tried not to show his distaste.

'Good, you got here,' he managed, as the split reached his throat. 'Not – not long.'

'What's happening?'

(Oh, she was doing it again, stroking his head, the decadence, that delicious, edible feeling, flowing through him, corrupting like sepsis.)

He rolled his eyes back, pressing his head into her hand. His guts ached, the Changes rolling and breaking in feverish waves.

'It hurts,' he moaned, another knife-twist wrenching something free that shouldn't be. 'Fuck me, it bloody *hurts*...' He looked down: his stomach bulged, skin in two flaps like an unbuttoned shirt, draped uselessly over an amniotic sac of anaconda coils. Mucus coated his hands as he tried to hold himself together, hands he didn't recognise as his.

(*His, or hers? Was there a difference? Can't tell, can't see, can't feel anymore.*)

'Ricky, what do I do? What's happening?'

His eyelashes fluttered involuntarily as he forced himself to focus on her face, and it took him a moment to realise why she appeared to be strobing.

(*What's that? Never seen that expression before. She worried, or what?*)

(*they call it 'concern'.*)

(*You in here too? Bloody hell, head's getting crowded, head's bursting.*)

That was a conscious thought too far. The pressure-pain shot into his skull, breaking over his brain beneath the bone. Thought evaporated. Skin split. Nerves screamed, wrenched apart. Synapse flares dotted his blank-eyed vision, turned in on himself, inside-out, ripped open. Things crunched into place.

He threw off his old name with his old skin, both too small for him now. They lay discarded on the kitchen floor as he stretched, setting his monstrous beauty free. At last, it tasted the air, opened its third eye, saw the glory of the wyrd as plainly as the dancing constellations of the sun-robbed sky.

He couldn't see Fairwood's wyrd: perhaps things were different for houses, even sentient ones. He looked instead for its essence, such a small thing, and there it was: a fragile, coal-dark glow, gleaming with oil-slick brilliance in the heart of the house.

He drew it into himself, absorbing it through the angles of his new existence. He had waited so long to answer the siren-call that drew him there. He had overcome the cruel curse that kept him from it, and now he was restored with it, both of them, beautiful.

(*Who did that?*)

Caroline Rickard was glowing like an ember, rivers of energy passing through her in the full spectrum of reds and oranges, vermillion bleeding into gilded tangerine, ice-blue-edged with the crackle of fear.

He was meshed with Fairwood, and Fairwood was intertwined with her. Still distinguishable, the way a climbing plant can be disentangled from a trellis, but if she was not careful, she would take root like ivy and then the disentangling would cut her free from the source of her life and being.

He saw into the threads of her wyrd, weaving before his eyes, speeding towards the infinite.

He saw what was coming, where it ended, where the final thread was cut, and as it crystallised in his mind so did something else, a forbidden thought, a deep, taboo desire.

He wanted to change it.

The wyrd bucked like a billowing curtain, throwing him down and out.

His beautiful, living, rippling skin shrank around him and bled out human dermis. Raw pink patches of new skin constricted, cling film-tight, dripping gelatinous residue as it leaked from the inside out. The world spun away, the kitchen solidified, reality returned to its usual number of dimensions. His limbs bound themselves to the usual number. He was naked and alone, shivering in the enormity of the universe.

Carrie was staring at him, covering her mouth with both hands, wide-eyed. He hadn't noticed the colours in them before, the flecks of green and ochre in the irises.

'It's bloody cold in here,' he croaked, gathering up his old skin-rags without any clear idea of what to do with them.

Carrie lowered her hands, pale with shock. She looked him over, lingering in several places south of his face. 'Oh my *God*. How... how can you be *that*? Where did— There were *coils with fucking faces in*— where— *Je-sus*.' She stopped. 'Do you... want to put your clothes back on?'

He remembered he'd been naked when she came in. No sense ripping his only clothes in the Change.

'Good thought.'

He handed her the old skin and she stood holding it in both hands as if she'd never seen a human shed before.

He dressed, wiping himself over with a tea towel as he dressed.

'What d'you think?' he asked.

Carrie held out the skin-rags.

(*Ah, his old skin would go well with the waste bags he'd saved when she was in that coma… two ingredients for something exciting that he'd find a good use for.*)

He grinned, taking it back from her.

'Well?'

She stared, stunned. A fair response.

He thought she needed some encouragement. 'Beautiful, ain't I?'

'*Beautiful?*' Carrie spat the word out like a rotten grape, her voice shaking. 'My God, Ricky that was *horrific.*'

Something writhed, unfamiliar, in his chest. (*No, familiar — bringing back thoughts of childhood, of family, of…*)

Carrie was watching his face, and she changed tack. 'I mean, majestic, yes, impressive—'

'Really?' The writhing wasn't physical. He couldn't control it. It surged up to his throat in a hard lump like his grandmother's trifle. He swallowed it back down, but it brought tears to his eyes. (*Fuck me, not this again.*)

'Really.' She let out a shaky breath, took a step towards him, and tentatively held out her arms. He eyed her, askance, but remembered on the lawn where she had held him, flung herself at him without a weapon or a curse, pressed herself into his chest and gripped his neck like a noose. This seemed less violent, and at least it was an offer this time.

His new skin tingled.

'Do I look the same?' he asked, inching closer. 'Do I look… like the old me?'

She nodded. Her eyes were wet too, pink with shock and, he hoped, regret at her first reaction. He could tell she was sorry for not seeing the beauty in him, but mistakes were to be learned from. She would see it the second time.

'You look great,' she said, dampness leaking into her voice.

(*You did that. You frightened her.*)

Even Fairwood sounded like him now. He accepted the admonishment and frowned.

'Bloody hell, love, come here.' He gave in to the lure of someone's touch on his new skin, but also in response to Fairwood's reprimand. Beauty could be frightening.

To his surprise she crumpled into him, shaking, but he didn't touch her in return. His grandmother had been the last to hug him, but that had been a long time ago.

'Your clothes smell,' she said, muffled, warm against his neck.

His grandmother still said this. He gave her the stock answer, not knowing where to put his hands. 'I'll wash 'em.'

He settled for patting her back twice and dropping his arms to his sides, but she didn't let go.

She was heron-slender, vixen-light. His mother would love to have her for her own, her own daughter-that-never-was, sit her in the chair in front of the dressing mirror and nail her hands to it when she fidgeted, and brush her hair for hours and hours until all the gold in it was spun cobweb-fine and she wasted away into beautiful bones.

But she'd be dead soon, anyway.

'Will you do the, the, you know.' His tongue disobeyed, colour rising to his cheeks.

She looked at him, uncomprehending.

He tried again, the writhing back, but this time of a different nature. 'The – you know, when you stroke my head like you do, I don't dislike it, I said I didn't.' He knew he was mumbling.

She stroked his head. Ripples of childish pleasure ran through him. His mother only stroked his head when she wanted something. The luxury was intoxicating.

He closed his eyes.

(*Who'll do this when she's dead? One week left, I can't change her wyrd, it can't be changed.*)

She pressed against his chest, the length of her warm through the fabric. Her arm was around his ribs, under his arm, her hand on his back. His mother had tried this once, not willing to take another dose, lured him in with affection and tried to stab him in the lung.

(*She don't have a knife, does she? She wouldn't.*)

The palm flat, splayed, unarmed, a star in the middle of his spine.

(*What's she doing?*)

Her breath caressed his chin. He could drink it.

He opened his eyes.

Carrie's were an ocean of hazel- and green-flecked blue, her eyelashes ruffled, skin masked with makeup that gave it a more even tone and hid the contusions administered by the fireplace. He could see her contours in detail, the true shape and the shape marred by puffiness, the light swelling spoiling the line of her cheek.

(Careful *with her, she's all flesh and fibre, not brick and stone.*)

(*She's so close, hell's bells and buckets of blood, she's so close, what do I do?*)

He froze.

Carrie gave him a smile of steel, kissed him once on the cheek like his never-sister as if to prove she wasn't afraid after all, and gave his head a final stroke. The chaste, firm brush of her lips set his face on fire.

'There. How's that?'

He released a breath.

'Yeah. That's all right.'

She took his hand in hers. 'Okay. Do you want to just… leave things here a minute, come into the other room, and we can – sit. Relax. I'll put the telly on, if you watch it, I don't know, or we could read or something. Can we just do that for a minute? Nothing eldritch, nothing – weird, nothing… involving tentacles?'

'I don't think they're tentacles,' he mumbled.

She cocked an eyebrow at him. 'I've got a ghost to worry about, mate, and a dead ex-boyfriend, can we not split hairs about your anatomy until after it's properly sunk in?'

He nodded. 'Not a word about this,' he warned. 'I don't want anyone knowing, not yet.'

'Okay.' She led him through into the living room, switched the television on, and flopped onto the sofa in what seemed like one fluid movement. He hesitated, but she grabbed a cushion and plumped it on her lap.

He grunted, misliking the flickering thing demanding their attention. Settling on the sofa with his back to it, he rested his head on the cushion so that his second mouth faced the screen, and, lulled into a doze by her gentle touch on his head, his eyes grew heavy enough for him to sleep.

Part 3

09–13 May

Deal with the Devil

In which Carrie gets off the hook and Ricky is useful

09 May

A full week had passed since the séance, and Phil had been 'missing' for six days. The gnawing in her stomach never went away. She had made no progress with the tongue search, but other things, driven by guilt and anxiety, sucked at her attention like a black hole. Like: what to tell the police when they came to interview her. What to say to her mum, how to tell her dad. If she should pack up and go, leave, take part of the house with her... but she couldn't do that.

Her money worries were temporarily put on hold, at least; Blackberry Antiques, a converted railway shed near Barker Crescent, had thrown her a lifeline in the form of enough cash to pay that month's bills, and there were more antiques in the well. Fairwood's avatar had reclaimed a few Charles II snuff boxes, and they occasionally appeared on the kitchen table oozing mud and slime. That was about the only thing going right.

The funny thing about keeping a secret of this magnitude, Carrie discovered, was that it didn't press against you *all* the time. At first, it was a bubble of disclosure waiting to burst behind her lips, as if her reply to an unexpected 'hello' would be, 'I'm housing a murderer!' and it would tumble out in the chipper, fake-chirpy tone she seemed to be adopting for all her interactions. Then hours would pass, and she'd forget.

She had gone to the doctors on Monday, a redbrick building on Mill Street where the surgery and pharmacy were down some steep steps, into a blindingly white corridor where she had half-expected to encounter a human centipede or something worse, but all that had happened was an appointment scheduled with Dr Monday in two weeks' time. She couldn't focus on learning any more about the history of the house, the ghost, or anything else.

One truth kept haunting her, dragging her into a spiral of guilt: her life was better without Phil in it.

She didn't watch the news all week, afraid of facing his mother's storm of grief and some heartfelt appeal, but the truth was missing persons rarely made the news. People disappeared from their lives all the time. The officer who interviewed her had probed the issue of debt and Phil's propensity to run out on his obligations. (What could she say? She told the truth.)

Mercy had invited her to the pub, and Carrie said yes, desperate to seem normal.

Then, on Wednesday, at three in the morning, as Fairwood breathed rhythmically in the deep hush of the night, Carrie's phone rang.

She peeled her eyes open, squinting at the flashing colours marring the peaceful darkness, assuming it was her alarm. The small inner voice woke first, scrabbling for a handle on the situation.

Oh God, what now, why's it, dark what's happening?

She fumbled the screen, not sure why it wouldn't turn off and why it sounded different. It wasn't the alarm, it was her ringtone.

Struggling up and turning on the lamp, a lance of pain shooting into her sleepy eyes, she managed to answer it before it went to voicemail.

'Hel—' she croaked, sandpaper-tongue sluggish, and cleared her throat. 'Hm! He-llo?'

'Carrie? Sorry to wake you. It's Tom. Tom Hoskins.' The voice was slurred, unsteady.

Carrie rubbed her face, avoiding the healing bruises. 'Tom?' (Phil's cousin.)

'The police were round this, this afternoon – they asked me if Phil had been violent to you that I knew of. Said, said they'd been over to see you.'

(*You never checked when Phil and I were together, did you Tommy? Never bothered once in all that time.*)

Carrie touched the last vestiges of bruising on her cheek.

'It's five past three,' she mumbled, remembering the police visit the day before. She thought she had done well, been as honest as she could (no need to lie, they would find out what a piece of work he was soon enough if they asked around), reiterated, in particular, that he owed money to some fairly nasty people. 'What's this really about? I couldn't tell them any more than I told you.' A jolt of adrenaline shocked her into clarity. 'Have they... found him yet?' (Ricky had said he'd been thorough, not even a forensics team would find a thing.)

'No.'

Relief flooded back.

A beat.

'He's not coming back, is he?' Tom slurred.

Carrie didn't know what to say. There was a moment of silence that stretched beyond the small glow of her lamp into the haunted shadows, falling away into a void of wordless guilt.

Then Tom sighed. 'Well, thank fuck for that,' he said, and hung up.

Not the epitaph Phil had wanted, Carrie guessed, but certainly the one he deserved. She held the phone to her ear for a few seconds, tapping the hard edge against her temple, her mind a dull blank.

I'm changing, she thought. *I'm different, somehow.*

A prickling washed over the side of her face as she put the phone back on the table. The duvet inched off her legs, tugged towards the floor by a small, invisible hand. Carrie snatched at it before her legs were completely exposed, tugging it back.

Something reached up from under her bed, a small, bony arm, pale and bloodless, hand buried under the bedclothes, groping over the top sheet for her ankle.

Carrie jerked her knees up under her chin, throwing the duvet off.

There was nothing there.

'Cut that out,' she ordered, trembling. 'It's three in the morning, stop it.'

There was a heavy, pregnant silence. It was not the silence of an empty room.

'I'm not looking under the bed,' Carrie said. 'Forget it. Go haunt the attic or something.'

She thought she heard a small sigh, a childish pout, and felt a tug at the corner of her undersheet.

'No! Stop it! All right, look, I'm *trying* okay, I'm looking for your tongue, I'm making progress, I promise…'

Something slithered underneath the rug, and a tube of lipstick dropped off her desk onto the floor.

'Okay, so I'm not doing very well, but I've got a job and… look, why don't you show Ricky your arms?' Carrie asked, rubbing the sleep out of her eyes. 'Maybe he'll know what the marks mean.'

There was a low hissing from the floorboards, and Carrie could make out a pale shape crouching under her chair, eyes burning in the darkness.

Another presence made itself felt, visible out of the corner of her eye, and the ghost slithered away with a soft hiss through the floor. Carrie whipped around to face the open door (*it was shut, I was sure I shut it*), and saw a figure in the dark.

Ricky was standing in the doorway, tendrils forming frond-like antlers over his head.

Carrie tried to swallow, recalling the Thing that had burgeoned through Ricky Porter's human skin in her kitchen, the creature of pulsing sapwood in eel-slick skin, peppered with round, scavenging mouths and all-seeing entomic eyes.

He was human and naked.

Good God, he's fit.

Of course he was. Moving bodies was hard work. She filed the observation away, unexpected spark of libido dying a quick death.

'How long have you been there?' she whispered.

He shrugged. 'Can't sleep.'

'Why are you naked?'

'What d'you mean? It's how I sleep. Or try to. Who was that?'

Carrie sighed.

'That was Tom. Phil's cousin.'

Ricky came in a little way, shadows playing over the contours of his humanoid body.

'What's the matter?' she asked.

His tendrils retreated with a slippery suck. The cherry-red of his eyes glowed. 'Nothing. Bellyache, that's all.'

He did look bloated, but it was hard to tell.

'Have you been at the frozen stuff?' Carrie's food budget was not lasting her as long as she needed it to, despite the antiques' sales. She had another cheque to go out for the window, and Joe Lin wasn't cheap. 'You're meant to defrost it.'

Ricky rolled his eyes, their eerie red glow producing an almost comical effect. 'Yeah, I know how a freezer works. I can feed myself.' He rubbed his stomach, coming all the way up to her bed. 'You got mice down there, you know that? They're a right treat, they are.'

'Bloody hell.' She made space for him to sit on the edge if he wanted, but instead, before she could protest, he pulled the edge of the duvet up and over himself, curling up beside her.

Carrie stiffened, stomach flipping.

'Oi! You can't just—' She shuffled away as the mattress depressed, threatening to tip her closer towards him. 'What the hell are you doing?'

He sniffed, making himself comfortable. His cold skin sucked the heat out of her.

'What's it look like I'm doing? Trying to get some bloody sleep.'

'Don't sound so bloody hard done by, you can't just – my God, you can't just— What is *wrong* with you?'

He rolled over, the red glowing in his eyes. 'Not allowed on the bloody furniture, am I? Richard Porter's an *outside* dog, is that what you mean?'

'You… you, you should at least *ask* first. For a start.'

'Oh.'

He turned onto his side with his back to her, the puckered lips at the back of his head firmly closed. Carrie stared at them, willing them to stay shut. He rolled over to face her, pressing his head into the top pillow and trying to get comfortable. 'I'll ask next time,' he said, muffled.

She gave up. 'Okay. Well. You do that.'

'It's cold and my belly aches.' He closed his eyes. 'Turn the light off, love.'

Carrie paused, then clicked off her lamp with bad grace. She lay rigid in the dark, next to the man, monster, Eldritch Thing that had killed her ex-boyfriend, dug out his spleen and kidneys, sliced him up while still alive and conscious.

Got rid of him.

She couldn't turn her back on him, but she didn't dare close her eyes either. As he relaxed, she heard his back lips part with a gentle smack, letting those muscular tendrils go slithering across the floor. He relinquished her duvet and let her take some back, draping an arm across her waist: an oddly familiar pressure. He grunted and shifted closer. Carrie wrinkled her nose and ducked under the stream of his fetid breath.

'God, you smell like a massacre in a pet shop.'

He chuckled and deliberately exhaled, angling his chin to hit her full in the face.

Carrie gagged in disgust and pushed him away.

'Eugh. No. You're not – you *have* to *ask* me before you do shit like this. How would you like it if I invaded your space without asking? Without any clothes on?'

'It's your house, ain't it? You do what you want. Anyway, I seen you without clothes on, that time with the flowers. You look basically the same.' Giggling to himself, he rolled away and back again, settling with her wrapped up close against him, a comforting dry heat generating between them. Carrie gave up and tucked her head under his chin, trying to figure out what to do with her other arm before the inevitable onslaught of pins and needles. It wasn't like he was going to *do* anything, and she'd probably wake up with all her organs.

That's not the point.

Her inner voice tried to make itself heard, but Ricky's energy was overpowering it.

This is fine, everything's normal, it's fine.

Carrie relaxed.

Eventually, they found a mutually least-awkward position with him on his back holding her into his bony chest, and Carrie wondered if he would consume her in the night, open up along his seam and absorb her whole. He gave her a small squeeze, as if testing her, trying to see if she was real, or really there. She felt like a living teddy-bear.

His belly groaned, bubbling with whatever disgusting furry cocktail he'd over-indulged in. Carrie rubbed the part of it she could reach, and he flinched away from her.

'Does that hurt?' she whispered.

'No.'

'Do you want me to stop touching you?'

He shook his head, keeping his eyes closed. His grip got firmer around her waist, as if he was steeling himself. She pressed her hand to his stomach again, his innards shifting under her palm.

He flinched when I touched his head, too, she remembered.

'Is... is that *nice*?' she tried again.

Ricky made a little gruff noise of assent, cracked and dry, the sound an oak would make if it could purr.

This is nuts, you know this is nuts.

Her inner voice managed one more opinion before it sank back into oblivion, and Carrie found herself following suit, sleep lapping at her consciousness and pulling her down. She stroked

Ricky's bare human skin until her dreams reclaimed her, soothing her own fears and what lay dormant underneath.

10 May

A few hours later, not too long after the dawn crept between the curtains, Carrie's alarm went off.

Fairwood had entered her dreams again in a form it knew she liked, her soothing protector, chasing away ghosts and shadows. It reminded her of the day they met, when she was hiding her cracks and fissures behind a brittle smile and it was a ruined effigy on a bed of weeds, waiting for her live-giving kiss. It enfolded her in its arms, hers forever, and as the alarm rang the weed-strewn bier fragmented beneath them into the wishing well, glittering like stained glass in their descent into its depths.

She woke pressed into Ricky's chest, wrapped up in a possessive embrace and cuddled against him like a favourite toy. Carrie stayed put for a moment, her alarm running out of steam and snoozing itself for five minutes. Ricky wasn't Fairwood – wasn't close. His chest rose and fell in a gentle snore, rocking her back into drowsiness.

She tapped his stomach to wake him up, but that seemed to have settled in the night. He smiled in his sleep, brow unfurrowed, deep in the undeserved rest of the clean-living innocent. She knew exactly what would wake him up: it felt mean, but a quick lesson in why boundaries were important wouldn't hurt him. She leaned in and planted a deliberate kiss on his cheek.

His eyes shot open.

Carrie recoiled as far as she could, trapped by his embrace.

Ricky realised he was holding onto her and let her go. He stared around the room, raising himself up on his elbows, remembered where he was, and dropped back down. 'Bloody hell, don't do that. What's the time?'

'Seven.'

'Fuck that.'

234

Carrie snorted. 'Aren't you an ascetic? Early mornings should be right up your street.'

'Yeah. Well.' He stretched, reached for her, and pulled her back down onto him. 'I fancy a little lie-in.'

Carrie settled back, warm and painfully aware how much she'd missed having someone there. Some*thing*. She found herself holding him tighter as she yawned.

'You should get yourself back out there,' Ricky said, placid from a good night's sleep. 'If you're a bit, you know. Frustrated. I could introduce you to Cousin Wes. He bats for whichever team'll have him.'

'I'm not—'

He shushed her, getting comfortable against the pillows. 'Five minutes.' He twitched his knee. 'And don't think that's for you, it just does that some mornings.'

He's not.

Carrie turned her head to stare down beyond his belly, burning with awkward, illicit curiosity.

Oh God, yes, he is.

She masked her discomfort with humour. 'Sure it's not just acclimatising?'

'Don't tease.' He frowned with his eyes shut. 'Are you teasing? I'm not good at... I'm not used to it. Gerald doesn't tease.'

'Who's Gerald?' Carrie asked, imagining another cousin.

Ricky tensed. 'Nobody.' He answered too fast, the tell of a terrible liar or a guilty man.

Carrie pulled away and gave him some space. 'It's okay, it's none of my business.'

Ricky grimaced. 'He – he ain't real, it's not... it's silly.'

'D'you mean like... an imaginary friend?' She could picture that. 'I used to have those when I was a kid. It's pretty normal for only children.'

'No,' Ricky drew his knees up and half sat, edging away from her. 'Not – he's not imaginary. He's just not real. It's stupid.'

Something clicked – the way he'd held onto her in the night, like a doll.

235

'*Oh*. Is he a – is Gerald a… toy? Like a teddy?'

'I made him.' Ricky couldn't look at her. 'Made him when I was ten, so he's not very good. I got better at the stitching and the stuffing, the skinning and that. He's had a few new limbs, hands, that sort of thing. Can't seem t'get rid of him. I still, um, still talk to him sometimes, you know. I know it's stupid.'

'It's not stupid.' Carrie didn't want to imagine what Gerald might be made of. 'I have a few teddies from when I was a kid. Look.' She pointed to the top of her wardrobe. The fluffy teddy with *I Love You* stitched into its large paws sat on the top, gathering dust. 'Mum got me that when I was, I don't know, five? I slept with it every night until I was thirteen, and that was only because we moved house and I lost her for a bit.' She watched him coming around, saw him struggling to believe her. 'I was devastated. Mum had moved out by then, so that made it worse. We found her in a box Dad had shoved in the garage.'

Ricky glanced shyly at her. 'My father said I was too old for him at twelve. Said he'd burn him.' His smile twisted in an echo of his grandmother's malevolence. 'I didn't let him, though.'

'Have you brought him here?' Carrie wondered what exactly was lurking in her cellars. 'I wouldn't mind.'

'I wasn't going to leave him *there*,' Ricky murmured. 'Brought him through the smuggler's tunnel. You can come and see him, if you like.'

Carrie held his gaze. 'Sure.'

Ricky studied her with the intensity of a naturalist who had found himself beside a rare and possibly rabid creature and wasn't sure what to do next.

He cleared his throat. 'All right.'

They got out of bed, kicking off the tangle of shared sheets.

Carrie followed him downstairs, Fairwood still peaceful and protective in the early morning light. Ricky was whistling a birdcall she didn't recognise. He looked over his bare shoulder and grinned.

The trapdoor to the coal cellar was open – Carrie felt its muted malevolence at the threshold to the utility room, that dark part of Fairwood's soul that needed soothing or catharsis.

'What happened down there?' she asked, as Ricky, still naked, padded down the narrow stone steps into the darkness.

'The cellar? It's where one of the Sauvants liked to call up things from Beyond. Nasty, ain't she? Bitter. You can feel it, can't you?'

Carrie hugged herself, thin pyjamas not warm enough for the chill in the air. It stank of week-old meat and old leather.

Ricky tugged at the dangling cord and the single forty-watt bulb glowed into life.

'There we are.'

He had brought, as promised, very little. A few dirty blankets were piled in one corner in a ragged nest, a fold-up worktable taking up space along one wall, bearing the weight of a few boxes.

'What're those?'

Ricky padded to where his grey, shapeless clothes were folded on the floor and slipped them on. She tried not to look as he dressed, the tracksuit and threadbare hoody clinging to him like another skin.

'Those? My knives, needles, stuff like that.'

He'd killed Phil with one or more of those, then. Her stomach flipped. Carrie turned her back on them, shivering, and came face to face with a broken nightmare.

Strapped to a wheel behind the door (how did he get it down here?) was a creature staring at her through Phil's eyes. She couldn't focus on the details at first – it was a composite sketch, mismatched and grotesque, yes, but whimsical – the kind of thing a horror-fascinated child might put together in a 'make your own Halloween monster' picture book of sliding tabs.

It towered above her, the deer-skull head one antler short and lolling, bloated leather body cracked with age and worn smooth in patches as broad as Ricky's forearms. Several animal skins formed its limbs, and a human had supplied the hands.

'This is… Gerald?' Carrie noticed the missing antler had been sheared off, snapped roughly from the base of the skull leaving a jagged spike.

'Yeah.' Ricky crossed the flagstones to stand behind her, hands on his hips. 'Haven't fixed him properly yet.'

Carrie stepped back, but Ricky didn't move. She knocked against him, his breath hot in her hair. 'You made him?' she asked, wondering why she wasn't scared.

His arm circled her with deliberate ownership, the way Phil had put his arm around her once, in front of an ex-girlfriend. 'Yeah. When I was a kid.'

Carrie figured it out at the same time Fairwood did.

The coal cellar, woken by the light, was unimpressed.

He's made a toy out of you.

Carrie shoved him off, and Ricky stumbled back, shocked.

'I never!' He protested, more to Fairwood than to her.

Wrapped himself around us, trying to take us over.

'I – that's not what I wanted…'

Carrie felt the rush of incendiary fury burning through her, coal-cold, coating her mind thick as charcoal ashes. Fairwood's darkest room found an outlet for its anger. The crypt beyond the thick walls sang out hymns of forgiveness and patience in vain. Carrie couldn't hear it.

'*Am I a toy to you?*'

Her voice scraped, guttural, over her throat.

Ricky shook his head in flat denial, the walls bucking around them in quickening beats. The table flew away from the wall and boxes tumbled to the floor, knives and cloth-rolls of needles spilling everywhere.

Gerald tipped forwards on his wheel as the wall pulsed behind him.

'Whoa! Whoa!' Ricky leapt to save the toppling Creature before it crushed Carrie. 'Watch it!'

Carrie jumped into the middle of the room below the swinging light bulb, shadows rotating around her.

'*You're a maggot in my belly, Richard Edwin Porter.*'

She didn't know why she said that.

Ricky forced the wheel back upright and leaned his weight against it, tendrils whipping out of the wrinkled lips and lashing across the room, missing her by inches.

'The fuck did you just say?'

Carrie was shaking. She couldn't stop. Every muscle spasmed out of her control.

'*No Pendle should set foot in this house.*'

'No, hang on, now wait, wait, *wait a minute...*' Ricky set Gerald safely upright and raised his hands, addressing the cellar and Carrie at once. 'I'm sorry, all right, I'm sorry, that what you want? I'm sorry!' He gestured at her and spoke to the ceiling. 'Look what you're doing to her, for fuck's sake, she can't take much more, leave her be!'

The anger washed out of her in a rush, taking her strength with it. She sank down onto the freezing stone, staring at him with residual hate. That, she was almost sure, was all her own.

'I'm *not* a toy,' she said, darting a glare at Gerald. 'I'm – you can't do that. I'm not, you can't, you can't *use* me like that.'

Ricky's lips parted, eyes wide. His tendrils floated above his head, writhing and knotting anxiously. 'I don't – I don't want to,' he mumbled, caught out like a naughty child. 'I don't *use*—'

'Don't lie, you're shit at it.' Carrie steeled herself and tried to stand. 'My God, Ricky, what have you done to us? You've... you're in my head, somehow. I'm not – I'm not *me*, I don't feel like me...'

'She's in there too,' Ricky pointed out, defensive. 'It ain't just me. And you're both in here—' he tapped his own forehead '—so stop making out like you're the only victims here. This wasn't what I signed up for, neither.' He folded his arms. 'Look, maybe it's just... taking a while to settle. Let's let it – let's give it a chance. Find our equilibrium. Bound to be teething troubles, right? No need to do anything drastic.'

'Like eviction?' Carrie wrapped her arms around herself and shuffled to the steps. 'Yeah, that would be bad for – oh, no, just one of us.'

'Yeah, all right, bloody hell.' He didn't touch her, but followed sheepishly up the steps.

'No, it's *not* all right. If you try and control us again, we're done.' Carrie realised that while some things that went without saying for everyone else, they apparently needed to be spelt out in neon letters for Ricky Porter. 'Boundaries. I have some. Stay out of my fucking head, and you can't just – I'm not your—' She lost track of what she wanted to say but made it to the washing machine so she could lean on it. 'You understand *why* we're pissed off, don't you?'

'Fine.' He faced her, pulling his hood up as the tendrils receded into the back of his skull. 'Look, let's call this probation, then, yeah? I know I'm pushy. I didn't mean to be. You're the boss. Give it six months.'

She wasn't sure if he was talking to her or the house, but she shook her head. 'Three.'

He didn't argue, which struck her as suspicious. 'Done. Three. Whatever you say. By then we'll have got a nice balance, and everyone will stay out of each other's heads, yeah?'

Carrie chewed her fingernail, forcing herself to relax, or at least to appear relaxed. He was watching her, eyes drawn to every little movement she made, as if he knew something she didn't.

'Okay.'

Ricky nodded. 'Deal?'

'Deal.' She shuddered one last time, stretched, and rubbed her face. 'God. I'll be late. Let's keep the ground rules in mind, yeah?'

'Yeah.' Ricky glanced down at his bare feet. 'Hey, look, I do owe you a favour still, if that'd smooth things over.'

Carrie side-eyed the trapdoor, where the cellar was still emanating distrust. 'Maybe.' A thought occurred to her and Fairwood at the same time. 'D'you think you can get a piece of Fairwood into Colonel Curtis's house? I don't know where he lives, but… I want to know what he's got to do with all of this bullshit.'

240

'Easy.' Ricky folded his arms. 'Course I can.' He paused. 'What's he got to do with anything?'

'He's… he's in the picture, too.'

Ricky's grin curved. 'What picture?'

'The—' Carrie frowned. 'This one.' She beckoned him into the kitchen and retrieved the picture Fairwood had rescued from Janet Varney's fireplace from a drawer. 'It's not… it's not great, but, that's the Colonel, isn't it?'

Ricky took it from her, squinting. 'What's this?'

'Janet had it. She tried to burn it. It's – I projected into her cottage, with Fairwood's avatar, and that's how I went into a trance and fainted or something.' She gestured at her healing bruises. 'You came over and told me about Phil, and I guess, I guess I didn't…' She couldn't remember the order things had happened in that day. That didn't feel right. She shook her head and let it go. He was grinning. 'Oh, God, have you – have you figured it out? You know something.'

Ricky licked his lips and handed the photograph back. 'Look. Leave this with me, yeah? I don't know what they *did*, but I think I got the general idea.'

'Who's *they*?' Carrie demanded.

He wouldn't answer. 'Let me sort it. Tell you after. If I do, new rules, yeah? If I fix this for you, I get to stay here, proper contract, signed and sealed, you and me, right? I sort this, an' I'm your official lodger, no booting me out wi'out a notice period, and we'll call this my first month's rent. Right?'

Again, he was talking to Fairwood, not to her. Carrie folded her arms. 'Okay. But as the lodger, you don't… we've got boundaries, right? Right?'

He rolled his eyes. 'Fine.'

She had to go to work. Leaving him lurking in the shadows of the utility room, Carrie ran upstairs to get dressed, trying not to think about what had just happened, or the murder weapons her new lodger had brought under her roof.

With Carrie at work, he had Fairwood all to himself again. There were books upstairs that he hadn't read yet, but he was saving escapism for another day. Today, it was just him and her. He soaked it up with a greedy thirst, stroking her beams and steps with bare palms, slipping back naked into the cellar with a clear object in mind. Not long now, and Carrie Rickard would be dead and he would be the sole living thing in its walls, the house's only occupant. His agreement with her wouldn't matter then.

Four days to go.

That thought didn't give him the same thrill of excitement as before. His guts twisted, but not in the same way. It troubled him.

'Just you and me, old girl,' Ricky murmured into the chill. 'Like it ought to be. If anything happens to her, d'you think −? I can be useful. I could stay.' He felt the house tremble, and added quickly, 'Just a question.'

(*You think we will find our equilibrium.*)

'Course we will. Course we will! You *wanted* me to come to you, didn't you?' He ran his hand along the walls, testing the perimeter. 'You remember, don't you? What old Sir Peter and his lot got up to? I mean, the Pendles suffered for that as much as anyone.' Ricky patted his rippling stomach. 'Where's the kid? No need to protect her from me.'

(*What do you want with her?*)

'A chat, that's all. You're sounding better already. More like yourself.'

There was a suspicious silence.

Ricky grimaced, aware his thoughts were not entirely his own. The thoughts of the Thing-That-Was-Also-Ricky, though, that was another matter. He had a level of detachment he didn't normally feel, a way of stepping outside his own head and into the distorted worlds beyond: Outside.

He giggled suddenly, clapping his hands together. 'I'm going mad, my love. Ain't that fucking perfect.'

The Crows creaked sarcasm.

(*How can you tell?*)

(*She's got a point.*)

'Look, send the kid in, will you? You heard your Lady and Mistress, she can't leave well enough alone. I thought Bishop the Younger was just a convenience for Gran, no one saw fit to mention the godfather.' Ricky crouched low near his filthy blankets and arranged himself, cross-legged, on the floor. He tugged a brown one over his lower half, its ragged ends splayed across the flagstones, and wrapped its grimy yellow counterpart around his head and shoulders. 'You know if you'd just told me the whole story from the start I'd 'a been much more helpful. Go on, I'm decent.'

The Crows breathed an eddy of cold air in reluctance.

(*What will you do with her?*)

Ricky grinned, a bubble of anticipation floating in his chest.

'I'm going to give you revenge against all those bastards in town,' he said. 'And our mute little miss can have her revenge at the same time, if she wants it.'

This piqued the house's interest. The cellar seemed to curve inwards, each wall intent on listening.

(*How?*)

(*Human waste, boiled down to the essence of physical rejection; old skin, the shedding of a past and an identity... knew I'd find a use for them.*)

'I have my little ways,' Ricky said, focusing on his deep, calming breaths.

Sinister Local History

On Friday night, dreading social engagements but craving normalcy and some sort of release, Carrie met up with Mercy for a drink at a pub in the dodgier end of town, the Snake and Feather. The Snake was too close to Hangman's Walk for comfort even though she only had the vaguest sense of what went on in that crooked Tudor street overlooking the sea, but Mercy assured her it was all right. They were meant to be meeting Tina.

By the time Carrie got there, the pub was already crowded. A pack of hirsute people gathered around the tables, dragging free chairs over to make up the numbers for their party, and a buzzing crowd was already pressing around the bar.

The boards were sticky under her feet, and no one could stand still for long without being jostled or having to duck out of the way. There were pints being carried back and fore, and glasses of what Carrie hoped was dark red wine, but there were also drinks that splashed onto the floor and fizzed into instant steam, adding a raw, acidic tang to the atmosphere.

Mercy kept a hand on Carrie's bag, pulling her deeper into the pub where Tina had elbowed her way to a table in the snug, a much quieter area with one older regular ensconced in the corner with a copy of the *Pagham-on-Sea Gazette* and chewing on the stem of his unlit pipe.

Tina's eyeliner had smudged, her eyes pink and glistening. She sat up straighter as they approached the table, putting away her grief with visible effort. Carrie wanted to ask what was wrong, but bit the question back, unsure if Tina would welcome the intrusion of a stranger. Tina shot Carrie a genuine smile, which settled it. Carrie controlled her urge to ask.

'Hey! Good to see you're up and about properly. How are things?'

That was a big question.

Leaving out the part where Ricky Porter had moved into her house and cuddled her at night like a stuffed animal, Carrie updated her on the ghost's activities, especially what it had written on her mirror.

Tina and Mercy leaned in, Tina's expressive round face a grimace of mild horror. It caused the only other occupant of the snug to fold up his newspaper abruptly and stump back out into the main bar, leaving them alone in the small back room.

Carrie waited until after he had gone before pulling out the photograph salvaged from Janet Varney's unsuccessful fire.

'Does anyone in this look familiar to either of you?' she asked, opening her diary to the pages protecting the picture.

To her surprise, Mercy frowned. 'That's – yeah. Wait. That's… I'm sure that's my gran. My dad's mum.'

'The strict religious one?' Tina put in. 'What was her name? Veracity?'

'Verity. Verity Hillsworth.' Mercy squinted at it more closely. 'I've never seen this before. What… what is this? Is it a play, or something?'

That hadn't occurred to Carrie. 'I don't think so,' she murmured. 'I mean, I guess it *could* be a scene or something. What's the Colonel doing here?'

The smudge on Mrs Hillsworth's arm was licked by flame and not easy to make out.

'Should I see what we've got at home?' Mercy leaned back, after a moment's fruitless study. 'I can dig around Dad's attic, see what there is of hers. Maybe there's some photo albums, or something.'

'Watch yourself,' Tina warned. 'Don't blurt out *why* to anyone, will you? If Carrie's being targeted because of something to do with this, something that happened with the History Society, it's probably best not to mention you're digging around yourself.'

'I don't blurt,' Mercy said, offended. 'Anyway, I can't die.'

Tina snorted.

Carrie couldn't help but laugh. 'At least we know it's a man,' she said. 'The ghost said 'kill *him*', so it must know there's a man behind it somewhere. So, not Beverley? Or, I mean, maybe it was one of her sisters behind the actual killing and the sisters are both dead… Or does it mean this mystery man has its tongue?'

Mercy frowned. 'So, who could that be? Guy wasn't even born then.'

'No, but maybe his dad.' Carrie had been thinking about this all week. 'Maybe this is about their parents, you know? Most of them in the society would have been kids or in their teens sixty years ago.' She drummed her fingers on the table, trying to keep her voice even, trying to breathe through the sudden tightening in her chest. 'I mean, they might be dead, by now. Or not members anymore.'

'My gran was the secretary of the society back then,' Mercy said unexpectedly. 'I mean, she's dead now, of course, but… I guess a lot of them are? It must be someone Mrs Wend is friendly with, in any case.'

Tina nursed her drink, her eyes on Carrie's face. 'Are you okay, Carrie?'

'No!' Carrie stopped pretending. 'No, I'm not bloody okay. Someone's trying to kill me, there's a man-eating soothsayer next door, and my house is alive. Did I leave anything out?' (*Dr Monday and his masks of skin are normal, Dr Monday has always been my doctor, Dr Monday has known me for years.*)

Mercy frowned down at the table, purple curls swinging forwards. 'You need to spend as little time as you can around Ricky Porter,' she advised. 'That family gets under your skin, like… like tar.' She looked at Tina for corroboration, and Carrie remembered Tina's friendship with Wesley Porter.

Mercy pursed her lips when Tina didn't back her up.

Tina shook her head, suddenly sullen, and pulled out an envelope from her bag. 'Look, I shouldn't be giving you this, but Jazz... well, he let me dig around in the basement where the old records are. Parsons will go *spare* if she finds out. I took photos on my phone, printed them off at home.'

'Oh wow.' Carrie pounced on them. 'What did you—' She pulled out the first photograph and wished she hadn't. 'Oh, God.'

'Yeah, it's grim. But it's the marks on the arms, look. You can see those really clearly.'

Carrie swallowed and made herself look. The grainy photo was black and white, but the markings on the girl's pale, bloodless arm stood out in livid contrast to her skin. They looked like numerals, but in a script she didn't recognise.

'What the hell is this?'

'These photos were never released,' Tina said, watching her. 'I don't think anyone understood what they were looking at, and the police force weren't particularly... diverse, let's say, back then.' For Carrie's benefit, she added, 'Human only.'

Mercy had grown pale.

'No,' she whispered.

Carrie frowned. 'Mez? What's wrong?'

Mercy sat back, shaking her head. 'I know what these are,' she whispered. 'It's a – it's a story. It's just a story. Oh—' She clapped a hand to her mouth, eyes wide and watering. '*Shit*. The chimney, *shit*.'

'What?' Tina leaned over and grabbed her wrist. 'What *is* it, Mez?'

Mercy lowered her hand, quivering. 'It's a fairy story, to scare us,' she whispered. '"Be good, or the devil will steal away your number."'

'Was Cathy a Resurrectionist?' Tina asked, not understanding.

Mercy shook her head. 'No. You have to... in the story, innocence is the secret ingredient to a, a, spell, I guess? Innocence is a character in the story, and she's hung in the dark and drained dry, and there's marks all over her, numbers, you know, special numbers, like equations…' She swallowed, not looking at the photograph. 'Those are… it reminds me of that, that's all. And it fits. But it's not possible. It's not. It's a story. A stupid story.'

'But you're right,' Carrie said slowly, collecting up the photographs. 'That makes sense. The chimney's dark, and convenient, and right under the chimney is the Pendle Stone, full of… energies. Arcane, eldritch, I don't know. Something that… you can use to access the Outside, whatever that is.'

'Do you think it worked?' Tina asked.

'No, of course not.' Mercy stood up abruptly, jolting the table. 'Hanging a child in a chimney isn't going to do anything. You can't steal people's numbers. That's ridiculous. Tragic, and ridiculous. But it wouldn't work. It's just a story.' She shook her head. 'I don't believe in it.'

'Mez—' Tina started, but Mercy was adamant.

Her pert nostrils flared. 'Okay. I'm buying this round. What's everyone having?'

'Mez…' Tina tried again but was defeated by Mercy's stiff determination. 'Rum and coke. Double.'

'House white's fine.' Carrie exchanged glances with Tina and slipped the photos away again into the envelope. 'Thanks.'

Mercy slid out of her seat, lacy skirt catching on the frayed green upholstery. She unstuck herself, shook her head and bounced out to the bar, putting Carrie in mind of a rainbow-haired fairy.

'I guess we're not talking about that anymore,' Carrie said, passing the envelope back.

'I guess not. Give her some time.' Tina sipped her drink, gave Carrie a friendly smile as if weighing her up, and promptly harpooned her. 'So, has your ex been back?'

Pinned to her seat, Carrie flinched. 'No,' she said. 'I hope he never does.'

Tina finished her half-full drink in two gulps and set it down firmly on a coaster. Her phone buzzed. She checked it and grinned. 'Wes. He's been getting *really* flirty since Burt broke up with me.' Her lips dropped. 'Burt picked up the rest of his stuff today. Sorry. I'm not... not feeling great about it.'

They shared an awkward, commiserating silence.

Mercy returned clutching three glasses, trying not to spill any of them as she negotiated the curtain. Carrie jumped up to help her, taking her glass of wine. Mercy leaned over to plonk a glass in front of Tina. 'Double rum and coke. Sal started making it before I even ordered, she assumed it was for you.' She gave her a pointed stare.

Tina gave her the middle finger and sipped her drink. 'Don't *you* start. Jazz is bad enough, thanks, he's like a mother hen.'

'Good. Just saying.' Mercy looked from Tina to Carrie and tucked her leg underneath her as she sat.

Tina scooped up her phone and buried it back in her bag. 'Right. Let's induct Carrie into the Underground and see if we can show her a good time before someone else tries to kill her.'

'Seconded,' Carrie said with feeling.

It wasn't long before the curtain of the snug was twitched aside, and in sauntered a man as lean as Ricky Porter if a foot taller, beer bottle in his hand, conspicuous in a plain black plastic mask covering the top half of his face, sharply dressed in a royal purple silk shirt and black skinny jeans.

Tina hailed him with a grin. 'Wes! You made it!'

'Sorry, Tee.' Wesley Porter went in for a warm hug. 'Would've been here earlier but I was running a quick errand when you texted. Family thing.'

Tina raised an eyebrow as they broke apart.

Wes raised his hands. 'Not selling, honest. Gone clean, on my Aunty's grave.'

'Yeah, you pass your gear on to one of your cousins to sell for you,' Tina remarked, unconvinced and unimpressed.

'Naun harmful, recreational only, give us a break, love.'

Carrie got the impression Wes was a much better liar than his cousin. It was the strangest thing, but after Wes stopped speaking she could remember what he'd said, but not what his voice sounded like.

'So, how's things?' Tina shifted along to make room for him, and Wes dragged a chair closer to hers than necessary.

'Yeah, all right thanks, apart from our soothsayer being an awkward sod for some reason. Insisted on coming to me instead of me going there, he's never done that before. Bloody weird. Only did me a bone-reading, that's all, nothing special. Gave him something he can sell to the party crowd.' He turned to the table, running his tongue over his lips as he spotted Carrie, now frozen and staring. The implication left her aghast.

Unbelievable! 'No sex, no drugs, no rock 'n' roll' my arse. What an absolute—

'*Hel-lo.* You must be Caroline.'

Carrie shook his hand. 'Carrie.' His palm was hot and dry. 'Is it Wesley?'

'Wes, please.' He finished his beer and set the bottle down. 'Don't mind my cousin, if he's been sniffing around. He doesn't get out much. Oh, speaking of getting out, sorry Charlie couldn't make it, she's got a date.' He made himself comfortable.

'Shame,' Tina said.

'Tee fancies my missus,' Wes said, dropping a hand under the table to rest on Tina's thigh, 'But I don't take it personally.'

Carrie noted Tina didn't brush him off.

'Right, let's get this over with.' Wes took off his mask, and Carrie held her breath. The surprise of his average appearance was a terrible anti-climax. She dropped her eyes to her glass and immediately forgot what he looked like.

Wait.

She raised her eyes again and fixed his face in her mind. When she looked away, she couldn't remember his eye colour, hair colour, face shape, the size of his nose.

Am I that drunk?

Not that drunk, no, but her frontal lobe was bathed in blissful numbness, and her thoughts felt more her own.

She caught Tina's eye and saw she was smirking.

No, I bet this is a thing, she thought. *All right, I'll play.*

'Go on,' Wes encouraged her. 'What's my hair like? Took me hours, this did.'

Carrie closed her eyes and guessed. She opened her eyes. She was wrong.

Mercy clapped. 'God, it's weird, isn't it? I'm getting another beer.' She slid clumsily by, knocking the table again.

'She's being subtle,' Wes said as she left. 'She doesn't like me. Anyway, Carrie, let's get to it. I figured I was coming over to be grilled.'

Tina shook her head. 'I think Carrie's earned a few answers, Wes.'

'Why's your Gran trying to kill me?' Carrie blurted out, fed up. 'And what's the deal with your face?'

Wes burst out laughing. He shook his head, long fingers toying with his mask. 'Gran's not trying to kill you, not that I know of. From what I can tell, Jan just wanted to scare you and it... got a bit out of hand. Gran was a bit pissed off because she, well, she was pretty close to Jan. I mean, she might have *reacted*—'

'I was nearly cursed to death.' Carrie scowled, noting how close he was to Tina. 'Dr Monday had to Sarcophagus Wrap me.'

'I'm not sure what that means,' Wes said slowly, nondescript voice easily carrying over the music, 'but Tee said all of this – it's got something to do with a ghost? Gran's got protection against stuff like that. If anything, she's just doing a friend of hers a favour, though I've no idea who that is.'

Carrie grated her teeth. 'I want some answers.'

'What d'you want, a potted history?' Wes exchanged glances with Tina, amused. 'Cor, she *is* new here. Yeah, okay. Right. Once upon a time...'

'Fuck's sake,' Tina muttered with a smirk, rolling her eyes, but Wes ignored her.

'*Once upon a time*, there were three sisters living at Bramble Cottage with their mother and father, pretty things they were, of course, and one day the eldest gets something in her head she can't quite winkle out. She strays into a place she shouldn't be, lured by all the stories and the strange lights there, and something flies in like a gnat through her lovely brown eye, gets stuck in her brain. She starts thinking of things that aren't there.' He gave her a sharp grin that reminded her of Ricky, but when she blinked, only Ricky's grin remained in her mind and Wes's slipped away.

'The middle sister likes history, fascinated by the long barrows up on Barrow Field she is, and one day she finds something she shouldn't find, a strange thing with odd carvings on it. The eldest lays it on the hearthstone and sings to it, songs she don't know. It feels right, somehow. And then, in the woods, the three sisters meet a man with three heads, which is probably the polite way of saying he was triply well-endowed, but this is only *partially* that kind of a story.'

Carrie wondered where this rambling tale was going and fairly sure she wasn't going to like it. Wes nodded, foot tapping under the table.

'So. The youngest sister feels left out, and she's the one who wants to go along with this man, but at this point the eldest isn't certain. He isn't really a man, you see, he's not human at all. But the youngest wants to go. There's a place in the woods – ripped up now for the new arable field, can't raise nothing there but sheep – where they met him. He wasn't there, you understand, probably never was there at all, he's a green shadow in their imaginations, he's the shifting darkness through the branches, the whisperings from the soil. He's not a real man. But they dance for him like he wants them to, around the fire they make there, and what do you know but they find themselves stripping down to their young milky flesh and writhing under the smoke.'

Wes flicked out an obscene tongue.

Carrie found herself rubbing the piece of The Crows in her pocket.

This is why we don't have Pendles in the house.
Can't imagine Ricky doing that, thank God.

Mercifully, she blinked and erased the memory of the tongue from her mind.

'They got themselves pregnant, of course,' Wes continued. 'Can't recall how, even now Gran'll say she can't remember. But they weren't the same after, and they took on married names, to be respectable. The youngest wanted to be first among the sisters, so she chose Mrs Foreman, you see, and the middle sister just wanted certainty and understanding, so she chose Mrs Shaw, sort of a pun. And the eldest, she was the one "wending her merry way" through the woods when the thought first came to her, and that's what she chose, something like a journey, something charming, something dignified, mysterious, a little romantic.' He paused, considering. 'Nothing romantic about the spawning, when it happened. And romantics tend not to last long in this world, but Gran, fair play to her, has lasted pretty well.'

Carrie let this wash over her, tingling with curiosity. 'So... that's why you're all... different? What are the Changes?'

Wes waved a hand in front of his face. 'Now you see us, now you don't.' He grinned, and Carrie tried to cement the image in her mind, the shape of his lips pared back against his teeth, the lift of his cheeks, the crinkling around his eyes – but then she blinked and wiped the picture clean.

'It's potluck. They start when we're about eighteen, but the signs are there before. Gran's the only sister left, now, the only shrine we can go to, no matter which branch of the family we're from. We do our libations, tug our forelocks, have a chat to old Gaffer in the side-to-side and down-below, wherever he is, and if we're very good and please him mightily, we'll get something a bit extra-special. Of course, when we were teens that wasn't cool. We all pretended not to take it seriously, happy to take what came, stick it to the Man, you know.' He snorted. 'Cousin Ricky was never one for peer pressure, he seemed to really care what he got, so we teased him about that.'

Carrie frowned. She started to dislike Wesley Porter's attitude.

Wes didn't seem to notice. 'Sometimes Gran lets others down there for scraps, just for fun. There's a few in this town with powers they shouldn't have, if it don't drive them to drink or turn 'em mad first. She likes to stir the pot a bit, add a bit of chaos.'

Carrie looked to Tina, whose expression had soured. She was lost in thought, staring at the table. Carrie decided not to delve too deeply into this at the moment.

'Right, so she's happy to help other people out and sometimes that involves what, doing rituals for them? Youth stuff, rejuvenation stuff, that kind of thing?' Carrie tried to remember what Ricky had said. 'The girl up the chimney... I want her to find peace. And stop tugging the duvet off me at three in the morning.'

Wes shrugged. 'Carrie... look, piece of advice, sincerely meant, okay? The Fifties are ancient history. Leave it all alone. Learn to survive in the *now*, instead. Don't let the soothsayer drag you out of the present, he's a little shit for that, too much staring into the wyrd and telling everyone their future is already built on the backs of the dead. Useful, don't get me wrong, but take what you need and walk away, don't let him in.' He tapped his forehead.

Carrie tightened her jaw, ready to come to Ricky's defence, but she didn't. He'd rather she kept his secrets than stirred things up by snapping at his cousin. She swallowed her annoyance. 'That doesn't solve my haunting. And someone has tried to kill me twice already, do I just forget about that?'

'Sure. Forget, forgive, move on. If anyone tries again, learn to be ready. Sod the ghost, call in an exorcist, banish her back to whatever crack she crawled out of.'

'Wes,' Tina nudged him, frowning. 'That's a person you're talking about. Or was.'

'Yeah, the one that cost us the Pendle Stone,' Wes muttered. 'Good thing I like you, Tee, your meddling Great-Aunt's still a sore spot for some of us.'

Carrie played dumb. 'Why does that matter, if your gran has a shrine anyway?'

'Not all of us like asking Gran for every little thing.' Wes scratched at a beer mat. 'She uses it against us. Holds it over us. Can't have a family row without her threatening to take our access away if we don't accept her adjudication. Then she goes and lets anybody down there, taking up grandad's favours, people who ain't even our own blood.' He grimaced, but even that left no lasting impression on her. 'Right, that's enough. That's my opinion and a bit of context for you, take it or leave it. I'm out for a good time, don't know about anyone else?'

'Sure.' Carrie raised her glass to meet his.

When Carrie went up to the bar to buy a round, sober enough to know she had no money but tipsy enough not to care, she spotted Guy Bishop across the bar. Carrie caught her breath. She hadn't seen him since he'd delivered the flowers and rambled about destiny.

He'd nearly killed her.

She pressed into a knot of people between him and her, but with limited success. Guy noticed her as she got served, meeting her glance with a start and a haunted stare.

Carrie couldn't wave or smile. She stared back.

The barmaid was asking her if she wanted anything else. She shook her head and paid with her card, hoping it wouldn't be declined. When it didn't, relief overrode her awkwardness. 'Do you know where the toilets are?'

'They're that way.' The barmaid pointed.

Carrie handed over the drinks to Wes, who had appeared behind her in his mask, wound her way through rowdy groups of carousing punters, and ducked into a smaller room with another bar, far quieter than the main pub. A wooden sign pointed the way to the toilets. She got halfway across the room when Guy called her name.

'Carrie?'

Fuck.

(*Get rid of him.*)

No Bishops...

Carrie pressed her hand to her forehead, her thoughts jumbled. In such quick succession they felt wrong, as if some weren't hers at all. The alcohol lapped at her consciousness, drowning out the others and letting her own bob to the surface.

She turned around. 'Hi, Guy.'

'You… my God. Carrie…'

That, and the shock on his face, told her all she needed to know.

'You've got some explaining to do,' Carrie said.

He came forwards, eyes glazed. 'I didn't know. I swear. I just… Beverley gave me the flowers. I didn't know you'd get ill.' The whites of his eyes were pink and glazed, and it looked like he'd been drinking for a while.

He slid into a seat, and Carrie decided, much to her bladder's annoyance, that her trip to the Ladies' was less urgent than finding out what he knew. She joined him at the table and crossed her legs.

'I don't… blame you. I'm not angry with you.' She managed a smile. 'Are you all right?'

Guy moved his hand. 'I'm, uh. Not so good. But Millennium Night came in at Ascot, five to two. Wish it had been ten to one.'

Phil used to talk odds. Carrie's bladder gave her a sharp nudge.

'I'm going to the loo,' she said abruptly. 'Wait, please? Don't go anywhere?'

He nodded, looking down.

She was as quick as she could be, but she paused at the vanity mirror over the sink and steadied herself.

He's not Phil. He's not. (For every problem there's an acidic solution.) *We can do this.*

For a moment her reflection shimmered and there were three faces in the mirror, two overlaid on hers. She blinked hard, rubbing her face.

(*We can do this.*)

(*I can do this.*)

I can do this.

She inhaled, exhaled, counted to five.

I'm too sober for this.

That thought sounded like something Tina might say, and it made Carrie grin. Her head was crowded enough as it was without picking up phrases from the medium as well.

She made it back to the smaller, quieter bar, where Guy was nursing another neat double.

'You want to talk to me?' she asked, sitting down. 'It looks like you could use someone to talk to.'

For a moment she thought he was going to refuse, but then he nodded, staring into his drink.

'You're all right? I'm glad you're all right, obviously. It's. I'm going to lose the shop.' He shook his head. 'I got… Beverley tried to help. She said she'd help, she said… if I did a few things for her, I could go into the cellar.' His lips twisted. 'I could go down there, and it wasn't… it didn't hurt. The first time was easy. Just some chanting. I was blindfolded, she used a prism, and told me not to look.' He chuckled. 'And that was it. I got lucky. I knew, just… knew. I could look at odds and I'd know who was going to win. Solved everything.'

'But I bet it wore off, after a while?' Carrie kept her tone as soft as she could, leaning in. 'And you had to go back?'

Guy's jaw fluttered. 'It was my fault, I got greedy, I suppose, I thought… the business was dad's *life* but we kept making losses…'

'What happened the second time?' Carrie asked.

'I had to look,' Guy whispered. 'I did what she said. I didn't… I didn't think it was harmful. Beverley wanted me to… get hold of some books for her, through my contacts. Specific books. So I did. And then, I went down to the cellar, to Mr Wend's shrine, and this time I had to look.'

(*Oh, the Outside. Yeah, that'll mess you up.*)

Carrie let the thought slide in and out of her head. It sounded like Ricky, but he wasn't in her head, not properly. It wasn't like he was reading her mind, more like her thoughts had morphed into his. They were intertwined in ways she wasn't sure she liked. Why was she only just noticing? It felt comfortable, as if she'd been thinking his thoughts for a while, but she couldn't put her finger on when that started.

'The Outside,' she said aloud, trusting the thought but not knowing what that meant.

Guy shuddered and downed half his drink in two swallows. He set the glass back down. 'It's a dimension,' he hissed down at the table, not looking at her. 'It's – outside our reality, *right next door*. I saw… I don't know what I saw. Not clearly.' He grabbed her hand, making her jump. 'The third time, that was worse. I didn't think it could get worse. But it was. *It looked at me*. Like it knew me. *Like it knew my name*.' He glanced around at the comforting beams, the Olde Worlde ambience. 'I couldn't, I couldn't go through with it. I'd done everything she asked, and she said it would get better *but I couldn't…*'

Carrie started to understand. 'That third time… Sorry, let's go back a bit. You delivered the flowers to me so she'd let you down the cellar again, a third time, and you hoped that would save your dad's shop?'

Guy nodded again.

'But you couldn't finish the ritual? But you still won some money…?'

'Yeah. Still won. She got Richard Porter, Ricky, you know him, to write down racing tips for me. I don't… I don't honestly remember much about that, about why I couldn't, you know. She had a nice medicinal bottle waiting, looked after me. She's good like that.'

I don't think she should have let him drink, Carrie thought.

'Dad doesn't like me drinking.' Guy gave her a wobbly smile, as if he'd read her mind. 'Doesn't like to be reminded of Mum.'

Carrie tried to smile but failed. 'I'm sorry.'

He shook his head with a warmer smile, drunk but steadier. 'I look like her,' he said, with a strange wistful pride. 'She was really pretty, my mum. She died when I was a kid. Car crash.'

Carrie pursed her lips, running her finger along her necklace chain until it hit the pendant, feeling closer to her own parents. She would text them as soon as this conversation was over.

'God, that's rough. I'm sorry.'

'No, it's all right. Long time ago, now.' But he didn't look at her.

'Look. Um. No hard feelings, yeah?' Carrie studied him, any anger she'd felt at his part in her ordeal drowned by pity. 'And let me know if there's anything I can do? I don't know what I *can* do, but I guess, if you want… support, maybe…?'

'Stop it.' Guy's head jerked up again. 'Stop looking, stop poking around. Stop. Just *stop.*' He stood with clumsy force, jolting the table like Mercy, and stumbled back into the main bar.

Carrie scraped her chair back.

'What was that about?' she asked out loud, then realised she wasn't in The Crows tonight and she was talking to herself. No one seemed to notice. She took her glass back through the main pub and into the snug to re-join the others, shaken.

The talk of 'Outside' chilled her. There was something wrong with him, something eating at his soul.

She *wanted* to leave it alone, but she wasn't sure the ghost would let her. She hoped Ricky Porter knew what he was doing.

Revenge Served Cold

In which Ricky finds a tongue and all hell breaks loose
11 May – Night

Ricky crouched down in the flowerbed of the Residential Home, watching the lights wink off one at a time. Let Carrie have her fun tonight and investigate the History Society at her leisure, he had other ideas. The photograph had been enlightening. There was only one person he could think of who tied the History Society together in such a neat group. Shame it had taken her a week to ask him, but then, she'd had other things on her mind.

As he waited, the magpies came home to roost.

(*Three for a funeral.*)

As omens went it was as subtle as a brick through a window: the lack of nuance was insulting. Finally, guided by the running threads in the wyrd coming to a natural cross-stitch, he strolled down the sloping grass towards Harry Bishop's room. The glass didn't bother him. He stood watching the old man's shape in bed, huddled under his quilt frail as a child. He dropped his hood, the back lips parting and the tendrils regurgitated upwards, vibrating against his bones. They spread over the glass, scratching along the pane.

Tap. Tap. Tap.

The glass cracked.

Ricky saw the figure tremble and wondered what it would be like to get off on fear, to truly enjoy it the way Uncle David did, or even his father. George Porter loved the sour taste of terror, that bitter taint to his meat. He loved the way the eyes widened, the pulse quickened, the rush of adrenaline pushing the quarry to greater feats, to run faster, climb higher, to fight for their life. Ricky had watched his cousins whipped into frenzies at the mere whiff of it.

What would it feel like to be the old man in the bed, praying this was a nightmare, praying the window-barrier would keep him out, hearing the crunch as the shards fell to pieces, seeing the figure with gorgon-antlers stepping through a mist of powdered glass?

(*This is all her, the things she would ask — let it go.*)

He heard the old man whimpering. Probably wouldn't get much sense out of him. He focused, looking around the room. Glass crunched under his trainers. His attention was arrested by the shelves along the opposite wall. Harry Bishop's books were packed end to end, books he had never been allowed to own, but this man had a small library within his feeble grasp. Ricky couldn't help himself. The tendrils floated around him as he turned to face them, drinking in the titles and the elderly spines, recalling summer days with Mrs Antram who taught him his letters at the library, a kind woman too bloody-minded to be afraid of George and Lettie Porter. That had been her fatal mistake.

(*"You want to be book-smart, eat the smart part of her,"* his father said standing over him with a fork, *"eat it all, every bit of it."*)

He'd kept her keys, though, and slipped back to the library after hours while his parents groaned pearl-green, safely bedridden after what he'd put in their food.

A hard, bitter lump rose up, seething and hot.

'*No!*' Harry Bishop croaked, wheezing, 'Not my books!'

Ricky turned. Tendrils trailed along the covers behind him, licking at poetry and prose. The taste of their jackets stirred up flint-edged greed, cutting deep into his viscera.

'Where's the bloody tongue, Harry?' he asked, gruff and grating. 'That's what I want. Just the tongue.'

'Wha-what tongue?' Harry Bishop had found his. He was quivering under the quilt, clawed hand shaking.

'Seriously?' Ricky pinched the bridge of his nose. 'Can we skip this bit and get to the part where you just hand it over?'

'I *know* you,' Harry croaked suddenly, levering himself painfully off the pillows. 'Richard Edwin Porter, you little gobshite. What d'you want with that, hey? Beverley would tan your hide for you—'

'She ain't here, is she?' Ricky snapped, knocking Hardy off the shelf.

(*Pretentious arsehole.*)

The volume thudded to the carpet, making Harry wince. Now he recognised his intruder as someone he had known since birth, his fear ebbed into contempt.

'You watch where you're putting those things and mind my first editions,' Harry snapped, taking a gasp of angry air. 'Illiterate little sod, you wait, if I could get out of this bed, scaring an old man...'

The dig at his lack of schooling struck Ricky's sensitive parts like an armour-piercing arrow. His tendrils lashed the air. He could feel his skin splitting under his clothes, his other form straining against the fleshy seams.

'Gran ain't here. Where's the fucking tongue, Harry? The little girl's tongue, you know exactly what I'm talking about. Who else would the Colonel stick his neck out for, if not for you?'

Harry twitched. 'What's the *matter* with you?' He fumbled for the bedside reading lamp, clicking it on. A cool evening breeze pushed the broken glass across the carpet. He squinted in the amber light, puzzling it out. 'Dear Lord, it's that house, isn't it?'

Ricky stiffened in denial. 'What about her?'

'It is. It's that *house*. That's it.' Harry's crooked finger jabbed in his direction. 'It changes a man, that vengeful place. The Rickard woman woke it up, didn't she, like I was afraid of, and it's got under your skin. Don't think I can't tell. I wrote the *book* on it.'

'What if it is?' Ricky tilted his chin. 'What if she does want her revenge, do you blame her? Lying there a ruin, a broken tormented thing, what do you expect? She chose me, an' she'll reward me, too.'

Harry Bishop laughed in cracked, wheezing gasps, coughing up mirth. 'Idiot boy! You never could see what was in front of you, all that farsight turning your brain. Fairwood won't give up the Pendle Stone to *you*, it's using you, can't you see that? Once it's got what it wants it'll reject you, keep you locked out for good.'

This missile, well-aimed, stung worse than the first.

Ricky Changed.

He couldn't help it.

He ripped off his clothes before he ruined them irrevocably, human skin shredding into raw, bloody rags with the pulsing pressure beneath. He let himself be seen in all his writhing beauty. His eyes opened onto the wyrd, myriad, legion.

Harry gagged on nothing, light years away.

'Christ!' he moaned, but Ricky wasn't that sort of saviour.

Where's the tongue, Harry?

He tore the truth from Harry Bishop's brain, taking it by the corner and ripping it out of his memory. His attention turned to an antique drinks' cabinet in the shape of a globe, lovingly painted but sun-bleached and cracked with age. A tendril went to work on the tiny keyhole, cunningly hidden by the pink lines traversing the north coast of Africa.

'Jesus!'

He isn't coming, Harry. It's just us.

The globe, under pressure from the suckers soft as gloves, groaned in rusty protest as he lifted the top half and the hollow innards gazed back at them for the first time in decades.

Found her.

He reached in and took out an anatomist's jar, in which some-thing unpleasant floated.

'Do it yourself!' Harry managed, voice enfeebled with terror, eyes streaming in the lamplight. 'Kill me yourself, Richard, you bloody coward, Christ, boy, what the hell have you done?'

The Thing-that-was-Ricky was not inclined to tell. Vengeance was not his to take. He was an agent of fate, not its assassin.

The jar smashed on the floor, filling the room with the stench of formaldehyde and botanical preservatives, something tangy on the air, greasy with static. The tongue flopped to the carpet, fish-like, and combusted.

Goodnight, Harry.

He was gone before the nurses got there, leaving the old bookseller to the fumes and the small fire blossoming on the floor.

It started softly: an owl ruffled its feathers on the roof, and hopped into flight, disturbed by a noise beneath it.

The attic windows rattled in their frames.

The murder of crows took flight in haste, a cawing storm of flapping wings against the moon, a bad omen.

And then, ringing out through the house and its grounds, swelling from the coal cellar to the upper rooms and bursting into the sky, came a roar of pure, ferocious, vengeful spite.

The binding spell was broken.

They were all going to pay.

–

Carrie and her merry company left the pub and headed for the centre.

'You're coming back to ours, right?' Wes asked Tina, his mask now replaced, giving him a dashing air of mystery. 'Charlie made me promise I'd ask.'

Tina played coy.

'Text her, give her a ring, ask her yourself,' Wes encouraged her as they got closer to the front of the taxi queue. 'Anyone else? The more the merrier.'

Mercy screeched with scandalised laughter.

'We're good, thanks,' Carrie said, realising he was serious.

Wes shrugged, passing around his hip flask.

Carrie took a swig of it without thinking, trying not to think about real life post-hangover, when bills would have to be paid, and the garden needed more attention, and the fact there was a homicidal ghost child in her house. But Fairwood was real, the small piece of it warm and solid, a reminder that the strange and miraculous could and did happen, Mercy was *still* talking happily about anything and everything, and Tina was trying to get a word in edgeways. When they all went their separate ways, she would be going home to Fairwood's anchored foundations, and the man-eating soothsayer in the cellar. A warm glow flowed through her, syrup-thick.

They shared a taxi, Mercy, Wes and Tina giving Carrie cash to cover their part of the ride. They dropped Mercy off first, still breathlessly chatting, then Wes and Tina a few streets away in an upmarket new build cul-de-sac, then around to Redditch Lane.

Carrie was feeling the wine now, and whatever Wes had passed around.

Never trust a Porter.

The ride was soothing, lulling her to sleep.

Halfway home, she was rudely jolted out of her drunken drowsiness.

A black ragged shape came hurtling out of the darkness, too fast for the driver to react. It collided with the windscreen, smashing square into the centre. The driver slammed on his brakes.

Carrie lurched forwards, the seatbelt jarring against her chest.

The driver let out a violent ejaculation in Arabic, thumping both hands on the wheel. His small, hand-painted Hamsa swung from the rear-view mirror, frantically warding off the evil eye but not, apparently, direct hits from foreign objects.

'You all right?' He checked his mirrors, turning on the taxi's hazards and dipping the headlights so as not to dazzle any other cars. 'Better check it hasn't smashed the glass,' he said.

Carrie sat frozen, blinking at the feathers stuck to the glass.

'It's a bad omen,' she whispered, reaching for the piece of tile.

Death and the Maiden

In which Ricky tells the truth

12 May

Carrie got in a few minutes after midnight, reeling a little from the wine and the shock, but largely annoyed. Pragmatism took over. She texted Tina and Mercy to let them know she was back, leaning against the door to absorb some of Fairwood's reassuring presence and hoping her annoyance leached into it, too.

Something's happened.

'Oh, *shush*. Shush a minute.' She meant to think it but said it out loud, flapping at the air with her free hand. She pressed send, wondering if she should have some water.

As she turned, an unexpected figure lurking in her hall startled her. Carrie yelped, jumping back against the door.

'You do know I live here now, right?' Ricky asked, offended.

She panted, clutching her chest. 'Shit, yes. Sorry.' She frowned, looking around. 'What's different? It feels wrong. Something's wrong.'

'Nothing.' Ricky was staring at her in a way she couldn't interpret.

'We hit a crow,' Carrie whispered. 'In the taxi. A crow. It flew into the windscreen. Broke its neck.' She shivered. 'Ricky, what have you done?'

'Nothing,' Ricky repeated, but she was sure he was lying.

He was a terrible liar.

'You lie to me again and we're *done*.' Carrie couldn't stop her voice trembling. 'What the hell did you *do*?' The adrenaline was wearing off, alcohol flooding back with a vengeance. 'I was having such a nice time! For the first time in, in, in *months*, I can't even remember... Then this *bloody...*' She gasped, trailing off.

Don't cry, don't you dare.

Her tears didn't listen.

Ricky watched her face crumple, his own eyes widening, reddening with his cheeks.

'I found the tongue,' he mumbled, fidgeting, edging closer. 'It's a long story...'

Carrie sniffed, gulping back a sob. 'Fuck off.'

'No, I really did. And, uh, look, I know you need the money, got some today.' He reached into his back pocket (his clothes looked more ragged than usual, as if he had torn them off and yanked them back on again in something of a hurry) and produced a wad of used twenties.

Carrie dropped her shoulders, still sniffing. 'Keep it.'

He scoffed. 'What for?'

'I don't know. Buy a new tracksuit.'

Ricky scowled, clearly uncomfortable with the concept.

Carrie sighed. 'I'll get one online for you, shall I?' She eyed the notes warily. 'I guess I don't want to know how you got it.'

'Nah, I wouldn't ask if I were you,' Ricky agreed, deadpan, stuffing the money away.

Despite everything, that made her laugh. 'You're such an arsehole, Ricky Porter.'

He didn't deny it. Sidling closer, her new lodger offered a tentative, steadying arm. 'You a bit pissed, love?' he asked, amused, without judgement.

Carrie shrugged unsteadily and, ignoring the arm, gave him a warm hug.

He didn't tense up as badly, or for as long.

'I'll take that as a yes.' He patted her on the back and propped his chin on her shoulder.

She rested against him, content.

'I love it here,' she murmured, letting him embrace her properly, soothed by his gentle rocking on the spot, which mimicked the gentle swaying of the whole reception hall. 'Can I have a glass of water, please?'

Ricky chuckled into her hair. 'You're a lot politer when you're pissed,' he said. 'It's your house, what're you asking me for?'

'Ricky, can you get me one, please?'

He sighed.

'Please?'

Ricky adjusted his grip and led her around the stairs, past the ticking grandfather clock and into the kitchen. He plopped her down in a chair and ran the tap.

Carrie beamed at him. At that moment, her world was a walled-in wonderland and she loved every imperial and metric measurement of it and all it contained. It overflowed in a grateful sigh as he handed her a glass of water.

'You're lovely, really.'

Ricky snorted. 'Bloody hell. Drink it all.'

She grinned, sipping it, in the mood to push her luck. 'Can I have some toast too?'

'I'm your lodger, not your bloody chef.' Ricky matched her grin, but for a moment, there was a shade of sadness in it, or regret. She blinked slowly, focusing, but he was already muttering something about white flour and salt content and putting two slices of bread into the toaster for her.

'What's wrong?' Carrie asked, leaning on her fist. 'Ricky? You okay?'

He had his back to her. 'Naun wrong with me, love.'

'Who *has* got something wrong with them, then?' She was catching on to the questions she needed to ask.

Ricky didn't answer.

He stood over the toaster in silence until it popped, and Carrie forgot she had asked a question at all.

'Have you enjoyed your life?' he asked finally, buttering it for her. 'In general, I mean.' He cleared his throat and put the plate on the table. 'I mean, this has been all right, hasn't it?'

Carrie squinted at the toast, then up at him. A vague recollection of Guy Bishop seated at the kitchen table rambling about destiny came back to her, with a fleeting sense of dread. 'Ricky, what're you even talking about?'

'Nothing.' Ricky shook his head. 'I'm chatting shit. Ignore me, eat your toast.'

She munched on it while he looked on, rubbing his neck at irregular intervals.

'Life's been good,' she said, not sure if that was strictly true or the molten butter dancing on her tongue. 'Oh my God, why does everything taste so much better when you're drunk, though?'

Ricky's snort turned into a delighted giggle. He drew up a chair. 'What's that like?'

'What? Getting pissed? Buttered toast?' She offered him her plate, but he shook his head.

'Nah. I mean, having a life you... *enjoyed.*' He folded his arms on the table. 'Apart from that arsehole I ate.'

Carrie couldn't help herself. 'You *ate* him, my God, Ricky, shit...' she trailed off, words dissolved in a geyser of laughter bubbling from the dark corner of her soul. 'Shh, shh, you ca-an't say that.'

Ricky leered, eyes bright. 'You're welcome.'

'We had some good times, too,' Carrie mumbled, trying to be fair. 'At the start. I don't know. My life's been... okay. I've always had friends. Always fitted in. Always just been—' she met his gaze '—fine.'

His lips twitched in a shaky smile. 'What about... tonight? Was there anything that could have made it... better?'

She frowned. 'Well. Apart from cheesy chips and a decent shag? Yeah, it was fun.'

Ricky swallowed, blushing. 'Good. Sorry I can't help out with the, er, the rest of it.'

'What the hell's the matter?' Carrie demanded, a prickle of suspicion penetrating to the front of her mind, willing herself sober. It didn't work. 'Is this—' She gestured at the plate of crumbs and attempted humour. 'Is this my last meal, or something?'

269

'Oh, shit, no.' Ricky shook his head. 'No, not yet.'

Something in the way he said it sent a shiver down her back. 'Ricky...'

'I saw your wyrd,' he blurted, cheeks strained and red.

Carrie pushed the plate away.

'I saw the threads of your fate, and I saw... I saw where they stop.' He looked like he was trying to stop himself, biting on the words as they tumbled out, but a soothsayer told the truth. 'I can't change it.'

'Stop?' Carrie echoed the terrible word, pronouncing it like a foreign syllable. 'What... what happens then?'

Ricky shook his head. 'I don't know.'

The image of the crow slamming into the windscreen popped back into her head, making her jump. She hardly dared ask, but she had to.

'How?'

'I can't see exactly. Could be a number of ways. It's the outcome that's certain.'

'When?'

He looked as if he was going to say the exact date, but he faltered. 'Soon.'

She realised she didn't want to know. 'How do I stop it?'

'You don't.'

She swallowed, not taking this in. 'What, so, that's it? I'm going to die?'

'Everyone dies.'

Carrie shook her head, open-mouthed. 'Why... how am I supposed to... how am I supposed to live knowing that? What do I do? I'm... I'm going to Dad and Ann's. First thing tomorrow. Shit, I've wasted... so much time, I – I thought I'd see Christmas... won't I? Why did you tell me at all?'

'Because.' Ricky knotted his fingers together. A slick smack of his second lips hailed the tendrils as they poured out over his head. 'It'll be because of me.'

Carrie's heart clenched.

A thin tendril snaked out like a questing root, tickling her cheek. She leaned away from it, blinking, not able to focus. It glided, worm-like, towards her earlobe.

'It won't hurt.'

'What—'

'If I don't, she'll leave, won't she? Spend her last days without us.' Ricky spoke to the house, which said nothing back.

Carrie flinched, wide-eyed. 'No! No—'

The tip slid smooth as a needle into her ear. There was a cold prick in her head, an ice-cream headache spun in a thin white line, and the warm glow returned with the loss of some other memory.

She frowned, staring at her plate.

'When did I make toast?'

Ricky's smile was sad. 'Come on, love. Bedtime.'

'Your cousin's a looker, isn't he?' Carrie said, trying not to slur. She stood and leaned against him. For some reason, she had an urge to cry. Tears streamed, blurring her vision, disconnected from a trigger.

'Which one? There's bloody hundreds.'

He was strong and lean, not like Fairwood's avatars, too much flesh moving under the surface. She nestled against him, leaning down to his shoulder level. He clicked his tongue (one of them) and adjusted his grip on her waist out of necessity.

'Wes,' she murmured, emotions subsiding, tears drying on her salty cheeks.

'Wes?' A pause. 'Oh! Oh, it was a *joke*.' His shoulder shook as he chuckled. 'Yeah, yeah, he is. Randy bastard. Did he try and give you one?'

Carrie snorted and let him sit her down on the stairs. 'I said no. He did offer.'

'Probably just as well.'

She grinned, and a tendril flicked against her skin, soaking up the salt from her pores. She brushed it away, still smiling. 'Tickles.'

'How about we get you to bed?' Ricky suggested, almost kind. 'Let's get you upstairs, love, and we'll talk in the morning.'

Carrie blinked heavily. 'I am a bit pissed, I think. It was such a good night, and then... more shit happened, and I can't... I really like them, and I want them to like me, and I can't tell them anything.' She sighed, wrapping her arms around him, safe inside The Crows where she had no secrets and could be entirely herself. He yielded, inching closer. 'I can talk to you,' she said, and then, sensible of his feelings on the subject of tools and toys, added, 'and you know you can talk to me.'

He gave her an awkward, out-of-character peck on the top of her head, rubbing her upper arm. 'Yeah, well. Come on, love. Up we get.'

Carrie struggled upright again, bone-tired and aware of the alcoholic buzz still tingling through her. Her mind was blissfully fogged, numb again, amenable to the idea of sleep.

'Were you saying something about... about omens or threads?' she asked, something vague slipping out of reach. 'Sorry. Sorry. I don't remember.'

'I say shit like that all the time.' Ricky rubbed her back.

The dead crow suddenly seemed a long time ago, fading into a murky mess of things she would rather not think about. The steps rocked.

'Easy, love.' He caught her as she stumbled up them.

'D'you want to sleep in my room?' she asked, after he deposited her at the bathroom door.

Ricky gave a shy, lopsided smile. 'If you want.'

'You're handsome when you smile,' Carrie added warmly, in the mood to give compliments.

He stopped smiling.

'Down, tiger.' Carrie shooed him across the corridor and closed the bathroom door on him. 'Go to bed. See you in a sec.'

He hovered, tense. 'This isn't... I don't want...'

'I *know*.'

She shut the door.

Her reflection watched her with whirlpool eyes, immobile in the mirror as she tugged the bobble out of her ponytail and located her toothbrush. All grown up, hair the wrong colour. Not her reflection at all.

'You can fuck off as well,' Carrie told it brusquely, with a savage squirt of toothpaste.

The mirror briefly misted over, and for once, something did as it was told.

This time was different.

When she climbed into bed with him, warm and soft and less inhibited, Ricky felt the shiver shooting through him and pooling, stiffening, in his groin.

Mine, he thought, and froze.

(*That's not me…*)

That house changes you, Harry Bishop warned him, gloating, imaginary. *It's using you, Ricky my boy, like you've been used your entire life—*

Ricky screwed his eyes shut, pressing her against him, fighting the war in his head. He had done exactly what the house wanted, hadn't he? Released the vengeful spirit, additionally imbued with all the rage and spite Fairwood kept contained, and now it was out in the world ready to exact revenge for both of them. He'd given The Crows exactly what she wanted. Now he could stay forever. Why wasn't it enough?

Save her.

Then they could both stay with Carrie forever.

Mine, he thought again, a lump of greed swelling around the unfamiliar burn of lust.

He'd had it once before, only once. He'd been fifteen. Cousin Wes, up and down for anything, even then, fingering Cousin Layla and sucking on her milky round tit, using that tongue of his, up against the wall behind Aunty Em's outhouse. They knew he was watching. She'd opened her eyes, cornflower blue, stared right at him, and it got her off. He'd always liked that colour.

He couldn't be certain what had seared its way into his crotch at that moment: Layla's big round eyes and greedy little moan, or Wesley grinning like the devil around that broad, pink muscle rippling over her breast.

273

Hell's bells and buckets of blood.

He'd blamed it on the cocktail of drugs and lager that got him through most family gatherings back then, exciting his teenage hormones. He wished he could go back to that, bury all this in something noxiously, euphorically chemical, but he couldn't.

It was too late for all that now.

This, though, this feeling: *this* was what *Fairwood* wanted. He was almost sure.

'You all right, love?' he murmured, her heat seeping into his core.

She made a soft sound not unlike one from Cousin Layla's repertoire and wriggled into a more comfortable position, a contented dead weight on his chest.

He rubbed her back in rhythmic circles.

I don't want to, he pleaded with Fairwood silently, staring at the sleeping ceiling …*I don't want that.*

Even his thoughts felt like Fairwood's, heavy and dense in his brain.

But you do, Ricky. You want what I say you want. We're entwined, but I am stronger now.

He held her closer, aware he was exuding a scent not his own – a loamy garden, a library in summer.

We don't need to fight about this, he begged her, a prisoner in his own head …*I gave you what you wanted…*

But Fairwood was angry and not inclined to listen.

(*Try and take me over, Richard Edwin Porter, would you?*
What good is my revenge without her?
You're a LODGER, you will follow the RULES.
SAVE HER.)

He wanted to. He really wanted to. But it didn't work that way.

(Wyrd bið ful aræd: it was gone midnight now and she had one more day.)

'Carrie, wake up,' he croaked aloud, shaking her. 'We had a deal! We had a deal, I kept to my end…'

She groaned in protest. Her groan vibrated back to his groin, quickening his breath.

'Carrie, bloody hell...'

'*What?*' She pulled away, blinking and groggy. 'What's the matter?'

Ricky felt Fairwood pressing in around him, glaring through knotholes. 'It's in my head,' he whispered. 'She's in my head, tell her not to.'

'What is?' She flopped back against the pillows and let him curl up into her. Her arms encircled him, the arms of the Owner, a protecting wall against The Crows.

'The house.' He let her stroke his head, the soothing sensations grounding him, helping him regain control of himself.

(*That's better.*)

Carrie was silent. He thought for a moment she had fallen back asleep, but her hand still stroked the top of his head and over his second mouth. It opened a crack, enough to allow two slim tendrils out. They looped loosely around her wrist for comfort, tasting hand soap and the boozy memory of the pub on her skin.

'The Crows thinks you haven't *really* chosen us,' she mumbled, syrupy-mint breath tickling his scalp. 'It thinks... you need controlling. Persuasion.'

'I don't,' Ricky insisted, writhing against her, itching to claw his way out of his own skins, all of them, wriggle raw and free out of the mesh and into someone else's destiny. 'We had a deal. Tell her I don't, she'll listen to you.'

'*Never trust a Porter,*' Carrie reminded him, drifting off.

Ricky lay rigid in the dark.

The burning in his lower gut hadn't gone away, but it wasn't lust anymore. Maybe he could absorb her after all, take her in and keep her warm under his coils. Better than burying her in the woods, having to dig her up to visit, staking her to the spot when she Rose. Better to hear her screaming in his head than not saying anything at all.

He lay sleepless as the house breathed around him, as Carrie's soft snores began, and the red embers in his eyes glowed with the promise of fire.

–

As dawn broke in streaks of peach and powdery cerulean, a cloud of flies buzzed above the slack jaw of Harry Bishop's severed head. A shard of a shaving mirror was still embedded in his neck.

The crows had landed silently on the grass but were keeping their distance. A breeze ruffled their feathers, but they stood silent on the lawn of the Residential Home, scattered about with glinting beady eyes.

Picking their way tentatively between the birds, Dr Monday and Detective Inspector Paula Parsons, suited up in case the forensics were worth using, and headed towards the decapitated cranium. Parsons had worked with Dr Monday before on several cases. They usually consulted in private, especially when the victim was what the good doctor termed an 'Overgrounder', but this was different. Dr Monday was wearing skin-mask twelve, the one with which DI Parsons was most familiar, to keep continuity.

Parsons had a takeaway cup of coffee in one hand, running the other lightly over her short, natural Afro, profoundly unhappy to be up this side of six-thirty.

'What do you think of this, then?' she asked him.

'It's the elder Mr Bishop,' he said. 'I'm certain.'

Parsons knew that much already. Harry had never had a smile for her in life, and the slack grimace was bitterly familiar.

Dr Monday consulted a notebook. 'Let's see. Miss Harris had one of her unhelpful premonitions, when was it? February, here it is. "Dark room, forward-slash grass."' He manipulated skin-mask twelve into an apologetic wince. 'Not a lot to go on, I'm afraid. That would match this, though – he wasn't killed here.'

Parsons wrinkled her brow and sipped her coffee. Maria would be going to bed now, locking the shutters of her club. She wouldn't be happy if this meant Parsons had to cancel date night.

'Remind me to sort out a psychic liaison officer or something. Bessie Haynes kept ringing in saying something about big black birds being omens of doom, and some kid rang up a few nights ago having hysterics about faces in mirrors. We might have put two and two together sooner. What's with the flies? That's not usual, even for here.'

Dr Monday found himself swallowing. 'Flies?' He turned his attention to the body. 'Ah. Yes.' He produced the orb, which floated pale and nearly invisible into the air. It hovered over the headless corpse, and the cloud of flies scattered into the sky as the orb approached. The orb floated about for a few moments, before returning to Dr Monday's inside jacket pocket.

'Oh.' Dr Monday frowned.

Behind him, a crow called twice.

Parsons shifted from foot to foot, glancing around at the birds with knitted brows. 'Why are they all *staring* like that?'

Dr Monday shook his head. 'I'm getting a lot of activity here.'

'As in, *paranormal* activity? Great.' She rolled her eyes. 'How do I arrest a ghost, exactly?'

Maria, ruby-nailed and bloody-lipped, would roll her own eyes at that.

Dr Monday shrugged. 'I am not entirely sure, Detective Inspector.'

'Well that bodes well.'

Dr Monday patted his pocket to reassure the orb. Parsons could see its vibrations through the fabric of his suit. 'It's angry, malevolent. I sense it has been contained for a time. That often magnifies a spirit's animosity.'

'*Could* a—' Parsons squinted down at the blood-soaked grass '—a ghost *really* have done... *this*?'

Dr Monday nodded. 'You would be surprised what a spirit can do to a physical being. It is quite fascinating. I have a series of papers published on the subject in *The Spectral Scalpel*, if you were interested—'

Parsons held up her hand. 'No, thank you.'

Dr Monday's skin-mask appeared a little crestfallen. 'Spectral Surgery is a very fascinating area. It's one of my specialisms, as a matter of fact.'

'I know, you've mentioned it once or twice.' Parsons set her lips and looked back at the corpse. 'I wish those bloody crows would get lost. It's like a Hitchcock film out here.'

'They are not going to bother us,' Monday said with some confidence. 'They sense the energy around the body. A sure sign of malevolent energies, I'm afraid.'

Bleary-eyed, Parsons looked up at him without gratitude. 'Cheers.'

'You're welcome.'

Parsons shot him a suspicious glare, but Dr Monday wasn't being sarcastic. She kneeled down beside the head. 'So, our ghostly visitor ripped Harry's head clean off. Why?'

'Well, that's the question, isn't it?' Dr Monday stepped away. 'Until we know *why*, I can't guarantee the efficacy of an exorcism, of course. And we would not want to dispel the spirit without giving proper thought to where it might be sent, or if it has the power to return. If its business here is so pressing, it may only be a temporary measure, and then we would be right back where we began, and it would gradually build up a tolerance to future rites.'

'Like antibiotic-resistant diseases?' Her coffee cup was no longer steaming into the air, grown cold in her hand. 'Right. Well. Let's not go at it half-cocked, then.'

Parsons went through into the ruined room, scorch marks still fresh on the carpet, and looked around her at the sum total of Harry Bishop's life. Dr Monday followed, his orb prepared to be useful.

'You know I have a… history with the Bishops, don't you?' she asked him, her voice tight and strained. She hadn't been out, then, and Guy had been like her in some ways, quiet and unhappy. She put the college years firmly behind her.

There were the musty old books she remembered, stacked high in corners in the Bishops' house, precarious towers of yellowed pages and leather binding you'd had to navigate to get to the bathroom. Then there were the odds and ends, the tasteful statuettes of hand-painted porcelain, the ones from the Bishops' own living room which Harry had never dusted. And even – she suppressed a gasp – the old globe from Harry's study. It was a giant, cracked, ancient thing, the kind on its own stand which took up a great deal of space and did very little except turn reluctantly when forced. It was so old it didn't even spin anymore. It had once been a drinks cabinet, but Harry didn't drink. His wife had, like a fish, until she'd wrapped her car around a tree. The whole earth in all its intricate detail was tilted to one side, the North Pole pointing at her from its compass circle.

'I remember this.' Parsons studied it. 'He'd never let me touch anything in his house. Acted like letting me through the door was doing me a favour.' She straightened up, tilting her head to one side.

'I'm sorry you were not accepted into the Bishops' home.' Dr Monday released his pet orb from his pocket. It hovered for a moment, as if uncertain of where to go, then began to circle.

Parsons snorted. 'Harry was a racist old prick.' She nodded at the en-suite, checking her white suit and shoe covers. 'Can you hear that? Let's see the bathroom.'

The door was ajar. A low buzzing was coming from inside.

'Je-sus...'

Flies crawled over one another in a fight for space as they explored the tiles and the towels. The old man's blood was everywhere, the flies swarming thickest on the globs of arterial spray and around the slick dark pool.

'Found the body, then.' Parsons shuddered. 'Oh, that's a bad one. Can we do something about those flies?'

Dr Monday closed the bathroom door.

'That's not what I meant.' Parsons sighed. 'Who the hell do I call? Is this something I'm going to have to turn over to your lot?'

'"My lot"? Ah – you mean the Hunters. I would rather not. I fear we would end up with trigger-happy Sam Maitland, and we are only dealing, so far as I can tell, with the spirit of a child. Magda will be able to confirm that.'

'Monday, we're dealing with a spirit who put a shaving mirror through an old man's neck.' Parsons spoke slowly, trying to come to terms with her own words. 'I need to sort this out.'

'I would suggest a verdict of suicide,' Dr Monday suggested. 'Dear me. This is very bad.' He shook his head. 'Unless the ghost is protected in some way, I think I can catch it before it does any more harm. I will do my best.' He pulled a pocket watch out of his pocket, and Parsons stared at it, aghast. 'Well – someone should inform poor Guy, of course. I will do what I can here, but I need to be back at the surgery by eight.'

Parsons exploded. 'My *God*, Monday! I can't tell Guy his father cut his own head off while shaving! What am I supposed to do about that mess in there?'

Police procedure was lost on Dr Monday. He stared at her. 'Forgive me. I didn't think.' He opened the door of the bathroom a crack, and the angry buzzing ate into Parsons like a buzz saw. 'I won't be a moment,' he promised, and, spats clicking on the tiles, he slid inside and the door snapped shut behind him.

Parsons closed her eyes. Telling the family about a bereavement was the worst part of the job. She didn't want to tell Guy at all, but it would be best coming from her. Date night was going to be a wash-out this evening.

Let the Past Burn

In which things unravel and Ricky says goodbye

13 May

Colonel Mark Curtis lived on the outskirts of Pagham-on-Sea, near the new estate. From the cottage, the estate was clearly visible – a sharp incongruity of concrete high rises surrounded by fields, and a high brick wall bristling with cameras and high-powered floodlights. The cottage was an outpost between the wall and the town, a short walk from Pagham Parkway station. Every night, the Colonel went for his patrol around the perimeter of that wall, checking the lights were on. He was the sole garrison, the thin red line, the one thing that stood between what was inside the shadows behind those walls and the empty shadows of the town. Fairwood could sense the purpose of the building, its functionality, its structure, its past. It read the layers of energies baked into the stone and architectural quirks like a three-dimensional map.

The Colonel was out. The cottage was empty and alone.

Cathy Ross came first, a small flutter of silent white through the large mirror. From her apron pocket, a small chip of tile tumbled out and bounced along the carpet.

Fairwood expanded from the small tile chip, angling itself into a corner by the skirting, and let itself meld with the cottage, feeling for hiding places and all the secrets Owners liked to keep. Carrie's curiosity had soaked into it like water into old wood: questions riddled its thoughts like woodworm in a beam.

From the mirror, a vengeful spectre with whirlpool eyes watched, the frame oozing flies.

'Hello,' Fairwood greeted her. 'He'll be back soon. Bit tougher than old Harry, I'd say.'

The malevolence of Cathy Ross, infused with the spite of The Crows, glared at the avatar through the glass.

'They'll catch you if you keep using mirrors like that,' Fairwood warned her, melting a hand through a painting and into the safe beyond. There was a clunk and a click of the lock mechanism. 'And after the Colonel there's at least one more to go. She'll be the toughest. And I can't help you there.'

Revenge, whispered Cathy Ross.

Fairwood dipped into the safe and rifled through the contents, eyes frosting over with data. The new broadband connection was worth the line rental. Anything outside of Fairwood's own experience could be downloaded.

The photograph was at the back, in a manila envelope.

It was a match to the one Janet Varney had tried to burn. The figures were clearer, unmarred by fire damage.

'Well, this isn't good,' Fairwood muttered, sliding it out. 'Better keep hold of this. He won't be needing it after today, anyway.'

The flies buzzed in a low drone, vibrating bodies swarming thick against the mirror glass.

–

Ricky's head pounded with pressure, a jack-hammer behind his eyes. It was the last day. Her last day.

Rising season was upon them.

He could feel the life in the soil below his feet, pushing up with greedy, thirsty fingers, the contamination taking root in long-dead flesh and marrowbone. His father would be recovering faster now, without daily dosing. He'd missed a few now, and Ricky couldn't face the struggle that would ensue to pour a fresh dose down his throat.

He couldn't go back home.

Bramble Cottage was no longer the broken-down border of his life, but Fairwood needed proof he meant it, proof he would respect her rules. He knew he was swapping one cage for another, but it was at least one *he'd* chosen.

He strolled back to the mouth of the smugglers' tunnel, spat on the skin of his latest palms (too smooth, too new for decent work) and dragged the bulging sack of bits and bones further away from the gaping hole. It was not a part of him, no reason to feel it was being cut off, no reason for the hollow in his chest. It was spring-cleaning, that was all. Not an amputation.

Antlers twitched as the skull bumped along the ground.

The Green Man tile bumped against his leg.

A leaden razor pulsed in his chest.

Gerald dragged a groove through The Chase and into the fields beyond it, trussed up limbs tight against the donkey hide.

The pyre was ready.

Gerald was silent, inanimate as ever, not one to fight against the web of destiny.

Even when Ricky bent his knees and hurled him up into place, there was no movement, no protest.

'It can't be helped,' Ricky said, gruff and panting. He dug out the Green Man and propped it up so Fairwood could see. 'Don't look at me like that. It's the only way she'll trust me.' Ricky glanced back at the Green Man. 'You think you got the Missus all to yourself, don't you?' he asked it, thinking of Carrie. 'Way I see it, that still ain't true. Not really. Look. This is my sacrifice. All for you. We go way back, you and me, right? Well – what's she burning then, if she loves you more'n I do?'

(*What?*)

Ricky took a step back. 'I'm just tellin' the truth,' he said sweetly. 'I'm giving up something. But she hasn't, has she? Not all of it.'

(*What do you mean?*)

'That fam'ly of hers… that necklace she wears, binding her to them, she hasn't taken it off, has she? Still a part of her she hasn't given up.'

(*No. No. You're trying to get between us…*)

'I'm not! I'm just saying I'm… I'm as committed as she is. I'm an asset. You *need* me to do the things she can't.'

He nodded, giving the flames their cue, and the pyre ignited in a rush of smoke and sparks. The heat flared against his skin.

'See?' His voice caught.

Gerald never moved when the flames licked his hide, never twitched except when the wood shifted and the skull sank, twisting sideways to stare mournfully at his creator and betrayer with dead, dun-coloured eyes.

For a brief moment, they reflected someone else behind Ricky, creeping up with long-limbed stealth. Spider-jointed arms reached for him in a dark rage, claws extended.

The flame-licked skull smiled, and Ricky turned too late.

–

Guy had a drink to face the day, just one. It was nice of Paula to tell him herself yesterday. Wouldn't tell him all of it, but he got the gist.

He poured himself a hair of the dog.

Beverley would say it was all right, even if his dad would disapprove.

Oh, no. His dad couldn't disapprove anymore.

A phone call saved him from pouring another.

Mark Curtis, on his way home from an early morning walk, inviting him over for lunch, telling him he shouldn't be on his own.

'I'll be round in ten,' Guy promised, putting up a front. Easy to do when you couldn't look the other person in the eye. Mark had been the first person he had told, once Paula had left. 'How are you holding up?'

'Oh, you know.' The sound of keys being pulled out of a pocket, jingling into the lock. 'It's *you* I'm worried about, son. It's a hell of a thing to happen. Hell of a thing. You don't sound too clever, you all right?'

'I'm fine,' Guy lied. It hadn't sunk in, even though he had been waiting for the news for months. He thought it would be peaceful, at night in bed, or sat up in his chair. He hadn't expected a house call from the Detective Inspector.

'If I ask you a straight question, will you tell me the truth?' An unusually tactful approach from the old duffer, Guy thought, even though he knew what the question was going to be.

'Sure.'

'I know you had a... little drop before the meeting this week. I just want to ask. Should I be worried?'

He meant, was it like before, should there be an intervention, did he need to go back to meetings, to a clinic, would his father be upset. No, of course not, his father was dead. Guy winced, rubbing the back of his neck.

'Has Beverley said something to you?'

'I want to hear it from you.'

Guy heard the door close. 'Are you home?'

'Just got in.' Keys dropped into the bowl. 'Come over when you're ready. We could have lunch.' A pause. A gentle nudge. 'I'm waiting on an answer, Guy.'

Guy sucked his teeth, holding back the tears. He hadn't cried for a long time – not since his mother died. He'd had to be strong for his dad, sitting up in his chair until four in the morning, reading the same page of the same book over and over and not seeing any of the words. He hadn't cried at the church, when the Methodist minister asked him to come up and say a few words. He'd made sure to smile and thank people for coming. It wasn't her, anyway, not her lying there. It was just a box with her name on it.

Then they'd got to the crematorium. Some well-meaning neighbour put their arm around his shoulders and said how beautiful the wreaths looked, and everything had fallen apart.

It felt like that now. His world, crumbling. Leaving nothing but empty space, no path, no signposts, no way back. The racing tips weren't enough, *bloody* Ricky Porter. Five to two, what shit odds were they? He was losing his dad's shop, the last bit of his dad, and his dad had died alone in fear. Taken from him, but not by the death they'd expected, not the one they'd prepared themselves for. It wasn't fair.

'I, um. I'm sorry, Uncle Mark.' He pressed the phone into his chest as he sniffed back the loss and cleared his throat. He raised the phone again. 'I'll be over in ten minutes.'

There was a sound of breaking glass on the other end.

'What the devil—'

There was an unearthly shriek, jarring in the speaker, full of hate and fury. Guy's phone battery drained from fifty-seven per cent to nothing and went dead.

'*Mark?* Uncle Mark!'

He held the power button down but it wouldn't come back on.

'*Shit!*'

He was out into the street and getting in his car, although he knew he wasn't all right to drive.

He broke at least three traffic laws racing through town, but he didn't care. He barely registered the journey, let alone the red lights.

The Colonel's car was parked in its usual place.

Red-eyed, he trampled the flowerbed and peered in through the living room window.

A fat black fly wrung its legs in consternation on the other side of the pane.

'*Mark!*'

The spare key was under a rock: Guy had used it several times, but in that moment, he couldn't remember which one. He heaved up the stones around the front door, spraying his jeans with soil, breaths ragged and shallow. The key revealed itself, chinking against stone, and Guy snatched it up, fumbling it. He got it into the keyhole on the fourth try.

His godfather was lying on his back in the living room, veins standing out on his throat and head, eyes bugging out at something no longer there.

Guy heaved.

Mark Curtis had been torn apart from the inside, as if something had seeped into his blood and birthed itself through his chest. He'd always been a powerful man, solid as a tree. Guy remembered being hoisted in a fireman's lift when he was fourteen, his dad looking on, not one for games. Those strong ribs were shattered and open, a gaping wound where his heart should have been. Guy looked up, sweat beading on his forehead, blood rushing away from his brain. The ceiling swam, a gory mess, with indescribable things clotting where they'd splattered.

A faint child's giggle made him jump, hairs prickling up over the back of his neck.

Could a little girl do this?

'I'm going to—' he started, threatening her, but the second heave cut him off with a watery gurgle.

He slapped a hand over his mouth and backed out of the living room, out of the door.

His phone was already in his hands, but he threw up first, over and over, until he was dry-heaving his grief into the ruined flowers.

Wiping his mouth with the back of his hand, eyes streaming, he leaned against the wall for support. His phone should still be dead, but it wasn't. He stared at it, the display reading the wrong date and time as it struggled back to life. It wasn't the police he called.

'Hello, dear.'

Guy breathed out. 'Beverley? Thank God, I– I need to talk to you.'

'Guy? What's the matter?' The voice that could reach him any time of day or night, regardless of signal, blew the dread away. Beverley Wend could solve any problem, fix any broken thing, right any wrong. Beverley Wend could make everything go away. 'Is this about your father?'

'Yes. No. It's… about Uncle Mark, the Colonel, it's – God. He's dead,' Guy said, breaking. He slumped against the wall in the dirt, staring at the patch of vomit beside him without really seeing it. 'I'm at Uncle Mark's house, and, and he's—' He broke off, gasping. 'He's gone.'

'It's not his time to go,' Beverley said, reasonable.

'Something ripped his heart clean out of his chest,' Guy rasped. 'Can he come, come back from that?'

There was a dead silence.

'Beverley? Can he?'

She didn't reply.

Guy lowered the phone from his ear, staring at the well-kept lawn that Colonel Curtis would no longer mow, the roses and lavender bushes he would no longer tend to.

It wasn't his time to go. The abyss wasn't due to open yet. And even when it did, he would be back.

Guy had imagined that scene a thousand times in his head, running it over like a chapter in a novel. He, Guy, would be older and white-haired. He would be gardening, maybe, or out for a slow stroll. He'd look up – his eyesight weaker, hearing no longer as sharp, but he'd see Colonel Curtis striding towards him with his usual confidence, bristling moustache the same as ever, and they'd shake hands. And Guy wouldn't die alone, no matter what happened, no matter who or what life swept away from him. And the Colonel would play chess with him the way they used to when Guy was a boy, and this time, Guy might even win.

Colonel Curtis had been loyal to the Bishops all the years he'd been in Pagham-on-Sea, generation after generation, getting to know them all as the decades came and went, a friendship the Colonel claimed went back before the Battle of Hastings, although the family line had gone through several family names since then. It didn't matter what they were called: the Colonel had always sought them out, the heirs to his friendship.

Bloodhound faithful, Harry had liked to say.

Loyal enough that, after the doctor's diagnosis, the Colonel was prepared to sacrifice even his honour for a dark ritual, a dirty secret, and give Harry a chance to live. To grow old. To have a child who would not, in their turn, leave the Colonel all alone.

288

'Bez? Please, I need your help,' Guy whispered. 'Please, Bez, I don't know, I don't know what to do. I did everything the way you told me to, I didn't... please, Beverley, please help him.'

When Beverley Wend spoke again, her voice was hard and cold. 'I *warned* them. I warned them all at the start what they'd be bringing on their heads. But our Eileen always knew best, didn't she? Always knew better than me.'

Guy shivered, swallowing his sobs. 'That ghost... it got Dad. And Mark. It's coming for you next, I know it will.'

'Don't worry about me. I've got some tricks, too. But I need you to pull yourself together, do you hear me? Pull yourself together and do as I say. Can you do that?'

Guy nodded, forgetting it was a phone call. He caught himself and verbalised it. 'Yes.'

'Burn it down.'

The dread pooled in Guy's sore stomach, whispering that this was, obscurely, his fault. He could hear Beverley in his hand.

'Guy? Guy, answer me.'

He raised the phone back to his ear. 'Burn... what down?'

'Fairwood House, of course.'

'Burn The Crows?' Guy repeated.

'Set her on fire,' Beverley said, in tones that brooked no argument. 'I'll deal with the spirit. But you deal with the house.'

'But...'

Beverley's rasp scythed through his head, loaded with years of disappointments and the endless rebellions of her spawn.

'*Not you too.*'

Guy struggled upright, lurching away from the wall. 'I – burn it down? I can't, it's cursed...'

'For the last time, Guy, it's *not cursed*. That's a *story*. There's a *protection* glamour on it that only affects *us*, and that's real old blood magic, it can't hurt *you*. It's a lot of things, that house, but it can't *curse* you.' Beverley sighed. 'It's under your skin, isn't it? Calls to you, somehow. I know. I've heard it, too. Now go over there, take some petrol, and set the damn thing on fire. That will take the strength out of this spirit, and it'll be therapeutic for you. Leave the girl in there, if you like, it will serve her right. Meddling like that, *this is her fault.*'

Guy shuddered, but the voice triggered something deep inside him, wrapped around his heart.

'This is her fault,' he mumbled, alone in the garden.

The echoes of childhood faded and died on the breeze.

'That's my boy.' Beverley hung up.

Guy stumbled back to his car and sat in it for a long time, gripping the steering wheel. When he rang the police to report the Colonel's body, the bottle of bourbon was already half-empty.

If I Can't Have You...

His mother stroked his head, humming the same three notes in a minor key.

He pressed his head into her palm, eyes still closed, savouring the moment. An obedient tear trickled down his cheek.

'That's my boy,' his mother crooned. 'That's my good boy.'

'Soup's ready, Lettie.'

Ricky opened his eyes, blinking the salt drops away. He was bound to a chair, which was laughable. His father couldn't hope to restrain him like that. He was too strong for them now. He strained against the bonds and the pain shot straight into his flesh. Ricky swore violently, earning him a sharp smack around the head from his scandalised mother. Her black mourning veil fluttered over him like a moth.

'Language, Richard!'

Ricky gritted his teeth, breathing hard through the stabbing waves in his torso. 'S-s-*sorry* Mum!' He clenched his jaw. 'It ain't right, it *hurts*...'

She was there, veil lifted, cheek to cheek. Decay filled his nostrils. 'Are you going to cry, my lovely good boy? Leak your salt for your mother?'

He tried not to, but the response was Pavlovian. In return for her rare, affectionate hand, tears spilled down his cheeks despite his attempts to hold them back. The pain eased as she traced a hand over the chains, a proboscis lapping at his tear ducts.

'That's it, help your mother get stronger,' his father said, the closest to approval he ever came.

Ricky sniffed, pleading silently.

His father was a spindly mass of shadow, but if he concentrated, he could see the older man's form underneath, the dirty string vest over a scrawny breastbone, the long limbs and the evil, watery stare.

'Doant you bother trying, son,' his father said, not unkindly. 'Granny Wend came to see us. I got you good.'

Ricky looked down. (*Shit me, he did an' all.*)

He was oozing between the chain links. The metal was oiled with something, probably something of Gran's. Could be she didn't trust Mr Wend or that she was jealous… the 'why' didn't matter. She'd never cared enough about his parents before, said he was being precocious, acting out, let it be. Ricky couldn't remember the last time Granny Wend had even asked about either of them.

She was doing this out of spite, not because she cared.

'I knowed you Changed again,' his father said. 'Could tell you got a new skin. No burns. No tattoos. New skin smell.' He drew his long nails along the wall, almost back to his old self. 'You all beautiful at last under there? Thought you could hide it from your own flesh and bone?'

Ricky looked down at the coils spilling out of his body, chained up on the floor.

(*I am bleedin' beautiful, and it ain't an 'it', father, it's me, me, me.*)

Ricky cursed his self-indulgence in staying at Fairwood for so long. His father needed more doses than his mother, and more frequently. He'd thought he could avoid them, safe at The Crows where they couldn't go.

He tried to Change, but he couldn't.

His father had ripped him open, punctured him, done something.

Pain spasmed through his guts, his beautiful coils, and he gasped with all his needle-sharp mouths.

'Look,' he gasped, falling into his father's broad accent to calm things down. 'Things... haven't been good wi'us, I know dat, I know it feather, an' some of it's all-along-o' me, I put my hand up to it. But all I want's a bit of *bloody appreciation*, and you *never listen to me!*' He hadn't meant to shout, but it burst out from his depths in a loud, guttural snarl.

His mother withdrew her hand.

His father heard what he wanted to hear. 'All-along-o' you is right,' he said in his deep ruminating growl, slipping deep into dialect. ''Tis all-along-o' you that your mother's so ampery.'

(*He's right, weak and decaying like cheese, she is.*)

'Feed him, George,' his mother begged, 'feed him his punishment.'

Ricky could smell the soup now. His punishment meal. Bits of his mother were in that soup. Bits that would never live long enough to spawn properly but would love to feed on living flesh, living brain, before they wriggled their last dance. Turn your mind to scrambled egg, they would, holey as Swiss cheese, like a foreigner's breakfast.

His face prickled with an odd sensation.

(*Is this what fear feels like?*)

'No! No, no, now hang on, hold on a minute, feather, feather doan' you be doing of it, doan' you bleedin' dare—'

'Blank as water, ye'll be,' his father gloated, scratching at his string vest. 'Disremember your own name.'

'My baby boy, back to me again,' crooned his mother. 'Start all over we will, and you'll be good as gold.'

He cricked his neck to seek her out, a looming presence in black lace and shadow. 'Mum...' His guts twisted. 'I'll be good now, Mum, I'll do what you say. Doant let him do it, Mum, please, please, Mum, I'll be good as gold.'

She shook her head. 'He's lying, George. Listen to him! Why couldn't we have had a girl, ruby-honest lips she'd have.'

The soft, susurrus words cut him deep.

'*You always say that,*' he hissed down at his chains, scraping the chair on the floor.

Fragments of a plan formed, shards of a broken mirror.

He breathed through the pain.

'I'll get you another live girl, mother. I know one.'

'You don't know any girls,' his father scoffed.

'I do.' He whipped his head around, the soup getting perilously close to his face now, borne by his father's elastic, clawed hands. 'Keep away, I'll disremember 'er, *don't*.'

The bowl paused, tilting towards him. Things bubbled to the surface, every bubble of scum alive with pale, kicking larvae-legs.

'If y' lie to me, boy, this goes in yer face,' his father warned, soft and low. 'They'll wriggle in how they like. Up yer nose, through yer eyes…' He sloshed the bowl on purpose, slopping a little of the living liquid over the rim. Something splashed on the bare skin of his hand. A sharp stab, like a horsefly bite, told him it was trying to burrow.

Gritting his teeth, he shook his hand under the chain that bound his wrist to the wooden chair arm, the burning spreading where the metal protested.

Behind him, his mother gave a soft little giggle not unlike his own.

'Let me loose!' he shouted. 'Let me loose, I'll go and get her for you!'

His father chuckled. 'He thinks we're stupid, Lettie.'

'He's not lying, George.'

'He ain't lying, no, but he ain't coming back. You bet he ain't.'

Ricky swallowed as the wriggling soup-spot finally plopped off his hand onto the floor, unsuccessful, and lay there like a flat, yellow tick. 'She's got yellow hair,' he said.

His mother went silent.

'Let me go, I'll go get her.'

'Will you bring her here?' his father asked.

(*Careful.*)

'I'll tell her you want to meet her. She's curious.'

The soup moved closer to his lips. He could smell the wriggling bits trying to find sustenance before they died. The contents of the bowl were humped at one end now, closest to him, even though the bowl was level.

(*Not my mind, not my mind, don't take that.*)

His father wasn't buying it, but his mother might.

'She's pretty, Mum, you'll like her, bright as a button she is. Yellow hair, soft skin, smells of sugar and summer.'

'He's *not* lying, George,' his mother whispered, and he could hear the longing in her voice. 'Oh, George, please. Please get me a girl. It's been so long since—'

He felt the tug in his chest before he heard the knock on the door.

(*Shit me, she isn't.*)

(*I never did that, I never.*)

He tried to twist his neck to see but he couldn't.

The bowl, at least, was withdrawn.

His mother was at the window, he could hear the lace against the net curtain. Today was the last day, the day he'd seen in the guts of the Blue Moon girl. It was going to be his fault after all.

'Oh, *George!*' his mother breathed, staring through the grimy glass at the visitor standing outside. 'She's *perfect!*'

–

Carrie played with the pendant of her necklace as she waited outside Bramble Cottage for an answer. A piece of brick was in her pocket this time, a kind of protective talisman. She had considered taking a knife with her, or a hammer, but the avatar was probably enough on its own.

What did you actually *see?* She thought, knocking the door.

He disappeared. One minute he was burning Gerald, then he was gone.

Carrie rolled her eyes, running the pendant along the chain.

'I hope this isn't going to be awful,' she murmured.

The door opened.

Carrie looked up at a middle-aged man in a string vest, took in his full lips and wide, straight nose – clearly a Porter, clearly

Ricky's father. Long, sinewy arms drooped down his sides, a lit cigarette between two long fingers.

'We don't buy at the door.'

'I'm not selling anything.' Carrie caught a glimpse of the cottage behind him – swept clean, bright, airy. No reek of decay or rot hit her, although she'd been braced for it.

'I'm… I'm a friend of your son's. I'm… Caroline.'

'Our son don't have no friends,' George Porter told her, dipping his balding head. 'What're you really here for?'

Carrie sighed, taking a leaf out of the soothsayer's playbook and telling the selective truth. 'Ricky said to drop by, he said he'd, um, do a bone-reading for me.'

'Did he? What you giving him?'

He hasn't seen me before, Carrie realised. *He doesn't know who I am.* No, of course not. They'd been upstairs, ill or something.

Carrie revelled in the ironic anonymity. 'Um. He said the first one was free. Like smack.' She watched George Porter's face.

Slowly, George stepped back from the door. 'He's not in, but you're welcome to come in and wait.'

Carrie smiled, and stepped into a very different space.

The cottage was clean, fixed up. The stench was gone – some of it may have been Gerald, but Carrie couldn't even smell mould. A wooden chair was pulled out from the table and facing away from it, which struck her as odd.

'Lettie, there's a girl here,' George announced in his gruff drawl. 'Caroline.'

Carrie turned.

Lettie Porter was a small, petite woman standing by the window in a long, black dress. Her brown hair was thin and lank, scraped back in a bun with a few stray threads hanging down her gaunt cheeks. She regarded Carrie with wide, brown eyes, full lips parted happily. Apart from the height difference, Carrie could have mistaken her and her husband for twins.

'Caroline! What a *beautiful* name.'

Carrie had honestly been expecting more tentacles and hoped her surprise didn't show. 'Are you Ricky's mother? Mrs Porter?'

'Yes, but call me Lettie, dear, please.' Lettie Porter also had the Porter nose, Carrie noted. Thinner lips, but the cheekbones reminded her of Mrs Wend. 'He won't be long.'

He doesn't live here anymore, Carrie thought, glancing at George Porter smoking in the corner. *He hasn't lived here for… a week, at least? Two? All his stuff is gone. Gerald is gone.*

Her gut told her to get out, and she listened. 'That's okay, I can… come back.'

'Oh, no, stay,' Lettie Porter entreated. 'You're just in time for soup.'

Carrie spotted a bowl on the table that she hadn't noticed before. 'I'm… thank you, but I've eaten.' She sensed George moving around the edge of the room, circling her. He was putting himself between her and the door.

Carrie plunged her hand into her pocket and rubbed the piece of brick.

Everything was wrong.

There was wallpaper on the walls, the net curtains were clean.

The chair, turned to face the wall instead of the table, kept drawing her attention and she didn't know why.

(*Bloody hell, piss* off *love!*)

Carrie heard it, punching into her head. It wasn't her thought. She wondered if she could get out of a window. 'Sorry – can I use your toilet?'

'Upstairs.' George pointed upwards. 'First on the left. There's water in the cistern, Lettie! Did you fill the bucket, woman?'

'Yes, George,' Lettie murmured, meek. 'If you could refill the cistern afterwards, dear, we'd be obliged, wouldn't we, George?'

'Obliged,' George Porter repeated, scratching his vest. 'Trouble with the water.'

Carrie nodded, and climbed up. The boards creaked heavily underfoot.

This isn't real, she realised. *None of it is.*

She paused at the top of the stairs, confronted by a narrow landing and a flat wall. To the right was a bedroom, door ajar, with an old-fashioned single bedframe in it, and not much else. Curious, she pushed the door open a little further, but there was nothing to see. It was austere, devoid of furniture except for the iron bedframe. The window was barred on the inside.

Ricky's old room?

She turned and went left, not trusting the floorboards although they looked and felt pretty solid. The bathroom was poky and narrow, a toilet and sink and an ancient tin bath hanging on the wall, straight out of the Forties. A metal pail of water, apparently drawn from the pump outside, was positioned under the sink. The room was spotlessly clean, but Carrie didn't trust her senses and couldn't put her finger on why. It had no window.

She made a point of slamming the bathroom door, but crept out into the room next door, the last of the only three rooms upstairs. This was Lettie and George's bedroom, a neat counterpane on the double bed, pillows plumped innocently against the wrought iron headboard. There was a dresser and a wardrobe, but nothing personal. Carrie crept around, Fairwood giving her a sixth sense for creaking floorboards that might give her away, and made it to the mullioned window. It lifted up – she knew that from the night of Janet's attack. She unscrewed the mechanism keeping it closed and heaved. It wouldn't budge.

She tried again.

(*Come on*, get on with it.)

Not my thought.

She heaved again, but the window was stuck.

(*What's taking her so long?*)

'I'm *trying*,' Carrie growled under her breath, and stopped. She turned, whispering as loud as she dared. '*Ricky?*'

(*At least it ain't my fault, I didn't bring her here, her choice to come.*)

Carrie tip-toed back to the bathroom, flushed the toilet and tipped the contents of the bucket into the cistern as requested, and came back down the stairs, empty bucket in hand.

'Thanks.' She wiped her hands down her jeans as if drying them. 'I'm from next door, by the way.'

George and Lettie were together, their backs to the front door. The chair, that oddly placed chair, had moved. Only a fraction, but it was now at a slight angle.

'What?' Lettie Porter's voice had a mellifluous quality, and for a moment her face was obscured as if by a dark mist. Carrie blinked and it faded, twisting through an angle with a wave of vertigo. She winced, frowning.

'I… own The Crows.'

The world twisted.

Carrie rocked through an angle in space, the cottage bending in front of her as her revelation caused George Porter to lose concentration. The shapes of Ricky's parents morphed in front of her. Carrie stumbled sideways against a patch of black mould on the wall.

She pulled away, inhaling the reek she remembered.

'What the pest are you doing here?' Ricky yelled at her, a bloody, chained mess in the kitchen chair.

Carrie gasped, shrinking away. 'Oh my *God!* What *happened* to you?'

The cottage snapped back and the mould disappeared beneath a skin of tight, clean wallpaper. Ricky was gone.

'This is how forensics never find anything,' Carrie mumbled, numb with shock. 'Isn't it? This isn't real. I don't know what you're doing, but this isn't real, is it?'

She judged the distance to the door but didn't fancy her chances against whatever George and Lettie *actually* were. Ricky was bad enough, or rather the Thing he really was under that tight human skin, that towering whirlwind of coils and slavering mouths and thousands and thousands of eyes… all wrapped in a tracksuit.

She started to laugh, like she had in the hospital the night Grampa Jim died.

'You're all mad,' she said, shoulders shaking. 'Your whole family, you're all fucking insane.'

'I like her, George,' Lettie Porter whispered, not taking her eyes off Carrie. 'Can we keep this one, I want her.'

Carrie bit down on her lip but couldn't help it. 'Mrs Porter, I'm sorry to have to tell you this, but your son's an arsehole.' She regained control, snorted, and shook her head. 'Did you know you... you ate my ex-boyfriend? He fed you my ex, in a pie. God! Sorry, sorry, I don't know why that's so funny. It's not funny.' She swallowed another snort. 'It's not funny.' She stopped. 'You haven't offered me any tea.'

Lettie and George looked at each other.

'George?'

'Go boil the kettle, Lettie.'

The cottage slipped back into how it actually was, a reeking shell in the woods, and the vertigo sensation rocked her back against the mould patch on the wall. Lettie Porter, fully veiled and solemn in black, slid off to the kitchen around the bloody body of her chained son.

George Porter in his string vest, a four-limbed tarantula of a man, watched her with baleful intensity, guarding the door.

'Don't eat the soup,' Ricky warned her, spitting a blood clot on the floor.

Carrie sobered, starting at him. 'What... what have you done now?'

'Oh, that's bloody *charming*.' Ricky nodded down at his shredded torso, thick cables of coils spilling onto the floor from his open intestines and chained in place of his legs. She couldn't tell where the human stopped or started, or how any of him held together. 'You call me an arsehole in front of my dear old mother, then you assume this is *my* fault? Well, fuck me very much, thanks a bloody lot.'

'*Richard!*' his mother hissed from the kitchen.

Ricky went red. 'Look at me, woman, I'm torn to shit and chained to a bloody chair, give me a break!'

His mother hissed around the door but said nothing else.

'Poisoned us, he did.' George gave her a wary look. 'That's what our lad's done. Been doing it for years, not that anyone cares. All over a toy, if you'd believe it. You should see his poor mother, the state of her. Wild, he was, wild. Drugs, drink, you name it, a bloody embarrassment, 'til he started taking his gift seriously.' He shot his son a glare and spat on the filthy floor. 'He's a man as ain't no account at all, were not for that.'

Ricky rolled his eyes, but his cheeks burned an ugly crimson.

George glanced from his son to the stranger by the stairs. Carrie sensed he was unsure and took her chance. There was no way she would get by him – those arms, dear God, those claws – but she might be able to get out of the bedroom window now she was seeing what was really there. Or find another way out. She might break something in the fall but it was worth the risk, wasn't it?

She jerked into action and sprinted up the stairs.

George Porter was too slow.

His claws raked the wall at the top of the stairs as she veered left across the rotten boards of the landing, trying not to see what the bathroom really looked like, and bulled her way into the master bedroom, slamming the door on those grasping, multi-jointed hands. Carrie heaved at the nearest heavy item of furniture, a chest of drawers, and rammed it against the door without looking at what had been leaning against it.

The girl's corpse hit the floor like a broken puppet, nailed to the wall by one arm.

'Oh *shit!*'

Carrie backed into the middle of the bedroom. Another girl was sat at the cracked vanity mirror in the later stages of decay. They may have been pretty, once. They had been dressed up like dolls in old-fashioned dresses, dusty hair in careful arrangements, as if someone had been playing with them. The source of the smell was now sickeningly apparent.

Carrie fought the nausea – no time for that – and pushed the seated girl off her stool. She threw the stool at the window, in this reality not mullioned at all but a single pane, cracked and dirty, and it shattered with a satisfying crash of glass.

Something grabbed her ankle.

Carrie looked down.

Another dead girl was gripping her with dry, hungry fingers, broken neck twisted up and mouth working furiously as she tried to pull herself closer.

'*Shit!*' Carrie kicked the zombie-girl in the head, shook her off and stumbled backwards.

Three others, decaying into the walls and crawling with insect larvae, were jolting slowly awake, following her progress. One reached out from its slumped position in a corner, surrounded by tatty embroidered cushions, but couldn't move.

Carrie froze. Her plan disappeared.

She stood rooted to the spot as she had done in her hallway the night Janet broke in, unable to think, unable to move.

Another tried to claw at her from the chair it was arranged in, thin dark hair curled and lacquered in place.

Go!

The one on the floor was scrabbling slowly at the floorboards but wasn't coming after her. She flinched back, but her thoughts were a mess.

'Leave my lovely girls alone,' Lettie Porter whispered through the keyhole.

The whisper chilled her, startling her into action.

Carrie blurted out the first thing that came into her head. 'If you come in here, I'll, I'll… I'll destroy them!'

With what, for fuck's sake?

The door rattled. The chest of drawers jerked.

Think! Why can't I bloody think?

'I mean it, Mrs Porter,' Carrie said, her voice high and strained. There was a rattling gasp from the one in the nest of cushions, drawing her attention. Carrie realised why it couldn't move, slotting together the details she had noted before. 'Oh my God, have you *nailed them all down?*'

'Had to,' Lettie Porter murmured.

'*Post* mortem, though, right?' Carrie backed up, her legs finally remembering how to move, albeit without much input from her brain.

There was a baffled silence.

Carrie rephrased. 'I mean, after they were dead.'

One of the zombie girls groaned at her.

'They kep' running away, crying for their other mothers,' Lettie whispered, sadly. 'Why should *other* mothers have such lovely little girls?' Her tone hardened. '*He* gets jealous of my girls. Takes dem from me, he does, for his liddle rituals and rites. I try to keep dem a-nigh me, but *he spoils it,* jealous, ungrateful child…'

Carrie didn't want to get into this. The scale of the Porters' disordered family life was getting to her.

'You lot need therapy. Or a lobotomy.'

The zombie nailed to the floor through her thigh bones moaned in what Carrie imagined was agreement.

'Yeah, what she said.' She shrugged off her jacket, balling it around her fists to protect herself and knocked out the rest of the window glass.

The door rattled again.

It was a long way down.

Carrie pulled out the brick chip and tossed it first. 'You better catch me,' she told it, as the chest of drawers thudded out of the way and the door slammed open.

She closed her eyes and squeezed out, shards raking her forearms, and tumbled awkwardly into the garden below.

Her stomach somersaulted as she plummeted, like a bad dream.

Fairwood caught her.

'You were doing fine,' Fairwood said, backing away from the cottage of horrors.

'Thanks.' Carrie wriggled free of her house's grasp and cast a look at the downstairs window. 'He's in a bad way, should we—'

Fairwood gave her a Look.

'Don't look at me like that,' Carrie said, breathless, ducking behind Fairwood's doppelganger form as George Porter leaned out of the broken window. Adrenaline coursed through her like a drug. 'He's… it seems a bit ungrateful to *leave* him there. *Watch out!*'

Unnatural claws raked at the avatar, or tried to – they got as far as an inch from Fairwood's head, and there was a sizzling sound, like frying sausages. George Porter shrieked, and the shadowy, elastic talons withdrew.

'Oh.' Carrie folded her arms. 'Protection still applies. Good to know.'

If she wasn't careful, she'd start laughing again, like a madwoman in a melodrama. She wouldn't be able to stop and they'd lock her in an attic and she'd spend her days trapped there with only dead girls to play with, like Lettie Porter. A dark giggle bubbled out, and she fought it down.

'Go,' Fairwood advised, pushing her towards the wall.

Carrie didn't need telling twice.

Leaving Fairwood to deal with Ricky Porter, she jumped over the garden wall and tore through The Chase towards her own boundary line.

–

Life was bearable again, numbed.

Guy stood on the back lawns looking up at The Crows, the casements and guttering, the attic gable high above like an unseeing eye. There was no movement from within, he had circled it twice to make sure.

Burn it down.

He had to break a window, throw in the bottle, light the rag.

Not in that order.

He'd never set a fire before. Where did you start one? Through the letterbox, but The Crows didn't have one. Had to be through a window.

He played with the lighter in his pocket. He'd had to buy one. Didn't smoke.

Guy had lost track of the time. The light was still golden, still warm.

Fairwood House was an icon of his childhood, the star of his made-up stories, the villain they'd all pretended to defeat. It was bricks and mortar, that was all, but it called to him, one broken thing to another. He couldn't remember when he'd first become aware of it, when the light glinting off the glass first became a signal, when its aura became palpable, magnetic. It had only gotten stronger as he'd gotten older.

Burn it down.

He squinted, shaking his head.

The bottle sloshed at his side.

He steeled himself, lighter half out of his pocket, when a shout caused him to turn.

Shit.

She was running across the lawns, Caroline, Carrie, cardigan off one shoulder, face red. She knew. She must know. No time. *Bitch.*

He tugged the lighter out, gripping it hard in his clammy palm.

'Guy!' She jogged to a panting halt some metres away, doubling over. 'Guy – Lettie Porter's, ha, she… she's batshit crazy. She needs… serious help.'

He squeezed the lighter harder.

'What – I was just… I came to see you.'

Carrie shook her head, straightening, glancing over her shoulder. 'They–they've got Ricky tied to a chair. And she's got dead girls in, in the bedroom – zombies – nailed to the, God, nailed to stuff. The walls, the floor, their *seats…*' She got her breath back. 'I wanted to get him out, but—' She stopped, looking back at him, seeing him properly. 'What are you doing here? Are you okay? After the other night, I—'

'Just came over,' he repeated, trying to make sense of what she was telling him, where she'd been. Why couldn't she leave things *alone*?

'We should… we should call the police, or something,' Carrie said. 'Shouldn't we?'

Guy caught himself reeling, unsteady. 'No. What for?'

'Oh, they'll do that switch thing.' Carrie tugged her cardigan around her more closely, half turning again to stare into the trees.

'It's so weird. Like I was in another, another version of the house, like a, parallel world or something, even they were different—'

'It's dimensional phasing.' Guy rubbed his thumb over the top of the lighter. 'Most of them can do it.'

She was looking at him in a way he didn't like, but he couldn't put his finger on why. Too many questions behind her eyes. Like his dad.

'What about the girls, the families must... must be going mad...'

'She only takes runaways,' Guy heard himself saying, before his brain caught up with his mouth. 'She doesn't like it if they have families to get back to.'

Carrie dropped her arms to her sides. 'What?'

'There's no point,' Guy said. 'They never find them. They never find anything.'

'No... What? "She only takes runaways", what... how do you *know* that?'

He took a step towards her, the bottle knocking against his leg.

Carrie backed away. 'You knew.'

He didn't have time for this. He had to burn it down, like Beverley wanted.

'You knew. Does everyone know? Does everyone just know everything?' Carrie shook her head. 'Fuck. Am I the only one making a fuss?'

'So don't make a fuss,' Guy said.

Now her eyes travelled to the bottle in his hand, to his closed fist.

'What... what are you doing?'

His nerve snapped.

Before she could react, he lunged forwards, striking her across the head and knocking her to the ground.

I Have You Now, My Pretty

In which Carrie's wyrd ends

13 May

Carrie groaned as pain thumped through her skull, not helped by the faint smell of car exhaust. Her mouth and throat were dusty and dry, but her clothes were wet. Her hair was wet, but it didn't feel like water. The smell was chokingly strong, headache-inducing. It took a moment for her to realize she was lying on something hard. She opened her eyes fully and saw the blood on the floor.

He had dragged her into the kitchen – the back door, she realised, the back door was unlocked – and dumped her in the back passage near the cellar door. It wasn't car exhaust she could smell. It was petrol.

There seemed to be a lot of blood. A small pool of it, a dripping trail leading away into the kitchen.

She tried to sit up but her wrists were stuck – no, bound. What with? She struggled. Her head spun, pounding.

This has really got to stop happening, she thought.

There seemed little point in screaming. She couldn't find her voice: her throat was too dry. It seemed like only yesterday Ricky Porter had accosted her over the fence, mere moments ago that she found the music box in the attic.

How the hell had it come to this?

All she'd done was buy a house.

A masculine, spicy fragrance made Carrie's heart flutter, then sink. Guy Bishop, pale even with his 'book lover's tan' as her dad called it, heaved her bodily over onto her bound wrists. She croaked out a pained yelp.

The reek of stale bourbon hit her over the petrol. At these closer quarters she recognised the smell of an all-nighter, the wildness of a gambler who had played to win and lost. She'd seen that look before.

He had rolled his shirt sleeves up, and Carrie wondered if his arms had ever seen the sunlight. She focused on a strong blue vein, swallowing her disbelief and trying to get to grips with her situation.

'I should've taken care of you myself, like Dad wanted,' Guy muttered, rambling feverishly. 'Never killed anyone before, never hit anyone before, I sell books, I'm not a fucking gangster, what the fuck, what the *actual fuck...*' He took a shuddering breath. 'Should have done it before, then Dad could have... could have died of natural bloody causes, not... not how he went. Not like that.' He shook his head, looking sick. 'Now Dad's... and, Mark – my *god*, I went to see him this morning... my *god*. Because *you* had to wake up that *fucking ghost.*'

She had always thought of Guy's brown eyes as being warm, but now all that warmth was fever rather than kindness. The same fever tinged his cheeks beneath his beard, giving his face its only flare of colour, aside from the dark circles under his eyes, puffy like bruises, as if grief and lack of sleep had been a double, physical blow.

'Guy, what's happened? What's wrong with you?'

He grimaced, red-faced. She saw the silver glint in his hand. The ceiling swam as she fought to focus.

'Guy, please, please don't. You don't have to do this.'

She had to keep him talking. Fairwood's avatar would be back, and the house would protect her, save itself.

What was taking so long?

'What happened? What happened with your dad? Guy, I'm so sorry. I – won't you talk to me? Tell me. Tell me what happened?'

Guy paused but didn't lower the lighter.

Carrie tried to moisten her lips and tasted blood and petrol. 'What... what actually happened in 1958?'

The temperature plummeted. She shuddered, her arms goose-bumped with the sudden chill, but Guy seemed not to notice. He was quiet for a moment, then backed off a pace, leaning into the doorjamb. She wriggled onto her side to see him, chest tight with fear. Something metallic and cold dug into her wrists. What was it? A belt buckle?

Where are they?

There was no sound from the kitchen. Fairwood's avatar wasn't anywhere around, the house's consciousness displaced and unable to help her without it. She shouldn't have left the cottage, she shouldn't have gone back alone.

'He was dying, my dad.' Guy was speaking so quietly she had to strain to hear him. 'He was only... only in his twenties. They couldn't do anything for him, the doctors. He was only human, so the Surgery wouldn't help.' He ground his teeth – she heard that, clearly, more clearly than his voice.

Something was forming on the ceiling above her, something shapeless and malevolent, drained of innocence and left for dead in the dark.

'Mrs Hillsworth had more years than she needed. I'm not saying it was right, what they did, I'm not *saying*...' He trailed off. 'Uncle Mark – he begged the Pendles to help, and Janet wanted to help too, she was about nineteen at the time and she'd do anything for Beverley but I think she had a thing for my dad, she was always... and Mrs Hillsworth didn't want to give her years up, but they said, they said when it was explained to her, she was fine, she did it gladly, except...' He swallowed. 'Except they had to...'

'They had to kill a little girl?' Carrie finished for him, unable to hide her disgust. She had seen the photographs, and Mrs Verity Hillsworth had looked far from glad.

Cathy Ross was with them now. Listening.

He was too drunk or too numb to notice the palpable oppression, crushing the breath out of her. Too lost in his own grief and the monstrous embrace of the past.

'It was – Dad didn't know about that part, I'm sure, he couldn't have. But they'd have arrested him, they'd have—' Guy broke off, shaking his head, but Carrie didn't think he believed it. 'Dad got the years from her, and then… medicine moved on, you know? Doctors *could* help. I know he was in a home and he was – he was really frail… but he had a good life, a better one, and I'm here because of that, and I—' He stopped. Carrie could feel him looking at her. 'I let him down.' He took a deep, audible breath. 'I let him down, because I didn't get rid of *you*.'

'Guy…' Carrie tried, but he jerked away from the door frame as if her pity burned like acid.

'He's dead because of *you*. They're *both* dead because of *you*.'

'Guy…' Carrie quivered, bracing herself.

He struck the lighter.

The low flame danced in his hand.

Carrie closed her eyes, screwed them tight, and thought of her family.

Cathy Ross rushed over her in a freezing blast of energy, forcing Guy off his feet. To Carrie, one moment he was on his feet and the next he wasn't there. She fought the pain in her head, forcing herself to sit and wriggle to the stairs. She tried to hook her hands on the edge of the last step, tugging at the belt to loosen it. Her hands came free, the leather edge grazing her skin. Her heels struck the trapdoor to the coal cellar as she struggled free.

She was on her feet in time to smell the smoke and see, through the open door of the utility room, a blazing pillar in the kitchen falling to its knees.

If that was Guy, he didn't scream.

He didn't make a sound. And then the curtains caught.

No.

This time, Carrie didn't freeze. She tried to run in to beat it out with something, anything, forgetting the petrol soaking into her clothes, dripping down the ends of her ponytail.

Something pushed her back – a dark force, gathered in the doorway like a thundercloud.

Carrie fought it, but it resisted.

'I can't do this,' Carrie whispered, holding her head. The cut felt superficial but the pressure behind her eyes was mounting. 'God, I can't do this, I can't do this, I can't, I can't...'

But she stumbled past the stairs and further along the old servants' corridor, falling through the connecting door that led back to the entrance hall, the world spinning in a maze of black spots and fragmented memory.

Carrie couldn't remember getting out. The lawn spiralled up to meet her hands, but she caught herself and staggered upright.

Where am I?

She saw Fairwood's avatar in the middle-distance, but her head was pounding. Petrol, smoke, blood, burning. All acrid in her labouring lungs.

She threw up.

Behind her, The Crows was on fire.

'No,' she coughed, staggering back towards the flames. '*No, no...*'

He caught hold of her, from nowhere.

'Cor, you look bad.'

Ricky Porter. She squinted up at him, and realised she was on the ground. Fairwood's form was smoking, crumbling, crawling across the grass towards her as flames licked out of its body.

'*No...*' She tried to reach it, but Ricky was holding her.

'Carrie, this is it,' Ricky told her. 'Make it count.'

She didn't know what he was talking about.

'What took you so long?'

He was gentle, his touch light.

She slumped over. 'Where... the hell have you been?'

His face, bloodied but familiar, floated above her in a blur. 'It's bloody hard work getting out of the cottage when the parentals don't want you to leave,' he said. 'If you'd left me there, your house would've saved you. It's not the way I thought it'd go, I got to be honest. I had something more direct in mind, when I saw it'd be my fault. But we can't change it now, can we?'

Carrie let the words wash over her, not understanding them. She tried to touch her head, but he pushed her hands back down.

'No, no. Doant. You're fucked. He got you good.' Ricky pulled her up a little. 'Carrie, this is important. Listen. You're dying. All right? Trying to fix it ain't going to work, it's a waste of time. I've seen it. But, maybe... maybe you can still save *her*, I don't know.'

Fairwood's burning avatar was reaching for her, leaving a charred strip of grass in its wake.

'My head hurts,' Carrie mumbled.

She was moving somehow, legs bumping uselessly on the grass. The world spun, a kaleidoscope of colour and confusion. Ricky was dragging her.

'Come on. One thing left to do. Make a wish.'

'What for?' She kicked at the grass, not sure if she should be helping him or fighting him off, but there was no fight in her.

He propped her up against the well.

Hadn't the well been further away?

Petrol still snarled in her nostrils.

Her life was going up in smoke and flames.

She tugged her necklace off clumsily, snapping the chain, and nearly dropped it into the grass. He pressed it into her hand, closing her fingers around the pendant.

The broken chain dangled, glinting.

She stared at it, thinking of her parents, not sure what was going on.

'Help me,' she said.

Ricky heaved her up, and the world lurched and spun from fire to wet stone. 'Bloody hell, I shouldn't be doing this, this is how you die. I *saw* it.'

Carrie tried to study him but couldn't focus. He had hold of her, stopping her from falling in. For a moment, she thought he was going to let go, a vague recollection of how the well worked swimming upstream into her mind.

Her anchor to humanity was in her hand.

'My head hurts,' she whispered, disorientated.

Ricky dug his fingertips deep into her arm and snarled in her ear. 'I can't change anything, *I saw it*. You end today. It *all* ends. *Make a bloody wish.*'

Carrie held her fist out over the well.

Her choices melted.

The wyrd weaved, warp and weft.

She opened her fist and her necklace dropped into the stony depths, plopping below the muddy water with barely a sound.

Carrie closed her eyes, thinking about Fairwood.

She made her wish, and the world went dark.

–

Her time was up.

If she didn't make a wish, he'd lose it all, the house would die, and all that would be left was Eglantine Valmai Pritchard's protection spell with no consciousness left to override it. That's what you got for letting the Welsh move in, with power in their bloody poetry.

He dug his fingertips deep into her arm and snarled in her ear. 'I can't change anything, *I saw it. Make a bloody wish.*'

Carrie held her fist out over the well.

Her lips didn't move. Her fist opened and the necklace dropped into the stony depths, plopping below the muddy water with barely a sound.

There was a bleed on her brain, slow but unstoppable, he could sense it, smell death creeping over her behind the telltale bruising around her eyes. She went limp in his arms, suddenly heavy.

(Wyrd bið ful aræd: *fate is inexorable.*)

He let her fall to the grass, the unfamiliar chest-cinching feeling squeezing like a vice. She was dead before she hit the ground.

The avatar was crawling towards them, a cracked and blackened husk, as the blaze spread from room to room.

Cathy Ross appeared in the kitchen window as he watched, outlined in fire. A small thing she was, a frail thing, a morsel of innocence hung up in the dark. A husk of vengeance burning her prison down.

'This wasn't the deal!' Ricky yelled. 'Oi! You little bitch! *This wasn't the fucking deal!*'

He looked down at Carrie.

She wasn't breathing. Her head lolled like one of his mother's doll-daughters.

He'd won. He'd got what he wanted. The future had steamed forth from the guts of the Blue Moon girl, telling him he would, telling him he would Change, he would get the Stone, he would get the house, and the rest was collateral damage.

He'd won, hadn't he? The only living thing in Fairwood. Master of all. Except he hadn't pictured it on fire, and Carrie wasn't breathing.

Ricky squirmed, battling something nameless and unfamiliar. It didn't feel like a victory.

It felt like a trick.

'What did you wish for?' he asked the lifeless body, but, like Gerald, she didn't reply.

He fought his quickening breaths, trying to think clearly. He could preserve her. He could stuff her skin, dress her up and keep her somewhere, or maybe he could let her Rise all mindless and starving and nail her to the floor like his mother did with her little favourites, for her own good. Yes. Yes, it wouldn't be the same, but he could still talk to her, muzzle her and sleep beside her, she wouldn't be warm but she'd be like his, his, his – *friend*. His chest seized, forcing out tears in a bitter sob.

'You said, you said, I'd get what I *wanted*,' he growled, panting, addressing the Voice in his head. 'You miserable old bastard, I'm fucking done, I'm *done*—'

The corpse burst into flames.

314

Ricky leapt back, tugging off his hoody and wrapping her in it, rolling her over, beating at the blooming roses of fire as they ripped through her clothes.

'Bloody hell!'

His human skin blistered and burnt, flaking off as what was underneath resisted the heat.

As he beat the fire out, the avatar stopped blazing, and the fire in the house also began to subside.

Cathy Ross's dead face distended in the window as she snarled, vaporised, and blew away into a cloud of black smoke. She wasn't gone, though, no, things like her were tough to get rid of. He'd find her. The window exploded outwards in a shower of broken shards.

'Fuck you,' Ricky muttered, hands red-raw.

He turned his attention back to Carrie's corpse, lying face down and smoking on the grass. He rubbed his face with both hands, ignoring the blistering pain in them. He had lost something he couldn't name. The void it left frightened him and he didn't know why.

He glanced behind him at Fairwood's avatar, sprawled on its belly with an outstretched arm reaching for Carrie. As he watched, the avatar crumbled into ash, leaving a charred shape on the lawn.

He rolled her over again onto her back and saw the bruising had disappeared, but now beneath her closed eyes the skin looked more like scorched wood.

'Shit.'

Carrie opened her eyes, window-pane grey. A network of broken capillaries spiderwebbed in one of them, matching the newly broken window.

He recoiled.

'Did it work?' she asked, oblivious.

'Shit me,' he breathed, taking her in. 'You ain't her.'

'What? Of course I am.' Carrie sat up. 'What? What's wrong?' She coughed up charcoal. 'Eugh, God. What happened? Are we okay? Did it work?'

He didn't want to touch her.

(*She won't be soft, won't be real, won't be what I wanted.*)

'What's the matter?' Carrie asked. 'Ricky, it's okay. Look. I'm fine. I told you, it was concussion, I blacked out or something but I'm fine, I feel totally fine now. How long was I out for?'

Concussion didn't work like that. She must know that, surely?

'What did you wish for?' He didn't like this feeling that clung to him like tar. Made him cold, like prey.

She smiled. 'It worked, right? I'm not dead, am I?'

'I don't know.' He lifted his blistered hand but couldn't touch her. 'You ain't breathing.'

Carrie cleared her throat. 'Of course I am, see?'

'No, you...'

She kneeled up and leaned closer, putting her cheek on his open palm. 'There. See? Calm down, mate.'

She was still soft.

Soft like fabric, soft like leather, soft like Gerald.

He relaxed.

'Yeah.' The relief caught in his throat. 'All right. I take it back.' He grinned, chest still tight. 'I liked your other eyes better.'

Carrie stood up.

'What are you talking about? I do feel a bit – I do feel weird. Different.'

She checked herself over carefully, running her hands down her charred clothes. He watched, following the path of her hands, wondering what she felt like now, if it was the same all over. That feeling was back – not fear, the other thing. Pooling in his groin again, unexpected.

(Is *this* me? Or *her*?)

It was fleeting and didn't matter.

'So, you were wrong,' Carrie said, with her familiar wry smile. 'The wyrd can be changed.'

He stepped back. She shouldn't be able to remember that. But she wasn't her, was she? Fairwood was speaking with her voice, remembering what he'd said, what he'd done.

'No. I was right.'

She shook her head. 'You can't have been, I'm... I'm fine. I'm fine, look at me.'

Her skin was like plaster, stippled with old scars: those eyes – grey and clear as glass.

Blank as water.

She looked over her shoulder for the avatar. 'Where's the... where's Fairwood?'

'I'm looking at her,' Ricky said.

EPILOGUE

Is This the End?

*In which Cathy pays Mrs Wend a visit and some things are wrapped up
to no-one's satisfaction*

14 May

Beverley Wend sat in the dark in the early hours of the morning,
waiting for a ghost.

She knew it was coming. She had spent the day preparing for
it, sensing its animosity approaching like a thunderstorm.

She had veiled all reflective surfaces in the room, except
for the mirror she wanted to use: an antique, rosewood frame
propped on a chair, angled perfectly to capture her entire body
as she sat sewing a costume for Maisie Wend-McVey's first school
concert.

The Colonel lay in the morgue, a soulless shell. He wouldn't
be going anywhere for a while, even if it was Rising season.

'They say seeing spectres in mirrors is all about reflections of
the self,' she said to her own reflection as the candle guttered
and the electric light dimmed. 'Now, I think there's something
in that. We look for apparitions in ourselves, don't we, searching
for contradictions, transgressions, something Other, I suppose...'
She paused, losing her train of thought for a moment as the lights
dipped and flickered. She took the time to put down her sewing,
the needle glinting slyly among the folds of silk, struck a match,
and lit a candle. A small smile curled over her lips. 'Yes, I *do* think
there's something in that. But not perhaps what *they* mean. *I* think
a spectre who travels through mirrors doesn't know who she is.

Doesn't know what to reflect. Has to steal and borrow. I'm sorry you never got to grow up, dear, I really am, but...' She tilted her head. 'Needs must, at the time. And you were so convenient, you see.'

Her teacup shattered in its saucer.

Mrs Wend regarded it calmly, watching the spread of tea leaves among the shards.

'Well, I don't need our Ricky to read *those*,' she said. 'Come on in, my dear. Don't be shy.'

Her reflection rose from the chair as Beverley sat facing it, her hands in her lap.

'How does it feel, to play at being old, to wear my skin? Even if it isn't real.'

Her reflection approached the glass with shuddering steps.

'That's it,' Beverley said sweetly, and now her eyes were as red as rubies. 'A little closer, dear, if you want to kill me. I'm afraid my Hector already did for my sister, Eileen, you remember her, of course, she was always one for luring the children.' She gave a fond laugh and stirred the tea leaves with a stiff finger.

Her reflection hesitated, then, carefully, stepped out of the mirror.

'That's it, my dear,' Beverley entreated, beckoning, and the electric lights flashed as the candle flame burned black. 'It will all be over soon. Won't that be nice?'

'Yeah,' a gruff voice said in the dark shadows of the room. 'That'll be bloody lovely.'

Beverley turned, startled.

Cathy Ross flew forwards with arms outstretched, and the lights went out.

16 May

Mercy was the first person Carrie called, once she'd had a couple of days for it all to start sinking in. She couldn't explain this to anyone else. She thought of her mum and dad, but for some

320

reason they got jumbled with other faces in her head, men with compasses and pencils, women with vision and ideas, all those who had constructed her over the years. She struggled to pick her most recent parents out of the crowd.

(*Most recent parents?*)

That couldn't be right.

She needed someone who had at least one foot in the human camp. Someone who could help her. Someone who would listen. Besides, she had something Mercy would want to see.

Mercy came over with Tina, a welcome addition even though Carrie realised Tina had not yet formally apologised for trespassing as a nine-year-old and chalking her initials on the kitchen wall. The quiet chant of forgiveness in her thirteenth-century soul encouraged her to let this go. She made them all tea, and they heard the story from the beginning. Carrie didn't leave anything out this time, although Tina's face told her she probably should have done.

'This is insane,' Tina said, evidently putting her feelings about Richard Edwin Porter to one side with heroic effort. Carrie could tell she had been dying to interrupt during those parts of the story. 'I mean… are you sure you're… you look different, like you're wearing makeup, but I wouldn't say you look—' she struggled for an appropriate word, '—inorganic.'

Carrie snorted. 'Hey! Wood isn't inorganic, thank you. But. Well. Look.'

She rolled up her sleeve and scratched at the scarring on her arm. Flecks of paint and plaster dust sprinkled onto her floorboards.

Tina and Mercy leaned in, horrified and fascinated.

'What do I *do*?'

Mercy shrugged, taking the high road of blind optimism. 'Well. I mean… I don't know. Maybe it… it might not affect you much?'

Carrie stared at her well-meaning new friend. 'Mercy? I'm an actual house.'

Tina raised a hand. 'Um. I know people who are actually dead, but they seem to manage. This is *technically* another form of that, isn't it? There're some undead support groups I could link you up with.'

Tina seemed more radiant than the first time Carrie had seen her. More confidant. She put this down to Wes and Charlie, and something warmed her chest where her heart used to be. The crypt's song glowed through her piping, filling her with gentle harmonies.

'I don't have a pulse, if that qualifies me,' Carrie said.

'Absolutely.' Tina sipped her mug of tea. 'There's quite a few in town who can relate to that part, at least. Though you might also qualify as a... sorry, not be indelicate, but as a "possessed object", and some of them are a bit funny about that.'

Mercy pulled a cushion onto her lap and hugged it to her chest, her mind running on another track. 'So,' she said, 'you said there was something else? Is it... is it about the History Society? Did you find out what the Cathy Ross thing was about?'

Carrie winced. 'Yeah. This survived the fire.' She pulled out the manila envelope that she – the other avatar – had taken from the Colonel's safe. 'I was going to give it to Carrie, I mean, me, to give to you, but then, um, you know. Arson.'

'There's hardly any trace of it,' Tina noted. 'The fire. How did you...'

Carrie smiled. 'I learned to fix myself. Had a bath. Filled in some gaps, you know. Sandpaper. I watched a YouTube video.'

'Are there many people who are houses, or...'

Carrie burst out laughing. 'No, it was a... it was a sculpture video. How to fix it if it's uneven, you know.'

Tina winced around a smile. 'Right. I wish I'd brought wine.'

Mercy took the envelope, her expression echoing Tina's sentiment. 'What's in it?'

'Just... just look.'

Tina put her mug down, waiting.

Mercy pulled out the photograph, an identical copy to the one Janet had tried to burn. She studied it, her face frozen.

'What?' Tina demanded finally after a long, tense pause. 'What *is* it? What's her number?'

'Ninety-eight.' Mercy handed the photograph to Carrie, who passed it to Tina for corroboration. The Resurrectionist stared down at her lap, sucking her cheek.

'Ninety-eight?' Tina pushed a stray strand of russet hair out of her eyes and frowned. 'Oh, shit. Yeah, I guess... I guess that does look a little bit like a nine—'

'She was thirty-two,' Mercy said. 'Thirty-two. Guy wasn't lying, was he? It's not just a story?' She put her hand under her top, where Carrie knew her own number was blotched onto her skin.

Tina pursed her lips and handed the photograph back.

'Do you... are you ready to tell us about it now?' Carrie asked, remembering Mercy's reaction in the pub.

Mercy's voice was flat. 'There's a story... a scary fairy tale. That's all. This witch wanted to live forever, so she stole away the years of people's lives and she was like a, like a Pied Piper figure, you know, she lived in this mountain and she lured young children away... she gets defeated in the end by Amaranth, the hero, and part of her spell was this horrible rhyme, I can't remember it now, but you have to take innocence and hang it in darkness and drain it of all its light... and then you have to open a way to the Other Side – we call it the Dark Place. Where we go, you know, when we die and come back.' She was shivering. Carrie put her arm around her, and they pressed closer together.

'And that's... that's what Guy said they did for his dad?' Tina glanced at Carrie. 'He was dying young, so they... stole someone else's life for him...?'

Mercy stared across the room. 'It's... it's not supposed to be real.' She lifted her top and revealed her birthmark. Carrie saw the blotchy port-wine stain on the side of her tummy more clearly this time at these close quarters, the number livid on her skin. 'Look at mine. I've got loads. If someone wanted to... they could take them. Ten, twenty. All of them. I could die on my next birthday.' She lowered her top and cuddled the cushion again.

Carrie shuddered at the violation, remembering the Colonel in the photograph with his triumphant hand on Verity Hillsworth's wrist. Her throat was dry as brick. 'No. They couldn't do it again. I think they needed the energies. The Pendle Stone, the hearthstone from the old gamekeepers' cottage. They needed that to open the, what was it? The Dark Place?'

'Yeah.'

'Well, that's tricky. I bet Mrs Wend's shrine in her cottage… I bet it's not strong enough, it's not *old* enough. This thing, it's part of me.' She touched her breastbone. 'I can *feel* it. The Pendles used to do magic, real magic, with it, for centuries. But the clan can't get at the Pendle Stone now, so they can't do it again. Well, Ricky can, but I know what he's doing with it, because…' She trailed off, biting back the words.

'It's *fine*, it's *fine* if you're not human,' Mercy said. 'I mean, I know it's not the same, but I'm not really, either. If it helps.'

Carrie pursed her lips, forcing the faces of her human parents to the forefront of her mind. They swam up through the crowd of architects and builders until she saw them clearly, the original creators of Caroline Rickard.

'I want to call my mum.'

Mercy looked like she was about to hug her, but thought better of it. 'I'm so, so sorry,' she whispered.

'Don't be. You warned me about the Wends, you warned me about Ricky. Tina said the séance wasn't a good idea… and I did it anyway, didn't I?' Carrie leaned away. 'I did it all anyway, and then… I couldn't stop. It was like… Ricky's right. I think… I think he's right about all of it, the wyrd, your destiny being unchangeable. People follow patterns they can't see, but they're there. And I—' She stopped. 'Do you think this was all supposed to happen? That it was all going to happen exactly like this, from the moment I saw this place?'

Tina shook her head, a dimple appearing in her cheek as she twisted her lips. 'No. I don't. I think there's a version where it's worse. Where you *really* died.'

Carrie looked at her, startled, but Tina shrugged.

'Well – you said Ricky told you, on the lawn, that it ended. He'd seen it end, that's what he told you.' Tina picked up her mug again, arching her eyebrows. 'I think you were *supposed* to die for good. You know. Not come back.'

Carrie frowned. 'He said that to her – to me – before,' she said, remembering. 'In the kitchen. She was – I was drunk, and... he told me I was going to die. Then he... put one of his... tendril things, into her – my – ear. And...' She struggled with the memory. 'And I forgot.' She shook her head. 'Fairwood didn't tell me. It didn't want me to know, and it told him – well, it bullied him – into trying to save me. But he shouldn't have. He's not supposed to interfere, is he? He's supposed to be an agent of destiny, or whatever the hell he calls himself. He's not supposed to...' She trailed off. 'Maybe it was just as well I did get to know him properly.'

'They're batshit, the whole family,' Tina said. '"Mad, bad and dangerous to know."'

'Like Byron?' Carrie joked, recognising the quote.

'Well, they're definitely into their sisters.'

Mercy sprayed her tea across the floor.

'Yeah, about the zombies Lettie Porter's got nailed to the floor...' Carrie patted Mercy on the back as she choked. 'Do you think we ought to... do something about that?'

'The police *never* find anything,' Tina said. 'The best we can hope for is that she doesn't get her hands on anyone new.'

'Like who?' Carrie asked. 'The homeless? Runaways? School kids? Randomers in their cars just... wrong road, wrong time?'

'Why do you think we moved away?' Tina put a defensive arm across her middle, tilting her head. 'Look, I'm not... I'm not proud that they did that. Mum and Dad wanted out. I felt awful, leaving everyone. Do you know what happened to, I think it's like eight percent, of people in my year at school? No, and neither does anyone else. Some are missing. Some are definitely dead. It's the luck of the draw around here. Burt never blamed me. But I shouldn't have left, we shouldn't have left. I don't think it's right.'

'There's nothing to blame you for,' Mercy said. 'I didn't know you felt like that, Tee, there's no reason for you to feel—'

Tina shook her head. 'Don't. I know. I know there isn't, but that *is* how I feel.'

'You're back now,' Carrie pointed out. 'Maybe that was inevitable, too.'

'Everyone's got *stuff* here, even if they are human,' Mercy said. 'That's... that's what Tee's trying to say. You don't fit in properly unless you have your own stuff. You won't *understand*.'

Carrie grinned. 'Thanks.'

'Well, when you need a bit of humanity, we're here.' Tina winked. 'I mean I say "humanity", no offence, Mez.'

'We're human-*passing*,' Mercy said primly, 'But I think Carrie knows what you mean.'

Carrie sighed. 'So. That's it, is it? I mean, I could try wishing myself human but...' She shrugged. 'Who knows if it'll work properly? What if that means I'd just end up a human *corpse*? And then there's the rest of it... Is that it then, we can't do anything about anyone or anything?'

'Well. That's not *exactly* true,' Tina said. 'We can get really drunk.'

'*Can* I get drunk?' Carrie wondered out loud.

'Only one way to find out.'

'Welcome to Pagham-on-Sea,' Mercy said, straight-faced.

Carrie's phone rang.

'Hold that thought.' Carrie struggled off the sofa and answered it. 'Hi Mum...'

Her mother's wail of relief was the herald to a massive rant at Carrie's failure to be in touch, how worried she'd been, and how Carrie's dad had rung her to ask if anything was wrong, but how would she know, Carrie never told her anything...

Carrie didn't mind.

She took the one-sided conversation into the kitchen, where the only trace of the fire was a dark patch on the floor tiles where Guy Bishop had stood. It wasn't as if he was the first person to die in the house, or even in the kitchen, but she tried not to look at it.

'I'm fine, Mum, I'm really sorry. I've been busy. With my job, making friends. You know.'

'So you *have* made friends, then,' her mother sniffed, teary and doubtful. 'I was *worried*, Caroline.'

'Had a minor house fire, but it's as good as new now.'

Her mother didn't take this well. '*What?* Oh my God, Caroline—'

'Everything's fine,' Carrie assured her. 'And I found myself a lodger, so I'm not on my own anymore. Fully vetted, and we get on really well.'

Through the kitchen window, a figure in grey was watching the house through the trees.

She smiled.

'Mum, I'm sorry, I'm going to ring you back, I've got people over. But I'm fine, I promise. Love you.'

'Caroline Rose, don't you *dare* hang up this phone—'

Carrie hung up.

She folded her arms, watching Ricky through all of her back windows at once.

(*Where the hell have you been?*)

(*Long story, but Gran's dead. Family's in a right state over it. Got a ghost in a jar here, bloody frisky she is. Tell you in a minute. Whose car is that out front?*)

(*Mercy and Tina are here.*)

(*All right. I'll go through the tunnel.*)

He disappeared from view, slipping between the trees.

Carrie smiled.

She wasn't going anywhere.